DEDICATION

I lovingly dedicate this book to Debbie...
friend forever, sister of my heart.

A NOVEL BY SHARLENE
MACLAREN

HER *Steadfast*
HEART

WHITAKER
HOUSE

Her Steadfast Heart

Sharlene MacLaren
www.sharlenemaclaren.com
sharlenemaclaren@yahoo.com

ISBN: 978-1-64123-584-6
eBook ISBN: 978-1-64123-585-3
Printed in the United States of America
© 2021 by Sharlene MacLaren

Whitaker House
1030 Hunt Valley Circle
New Kensington, PA 15068
www.whitakerhouse.com

Library of Congress Cataloging-in-Publication Data
Names: MacLaren, Sharlene, 1948- author.
Title: Her steadfast heart / Sharlene MacLaren.
Description: New Kensington, PA : Whitaker House, [2021] | Summary:
    "Romance novel set in the Civil War era centering on a widower serving
    in the Union army who advertises for a temporary wife to care for his
    four children and the woman who answers that ad"— Provided by
    publisher.
Identifiers: LCCN 2020048210 (print) | LCCN 2020048211 (ebook) | ISBN
    9781641235846 (trade paperback) | ISBN 9781641235853 (ebook)
Subjects: LCSH: United States—History—Civil War, 1861-1865—Fiction. |
    GSAFD: Love stories. | Historical fiction. | Christian fiction.
Classification: LCC PS3613.A27356 H47 2021 (print) | LCC PS3613.A27356
    (ebook) | DDC 813/.6—dc23
LC record available at https://lccn.loc.gov/2020048210
LC ebook record available at https://lccn.loc.gov/2020048211

1 2 3 4 5 6 7 8 9 10 11 ⊔⊔ 28 27 26 25 24 23 22 21

1

June 1864 · Lebanon, Ohio

Captain Joseph Fuller stepped down from the train, planted his feet on Deerfield Station's wooden platform in South Lebanon, Ohio, and observed the crowd gathered around him, seeking out a familiar face. Seeing none, he gazed upward for a moment, squinting at a wispy cloud creeping slowly past the brilliant sun. The sky could not be bluer, and any normal soul would take joy at the sight of it. However, he hadn't considered himself normal for quite some time, so the azure sky did little to lift his spirits. Someone bumped against him and muttered, "Pardon, soldier," before he realized he stood in the path of another passenger, a burly fellow who'd smoked a cigar the entire time on the last leg of the trip from Cincinnati to Lebanon. He moved to the side, breathed deep of the day's fresh air, and hefted the strap of his knapsack over his shoulder.

"Here's y'r valise, Captain," said the driver, dropping the thing on the ground so that the dust flew. In it were a spare set of trousers and a shirt, some underclothes, and his tooth powder and brush.

"Thank you." Joseph picked up the valise by its worn handle and set off toward the row of waiting stagecoaches, one of which would deliver him to Lebanon House, where he hoped to find one of his brothers waiting to drive him to the family farm. That old sun seared through the thick fabric of his worn woolen uniform, heating his shoulders till he swore it would burn holes straight through the fabric. Nothing unusual about that though. He'd spent thousands of hours marching up and down trails on hot summer days. Probably sweated buckets too whilst fighting for the Union!

An annoying pebble slipped through the hole in the toe of his scuffed leather boot as he slogged across the gravelly path toward the nearest stage, but he'd ignore it till he got home. He'd have to stop by Ma's house first to visit a spell before heading to his white two-story farmhouse. He knew just the sight of the wide steps leading up to the covered porch would probably put a small spot of warmth at the center of his heart. He wasn't sure if his rowdy bunch of kids would be at the main house with Ma or with his sister-in-law Cristina, but he'd round them up from somewhere and take them home with him.

Before he could speak to the stagecoach driver, who stood at the ready to offer train passengers a ride to their next stop, he heard a male voice call out, "Joey, wait up!" He spun around to find his older brother Jack jogging toward him. Jack reached him with an outstretched arm to shake his hand, but quickly grabbed Joey into a bear hug instead. "Welcome home, brother," Jack said, setting him back and squeezing both his shoulders in a vice-like hold, providing Joey with his first smile of the day. "I've been in town buying supplies, but I timed my errands around the train's arrival from Cincinnati. I see I'm a few minutes late."

"Don't worry about it. I wasn't expecting a welcoming party. Actually, I thought you'd be picking me up over at the Lebanon House Station."

"Naw, I decided the extra drive would be nice. Gives us time to talk before your kids and Ma start monopolizing your time. How long you home for?"

"I was due a two-week furlough, so I'm using it."

The two stood and gazed at each other for a couple moments before Jack slapped Joey on the arm and said, "Well, come on then. My rig's parked over there."

Once at the two-horse wagon, both climbed aboard the high seat and settled in for the six-mile jaunt to the Fuller Family Farm.

"So, Ma told you about my predicament I presume," Joey said after Jack veered onto the main road.

"She did. Both Cristina and I have been doing what we can till you could make it home and see to other arrangements. Isn't this about the fourth or fifth nanny to have quit on you?"

"Fifth, I believe. Even I've lost count." His children were a bit more than a handful, sometimes downright unruly, and he'd had a hard time managing them since his wife Sarah Beth's passing some three and a half years ago. He often wondered if he'd made a big mistake in leaving them for the sake of the Union just months after her passing. In fact, the question haunted him. *Had he joined for the right reasons, or had he looked at the opportunity to serve his country as a means for escaping his family responsibilities?* His kids had grown so much, especially Isaac, and it pained him to think of all that he'd missed. Still, he'd made a commitment to his country, so there'd been little he could do but see that obligation through.

"How's Ma doing with that broken leg?" he asked, wanting to go a different direction with his thoughts.

"She's feisty as ever, trying not to let that wheelchair slow her down, and for the most part, it doesn't. Doc says she's healing well. Maybe another month or so in the cast. She, of course, blames those two last steps on the stairs. She swears they weren't there before." That gave Joey a chuckle. "Ma hates that she couldn't just take over the care of your kids, but that leg…"

"I totally understand. I don't want to make my children her responsibility, never have. It's enough that she and Cristina chip in as much as they do. I appreciate it." He removed his hat and drove his big hand through his fresh-cut hair. He'd had to make himself at least halfway presentable to his mother before walking through her door. Of course, that hot train ride hadn't done much for his sweltering body. "Are my kids at Ma's now?"

"No, they're actually at my house playing with their cousins. You can get them after you've had some time with Ma."

"Sounds good." He took a gander at familiar territory as the wagon bounced along. He placed his hat back on his head. "It's always good to get back home."

"You don't have much longer. Isn't your discharge date coming up?"

"Actually, middle October. Don't recall the exact date. You're right, it's coming up on me."

"You must be looking forward to it."

"It will be good to have fulfilled my commitment with the Army, but life on the field is so hectic, I haven't had time to think about my discharge."

A long-tailed weasel darted in front of them, probably searching out its supper. "War sure is an ugly thing," said Jack. "But despite the death and destruction, this one's been especially necessary."

"True enough. How's Cristina? And when's your baby due?" Joey didn't feel like talking about the war. Too many other things filling his mind.

"She's feeling well now that she's finally stopped retching. These last few months will go fast. Doc says probably early to mid-November, but only God and that little one knows for sure. I've built a crib, and we've converted one of the spare rooms down the hall into a nursery."

Joey gave a wistful nod of the head. "You and Cristina make for a perfect little family."

"I'll admit the Lord has blessed us."

Joey refrained from any further comments. He didn't wish to get into any sort of religious talk with his brother. He'd get enough of that from Ma.

"You got anything in mind for finding your next nanny?" Jack asked. "Haven't you about exhausted your resources around town?"

"Sure have. I'm afraid my kids' reputation precedes them. I got some ideas, one in particular."

Jack stayed focused on the road. They hit another rut in the road, and the two knocked against each other. "Sheesh, can't you see them things coming?" Joey asked.

"You wanna take the reins?" Jack asked.

"I'd probably do a better job."

"Doubt it. I've always been the better handler."

"Just because you're older doesn't make you the expert."

They sparred for a while, each trying to outdo the other with playful insults. Soon they reached the road on which the Fuller property came into view. In the distance, Joey spotted the familiar silos and barns in the distance and knew it wouldn't be long till they reached the narrow, well-driven, two-track road with the customized sign over the entrance reading "Fuller Family Farms." His gut lurched. He thought about the idea he had stored in his head and couldn't help but worry about Ma's reaction to it.

"You mentioned a while back that you got a plan in place for what to do with your kids. Mind if I ask what it is?"

"You'll find out soon enough. Matter of fact, you should probably be sitting close to Ma when I tell her about it. You may need to pick her up off the floor."

2

June, 1864 · Columbus, Ohio

Faith Haviland swept a few strands of damp hair off her forehead, irritated by how it had escaped the neat bun of this morning. She shoveled more dishes into the sink and set to washing them as fast as possible to prepare for the supper crowd that would soon descend upon Daybreak Diner. It wasn't a fairytale job by any means, but, alas, it was a job, and many would clamor for it if her Aunt Martha ever hung up a "Help Wanted" sign in the window. Her aunt, who happened to be her father's younger sister, owned and operated the establishment and often stated her wish for Faith to one day take it over. Faith shuddered at the prospect of telling Martha she'd been entertaining the idea of leaving Columbus. Martha wouldn't like the news, but Faith couldn't worry about that. Things had grown too tedious in her hometown, and too many found it their job to remind her of the unfortunate event of her canceled wedding. Add to that the troublesome, if not peculiarly obsessive, behavior of Stuart Porter, and tedious hardly described it. Ever since her fiancé's departure with her best friend just two weeks before their April 15 wedding day, Mr. Porter had started closing in on her, insisting he would marry her in an instant if she'd simply agree.

For as long as she could recall, the man had outwardly admired her, even though she had done nothing to encourage it. Nothing about him appealed to her. First, he didn't serve the Lord; second, he was an obsessive drinker; third, he came off as pushy and persistent; and finally, he resembled a goose with his nose sticking out like a beak. Not that looks meant all that much—goodness, she didn't consider herself any major prize—but it was all the other things thrown in. The man was almost twenty years older than she and widowed to boot. At least, that was the rumor anyway. No one had really known his wife, only that she was there one day and gone the next. Some said she'd died, and others said she'd left him for another man. Whatever the case, it'd been a mysterious event that few knew anything about, and if they did, no one discussed it much, probably mostly from lack of caring.

"I think that dish is clean now." Faith gave a jolt at the sound of her aunt's voice.

"Oh! I guess my mind got all taken up with woolgathering."

Martha gave a jovial laugh, and while washing the last plate, Faith envisioned the woman's chubby, round face, her lips turned up in a wide smile to reveal that missing top tooth, and her graying hair falling at the temples, as Faith's was prone to do. She dried the dish and put it on the eye-level shelf with the rest of the plates.

"And what sort of thoughts were wrapped up in that woolgathering?"

Faith dipped a clean washrag into the pan of dish water, wrung it out, and started wiping crumbs off the food counters. "I don't know. Nothing in particular, I suppose."

"Uh-huh. I've seen that expression of contemplation in your face before."

Faith smiled. "Have you?" It wouldn't be long before customers would come sauntering through the door in need of this evening's fare: chicken stew, mashed potatoes, carrots, sliced tomatoes, and rolls hot from the oven. She used to love her job—visiting with patrons, serving them tasty meals, and listening to their oohs of approval—but after several years, it was more a chore than anything to drag herself to work to fulfill her ten-hour shifts. A restless spirit had been calling her to something bigger, something different, but she knew not what because God had yet to reveal it. Her recent heartbreak had led her down a path of rediscovery, and leaving Columbus played into that. Why, she didn't even have any further interest in adding to her Victorian button string, even though folks had continued to give buttons to her. Her canceled wedding plans put a big damper on that.

"Well, whatever was on y'r pretty little mind, I s'pose it's time we start thinking about this next wave of customers. I'll go flip that sign around on the door."

"It's not quite five yet, Auntie."

"No, but we're startin' to accumulate a crowd out there."

Faith turned her gaze to the front window, where indeed a host of folks had situated themselves in front of the door. Upon a closer perusal, her stomach dropped to the dusty shoe that poked out from her muslin skirt with the ruffled hem. "Oh, drat, that horrid Mr. Porter is out there. I've told him several times I'm not interested in courting him. That one date a few weeks ago was enough for me."

"I told you if you accepted, he'd start nagging you."

"I thought that one time would be enough to make him see how very unsuited we are for one another. I even came right out and told him I wasn't interested, and then his trying to kiss me even after I made my feelings known really settled it for me." She shuddered at the memory.

"Well, if he becomes a pest, I'll tell him to leave. I've done it to other customers, and I can do it to him."

"Auntie, you're the berries." Faith stifled a little laugh, then walked back to the kitchen to retrieve the necessary dishes. The food aromas made her own stomach growl, and she looked forward to a lull when she and Aunt Martha could also eat.

Martha walked to the door, turned the sign around so it read "Open," and unlocked the door. The bell above it gave a loud jangle as the first of the supper crowd entered. They were a vocal bunch as regulars greeted each other, some remarking on the wonderful smells and others commenting on the night's menu. As was customary, all made their way to one of the eighteen tables, then immediately took to sipping on the glasses of water waiting there for them, or taking up the weekly newspaper Martha always provided for her customers' reading pleasure. Suppertime at the diner was a cheery time for most, and normally, Faith freely added to the friendly chatter—except on nights when Stuart Porter showed up to unsettle her nerves. Even now, a tiny glance in his direction revealed a pair of hungry, googly eyes seeking her out. Oh, how wretchedly uncomfortable he made her. Martha approached the fellow's table, so Faith watched to see how things would unfold. She overheard Stuart say, "I'll wait for Faith, thank you. Would you send her over please?" Martha then bent toward him and made an inaudible comment to which he commented back. Although it pained her greatly to intervene, Faith quickly walked over.

"Aunt Martha, I'll see to Mr. Porter." Martha threw her a probing glance, but then walked away at Faith's insistence, stopping just briefly along the way to say hello to a few regulars. Soon, she would begin filling dinner plates with tonight's cuisine and then start delivering them to famished folks. It would be Faith's job to refill water glasses and coffee cups throughout the evening, see to customers' needs, and then start clearing and cleaning tables of outgoing patrons to make way for the new. They had a routine system.

Hiding her annoyance at Stuart, Faith straightened and gave him a stiff smile. "Would you like some coffee to go with your dinner, Mr. Porter?"

He reached out to snag her wrist but only managed to brush it because she quickly put both hands behind her and clasped them tight. He gave her a confident smile. "You should know by now to call me by my first name, Faith. We did go on a date if you recall."

She cleared her throat and said in a hushed tone. "Yes, we did. I agreed to accompany you to the theater when the musical troupe came through town, but I made it clear it was to be our last date, especially after you forced a kiss upon me."

"I acted inappropriately. Surely, I deserve another chance to prove myself."

"I'm sorry, no, Mr. Porter."

He raised both eyebrows and gave a low chortle. "We shall see. I do not give up easily. I understand a traveling troupe will be putting on three stage performances next weekend at Hartford Hall. Now, if I promise to be on my best behavior, could I count on you to come along with me?"

She gawked at him for all of five seconds. "No, Mr. Porter, you may not, but I'm sure if you look around a bit, you'll find some fine young lady to accompany you." It proved difficult to keep her tone civil. *Lord, help me.*

His face took on a distinct red tinge, whether from anger or embarrassment she couldn't say. "But I'm not interested in anyone else. It's always been you, Faith—for as long as I can remember. Even when you were engaged to be married to that ghastly fellow, I still believed we were meant to be together."

That sent a bit of chill up her spine. "You know, Mr. Porter, I think you should leave. I really do. This is my job, and I have to get back to work."

He snagged hold of her wrist before she had a chance to escape and leaned close. "Just one more date, Faith?"

"No!" She wriggled to get out of his hold, but he refused to release her. "Let go of me," she said in a hissing whisper, but he clung tighter, giving her a hard stare.

"Hey, you havin' a problem with Mr. Porter, Miss Faith?"

Mr. Hardy, an elderly gentleman sitting at the next table over, had turned himself full around to glare at Stuart. His wife also scowled at him. *Great, they'd made a scene.* Just what Faith didn't want.

Stuart dropped Faith's hand at last, then took up his water glass for a quick swallow. He set the glass back down, then, with an icy smile at those around him, he pushed back in his chair and rose. "No problem at all, Mr. Hardy." He tipped his hat at Faith. "Until next time," he whispered, brushing past her and heading for the door. She heaved a sigh when he walked out, but the cold way in which he'd said, "Until next time" sent a prickle on the back of her neck.

"Oh, I can't stand that man," mumbled Mrs. Hardy. "There's something about him I just don't trust. I buy my meat at Weber Butcher Shop on the other side of town for that very reason." She reached into her pocket. "Here, maybe this will make you feel better." She withdrew a large four-holed silver button. "I've been carrying it around for a few days, waiting for the right opportunity to give it to you." Faith smiled at the dear woman and took the small token. Truly, the last thing she wanted was another button for her silly string, but she had to be cordial. "Thank you kindly, ma'am. I shall treasure it."

Stuart banged around his butcher shop, which was closed for business now, but in need of some tending before he could head upstairs to his living quarters. He had purchased the building some twenty years ago after marrying Opal Tindle. Thankfully, she'd inherited a decent dowry from her deceased parents. Stuart's father had been a butcher, though a drunken one, which had led to Stuart's interest in the trade. An only child, he'd grown up taking care of his sickly mother until she passed, then shortly after, around age seventeen, set out on his own, moving to the next town over, Lima, Ohio, where he quickly acquired a job working for a butcher. That's when he met Opal. They dated for a while and then married, both young and lacking life experiences. Truthfully, he'd never even loved her, but he did love the dowry her parents had left her. The couple lived in Lima for a few years, but then Opal grew deathly ill with some sort of lung ailment that required lots of medical attention and his almost continuous care. What a bother she'd become, not to mention an annoyance. He'd spent the better share of his childhood taking care of his sick mother, and now he had a sickly wife who required constant care? The whole thing had nearly been his undoing—until he'd found a solution. He sniffed at the memory, then went in search of a bottle of brew with which to help settle his nerves and possibly relieve some of his anger.

He uncorked the bottle and took a good swig, letting it burn its way down to his gut before he took another big swallow. Ahh, already he felt better, although still plenty mad at Faith Haviland for her utter disrespect.

With the bottle in one hand and a wet rag in the other, he swiped at the front counter, then moved into the other room and opened the giant icebox that held several slabs of meat. Some meat was curing in the back room, but when customers ordered certain cuts, he stored them here until the time of purchase. He took mental inventory then closed the door tight. He took pride in his shop, had since purchasing it with Opal's dowry. Of course, she'd been sick when he'd moved her away from Lima. She hadn't really felt like moving, but he'd given her little choice. An opportunity had come up in Columbus to buy the shop, and he wasn't about to pass it up. They set up housekeeping in the apartment over the butcher shop, and Opal pretty much stayed holed up there, coughing and getting more sickly with each passing day. She'd asked to see a doctor in Columbus because her doctor in Lima had suggested it, but he'd been so busy setting up his new business that he'd failed to find her one.

One day when he'd come upon her crying upstairs, she'd said she wished she were dead, that life with him had brought nothing but misery. He never helped her, showed no sympathy for her plight, and rarely even talked to her, she'd complained.

She wished she were dead?

For days, he'd pondered her wish…and so one day, he'd done the only thing he could for her—ended her misery. She had, after all, asked for it.

At least, her absence had freed him up to start looking for a different woman. Faith Haviland, the blacksmith's daughter, was a mere girl the first time he noticed her, already a beauty in his eyes but too young. For years, he pined for her, watching her from afar. She had an older sister, but she hadn't attracted him in the way Faith had, with her big blue eyes and long blond braids, her skirts blowing in the wind, and her smile enough to set the sun to shining. He'd waited a long time for her to grow up, and when she finally did, he started watching her comings and goings until he figured out her routine. She'd started working at her aunt's diner, so from time to time, he'd go in and strike up conversations with her. He'd even invited her to take a walk with him one day after her shift ended to which she'd laughed and brushed him off. After that, she had started dating boys her age, one after another—and he began giving up on her—until that fellow she'd intended to marry left her just weeks before their wedding. What luck! With renewed interest, he resumed his pursuit of her, but this time with a great deal more determination.

Distracted, he picked up one of his knives and ran his index finger along the blade, shifting nervously at its smooth surface. He held it up close to see his blurred reflection and imagined the frown pulling at his smooth-shaven face. He'd taken great pains to ready himself for supper, to make himself look extra presentable for Faith, only to be turned away.

Perhaps this called for more drastic measures, ones that involved kissing her with more intent and making himself more difficult to resist. He could insist on walking her to or from work—or driving her home in his carriage, whichever she preferred. He might even start waiting for her outside the diner at closing time and not taking no for an answer. Surely, his persistence would pay off, and she'd finally take notice.

He would have to think on this for a few days—until he came up with a foolproof plan.

3

"Y ou're going to what?" Laura Fuller sat rigid, both hands clutching the sides of her wheelchair, her face a picture of shock. Her broken leg pointed straight out as it rested on an ottoman. "That's a ridiculous notion, Joseph Allen Fuller! You can't marry someone you don't even know just because you don't have a current nanny. And what makes you think this—this wretched idea of procuring an annulment after your discharge and then paying said wife a hefty fee for her effort will woo anyone any more than hiring another nanny?"

Joey glanced across the living room at his older brother, who was sitting on the sofa, his arms stretched out across the back. All Jack did was lift his brow and shrug his shoulders. *What good was he?* "I have exhausted all my resources, Mother." Joey sat on a chair facing his mother, his hands clasped between his spread knees as he leaned in. "There isn't another woman in town who would take on this job. Gossip flies fast around here, and by now, the whole town thinks my children are nothing but a bunch of wild, abandoned monkeys."

"Well…," Jack drawled.

Joey quickly pointed a long finger at him. "Don't—you—say—another—word!"

Jack gave a belly laugh. "I haven't said anything yet."

"But you were about to. You were going to agree with what I just said—about them acting like monkeys."

"Stop calling my grandchildren monkeys," Laura said. "They are merely testing every nanny who comes along to see if she'll stay. They are insecure and unsure of their futures. It has been a while since anyone stayed long enough to make them comfortable. You know I would take over their care if I could."

Joey stuffed his anxious nerves back into his chest. "Ma, I don't expect you to watch my four kids."

"Well, I've done it in the past."

"Sure, when you weren't contending with a broken leg."

She lowered her head and fingered a piece of lint on her skirt. She might be laid up, but she still managed to dress herself and do her hair up into a perfect bun with a fancy comb. "It's true they would be a bit much for me to handle at this time."

"Apparently, they're too much for an able-bodied woman, let alone one with a broken leg. I have heard a few nightmarish stories from those who have quit on me—Isaac being the biggest problem but the youngers learning from him. He is no role model, that's for sure. One woman told me Isaac poured pepper into her coffee, which gave her a terrible sneezing fit that lasted nearly an hour. Another said he climbed down a ladder from the second-story window one night after bedtime. And yet another reported he threw flour all over the pantry floor." Joey sighed. "I could go on."

Laura raised her head and gave a woeful expression. "Oh, dear. They can be stinkers, I'll not argue that."

The front door opened, and in walked Jesse, the youngest of the three brothers. Joey stood up and Jesse's mouth formed a wide grin as he strolled from the entryway and across the parlor to embrace his brother. After the quick hug, he held Joey at arm's length and studied him. "Why do I get the feeling I walked into a less than cheery conversation?" He glanced at his mother and then Jack. "What's going on?"

"Tell him, Joseph," Laura insisted.

Joey stood there, mouth gaping, unsure where to start and not looking forward to repeating the whole scenario. "Ma will tell you later."

"Joey's going to advertise for a wife," Jack blurted.

"No kidding," Jesse replied without missing a beat, showing neither shock nor mortification. "Going that route rather than hiring another nanny, huh?"

"Is that all you have to say, Jesse David Fuller!? Tell him what a terrible idea it is! You're the one with the most level head."

"I resent that, Ma," Jack said with a gleam in his eye.

"I'd just as soon hear his reasoning, Ma. Best to listen first, then form an opinion," Jesse answered.

"Hmm, maybe he *is* the most levelheaded," mumbled Jack.

Joey went ahead and repeated his plan, noting that his mother's grimace stayed firmly in place throughout the retelling.

After his recitation, Joey scratched the side of his nose and sat back down. Jesse took a seat on the sofa next to Jack. "So, how do you plan to carry this out?" Jack asked. Their mother scowled and impatiently tapped on the arms of her wheelchair.

"I plan to send a wire to the *Columbus Dispatch* tomorrow and ask them to place an ad for me. I'll also pay extra to have them make posters to place in prominent locations."

"Hmm, so I guess Jesse and I will be getting a temporary sister-in-law, huh?" Jack didn't bother holding back his grin. "What if you end up with a toothless, barn-sized woman with no hair?"

"I frankly don't care what she looks like as long as she can carry out her duties for the next four months with a promise to stay put."

Laura bit her lip. "Oh, Joseph, I don't feel good about this. This is not how God intended marriage to be," she said, her voice filled with pleading.

"Ma, don't start preaching at me."

"Well, you need some good preaching!" Her hazel eyes flashed. "Have you even thought about the ramifications this could have for your children? What sort of morals are you passing down?"

"It's not like I'm going to treat her any differently than all the other nannies I've hired. I'm just putting a legal stipulation on this arrangement so that she'll be less apt to desert her post."

Laura shook her head then tipped it at Jack and then Jesse. "Can't either of you talk some sense into your brother?"

Jack laughed. "Are you serious, Ma? You should know by now that Joey lives by his own rules. Always has."

Laura shook her head regretfully. "That's true. Ever since childhood he's had a head as hard as granite."

"Stubborn as a hammer iron too," said Jesse.

"Okay, everybody, you can stop talking about me as if I'm not right here. I happen to think this plan will work if I can find someone capable of handling my kids."

"And how will you know that if you marry a stranger? You thought the others capable too, but found out after a few months' time that you were wrong."

Joey rubbed his temple. "I don't *know* it, but I still think this is the best possible way to handle the hiring of my next nanny. I think the legalities of the agreement will be of great benefit. I don't know why I didn't think of it earlier."

"I think you should give it more thought, son."

"I've only been granted a two-week furlough. I have to act fast."

She scowled. "Have you prayed about this at all?"

Joey shifted his weight and gave a low chuckle. "I'm leaving that up to you, Ma. You've got better connections."

A mere hour later, Joey reunited with his children. They had been playing a game of tag with their cousins when Jack drove his rig onto the long drive leading up to his sprawling single-story house. As soon as the children noticed the incoming wagon, they dropped what they were doing and ran in their direction.

"Daddy!" and "Uncle Joey!" came the squeals of all six youngsters as they trotted over, dirt and grime on all of their faces.

As soon as Jack reined in the horses, Joey jumped down and dropped to his knees, then opened his arms. They all tried to wheedle in close.

"Step back, Elias and Catherina." Jack gently coaxed his children to the side. "Your cousins want to hug their daddy."

"How long you home for?" Thirteen-year-old Isaac quickly stepped out of his father's embrace, and was mimicked by eleven-year-old Franklin. It pained Joey to know that his sons had passed the point of wanting much outward show of affection. It was the younger two, eight-year-old Beth and five-year-old Miriam, who lingered the longest.

"Not long, I'm afraid. Just a couple of weeks."

"That ain't very long," whined Franklin. "How comes you never stay long?"

Joey stretched out his arm and patted his son's sandy-colored head. "I know. That's because there's a war going on, and I have very important responsibilities."

"I hate the war," said Beth.

"Me too, honey, but it's got to be fought."

"What's war?" little Miriam wanted to know.

"It's fightin' and killin'," Isaac offered in a loud whoop. He situated his arms as if he held a rifle, then pointed his imaginary weapon into the distance and fired, mouthing all the appropriate noises. At least he hadn't pointed it at any of his cousins or siblings, noted Joey. That was one positive.

He decided to change the subject. He raised himself from his kneeling position and directed his next comment at all four of his children, Jack and his kids looking on. "Anything new around here?" He slanted his head and narrowed his eyes as he let his gaze move from one to the other.

"Yeah, their nanny quit," said Catherina.

"Catherina," said Jack, "Uncle Joey wasn't talking to you."

"Well, what do you know? She's absolutely right." Joey's eyes continued roving from one child to the other. "And why do you suppose she quit?"

"They—" This time, Jack shushed his daughter with a palm over her mouth. Her wide eyes shone bright above his hand.

Joey's four children all stood wordless, as if they hadn't a single clue. He might have laughed at their innocent young faces if he hadn't been so frustrated with them.

The door to Jack's house opened and shut just then, and out stepped Joey's sister-in-law Cristina. She put a hand to her eyes to shade them and then gave a shout. "Joseph! Welcome home. Would you like to stay for supper? I've made plenty."

Joey perused Jack's face and earned a nod from him. "You best stay," Jack said. "I doubt you have much food in your house to rustle up. When you go into town tomorrow, you can pick up a few supplies to hold you over."

Joey looked at Cristina and waved. "Okay then, sister," he called out. "Don't mind if we do."

Their supper of venison steak, potatoes, carrots, and cornbread was a jovial affair filled with plenty of chatter and goodhearted fun. To his surprise, Isaac behaved in his presence, perhaps because he sensed the stern lecture that was sure to come before bedtime. After supper, the children, with the exception of Catherina and Beth, went outside to resume their play. The girls cleaned up, and Jack and Joey retired to the living room, away from the kitchen clamor.

"You been thinkin' about that ad you're going to place?"

"Yeah, it's on my mind. I'll keep it simple as possible—something like: *Union captain seeking temporary wife to care for four children under thirteen. Will offer hefty settlement and hasty annulment upon October release from army.*"

Jack slanted his head to one side and issued him a thoughtful countenance. "That's simple enough. You think that'll be enough to woo the right person? You sure you don't want to tack on '*Must not look like the back end of mule*'?"

At this, Joey cut loose a good laugh. "I told you I don't care what she looks like, but it might be easier for me to say 'I do' to an attractive face than one looking like a mule's back side."

At half past seven, Joey rode with his brother over to one of the storage barns to select a rig for his two-week stay, then while Joey wiped the dusty thing down, Jack rode to another barn. Within fifteen minutes or so, Jack returned with a couple good, strong horses in tow for hitching to the rig.

By eight o'clock, they all bid each other a good night's rest, and Joey and his brood started the trek across the wide-open field to their two-story house on the north side of the Fuller farm. *It would feel good to be home*, he mused. The house, upon entering, was dim and quiet, as expected, so before doing anything else, Joey reached for the cast iron safety matchbox on the top of the bookcase not far from the door. He withdrew a match, struck it on the enamel finish, and quickly lit the lamp next to the door. He then walked about the house and lit a few more lamps to ensure plenty of lighting when nighttime set in. Placing the matchbox back in its rightful place on the fireplace mantel, he turned to face his children, who all looked sufficiently prepared for what they surely knew was coming. He rubbed his hands together. "All right then, I want you all to go upstairs, put on your nightclothes, then thoroughly wash your hands and faces and brush your teeth with plenty of tooth powder. Once done, march yourselves back downstairs so we can have a good talk."

They stood staring at him for one long moment, Miriam's big eyes going moist in the corners.

"Don't just stand there. Just go upstairs and do as I say. Now."

As if someone had just lit a match under their bottoms, they turned in an instant and scooted upstairs. Joey went to the kitchen to brew a pot of strong, black coffee. He would surely need it.

Twenty minutes later, a tin mug of hot coffee in hand, he found his four youngsters all sitting quietly huddled together on the old worn-out divan. He couldn't help the smile that escaped. "Thank you for minding me without argument. Now then, let me have a seat here across from you so we can talk a bit. I'll direct my question to Isaac, and I would like him alone to answer me."

"Yes, sir," they said in unison. Even little Miriam gave a stiff nod and pulled her small frame a little straighter.

"Isaac, explain to me why your latest nanny, Miss Wiggens, did not stay longer than three months."

At first, Isaac shrugged, but when Joey tightened his brow, sending him the sternest face he could muster, the boy started talking.

"She was mean, Pa."

"No, that is not what I asked you. Why did she leave?"

"Because she didn't like us, I guess."

"And why didn't she like you?"

"I don't know."

"You *know* there's a reason, and I'm certain it's the same one for why all the others before her didn't last longer than five months. To date, only one has made it longer than six months, and in the meantime, your aunt and your grandmother have had to assume responsibility for you until I found someone new. Your behavior has been a huge hindrance to me."

"What's 'hen-da-rans'?" asked Miriam, carefully trying to pronounce the word.

"It means we ain't been good," said Franklin.

"I been good," she squeaked.

"I'm not placing the blame on you, honey. Come here and sit on my lap." The child leaped from her seat and ran across the space that separated them, then quickly climbed up. Joey gathered his youngest child in his arms and kissed her downy head.

"She's done stuff, Daddy," Isaac whined. "Like she poured a teaspoon of cocoa powder onto Miss Wiggens' apron."

Joey pulled away from his daughter with a frown. "Did you do that, Miriam?"

Her little face screwed up into a frown. "I don't know."

"You do too know," Franklin insisted.

"Yeah, well Beth tol' me t' do it. 'Member, Beth?"

Beth's eyes cut to the floor as she twiddled her thumbs in her lap.

"Beth," Joey said. "Why would you do that?"

With tears in her eyes, she said, "Isaac and Franklin always tell us what to do."

"We don't neither," said Franklin.

"I'm not the only one who acts bad," said Isaac. "We don't like the nannies you pick. They always yell at us. That one before Miss Wiggens always slapped my face."

Joey frowned. "That's disturbing. Why didn't you tell me?"

"'Cause you ain't ever home," Isaac responded, his voice choking up.

But a glance over at his oldest son told him that the boy was made of sterner stuff than he let on. And Joey wouldn't allow Isaac to make him feel guilty for serving his country. He also didn't doubt for a minute that the boys egged on their sisters…but he didn't wish to pit them against each other either.

They talked on a bit longer, each trying to defend his or her position, until Joey resolved he'd never reach the whole truth of the matter. Good heavens, Miss Wiggens hadn't even given him a list of grievances; she had merely told his mother that she was leaving her post—"And good luck to Captain Fuller in finding someone who can last as long as I did!"

At this point, Joey really had no alternative. "All right, listen to me. We are going to put an end to this problem of nannies."

For a change, his children all sat mute…until Franklin broke the silence. "We are?"

"Yes, we are. The next lady I bring in here will be staying until I am mustered out of the Army in mid-October. You will *not* chase her out of the house. You *will* mind your manners, and you will *not* complain about it. You will do *exactly* as she says, and if I hear that you're not obeying the rules, there will be *consequences* to pay upon my return. You will eat what she feeds you. You will rise in the morning when she tells you to and you will go to bed as told. And you will *not* cause any trouble for her. Understand?"

The three children facing him all gave their heads a sober, somber nod, whereas Miriam lay lazily in his arms, as if none of this applied to her.

"And do you want to know why?" This he asked with as harsh a tone as he could deliver.

They all moved their heads slowly up and down.

"Because the next nanny will be your stepmother."

Joey probably should have delivered that bit of news with a little more delicacy, but sometimes the straightforward approach was best. His sons and Beth stared silently at him with wide eyes and slack jaws. Little Miriam drew away from him, a confused expression on her face.

He collected himself, took a deep swallow, and then drew in a cavernous breath. "You *do* know what a stepmother is, don't you?"

"Daddy, we ain't dumb," said Isaac.

Miriam tugged at Joey's sleeve and looked up at him, blinking. "I must be dumb, Daddy, 'cause I don't know."

He couldn't hold back a little smile. "It's somebody that will be like a—a second mother to you. She might not stay after I am released from the army, but she will stay at least until I come home." He pulled Miriam back into his arms and she soon fell fast asleep. His little darling was tired.

"What is *that* supposed to mean?" asked Isaac. "You're goin' t' marry someone then divorce her?"

"Well, I don't want to put it exactly like that."

"Why'd you say she might not stay then?"

"Well, because she will have just met me. She might not like me."

"Or you might not like her," Franklin suggested.

"We're going to—to work out a—sort of arrangement. If I can find someone to agree to it that is."

"That's stupid!" Isaac never had been one to mince words.

"It might very well be, but you children leave me no options. A legal agreement between a lady and me will prevent her from abandoning her responsibilities here."

They all sat in stark silence for a solid minute while letting this new twist settle in their heads. But the silence didn't last long. "I don't want no dumb stepmother," Isaac blurted, jumping to his feet and turning a couple of circles, his face going red as a tomato.

"Me neither," echoed Franklin.

"She'll be worse than the rest," said Isaac.

"Not if I can help it," Joey countered.

"What's her name?" Beth asked, her tone curious but equally irritated.

He paused to find a way to answer her question.

Isaac picked up on it. "Yeah, what's her name?"

More silence while he tried to form his answer.

"Daddy, don't you even know her name?" asked Beth.

He gave them all equal time as he gazed from one to the other. "I— haven't met her yet."

"What?" the three said in unison.

"How can you marry someone you don't know?" asked Isaac.

"I'll be sure to make the best possible choice of all the women who apply for the position."

"Wait." Isaac slowly sat back down and gave his head a shake. "You're hiring somebody to be our stepmother? I don't get it."

Joey drew in a deep breath and then blew it out, shaking his head. "Don't worry. I'll not do anything that will cause you harm. You are my first priority."

"If we're your first priority, how come you're givin' all your attention to the war?" Isaac demanded. *Why did the oldest have to be the one to come up with all the toughest questions?* The other two sat staring at him, clearly anxious for his response. Joey shifted the sleeping girl in his arms.

"You will always be my highest priority. I love you all so very much! But this war is important; we must preserve our country and keep it strong, or everything our founding fathers struggled to create will fall apart. I will only be gone for a little bit more time. In a matter of months, I'll be back home again, and it will be just us."

"And that stepmother," put in Franklin.

"Well, we will see where all that goes after I muster out of the army. Don't trouble yourselves with it now."

They all just gawked at Joey—as if he'd lost the last of his wits. And maybe he had. Only time would tell if his far-fetched notion would grow wings and fly. If it didn't, well, then he was back to square one—right where he didn't want to be.

4

$\mathcal{F}$aith scurried around to ready herself for work. Her mother was in the kitchen downstairs making coffee and frying bacon and eggs if the smells coming up through the floor register were any indication. She sat down in front of the mirror at her vanity table to finish her updo, satisfied that it would stay put for at least the first few hours of the day. She flattened out the sides and inserted a couple of fancy combs, then applied just a hint of color to her cheeks. She sat back to peruse her reflection. *You're no beauty*, she thought ruefully, not for the first time. She had big blue eyes that, in her opinion, were not proportionate to the rest of her face and blond hair that could do with a little less sunshine due to its bleached tinge. She always wore hats in the garden to protect her skin and hair from the harsh rays, but it didn't do much good. In fact, her arms and face had tanned from the sun, something most women considered quite unladylike. She smiled at herself and decided she was content with the condition of her teeth. At least they weren't overly big like her eyes, and they were straight for the most part and shimmery white. Her ears were fine, as was her nose, but she still didn't view her looks as anything out of the ordinary, never mind that Papa often said she had the most beautiful face in all of Columbus. Fathers had to say things like that to their unmarried daughters.

If she was so stunning, why had Frederick Holland left her just two weeks before their April wedding? And why had her best friend Dianna betrayed her after spending so much time with her, helping her choose her long, flowing white dress with the endless train and even assisting her in writing out the invitations? It wasn't until closer to the date that Dianna started withdrawing from her and Frederick grew more distant and less affectionate. How could she have been so blind? After the fact, Faith began to recall her fiancé and best friend laughing together on various occasions, huddling close in quiet conversation, and even seeking each other out in large crowds. She'd always surmised they were planning one surprise or another for her upcoming wedding, but instead, they'd been planning their *own* little surprise. How foolish of her to be so trusting! She'd cried off and on for a few weeks after reading the short letter of apology from Frederick, who claimed to have unintentionally fallen in love with Dianna and now planned to marry *her* instead.

The shock had nearly killed Faith—but not her faith. She'd never even missed a day of work, nor had she wasted much time feeling sorry for herself. In fact, with head held high, she'd returned the wedding dress one week after the dreaded letter, thankful that the shopkeeper declared she'd no doubt find another buyer for it yet that week. Yes, by God's grace alone, she'd started moving on. Unfortunately, the townsfolk had not, and their sorrowful stares, well-meaning remarks, and continued notes of sympathy had wearied her. They'd even continued to offer her buttons for her Victorian button string, thinking the small tokens would somehow aid in her healing. Little did they know that each burnished, sparkling glass, or polished shell button only made the sting in her heart more poignant.

She stood up, gave her bedroom a final inspection, then released a gentle sigh before stepping out into the hallway and walking down the carpeted corridor to the stairs that would lead to the foyer. The hem of her skirt might've brushed the floor were it not for the raised heels of her laced-up shoes. She entered the kitchen. "Good morning, Mama."

Audrey Haviland's skirt flared slightly when she turned to greet her daughter. "Good morning, dear. Did you sleep well?"

"I did, thank you." She picked up a slice of browned bacon and let it crumble and melt in her mouth. In less than thirty minutes, she and Aunt Martha would be standing at the big stove in the diner, frying eggs, bacon, and potatoes, their usual morning meal. There would also be a big kettle of oatmeal warming on the stove for those who chose to eat a lighter fare. There might even be griddle cakes resting on a warming tray. "Has Papa already gone to work?"

From behind, she felt the wisp of a kiss on her cheek. "Not yet, sunshine." An instant balm settled in her chest at the sight of her father's bearded face, twinkling blue eyes, and warm smile. Albert took his seat at the round kitchen table, a cup of freshly brewed coffee already waiting for him. Audrey always stayed one step ahead of her husband. He wore his usual work attire, suitable for a long day at his business, the aptly named Haviland & Sons Blacksmith Shop. There were only two other blacksmiths in Columbus, neither of which had the same level of skill and expertise, nor Albert's fine, long-standing reputation.

"Are you off to work?"

"Yes, Papa, although I must say I'd rather sit a spell with you and Mama. I'm getting weary of everyone asking for the hundredth time whether I've yet heard from Frederick and Dianna. And the buttons—oh, Mama, they keep filling my pockets. Can't folks tell I'm no longer interested in collecting for that ridiculous button string?"

"It's not ridiculous, dear. You should continue the collection, for now it has become a lovely hobby. Someday, before your wedding day, you'll receive your thousandth button." She smiled brightly and clasped her hands together. "And may it come from your betrothed and not some ordinary person."

"Mother, my wedding day has long passed."

Audrey stood up straight, pursed her lips, and stuck out her fine little chin. "There will be another." Without giving Faith a second to respond, she went on. "Now then, folks do mean well. You shouldn't let their small acts of kindness and gentle words of sympathy concern you so." She set a plate of food in front of Albert and then turned to spoon a plateful for herself. As usual, he would wait until she seated herself before offering the breakfast prayer.

"Folks do mean well, dear wife, but they should know by now to let the whole thing rest. It's a subject that's grown old and need not be resurrected over and over," Albert said, ever able to see things Faith's way. "Has that Porter fellow quit pestering you?"

A rock-like knot formed in her chest. "I have not seen or heard from him for four days now, and that is a record. As I mentioned to you earlier, our last conversation was most unpleasant, and I had to be very direct with him. He became rude, and several in the restaurant stood up for me. But since then, he's left me alone."

"Good," Albert said. "I'll not put up with him bothering you. Even your brother Thomas said he'll take the man's head off if he keeps up his improper behavior. We should pray for his soul, of course, but we're not obligated to like him while we do it. I'll leave that part to God."

She giggled. "Oh, Papa, I do so love you. Thank Thomas for me today. It's nice to know someone besides God Almighty is looking after me. I must go now. Both of you have a wonderful day."

They said their goodbyes, and Faith headed to work, enjoying the pre-dawn stillness. It was dark as midnight, save for the low-burning streetlamps that served to mark her path. Not even the birds had awakened, nor had the moon completely vanished. Her heels made a clicking sound on the cobblestone sidewalk as she neared City Park at Deshler Street. With six or seven blocks to go and time on her hands, she slowed her pace and set to praying about her day, asking God to bless it and to bless those with whom she talked. She prayed too that those who wished to blather on about Frederick and Dianna might at last find the subject too boring to discuss.

A rustling sound in the bushes just feet ahead of her put her on alert. At once, a silhouette of a man emerged from the park and started to advance. She had to squint in the dark to make out the figure…and recognized Stuart Porter's tall frame. "Good morning, Faith," he said in his low, rough voice. "You look so pretty this morning."

He smelled of alcohol. An unsettling feeling had her looking over her shoulder. "What in the world are you doing here? You startled me." She stepped up her pace.

"I thought I would walk you to work."

"You've been drinking, and I don't need an escort, Mr. Porter." *So he'd been waiting in the park for her to pass by?*

He gave an unfriendly laugh, which made her stomach twist in a nervous knot. She kept walking, but then he suddenly took hold of her arm and squeezed. "I think it's time you learned to be a little more polite to me, Faith."

"Stop it this instant! Let me go!" She tried twisting out of his hold, but he only held on tighter.

"Just relax, would you?" he asked.

She stopped and, with all the courage she could muster, stared up at him. "Let go of me right now, Stuart Porter."

Rather than obey, he tossed back his head and laughed. "You are a feisty one, F-Faith. Feisty Faith. Maybe I shall start calling you that."

"You're drunk, Stuart Porter. What is *wrong* with you?" All the while, he kept squeezing her arm, and the pain was beginning to get to her. "You're hurting me, Mr. Porter." Again, she tried to wriggle free.

He gave a low chortle. "I'm sh-sorry. I don't mean to hurt you, but you're not cooperating. I—I didn't want to force a kiss on you, Faith, but you give me no choice."

"What?" She jerked back her head. "Don't be ridicu—"

In an instant, he yanked her chest up close to his, pinning her free arm between them as he pressed his cold, hard, smelly mouth against hers, one hand still clenching her arm just under her elbow, and the other pressed hard at the center of her back, hauling her close. He tried to part her lips, but she shook her head back and forth to avoid his kiss, fighting with all her might. She wriggled to free the one hand that was pinned between them and then scratched the side of his face. Then with the pointed toe of her shoe, she kicked him hard in the shin. That got his attention, and in response, he took a tiny step back, growled, then drew back his fist and threw a hard punch to her mouth, knocking her to the ground.

Stunned, Faith sought to catch her bearings and her breath, knowing that if she didn't escape him soon, she could be in even bigger trouble. She clawed at the ground, grabbing a fistful of dirt, and when he yanked her back up by the arm, she threw the dirt into his eyes, setting him off balance.

"Hey, what's going on over there?" boomed a male voice in an approaching wagon.

"Help!" Faith screamed and set off on a run toward the wagon, despite feeling dizzy and faint. The wagoner drew his horse to a stop and instantly reached down a hand to help her up. Once on the wagon seat, Faith looked back and discovered Stuart had vanished. She thanked God for her unknown rescuer.

"You all right, ma'am?" he asked.

"Yes, yes, thank you so much for stopping. Please, please—would you mind taking me to Daybreak Diner? I must get to work."

"Um, sure, but…don't you want me to take you to Sheriff Mumford's office instead?"

Her mind was a blur of terror and confusion. She knew the sheriff's office *ought* to be her first stop, but what she really wished to do was collect herself beforehand, and oddly, the restaurant seemed the best place for now. "No—I—I need to get to the diner. My aunt can't handle things alone."

The middle-aged stranger shook his head. "All right then." He set the horses in motion. "Who was that fellow anyway?"

Without hesitation, she answered. "Stuart Porter." Breathless, she put a hand to her already swollen mouth. She ran her tongue around the inside of her mouth and was relieved to find that all of her teeth were intact.

"The butcher?" he asked.

"Yes, he—he wanted to walk me to work, and when I refused him, he became forceful. I don't know what possessed him—other than he'd been drinking. He stunk to high heaven."

"Humph, well, you best report him. The fellow needs to sit in jail for a few days."

They rode the rest of the way in silence.

$\mathcal{Y}$ou *must* report him to Sheriff Mumford," Aunt Martha whispered later in the kitchen. Over the past hour, Faith had gotten a number of stares from patrons, some asking what had happened and others keeping their questions to themselves. "Look at your mouth. You have a fat lip, and it's gettin' worse. If you don't go to the sheriff, I will."

"Then you go. I'm afraid to leave the restaurant." Perhaps she should have listened to the fellow who'd driven her to the diner, whose name she'd never learned, when he'd offered to drive her straight to the sheriff's office. But she'd not been thinking straight.

"Miss Haviland, excuse me, ma'am." It was Mr. Carver, one of their regulars, standing at the counter. "I couldn't help but overhear you and Miss Martha talkin', and I was wonderin', do you want me to go get the sheriff for y'? I can direct him here, and once he arrives, you'll be in safe hands."

Faith opened her mouth to answer, but Martha beat her to it. "That would be mighty nice of you, Mr. Carver."

"I'll be happy to help in any way I can," chimed in Mrs. Goldberg, who walked up next to Mr. Carver. "I used to wait tables in Sandusky before we moved here last year. I'd be able to relieve you if you need to go home for the rest of the day, Miss Haviland—or even for the next few days. I'm mighty capable in the kitchen, Miss Martha."

"Oh, my goodness, I'd be much obliged, Mrs. Goldberg," said Martha.

"Please, call me Florence. I been tellin' my husband, the new owner at Village Feed Store, how I'd like to find me a job again. I'm tired of bein' in the house all day stitchin', knittin', cleaning, and cooking. It's just the two of us, and a house can only get so clean, you know."

"In fact, I've been considering puttin' a sign on the window to advertise for a part-time helper," said Martha. "Perhaps we can work together awhile, and if you find you like it, you can start workin' here more regular like."

The woman's gray head bobbed up and down as she gave a full-toothed smile. "I would love that. I been prayin' about findin' something."

Faith couldn't believe her ears. Was God already laying the groundwork for her to quit her job and head for parts unknown? Stuart's unexpected attack on her this morning had convinced her even more that she needed to leave Columbus. Even if he did go to jail, how long could they legally hold him? He'd assaulted her, yes, but his attack hadn't resulted in anything more than a swollen mouth and a sore body from having fallen to the hard ground. She shuddered to think what he might do next. Lord, have mercy.

Sheriff Mumford arrived within twenty minutes, and quick as a dart, he and his deputy ushered her out the back door into the alley where he'd parked his waiting police wagon. She'd barely had time enough to say goodbye to Aunt Martha.

"I am sorry to have whisked you away so quickly, miss," Sheriff Mumford said. "But I wanted to get you out of there. I understand some fellow assaulted you this morning, and you never can tell where he might be lurking. One of my deputies went to retrieve your father. You might need the extra support."

Her heart pounded faster than a sprinting horse. "Thank you."

At the sheriff's office, the sheriff and one detective asked several straightforward questions—name of her attacker, did she know what had provoked him, was there a previous history of problems with him, did she need to see a doctor, and what were the extent of her injuries? With God's help, she managed to stay calm throughout the interview, answering each question as best she could.

"Thank you for your time, miss. A couple of deputies have gone to his shop to make an arrest. If he's not there, then we'll find him. In the meantime, I'd suggest you lie low, no going out or even working at the diner until he's in custody. I'll have Deputy Ernest Cook here escort you back to your place. Will there be someone there?"

"I'm taking the rest of the day off, Sheriff," her father said. "My wife and I will keep our eye out for any trouble."

"That's good. I'd lock things up tight and stay on guard until we have this feller in custody. I presume you plan to press charges, Miss Haviland."

She nodded. "Yes, I don't want him doing this to anyone else."

Stuart hid in the blackness of the attic situated off one of the spare rooms, the smells of musty clothes and old relics overcoming his senses. He lay still, wool blankets and old quilts heaped atop him, his body surrounded by crates and cartons. He tried shallow breathing so as not to give himself away, his eyes buttoned shut, his body unmoving. He'd known it wouldn't take long for the authorities to walk into his business and then climb the stairs to his residence, but with a little luck, they'd give up looking for him and figure he'd already skipped town. Which would be the case just as soon as they vacated his place. "Don't see nuthin' in here."

He recognized the voice as belonging to Duke Shepard, one of Sheriff Mumford's deputies. He pictured the fool holding a lantern high in the old attic.

"It's plenty spooky in here," said another man whose voice was unfamiliar. "And hotter 'n a cat afire."

"Yeah, he ain't up here. Who's gonna hide in an oven?"

"Shall we dig around a bit?"

"Naw. We'll just go back to the office and report him having already made tracks out o' town."

"Yeah, his shop looks closed up tight as a drum. Don't look like he planned to do any business today—or tomorrow, for that matter. Wonder what sort o' trick he's up to."

"I don't know, but I never have trusted that feller. I've heard stories."

"Such as?"

"For one, whatever happened to his wife?"

"I didn't even know he was married."

"Exactly. Most don't. But he was at one time."

"Oh yeah? Maybe she left him."

"That's the story. Or maybe—who knows? Maybe it's something more sinister."

"Now y're givin' me the quivers."

"Yeah, let's get. He ain't here."

Lying as still as a dead jackrabbit, Stuart waited for the sounds of retreating footsteps descending the stairs. At the final slam of the front door downstairs, he finally dared to move. Shoving the heavy blankets off him, he sat up and gasped for a good breath, the heavy air threatening to steal his last one. He swiped at his drenched brow, then pushed the bedding the rest of the way off him and stood. He had to work fast lest the sheriff himself come back to do a more thorough search. Those fool deputies were worth about as much as two cracked eggs.

One thing they'd been right about, though, was the fact he'd closed up shop. Not knowing exactly how things would go this morning with Faith, he'd devised a plan for skipping town for a few days—maybe even weeks—until things blew over. He hadn't intended to hit her. He'd really only wanted to steal a few kisses—but she'd hauled off and scratched his face and then kicked him, which made him react. Okay, so maybe he shouldn't have punched her. He'd pay for that for sure. Fool woman!

He had to get out of town, but not quite yet. First, he had to find out what Faith's intentions were. Did she plan to press charges or let the thing blow over? Whatever the case, he wouldn't—no, he *couldn't*—go to jail. The idea of his being trapped in a cell called up memories of his childhood, when his father locked him in a closet for the smallest infractions. No, sir. No jail time for him.

He had to think—and think fast. But first, he needed a good stiff drink.

∽

Audrey stood on the front porch wringing her hands when Deputy Cook pulled his wagon up to the Havilands' house. Betty Jenkins, a neighbor lady, was standing next to her and Faith inwardly groaned.

"Faith, are you all right?" Audrey called out. "Mrs. Jenkins here just reported to me that that awful Stuart Porter attacked you on your way to work this morning. It's all over town." She hurried down the steps and over to the wagon. "Oh, my goodness, daughter, look at you! What did he do to your mouth?"

"I'd best be off I guess," Mrs. Jenkins said and scurried away—no doubt ready to spread more scuttlebutt around town.

Albert arrived just then and parked his wagon behind the deputy's. He jumped to the ground and went over to help Faith down. "Thank you for seeing her safely home, Mr. Cook," he told the deputy.

"Is that awful Stuart Porter behind bars yet?" Audrey asked.

"Not yet, ma'am," the deputy replied. "But don't you worry, he will be." He tipped his hat to the Havilands. "Afternoon, folks," he said. Clicking to his horse, he set off down the road.

Faith held tightly onto her father's arm as they went into the house. It was still early in the day, a quarter past two, and Faith's stomach was doing flip-flops. *Had she even had anything to eat today?* She couldn't remember.

"Here, dear, sit yourself down," Audrey said as soon as they walked into the living room. Faith lowered herself to the sofa, her mother quickly sidling up next to her. "Tell me what happened this morning and also what the sheriff said about the situation."

Faith looked over at Albert, feeling panic rising inside her. *Mama will surely not let her out of the house if she hears what happened!* Her father nodded at her. He understood. He sat down in the chair across from them and gave Audrey an abbreviated version of the morning's events.

Audrey squeezed her daughter's hand, and Faith saw her mother's gray eyes fill with tears. "What if that awful beast comes knocking on our door in the middle of the night?"

"That's highly unlikely, dear," Albert said. "But to be safe, we'll be locking things up tight tonight at the sheriff's suggestion, and I'll have my rifle at the ready. After the deputy took Faith outside to help her into his wagon, the sheriff told me confidentially that he's never fully trusted Stuart Porter. He mentioned something about the mysterious disappearance of his wife…"

Faith's spine prickled. "I've never heard anything about his having a wife!"

"Apparently, most don't know, but some folks say when he first moved to Columbus some twenty years ago, he came with a wife—but no one ever met her. Word was she suffered some sort of horrid illness, but whether she died from it or simply left her husband to seek treatment and never returned is a mystery. Sheriff Mumford told me they did do as thorough an investigation as they could years ago, but that the case went cold when they couldn't find an ounce of proof of any foul play. Some say Porter told them his wife left him for another man, while others say he told them the dreaded disease took her last breath. It's unclear—and there's no record of her death in court files."

More shivers skipped up and down Faith's spine. The recollection of what Stuart had done to her that morning and the worry that he might accost her again made her stomach queasy. *Lord, lead authorities to Stuart, and in the interim, please keep us all safe.*

Toward dusk, Faith stood over the stove, boiling water in the kettle to make a cup of tea. She'd been mulling over the day's events. The open window in the kitchen blew in a nice summer breeze, cooling her skin and helping to calm her nerves. Her mother, on the other hand, scurried about the place like a leaf in a whirlwind, every so often taking a piece of paper out of her apron pocket, then quickly stuffing it back inside.

"Mama, settle down. Everything will be fine." She picked up the kettle and carefully poured the steaming water.

Audrey threw a worried glance at the open window. "We should probably close that. You know what the sheriff said about keeping the house tightly secured."

"It's too stuffy not to let in a little air. Mr. Porter would not come snooping while it's still daylight."

Audrey continued to fidget with the paper in her pocket, her eyes darting from Faith to the yard outside. "I hope you're right."

Finally, Faith's curiosity got the better of her. "What have you got there?"

"What?" Her mother's head shot up. "Where?"

"In your pocket. What have you got? You keep taking it out and putting it back. What is it?"

"Oh! This?" She withdrew the paper and slowly started to unfold it, then she pressed the rather large, wrinkled sheet to her chest. "You know I've never been thrilled with the idea of you leaving Columbus. If you went, a piece of my heart would follow you."

"What exactly are you getting at, dear?" Albert sauntered in with a rolled-up newspaper tucked under his armpit.

"Well, I…" Audrey began. "I found this when I went to market yesterday."

"What is it?" Faith asked.

"Yes, what is it?" Albert repeated.

Audrey thrust the paper at Faith, but her father snatched it away with a smile and began perusing it.

His eyes crinkled, his smile faded, and for a few seconds, he said nothing. Soon though, he raised his head and regarded his wife. "You can't be serious, Audrey." He handed the sheet of paper over to Faith.

She took it and read it in silence. The headline said it all: "WANTED: Temporary Wife to Care for Four Children. *Healthy Monetary Allowance after Speedy Annulment.*"

Faith shot her parents a nervous glance then quickly reread the newspaper announcement. She slowly lowered the paper and raised her eyebrows at her parents. Audrey's eyes implored while Albert's probed.

"This is quite unthinkable," Faith said finally.

"My thoughts exactly," said Albert.

"Yes, it is a far-fetched notion," agreed Audrey.

"On the other hand..." Faith raised the printed advertisement and read it again, this time aloud:

WANTED: Temporary Wife to Care for Four Children. *Healthy Monetary Allowance after Speedy Annulment.* Widowed Army officer with four children, ages 5 to 13, requires caregiver for next four months. After captain's discharge date of October 15, wife shall be granted a healthy financial stipend and a speedy annulment. Make haste and reply to Captain Joseph Fuller, Fuller Family Farms, Lebanon, Ohio. Chosen applicant will receive two-way train tickets. Should applicant fit requirements and desire to marry, wedding will transpire immediately. If applicant does not wish to marry, she may take advantage of return ticket. *Please be aware*: this arrangement is legal and binding. Wife shall be obliged to stay until the captain's day of discharge. Announcement 236. *Columbus Dispatch.*

For several moments, Faith reread and pondered. Finally, she refolded the advertisement, clutched it in her closed hand, and gaped at her parents.

"What are you thinking?" Audrey asked.

"I don't know what to think. He's an army captain in need of someone to watch his four children until his time of discharge." Her heart thumped with a mixture of curiosity and terror. *How could she possibly entertain such a wild notion?*

"Lebanon is not that far away, perhaps a six-hour train ride. And he did mention sending a two-way ticket," Audrey said.

"Mama, how could I do such a thing—marry someone I don't love?"

"Yes, how could she?" her father asked. "It would be foolhardy."

"Not necessarily. People marry for convenience all the time. Why, look at Harv and Mary Ballister, who married just after both their spouses passed. They barely knew each other, but Harv had two children, and Mary had three—and no means for caring for them. Harv at least had a lucrative business, so he had the means. I see them at church every Sunday, and they appear happy. Another thing, Faith, if you never consummate the marriage, a judge will grant an annulment."

"Mother!" Faith's face went as hot as that tea she'd just sipped. "I don't wish to discuss that aspect."

"Well, it does happen, Faith. Once two people marry…"

"Mama, I know what happens after two people marry." Her father shifted his weight and glanced at the floor, obviously embarrassed. "But in this case, of course, it would not happen! Besides, it sounds like he will be on the battlefield whilst I watch over his four children."

"All right then, all the easier for you to part ways when the time comes."

"But that would put me right back here in Columbus, and by then, I'm certain Stuart Porter will be free to roam the streets again and cause me problems."

"But if your stipend is healthy enough, perhaps you could start anew somewhere else," Audrey said. "Lebanon, or even somewhere east. You've always wanted to see new places."

Faith's mind filled with all manner of thoughts as she tried to weigh the pros and cons. "I—I suppose I can't truly make any sort of decision unless I actually meet the man."

"I wouldn't want you marrying anyone even for one week if you thought him totally wrong for you," Albert said. "You've already endured a terrible heartbreak. I shouldn't wish that on you again. Perhaps I should accompany you."

Audrey gave her hands a clap. "Yes, Albert, that is a fine idea."

Faith tensed, her throat going as dry as corn flour. "But you would not be the one applying for the position, Papa. Your coming along might very well make him think me incapable of tending his children. I would need to make a good first impression."

"Humph, I suppose that's true," Albert replied.

Audrey clasped her hands together and glanced from Faith to Albert and then back at Faith. "So, dear, would you seriously consider this proposition? I think it might be a good thing for you."

"I—I don't know. Perhaps I would." Faith put a hand over her mouth. "Oh, dear, did I just say that?"

"I believe you did," Audrey said.

Faith took a deep breath and pulled her shoulders straight. "If it is meant to be, it will be. I shall trust the Lord through it all."

Behind Albert's dark beard, a tiny smile emerged. "Your mother and I will both remain in prayer until you've come to a proper decision."

"And I shall be as well," Faith assured them.

Oh, Lord, grant me clear direction—that I may make a wise choice, one that pleases You.

6

*J*oey's chest fluttered with apprehension as he caught sight of a stagecoach, no doubt *hers*, come flying over a distant peak. The rolling coach bounced along, and he could only imagine the splattering mud coming from the wheels as a result of this morning's three-hour downpour that had drenched everything in sight. Now, however, the sun peeked through puffy clouds, giving a wisp of hope that a lovely afternoon awaited. He swallowed hard and tried to tamp down his jitters. Good grief, he hadn't been this nervous since the Battle of Atlanta a year ago.

He removed his hat and smoothed down his hair, then slammed the blamed thing back on his head. *Why should he care so much about his appearance?* For all he knew, the woman about to disembark from the stagecoach wouldn't give a care how he looked, so why should he? No doubt his promise of a speedy annulment and the healthy stipend had been all she'd needed to convince her to take the trip. Of course, she'd been his *only* applicant, so apparently, his ad hadn't been all that convincing. Fleetingly, he wondered what he'd gotten himself into—and he wasn't the only one. Ma thought he'd lost all the screws in his upper story. Jesse's words of a few days ago rebounded in his brain. *"What if you end up with a toothless, barn-sized woman with no hair?"* That thought had occurred to him, but he brushed it aside and hoped for the best. This was nothing but a big, irresponsible risk, and not only was he playing the silly game, he might very well be putting his children in harm's way. She could be a mean old sourpuss. If he'd been a praying man like his brothers, he probably would've sought help from the Almighty.

Isaac was his biggest concern. Franklin, Beth, and Miriam would probably adapt in time, but Isaac? Just this morning, while standing at the sink halfheartedly washing dishes while Franklin stood beside him to dry them, Isaac had declared he already hated *"the new maid."*

"She is not to be called a maid, Isaac, and don't throw around the word hate, as if it were a natural emotion. You don't even know her. She will be the new nanny, just like all the others, and you will treat her with respect. Understood?"

"You said she'd be our stepmom. That's different than a nanny."

"Well, yes, it is, and all the more reason for respect."

To that the boy had said nothing, just kept moving his wet cloth across the same plate. "Hurry up!" Franklin had said. "I been standin' here for five minutes whilst you wash that same dumb dish. I wanna go outside sometime today."

Joey shook his head at the memory and turned his attention back to the approaching stagecoach.

⌒

"Lebanon House Station, coming up!" called the stagecoach driver from his high perch.

Faith's nerves stood up like a thousand little soldiers. She glanced around the stagecoach, where she and five other passengers were squeezed as tightly together as a cluster of gooseberries. She would be so relieved to finally arrive. Her long train ride from Columbus to Deerfield Station began early that morning, and this last little jaunt from Deerfield to Lebanon House made her about as tired as an old shoe. On the one hand, the driver's words cheered her, but on the other, fear of what awaited her made her quiver with worry. She put two fingers to her upper lip and was thankful that most of the swelling caused by Stuart Porter's fist had gone down. It was still noticeable if one looked closely and the abrasion inside her mouth was tender. *At least no one could see that.*

What would Joseph Fuller look like, and how would she recognize him? She formed a quick prayer for courage and tried to see out the windows, but the men on both sides of her blocked her view. Quite certain she was doing God's bidding, she tried to take in several deep breaths to calm herself, but nothing helped. With the stench of close bodies and the overwhelming heaviness in the air, she decided if she arrived in Lebanon before melting, it would be a miracle.

As the time for meeting Captain Fuller drew close, more doubts stormed her mind. *What if she'd jumped ahead of God's leading? What if she'd misread the direction she perceived Him nudging her to go? What if she wasn't even cut out to take care of four children ages thirteen and under?* She thought about her family and how her mother's firm resolve had helped hold her own emotions at bay.

Audrey had given Faith a quick hug at the station that morning, stepped back, and said, "Now you send us a wire just as soon as you make your final decision. Your papa and I will be praying for you. Remember, trust God in this, and He will close and open doors."

Besides Mama and Papa, her sister and brothers had also seen her off at the station, all wearing reserved expressions yet assuring her they'd stand by her no matter what. Her eldest brother Thomas, ever the watchful one, reminded her that the authorities still hadn't located Stuart Porter and she ought to bear that in mind whenever she took the Fuller children anywhere…if she married their father, that is. His words had set her heart into a regular tailspin. Folks everywhere had grown leery since news of Stuart Porter's attack on Faith, and none wished to have a face-to-face encounter with him. Mothers held extra tight to their children's hands, women traveled in pairs, youngsters didn't play on the streets alone, and the men kept their firearms handy while riding through town.

Albert had offered his final bit of wisdom when he'd put a strong arm around her shoulder and told her to put her trust in God rather than worry about Stuart Porter. "Porter has no idea you're traveling to Lebanon, and I can't imagine how he'd ever find out. Your whereabouts are not public news." His soothing words did help to calm her…a little.

Several hours later, with exactly three train stops at various stations along the way, and now this final stagecoach ride into downtown Lebanon, Faith gave her fellow passengers one final inspection. The two men seated on either side of her had kept up a constant conversation about politics, business, and the economy since leaving Deerfield Station, ignoring Faith for the most part and talking over her head. Across from them sat three women, one elderly and the other two middle-aged and heavyset. The oldest had divulged that she was returning from a lengthy visit with her daughter's family in Westerville, Ohio. The other women had spent most of the trip napping. Thankfully no one asked Faith why she was visiting Lebanon. The last thing she wished to do was explain that she was on her way to meet her future husband.

Joseph watched as, one by one, passengers started disembarking the stage. First came an elderly woman whose waiting husband stood at the ready to help her down. Two gentlemen wearing business suits and carrying portfolios came next, and after them, two portly women, one of whom wore a huge feathered hat and a giant hoop skirt. The driver put out a hand to assist the one with the hat, but she ignored it, so he helped down the woman following her. The lady with the massive hat immediately laid eyes on Joey as soon as her shiny black leather shoes touched the ground.

"Might you be the one I'm to meet?" she asked, approaching him without hesitation. "My, it was a long train ride! I feel as if I've been riding for days and not mere hours. Have you been standing here long? I am quite prepared to assume the task at hand, and as I mentioned in my return letter to you, I do have plenty of experience."

Letter? Experience? "I—are you—?" His stomach dropped to his boots, and he found himself quite speechless. Jesse's words about the possibility of his bride being a barn-sized, toothless woman returned to haunt him yet again. *Was his worst nightmare coming to fruition?*

When he didn't finish his sentence, the woman switched her body weight to her other foot, and she placed one gloved hand on a round hip, the other hand holding tight to a medium-sized valise. "You are the son of old Mr. Curtis, are you not? As a full-fledged nursemaid of the elderly, I am here to care for Gerald Curtis in his final days on earth."

Relief in the form of a huge mass of air whistled past his lips. "No, ma'am, 'fraid not, but I do know Gerald Curtis." He glanced off. "In fact, there's his son now." He waved at the approaching man who smiled and returned the gesture, and with nary a thank-you, the woman set off to meet him, satchel in hand. Joey turned and studied his surroundings. The woman who'd followed the hat lady off the stage had already connected with a younger woman and a child. Stumped, he wondered what had become of his bride-to-be. The stage driver had stepped off to the side to engage in conversation with another driver, seemingly unaware of his missing passenger.

Confused thoughts ran through Joey's head. *Had he mixed up arrival times?* He pulled out the telegram he'd received just yesterday and reread it. "Arriving at Deerfield Station at 12:30 p.m. and by stage at Lebanon House Station by 1:30 p.m.," the note clearly stated. He checked his pocket watch, which now read twenty minutes before one o'clock. A bit of a racket ensued aboard the stagecoach, so he moved closer—just in time to see a slender woman in a long summer dress with scooped neck and puffy sleeves emerge carrying a medium-size bag. Most of her face was hidden in the shadow of her hat brim so he couldn't make out her features.

She lifted her face, and a lovely pair of large eyes alighted on him, though the shade from her hat prevented him from determining their color. He guessed her to be about five and a half feet tall but weighing about as much as a sack of feathers.

She stood staring long and hard at him, the brim of her hat still hiding her expression. The driver quickly stepped up. "Oh, pardon, miss. I thought I'd already helped all the lady passengers down."

She waved a gloved hand at him. "It's quite all right. I'm afraid I lost my button string for a minute, and then when I found it, I realized I'd lost a couple of buttons from it as well. They rolled under the seat, so I had to get them before I could disembark." She accepted the driver's hand and stepped to the ground.

"Your button string, miss?" the driver asked, mystified.

The slender young woman shook her head. "Yes, my button string, but never mind. I procured it easily enough, even though it did take a bit of stretching on my part. All is well, thank you."

"That's good. I'll fetch y'r other bag under the coach." While the driver's back was to them as he stooped to drag out another piece of luggage, Joey and the young woman gaped at each other. The driver set her large suitcase on the ground beside her, then excused himself to talk to the livery boy who'd come to tend his horses.

Joey took another step forward and extended a hand. "Miss Haviland, I presume?" he asked.

"Yes, and Captain Fuller, *I* presume?"

"That is correct. My name is Joseph, but you may call me Joey if you prefer."

She nodded and shook his hand. With the formalities out of the way, she quickly put her hands to her sides and lifted her chin a tad higher, at last revealing an oval face and lightly freckled nose. Joey now noted the azure blue of her eyes, which sparkled in the sunlight. He detected a swollen lip but decided now wasn't quite the time to ask about it.

She perused him top to bottom. "Well. It's nice to meet you, sir."

"Everyone's called me Joey since boyhood, although my mother calls me Joseph and sometimes Joseph Allen if she has a gripe with me." This he said to eke a smile from her, but none came. His jitters escalated. She was a pretty thing, but slender as a pine twig, making him question how she'd ever manage his overactive brood. *What if she agreed to the marriage, but realized too late that she wasn't up to the task?* He'd only be here a few more days to help her adapt, but after that, she'd be on her own.

She scrutinized the town and then her immediate surroundings. "Where are the children?"

"Oh, they're back at the big house—my mother's house, I should say. I thought meeting them here might be a bit too chaotic."

"I see."

Joey picked up her valise so that now he held two pieces of luggage.

"Should I choose to stay, I shall send for my trunk later," she said.

"Of course." He couldn't help but stare. She was prettier than he'd expected her to be, with the exception of that swollen lip, which begged the question—why hadn't anyone else snagged her up? *Was she a difficult woman? Did she have some hidden affliction? Was she a weakling?* By the look of her, she hadn't milked any cows or mucked any stalls of late. Questions flew through his mind until he finally said, "Well, shall we go then? We can talk on the way to the farm. It's just a few miles' drive. You can take my arm if you choose, although you might find yourself bumping against your suitcase." He tried to crook his arm, but she didn't take it, so they advanced to his waiting buggy side by side and without a bit of conversation.

Whoo boy! Isaac had better be on his best behavior. Joey could imagine her running at the first hint of his naughtiness.

7

Captain Joseph Fuller certainly didn't lack in good looks, with his broad build, towering height, and dark brown hair and eyes...but those attributes weren't enough to sway Faith's good sense. No siree. She'd already cowered under the brutal hands of Stuart Porter and endured a painful rejection by Frederick Holland. She wouldn't be caught off guard again. She had come to Lebanon to see if she could feel right about marrying a man she didn't know, and meeting his children was a paramount factor in that decision. Sitting beside Captain Fuller on the front buggy seat, she sat up straight, making herself as tall as she could, and tried to keep some space between them so as not to bump against his sturdy frame as they jostled along, the seat springs complaining under their weight.

"Tell me about your family in Columbus," he said as he steered his horses down Lebanon's main thoroughfare.

"All right, but then you must tell me about your family."

"Fair enough."

"I have three siblings, two older brothers and an older sister. They are all married with children. My father and brothers own and operate Haviland and Sons Blacksmith Shop, while my mother keeps house and tends to her large gardens. I've been working with my aunt in her restaurant, Daybreak Diner, for a number of years while living at home with my parents, but it was high time I moved on with my life. When I saw your ad, I decided to apply. Have you had many applicants?"

"Not many," was his short response. "So, you've never married then?"

"No."

She kept her eyes trained on the road ahead but felt his gaze upon her. He'd spread his knees and rested his elbows on them, holding loosely to the reins. Evidently, his horses had taken this path countless times and needed no prodding or guidance. "I can't believe you've managed to escape marriage. Those Columbus men are fools."

Her face went hot, and not from the heat of day. "I nearly married this past spring, but my betrothed chose someone else the last minute. However, that's a boring story. 'Tis your turn to talk. When did your wife pass, if I may be so blunt?"

"My wife, ur, Sarah Beth, died of a cancerous tumor in February of sixty-one."

"Oh, I'm so sorry. That must have been terrible for you and your children."

He peered straight ahead. "Yes. Quite. I swore I'd never marry again, but here I am making you a proposition."

"Well, you needn't worry. You did say it was temporary."

"Indeed I did."

Faith waited to see if he'd expound on the subject of his wife's death, but he did not. She hurried ahead. "Tell me about your children."

"Ah, my children. You'll meet them soon enough."

"The ad mentioned four of them, with the oldest being thirteen. Are there both boys and girls? What are their names?"

"Yes, two boys and two girls. Isaac is thirteen. You'll find him the most…well, busy, of the four. He is primarily the reason I've not been able to hold onto former nannies. Actually, to be honest, he's just plain naughty. Then there's Franklin, who's eleven and easily swayed by Isaac's antics, Beth who's eight, and the baby, Miriam."

"Baby?"

"Not an infant, but the youngest. She's five."

"I see. Well, they sound lovely despite what you say about the two boys. I'm anxious to meet them—if I pass muster, that is."

He turned his russet brown eyes on her and gave a half grin. "Lovely? If you pass muster?"

"I'm not sure how you plan to handle this application process. You probably have others who are also vying for the position."

"Let's just say all others were eliminated."

"Oh?"

"I mean…er, my posted ad did not muster a whole lot of interest."

"I see. So those who did apply have already lost their standing?"

"You could say that."

They hit a hole in the road, which tossed Faith against Captain Fuller, nearly landing her in his lap. She grabbed hold of a support pole to the right of her and pulled herself upright. With her free hand, she smoothed out her skirt then did a quick readjustment of her floral hat.

"You all right?" he asked.

"Yes, just fine, thank you."

"There are a few potholes here and there, and after a good soaking rain, such as the one we had this morning, new ones seem to show up."

"I can see that. The countryside is beautiful. I've never visited Lebanon before. It seems quite pleasant."

"It's a tidy little town. You'll find everything you need in the way of supplies."

"Have you been to Columbus much?"

"Several times."

He didn't elaborate, so she continued looking out over the landscape. Soon she found him staring at her and wondered if he were too embarrassed to mention her swollen lip. She instinctively touched two fingers to it. "I—I imagine you've been wondering what happened to my lip."

"It's been a lingering question since I first met you at the station, yes."

"Well, then I should probably explain. I—well, I had an encounter with someone."

"You mean you accidentally collided with another person?"

"No. Not quite."

Captain Fuller's head jerked back. "You don't mean someone hit you—on purpose."

"I'm afraid I do."

"Not a man, I hope."

"I'm afraid so. Oh, I hate that my first meeting with you involves having to explain this—this misfortune."

"What in tarnation—why would someone hit you, and a man in particular?"

"I'll be honest, it came as quite a shock to me. There is a certain fellow in Columbus who is rather obsessed with me, especially since my fiancé Frederick ended our engagement. I made the mistake of appeasing him with one date, and ever since then, he's hounded me mercilessly for a second date. The other morning, he stepped out from some bushes and told me he wished to walk me to work. It was still dark, but he'd been lurking there waiting for me. I immediately smelled liquor on him and told him I had no need for an escort, but he persisted. I tried to walk past him, and that's when he grabbed me and started forcing himself on me, attempting to grope me and kiss me. I managed to scratch his face and kick him after which he gave me his fist and knocked me to the ground."

"He slugged you. In the mouth." Captain Fuller's own mouth gaped, and she worried he might catch a fly or two.

"That's right, sir."

"I trust law enforcement has him in custody. The fellow deserves jail time."

"Um—I'm afraid they can't find him."

"Are you serious? What sort of incompetent sheriff's department does Columbus have?"

"I'm confident they'll locate him. I have faith in our sheriff."

His dark eyebrows crumpled as he leaned in to study her swollen lip, his elbow bumping against her as they jostled along. "That nasty skunk landed you a good one. I'd like to get my hands on him. How did you manage to escape him?"

"By God's divine intervention, a gentleman was driving by and called out, asking what was going on. I scrambled up from the ground and ran to the man, and he helped me into his wagon. When I looked back, Stuart Porter was gone. Vanished. He knew he was in trouble."

"The miscreant's name is Stuart Porter?"

"Yes, and that's the last anyone has seen of him. Sheriff Mumford and his deputies have kept up their search, however."

"I see. Well, at least they're hunting for him."

"Yes, but I worry that even if they catch him, there won't be much they can do. He might spend a few nights in jail at best."

"He'll spend longer than that. He's already racked up a couple of charges, assault and battery and evading the law. If he resists arrest once they catch him, there'll be a third count against him."

"I hope you're right."

"What about this fiancé who left you at the altar? Is he long gone?"

"Yes, as I said earlier, that's another story."

"I'm not bored if that's what you think." He offered her a little smile. "Tell me about it."

"It's not terribly interesting, so stop me if you start to nod off."

He chuckled. "I'll try not to be too obvious."

She went on to tell him how Frederick Holland had run off with her best friend just two weeks before the wedding and the details leading up to it. She tried to keep the story short, not wanting their first visit to be all about her various woes. *Good gracious, he might start considering her a risk to his children.* After going on a bit, she said, "In truth, I'm long over it. It caused a great deal of embarrassment, but by God's grace and strength, I've put it behind me."

Captain Fuller did not readily reply, just kept his eyes on the road while shaking his head, probably pondering her sorry life. "So, let me guess," he said after a long moment. "Your coming to Lebanon had multiple purposes: escaping that infuriating monster who attacked you, leaving behind the embarrassment of betrayal, and earning the promised financial settlement I'm offering after the fulfillment of your commitment."

She swiveled on the seat to look up at him, her brow wrinkling. "I wouldn't blame you for turning around and putting me right back on that stage. In fact, I'm prepared to use that return ticket you sent me if you wish to be rid of me. I admit some of what you say is true, but I do have other reasons, one of which is that I'm twenty-six and well past the age for living under my parents' roof. Ever since my failed engagement, I've been wanting to leave Columbus. I just wasn't sure where the Lord wanted me to go and what He had in mind for me. I pray about everything, you see."

"I sort of picked up on that." Though it was faint, she noted the makings of a small grin. "I don't wish to be rid of you—not at the moment, anyway." He chuckled, and she relaxed. "And so, when your time here has ended, you'll retreat to yet another town?"

"Well, your advertisement coming to my attention only a few days ago has left me with little time to determine just what I'll do next or where I'll go. I'll wait on the Lord for those answers."

"Thankfully, should you decide to go through with this arrangement, you'll have some time to plan."

"Yes, I thought the same."

"And seeing as your circumstances back home are less than ideal, it would be to your advantage to marry me." Now there was a teasing glint in his eye to add to that chuckle.

"You may have a point, Captain."

They rode along for a bit, the cooling breezes drying her perspiring brow and the scent of wildflowers a pleasant distraction. In time, he broke the silence. "What is the story on that button string you mentioned back at the station? What exactly is a button string?"

"Oh, that." She gave a little laugh. "Have you never heard of one?"

"Can't say I have."

"I suppose, being a man, you wouldn't. It's a rather old tradition carried down from England. My grandmother passed it down to my mother and my mother to me. It's said even Queen Victoria has one. It's rather silly, I suppose, but a tradition in certain family circles. My mother started me on my collection of buttons when I was about twelve. The idea is to collect them as gifts from friends and relatives, buttons of all colors and sizes, and string them on a chain of sorts. I use a strong silk string for connecting them, the sort that some fishermen use. I would never wear it, as it's starting to get heavy, but some of the buttons are quite lovely. The hope of every young woman is to collect a total of nine-hundred-ninety-nine buttons, but then stop collecting and wait for her husband-to-be to give her the one-thousandth button on her wedding day." She blushed a little. "And if you're about to ask me if Frederick Holland, my fiancé, was prepared to present me with my thousandth button, the answer would be no. I'm afraid I did not reach the required number. As I said, it's a rather silly tradition, but I suppose it's been fun nonetheless. My grandmother, having come from England, started her collection as a young girl, so it was only natural that she would also carry on the tradition with my mother, and then my mother with me."

Captain Fuller appeared to be mildly interested, for he flashed a winsome smile. "Well, you keep collecting them. You never can tell. Perhaps one day you'll get to that nine-hundred-ninety-ninth button, and will be caught holding your breath just waiting for that very last button to complete your chain."

"Hah! It is rather humorous how after my fiancé skipped town, several ladies who knew about my collection started slipping additional buttons to me—as if that would help to cheer my spirits. I'm afraid it did the opposite. The last thing I wanted to do after Frederick left was collect more buttons for that wretched chain."

"And yet you brought it with you."

"I know." Faith sighed. "I suppose it's become a part of me. The thought of leaving it behind didn't sit well, no matter that it is a constant reminder of my failed engagement."

"Humph, I think I see what you mean. It's sort of like that for me when I look at the portrait of Sarah Beth I have hanging in my living room. At times, I wonder if I shouldn't take it down, but then it does give me a certain sense of peace when I walk by and happen to glance up at it. She was a lovely woman, my wife."

"I am truly sorry for your loss."

"I appreciate that."

After a few more dips and bumps in the road, she asked, "How many nannies have you had in the past?"

"Probably a few too many to count. My mother has usually managed to find replacements for me, but I've had to come home on a couple of occasions to procure one. It's been somewhat of a nuisance. I hope you'll manage to stay for the duration—that is if you agree to marry me."

She dodged the comment. "Do you have siblings?"

"Two brothers. The oldest is Jack. He has two stepchildren with his wife, Cristina, who was widowed, and now they are expecting a third child in November. And then there's Jesse, who's younger than me. He's not married and lives in the main house with my mother Laura. My father passed in '58. You'll meet everyone soon enough."

She let that bit of information settle. "Your family, what do they all think of this whole, um, arrangement? You must admit it's rather rare that a gentleman would seek a wife by way of a public advertisement."

"And perhaps rarer that a woman would show interest," he said with a twinkle in his eye.

"You are right about that."

"As for my family, they're all skeptical, my mother most of all. Don't be surprised if she doesn't give you the most ardent of welcomes."

"I understand. My family has not been completely in favor either."

"I'll admit I'm surprised you at least agreed to meet me. Weren't you a bit worried I might be dangerous?"

A nervous giggle escaped her. "It crossed my mind."

"And now?"

She thought a moment. "I've managed to relax some since meeting you."

"Good. I hope you at least realize I'm nothing like that scoundrel Stuart Porter."

"I've come to discover the truth of that." Faith smiled. "And there *is* the matter of that return ticket to Columbus."

"Ah, yes, the return ticket. Well, I don't want you feeling trapped, of course, but now that you've divulged a bit of your story, it seems to me you might be just as eager to make this arrangement work as I am."

"You could be right."

She felt his eyes come to rest on her. "The other nannies were all a bit, um, sturdier looking than you."

She raised her chin and looked into his dark brown eyes. "Really. And yet, despite their stature, they failed. I'll thank you not to make any prejudgments of me."

His brows shot upward, and she thought she caught the beginnings of another smile. "Yes, Miss Haviland." He steered his team around a large puddle, causing her to rock against him. She pulled herself upright.

Up ahead, four deer dashed across the road, disappearing into the cornfield—while at the same time, a band of blackbirds made a scuttling sound with their wings and rose to the sky in a large flurry. Midday sunshine burnt hot spots into her shoulders, and she longed to remove her traveling jacket, but didn't think it proper.

"If my mother had been well enough, she probably would've taken over the care of my children until my discharge," Captain Fuller offered after a brief silence. "But she broke her leg a while back and is confined to a wheelchair until it heals."

"Oh dear, that's too bad."

"Don't worry, she manages just fine by ordering everyone around."

"I hope you won't mind if I ask one more question."

"Not at all."

"Do you adhere to any sort of faith—in God, that is?"

She had to ask it, for it could mean the difference between accepting this outlandish proposal...or using that return ticket to Columbus.

He seemed to mull over his response, then wriggled a bit in his seat. At last, he cleared his throat. "My mother and brothers are firm in their faith, and they all attend services at Community Methodist Church in downtown Lebanon."

"And you?"

"I—do not. Will that be a problem?"

"It could be."

"I know the way of salvation if that is any consolation, even made a profession of faith as a young lad, but—well, I have a hard time believing a loving God could allow such grief in a person's life. It's turned me sour toward God."

"I presume you're talking about the loss of your wife."

"That—and all the hatred surrounding this dreaded war. Our country is divided, and I don't know when or if we'll see an end to it. How could God allow such travesty—all this killing and disease?"

"For the greater good, I suppose." She carefully considered her words before continuing. "I don't know. I don't have any pat answers, and I certainly don't know how this war is going to turn out, but not knowing doesn't make me waver in my faith. I know that God is ultimately in control of everything."

He merely nodded but said nothing more, and so their discussion ended—until they turned down a long drive and passed under a sign reading "Fuller Family Farms." Faith broke the silence. "Oh, my stars in heaven, what a lovely sight!" she exclaimed. "There's corn and wheat as far as my eyes can see. And the house—how very stately. Is that the main house you mentioned earlier?"

"Indeed it is." At the end of the drive, he set the brake, then turned to face her. "It's a big farm, but we are a humble family. I think you'll like everyone."

"But will they approve of me?" she asked, trying to quell her sudden nerves.

"It's not my brothers or even my mother I'm concerned about. It's my children. I'm worried they will make a bad impression on you."

She flicked her wrist. "Goodness, don't worry about that." But his comment only made her nervous stomach tingle the more.

"Shall we go inside?"

She eked out the tiniest smile and grew suddenly nervous. "Yes, of course."

Who was this man she considered marrying? And had she lost her last drop of common sense?

8

Just as Joey had feared, the second he raised his hands to help Faith down from the wagon, the entire Fuller clan, including his children and Jack's, all came running from the house. "Well, I guess the welcoming committee has arrived," he said, embarrassed by the hoopla. He put his hands to her small waist and hoisted her down. *Good grief, did she weigh any more than a sack of flour?*

"Hi, Uncle Joey. Is this her?" his nephew Elias asked without a trace of decorum.

He should have stipulated wanting only *his* children at the house. Miss Haviland must surely think his family a bit batty from the way all the children ran in circles, squealing and carrying on like some kind of circus act.

"Attention, everyone." His whole family instantly hushed. "Let me introduce you to Faith Haviland."

"Hello, Faith," the adults said in unison.

"Hello to all of you," she returned.

The children mostly stood and stared—except for Isaac. Up to his usual antics, he pulled Catherina's braid, making her screech and run to her mother. Then, Franklin started kicking at the dirt, seemingly to see how high he could make the dust fly, and little Miriam was whining about something. Beth did nothing but gawk at Faith, who stood beside him looking nonplused. His pregnant sister-in-law Cristina bent over to attend to Miriam, while Jack and Jesse looked on with interest, both wearing slanted grins. His mother, while absent from the hubbub in the yard, sat in the doorway to her home, one arm resting on her wheelchair, the other up to shield her eyes from the sun. While he couldn't get a good look at her expression, Joey did notice she wasn't smiling. *Great.*

Isaac had already started sizing up Faith, probably trying to figure out a good way to scare her off. He would have to have a good, long chat with the boy before entrusting him to this woman he wasn't at all sure could handle him.

Jack spoke first. "Well, good gravy, let's not all stand outside in this heat. Come on in." Once inside, Cristina beckoned to Beth, and the two disappeared to the kitchen while the rest found places to sit in the living room. Joey and Faith settled on the divan, Jesse casually dropped into one of the chairs, and the children gathered around on the floor, all staring wide-eyed from Joey to Faith. Jack pushed Laura's wheelchair into the living room and positioned her next to the expansive fireplace, directly across from Joey and Faith, pushing a small footstool up close so she could rest her leg there. She'd only nodded and said hello to Faith, and Joey wondered what thoughts raced through her mind.

"How was your trip from Columbus, Miss Haviland?" Jesse asked first.

She sat straight as a pin, hands folded in her lap, her floral hat tipped slightly and blond hair flowing past her shoulders. She directed her gaze at Jesse and offered a friendly enough smile. "Fine, thank you, if not a bit cramped. I was happy to arrive."

"Ouch! Stop it, Isaac!" Catherina squealed from her station on the floor. Isaac, sitting behind her, had either pinched her, pulled her braid again, or poked her in the back.

"Isaac, that's enough," said Joey, not knowing exactly what the boy had done but feeling the tension mounting in his neck. The last thing he needed now was for Isaac to put on a display of bad behavior before Faith had the first chance to get to know his family.

"Why is your lip all big?" Miriam blurted out.

"Funny, I asked her the same thing," Joey hurried to say, focusing most of his attention on Miriam, even though everyone else's eyes had landed on him too. "She knocked into something hard. But we needn't embarrass Miss Haviland with unnecessary questions about it. She is already quite humiliated by it."

"She prob'ly tripped over her own shoe," groused Isaac.

"Isaac," Joey warned.

"What'd she do, hit a door?" asked Franklin, grinning as if he'd just said something funny.

"Ha! Quite the contrary," Miss Haviland inserted with a little giggle. "Granted, I can be quite clumsy, but not this time. A fellow rammed into me, but I can assure you I'll be just fine. I was walking to work when it happened."

"He must have been as big as a house," Catherina speculated.

Faith laughed, which put everyone at ease. "Indeed. Thankfully, I am no worse for the wear."

Joey grinned. He would have to commend her later for her quick response to Miriam's question about her swollen lip.

"Where'd y' work?" asked Franklin.

"In a restaurant that my aunt owns."

"I wish I worked in a restaurant," chimed in Elias. "I'd be able to eat whatever I wanted."

At that moment, Cristina came into the room carrying a pitcher of red punch—strawberry, no doubt—and a dozen small glasses on an oblong pewter tray. Beth walked proudly behind her aunt bearing another tray holding a plate of one-inch square lemon cookie bars and some napkins. The children leaped up to grab the refreshments, Elias beating everyone else.

"Tell us about your family, Miss Haviland," said Cristina as everyone sat back down with their glasses of punch and tangy lemon squares balanced on napkins.

Without missing a beat, Faith reiterated what she'd told Joey on the wagon ride home, only this time, she expounded a bit more, mentioning her brothers' wives and her sister's husband and the dozen nieces and nephews she had. She told about her father's and brothers' blacksmith shop, the church the Havilands all attended in Columbus, her personal walk with God, and the importance she placed on her family. He couldn't help but notice the way his mother's eyebrows shot up at Faith's words and how her chin lifted a tad, and then a hint of a smile washed over her otherwise muted face. *Had his wife-to-be started winning over his mother?*

"I see you're named quite aptly," Laura said.

"Thank you, that's what my father often says. My parents named me Faith because of their own faith in God."

More topics of discussion arose, most of them general, and then Jack announced it was time to take his family home so their mother, Joey, and Faith could become better acquainted. Cristina announced that she and Jack would host everyone at their house for dinner around six o'clock. She and the three girls quickly gathered up napkins and glasses to take to the kitchen. Jesse mentioned his need to go out to the birthing barn to check on a couple of cows getting ready to calve—and naturally, the boys decided to go with him. Out the door they all flew, with Jesse promising to drive Isaac and Franklin home later. That left Beth and Miriam, and so Cristina quickly invited Joey's girls to her house to play with Catherina and help in the kitchen with dinner.

Outside, the last sounds of his family's voices and squeaking wagon wheels faded into nothing. Soon, all was quiet except for the chirping birds and cows lowing in the distance. Both Laura and Faith had their hands clasped in their laps. Joey fiddled with a loose thread on his pants and anxiously bounced his knee up and down.

"I'm sorry to hear you broke your leg, ma'am. Is it healing well?" Faith quickly put in.

"Yes, it's coming along fine, thank you. The doctor said only a few more weeks before I should be able to put a bit of weight on it—with the use of a pair of crutches, mind you. It sure is a nuisance though."

"I can imagine," Faith said.

His mother, though handicapped, certainly succeeded in keeping herself more than presentable, dressed as she was today in her lovely blue satin gown and her hair done up in a perfect bun with those two fancy combs holding everything in place. Joey turned to Faith, quirked his brow, and grinned. "My mother is a very meticulous housekeeper, so to say this broken leg is a nuisance to her is quite an understatement."

Laura waved him off and gave Faith a good perusal. "You certainly are a pretty thing. Joseph's brothers teased that you might be toothless and as broad as a barn."

"Mother..."

"Well, it's true." Laura smiled and set her eyes on Faith. "I'm most happy to hear you are a woman of faith, Faith." She giggled a little. "I do so love your name, but did I already mention that?" She moistened her lips and went on. "I don't know if Joseph told you how silly I thought it was of him to post an advertisement for a bride."

"He did say something to that effect."

"Well, it's not that I think your marrying my son is a terribly bad idea, Miss Haviland. He can be quite gentlemanly when he puts his mind to it."

"Thank you for that vote of confidence, Ma."

"I wasn't talking to you."

Duly reprimanded, Joey sat back, shook his head, and gritted his teeth.

"Now then, Miss Haviland, are you confident in your ability to care for four energetic, sometimes disrespectful, often rowdy, and very rambunctious children?"

"Not at all, ma'am," Faith answered just as calm as a clam. Joey held his breath. "But I do know that through Christ, I can do all things, and so I shall lean on Him to help me; that is, if I decide to marry your son. I've already taken note of Isaac's lack of self-discipline, and I realize his behavior leaves a bit to be desired."

Laura's graying eyebrows wiggled as she raised one shoulder and tilted her chin upward. "Well, I'm impressed with you, my dear."

"Please know I have prayed about this and will continue to do so."

"And you should know I've been doing the same. I want what's best for my grandchildren. And my son, of course." Laura smiled broadly now. "Perhaps, if anything, you will be exactly what my son and his children need. If you should decide to go through with this arrangement, then you have my blessing."

"Thank you, Mrs. Fuller. I appreciate that."

Joey breathed a little sigh. "As do I, Mother." Then he turned to Faith. "Shall we go?" He stood and extended his hand to her.

"You're leaving so soon?" Laura protested.

Faith took his hand to stand, and he noted the lack of calluses. *Was she even fit to be a farmer's wife?* "I'm afraid so, Ma. Miss Haviland and I have much to figure out in the coming hours. I want to give her a tour of the farm and then show her around my house before the children get home. If all goes well, we'll visit the judge tomorrow."

"Just to talk to him, not to wed," Laura said. "Correct?"

"No, to wed."

"Tomorrow?" his mother and Faith both said in unison.

"My time at home is growing shorter," Joey said, directing his gaze mostly at Faith. "Don't worry, we will have talked it through enough to both be comfortable." Then to Laura, he said, "We'll see you at Jack's for supper, Ma, unless you're planning to stay home."

"No, of course I'm coming. Jesse and a couple of the hired hands have been helping me navigate getting up to the wagon. I'll see you again tonight, dear," she told Faith.

"Goodbye, ma'am. It was lovely meeting you," she managed before Joey opened the door and ushered her out to his waiting rig.

"And you, dear," Laura called out.

Joey gave Faith a hand and she moved her skirts to one side and stepped up into the wagon. She sat down while he hurried around the front and then climbed up beside her. Once seated on the squeaky old leather seat, he allowed a sigh to whistle out of him. "Well, that was a bit of a whirlwind visit, wasn't it?"

"Yes, and a very hasty exit I might add."

"My mother would belabor the whole matter of this marriage until evening if I gave her the chance."

"I see. But in the end, she did seem quite agreeable about our getting married."

"Yes, you quite impressed her. I hope the rest of my family earned your approval."

"Everyone was very friendly and accepting. Even the children were delightful."

"I'm glad you thought so." He picked up the reins and directed his horses to begin the trek toward home.

"Regarding tomorrow," Faith said after the horses reached a well-traveled two-track path that followed one edge of the cornfield. "I don't see why we must marry so soon."

"I had a feeling you might object to that, but as I told my mother, my time here is short. I only have a few days remaining before I must report back to my post. I think it would be best to marry well in advance of my leaving. I want to ensure that you are well situated and that the children have a clear understanding of your position in the home."

"I see. Well, I suppose that makes sense."

"You'll accept the challenge then?"

She brushed a stray leaf off her lap and cleared her throat. "Well, I'll have to hear the details of the arrangement before I decide—and then get to know the children a bit better."

"Yes, of course."

"You mentioned a stipend—at the end."

"I did. We can discuss that in full when we reach the house. I have even drawn up a contract of sorts."

"I see."

"First, though, let me take you on a little jaunt around the property."

She sat a little straighter and smiled, revealing a gleaming row of top teeth. "I would very much enjoy that."

He swallowed hard, realizing the step he hoped to take with this woman was no small act. He could only hope she wouldn't choose to take advantage of that ticket back to Columbus tomorrow. If he'd been a praying man, right then would have been a good time to utter a few words.

9

Captain Fuller's house had a large wraparound porch, the kind a woman dreams of having, and two stately pillars on each side of the steps leading to the front door. It wasn't as grand a house as his mother's, and some of the siding looked in need of repair, but it didn't pale much. After taking a tour of the property and barns and seeing all the livestock and farm equipment, Faith reckoned the Fuller Family Farm was no small operation. Even in wartime, they'd obviously managed to keep the business running well and probably sold to many marketplaces, using the railroad for shipments. Perhaps one of the captain's problems with his children was that they'd never had to lift a finger to get whatever they wanted. She knew there had to be more to it, his absence in their lives no doubt playing a large part. It would take some time to get to the bottom of things—if she stayed, that is. The Fuller children would benefit greatly from stability. Her heart went out to them when considering all the changes they'd undergone in their brief lifetimes, what with the loss of their beloved mother and their father off to war. Why, it was almost enough to convince her to sign on the line this very minute. *Almost.*

"After you, Miss Haviland," Captain Fuller said, his deep voice startling her back to the present as he stood there with the front door open.

She entered a parlor room, where a small bench stood pushed up against the wall and a table next to it held a small vase of fresh-cut flowers. She absently wondered if Captain Fuller had been the one to arrange the bouquet. A dozen coat hooks protruded from the wall to her left and a couple of lightweight jackets and an umbrella hung there.

Captain Fuller gave a sweeping motion with his hand. "Welcome to my home." He stepped ahead of her and gestured for her to follow. "This is the foyer, of course." He kept walking. "Here on the right is the library." He paused at the doorway to both rooms. The large library held floor-to-ceiling shelves filled with books of all sizes, many with aged bindings. *What an intriguing room!* Up against one wall stood an oak desk with an office chair pushed under it. "It serves as my office too. I store files and important documents here, and when I'm home and fully engaged in the farm, I do a lot of the paperwork, including payroll."

He moved on, past the tall staircase. "To your left is the dining room. As you can see, it's large enough to seat a good number. That table does have leaves for extra seating. They're stored behind the bureau. And over here"—he directed her to the right— "is the living room." It housed a massive stone fireplace over which hung a bigger than life portrait of a beautiful woman with sandy colored hair. "My wife Sarah Beth," he stated matter-of-factly, as if reading her mind. She noted how he referred to her as if she still lived.

"She's lovely."

He paused for a moment and stared up. "Yes, she is. Or rather, she *was.*"

She took to glancing around the rest of the room, the furnishings of which showed signs of disrepair. She envisioned his children spilling food and beverages there or jumping on cushions, just generally misbehaving. She also noted one of the windows missing half its drapes and surmised it'd probably happened during a bit of horseplay—or perhaps during a fit of anger. Its rod was crooked, as if someone had pulled down the heavy fabric. If she did accept Captain Fuller's proposal of marriage, she would have to see what she could do to restore order to the house. But then she might be jumping ahead of herself to presume she had the right. Frankly, the house needed new paint and wallpaper, not to mention furniture.

"Over here's the kitchen," he said, pointing through an archway toward the back of the house. "There's a nook there." He pointed at a table and chairs nestled into a lovely bay window overlooking the backyard, where stood several sheds, a fenced-in pasture, barns, and off in the distance, low, rolling hills. A large oak tree provided plenty of shade, and on one of its thick branches hung a long rope swing with a wooden seat. "We eat our breakfast there most every morning. Then off to the side of the kitchen, you'll find a large pantry and another room for storing large items such as kettles and pots, and so on. There's also a laundry tub back there with an inside pump handle, and clothes lines in the side yard. All the bedrooms are on the second floor, of course." She couldn't help but wonder where she'd sleep. Surely, he had enough rooms upstairs that she could have her own space. If she married him temporarily, she'd make it clear as glass she'd not be sharing a room with him. In fact, the very notion of it made her flush with embarrassment.

She glanced around, admiring all the conveniences. Her parents' home was equally nice, but smaller, nestled as it was in the heart of town. Faith wasn't accustomed to wide open spaces, but she visualized herself enjoying it. She walked to the back door in the kitchen and turned her attention once again to the great outdoors. A herd of cows grazed in a distant pasture, but she didn't know if they belonged to the Fullers or a neighboring farmer. Chickens roamed freely outside and a large dog lay oblivious in the shade, no doubt having seen younger days.

"This is really quite lovely," she said, staring out. "I've always lived in the city, so farm life is foreign to me. I do love to garden though. That one yonder looks desperate for attention."

"Yes, it's been sorely neglected." He stepped up behind her. "Do you think you could get used to this?" The deep timbre of his voice, combined with his airy breath, set off a chill at the back of her neck.

She continued surveying the property, pretending his company didn't affect her. "Perhaps. Of course, it would only be for a few months, so I shan't get *too* used to it."

"True. Speaking of which, shall we go sit in the living room so we can talk business?" He stepped back, and she turned. He made another sweeping motion with his hand, so she slipped past him and walked back through the arch to the living room. "Our family lawyer drew up some legal papers pertaining to our arrangement," he said. "I only have for you to look them over and sign if you approve."

It was all so formal…and she questioned her level of common sense. *How could she possibly marry someone in name only?* But just as quickly, the thought reverberated in her head that Sheriff Mumford had not yet jailed Stuart Porter—and the thought of him running free further cemented in her mind the need to marry, if only for the chance to go into hiding.

⌒

"What sort of trouble did you get yourself into, Stuart? You been keepin' y'r nose clean for the past several years, ain't y? At least since Opal's demise. You can't stay here for more than a few days. I'm short on supplies. What did you do? Who's mindin' y'r butcher shop?"

For the moment, Stuart ignored his cousin's monotonous rambling questions and raised the bottle of brew he'd brought with him to his mouth to take another deep swallow, letting the liquid burn clear to the pit of his stomach and land with a fiery scorch. He stood at the back of Leon Porter's house, made a swipe with his sleeve across his wet mouth, and stared out the window at the outbuildings. Situated on several acres some fifteen miles outside of Columbus and surrounded by woods, wheat fields, and a rippling creek, his cousin's house and property would make for the perfect hideout, at least until he planned his next move. How it rankled him that Faith had left town—with the possibility of marrying some idiotic farmer, one Captain Joseph Fuller. Stupid sheriff and his inept deputies! They hadn't even seen him standing in the shadows at the train depot early that morning, disguised as he was, wearing a droopy hat and an overlarge trench coat stuffed with rags to make him look heavier. He took another swig of brew and scratched his chin where his growing whiskers created an awful itch.

He moved away from the window and peered around the house. For an old house, his cousin did a decent job of keeping it up. It wasn't fancy, but overall Leon did well for himself, hermit that he was. His stomach churned, not only from the brew, but from angst.

"You shouldn't drink so much, Stu. You're turning out just like your father."

"Don't say that," he spat. "I ain't nothin' like him!"

"All right, all right, just calm down. You didn't answer my question. What'd you do in Columbus to make you come here to hide out?"

"Nothin' much," he mumbled, taking another long drink.

"Yeah, right. You didn't do much to Opal either, and then she up and died real mysterious like."

"Opal died of natural causes."

"So you say. You never told me how she died."

He glared at his cousin, lifting one side of his lip in a sneer. "Don't forget you helped me bury her body, so y're an accessory." He turned back to the window to gaze out through blurred eyes. A dozen chickens pecked at the ground. Further out, pigs waddled in a muddy pasture, a couple of cows and horses munched on sparse grass in a wire enclosure, and some goats played in a fenced area. The only appealing thing Stuart spied was a nice looking vegetable garden. Leon always had enjoyed gardening, and good thing, since he wasn't good for much else.

"An accessory to what—if she died of natural causes?" Leon sputtered, his voice sounding distant to Stuart's ears. "To this day, I regret that I helped you bury her."

Stuart grinned and slowly lifted his gaze to squint at his cousin. "You ever think about reportin' me, I'll just tell 'em about the part you played."

"I had nothin' t' do with her passing."

"Me neither, so just drop it, would you?"

Leon picked up a single dirty dish and shuffled across the room to drop it into a pan of dishwater. "So what did you do, Leon? Why are you havin' to hang out here?"

"Like I said, it wasn't much. I was fixin' t' have a little fun with my woman the other morning. She was walkin' to work, and I stepped out from behind some bushes to greet her. She didn't much like that I'd surprised her and said, in essence, that she wanted nothin' to do with me. It made me mad, so I roughed her up a little. All I wanted was a little kiss. Was that asking too much? Anyway, the little wretch kicked me and scratched my face. Look." He turned his face to the side so that Leon could peruse the injurious scratch marks. "So I hit her and knocked her down. I didn't mean for it to go quite that far, but it happened. I started to help her up just as some fellow came along on his wagon. He yelled out, and she took that opportunity to escape to his wagon. Course, I scrambled out of sight."

"You called her your woman, Stuart. Don't sound like something you'd do to a gal you care about."

Anger sprouted inside him, so he took another fast swig of bitter brew. "All right, she's not exactly my woman. Yet."

"You shouldn't have hit her, Stu. That's assault. They might throw you in the clink for a few days for that."

"I'm not going in no jail cell, not even for a minute. You know how I hate cramped places." Anger blustered up in him.

"Yeah, I know. Your pa locked you in a closet a few times. So who is this lady anyway?"

"Her name's Faith. She's beautiful." Just thinking about her made his heart flutter with excitement. "She's off in Lebanon right now. Saw her leave on the train."

"How'd you see her leave if you're in hiding?"

"I have my ways."

"What's she doin' in Lebanon? Did you scare her off?"

"I may have. I overheard a conversation between her and her parents. I snuck onto their property and hid in some bushes under an open window and eavesdropped." He laughed a little. "Clever, ain't I?"

Leon shook his head. "Stuart, you need to go back to Columbus, turn yourself in, do your time, which probably won't be much, and then go back to living a normal life. It wouldn't hurt for you to start going to church either."

"Don't start preaching at me. I don't want to hear any of your religious talk. And I've come this far. I'm not going to turn myself in—not just yet anyway. I've got to try with her one more time, even if it means her turning me down."

"You hit her, Stu. You think knocking her around is going to make her fall in love with you? Besides, you're a drunk. Look at you."

Stuart laughed. "Before it's all said an' done, she'll be bowing to my every want."

"Uh-huh, because you're so doggone irresistible."

Stuart took another drink then wiped his mouth again. "I might need your help, Leon."

In an instant, Leon raised both his hands. "Nuh-uh, forget it. I'm not gettin' involved in any of your crimes."

"This isn't no crime, and what if I said there's money in it?"

"I just told you I regretted helping you bury y'r wife, and I don't want a single cent from you."

"Look, all I want y' to do is go into town and snoop around a little. Ask folks what they know about the butcher shop bein' closed. Find out how hard the sheriff's lookin' for me. Hardly a soul in town knows we're cousins. I brought a stash of bills and gold coins with me. I'll reward you real good for your time and effort."

At that, Leon's eyes lit up like two hot coals. "You're crazy, Stu, always have been. You an' me, we never did have anything in common, and now that we're middle-aged, we have less in common than ever."

"An' that's why we always got along."

"Yeah, all went well between us long as I let you make all the rules."

Stuart laughed and pointed a finger at him. "And you followed 'em." He drank and laughed, drank and laughed, then held the bottle away from him for a moment to let his fuzzy mind wander a tad. "'Member the time we broke into old man Harris's hardware store on Murphy

Street? What were we, ten, eleven? I managed to get the money drawer open about the same time we heard Harris fumbling at the back door. It was stuck, 'member? Which gave us just enough time to dart back out the front with a wad o' money."

"Of which you kept the bigger share even though *I'm* the one who broke the window to get in, you rotten cheat."

That broke the ice between them and spurred on a few more stories of their malicious antics as kids. Neither had ever had much in the way of discipline, having free rein about town while their fathers drank their guts out in one saloon after another.

After a time, the two men quieted. "I settled down since then," said Leon.

"Yeah, me too."

"Oh, pfft. You haven't settled down. You might be takin' a break just to hide your true character, but you won't ever be settled down, no sir. What made you think you could win yourself a woman anyway? You already had one in Opal, and we both know that didn't go well. Why'd you get rid o' her, anyway?"

He scoffed. "She wasn't good f'r much. She couldn't cook, her cleanin' skills were limited, she slept too much, and she turned out t' be a sickly thing."

"What was wrong with her?"

He shrugged. "The doc in Lima never could figure it out. He just kept givin' her more an' more medicine for her cough. She had some sort o' lung disease." Stuart laughed to himself, a guttural sound. "Woman was pure miserable. She needed help t' the other side."

"The other side? What do y' mean by that? You gave her somethin' to help her die?"

"Pssh. Weren't much." He guzzled the last of his rancid whiskey then set down the bottle with a plunk. His insides felt overcooked. He stared at Leon through fogged eyes. "I don't know what's in that putrid potion, but sure was awful. Guess it's been sittin' on my shelf longer than I thought. Got me a bunch more in my bag. Ol' Stuart don't go nowhere unprepared."

Leon moved a little closer and got blurrier the closer he came. "You said you helped Opal to the other side?"

"Yeah, I did her a favor. I just gave her what the doctor already prescribed. You know what they say. The only difference between medicine and poison is the dose."

Leon scowled. "So you gave her enough to kill her."

"She was already dying." Stuart's words came off slurred, but he couldn't help it. His head and mouth weren't working right.

"You need God, cousin. You're heading down the wrong path."

"I told you not to preach at me!"

"How did you explain Opal's disappearance? Didn't folks wonder why you didn't have a funeral for her?"

Stuart cackled. "No, I told anybody who asked she ran away. But most folks didn't even know I was married." He gave a loud belch. "I think I need to go lie down." He staggered across the room to the old sofa. Once there, he fell into it. "Wake me up before you go."

"Before I go?"

"Before you go to Columbus."

"I'm not going to Columbus for you."

"Yeah, you will. We're family." And with those final words, he passed out.

⌒

"This is the paper my attorney drew up. It's really quite straightforward. Feel free to read it as thoroughly as you please."

Faith took the single piece of paper in hand and set to reading it. While she perused the document in the wingback chair, he situated himself in an identical chair across from her and watched her read. A tiny muscle flicked in her jaw, and she cleared her throat halfway through. Once her eyebrows wiggled, and then when she got to the bottom of the paper, her jaw dropped. "That's a hefty amount of money. Are you sure you can afford it?"

Joey smiled. "Quite sure. After the annulment, you might wish to set up housekeeping somewhere else. Perhaps this small sum can at least give you a head start."

"Yes, perhaps."

Her expression went thoughtful, and so before she had much time to mull over the contents of the contract, Joey handed her a pen. "You can just sign right there on that line." He pointed to the spot.

"Yes, but I need to spend more time with the children."

"It won't hurt you to sign the paper. It doesn't bind you to me. It's the vows we say tomorrow that will do that. Signing this is just a formality."

She squinted at the paper. "Just the same, I believe I'll ponder it and pray a bit more tonight after I read my Bible. By the way, where should I put my belongings?"

"Oh, yes, your suitcases. Just sit here and make yourself at home while I retrieve them from the back of the wagon. The bedroom is upstairs." He left her then and noted that she'd picked up the document to read it again, no doubt looking for a loophole. Of course, there weren't any, but he couldn't blame her for making sure.

Joey returned moments later only to find her in the library scanning book titles, her hands clasped behind her. She was every bit as lovely facing away, her blond hair falling around her shoulders, most of its morning curl gone. *Had she done her hair up in rags the night before to curl it? Did she always wear it down, or did she like to pin it in a round bun at the top of her head?* He could just envision it flying every which direction on days when she would go outside to hang clothes or pull weeds or push Miriam on the rope swing. For just the slightest instant, he tried to imagine how soft her hair might be, then just as quickly chided himself. The only touching between them wouldn't happen intentionally. He'd see to that, and he surmised she would as well. He set her two pieces of luggage down and cleared his throat. She spun around.

"Oh, I didn't hear you come back in. I was just perusing your library. I hope you don't mind."

"Not at all. Did you find any titles that interested you?"

"Indeed I did. And I see several I'm sure the children would enjoy. Do they like bedtime stories?"

"I wouldn't know."

"Whatever do you mean? You don't read to them?"

"Their mother often did."

"But you're their father! Surely, they'd enjoy a story from their own daddy."

Joey lifted his shoulders in a simple shrug. "I never thought about it."

"Well, that's ridiculous. Children need as much time with their fathers as they do their mothers." As soon as she uttered the words, she put a flat palm to her mouth, as if to clamp it shut. "I'm sorry. That was quite forward of me."

"Don't trouble yourself. I'm aware my parenting skills leave much to be desired."

She shifted from one foot to the other and sniffed. "It's never too late, you know."

"No? I can't bring their mother back."

"That is not what I meant, Captain Fuller. It's not too late for you to start showing the children more attention."

"Well, I'll be leaving in a matter of days, so that's not something I have a whole lot of time to perfect, I'm afraid."

"You should make every effort in the time you have remaining to do as much as you can, sir."

He grinned down at her and tilted his head forward. "Is my potential wife already taking the reins in this upcoming marriage?"

Her pretty face took on a pinkish hue. "Not in the least. I'm merely making a suggestion."

"I'll take your suggestion into consideration then, as long as you bear in mind it might not make a whole lot of difference, especially where Isaac is concerned. The boy has a stubborn streak—if not a bitter one."

"Then we will do what we can to sweeten his disposition."

"*We* will? It's sounding more and more like you might be staying on, Miss Haviland."

"We'll see." Her expression remained stoic, and then she gave him her back and continued her examination of his many volumes of books. Hmm. Besides being quite pretty, this Faith Haviland could very well prove to be a spirited individual. Isaac might have met his match. Shoot, *he* might have as well!

aith lay in bed and stared at the high ceiling, exhausted from the last few days—everything from Stuart's attack, to dealing with the sheriff, to making a crucial decision concerning her future, and then to rising early yesterday to prepare for her day of packing and saying her goodbyes to Aunt Martha and the others at the restaurant, and finally, visiting her nieces, nephews, and family members. Add to that boarding the train this morning and then the stage at Deerfield Station to at last meet Joseph Fuller and his entire family today, and then trying to acclimate herself to a strange new environment. What a whirlwind!

She had just closed her Bible after placing a dried flower in the pages to hold her spot and then set it on the bedside stand next to her. Captain Fuller had given her his own bedroom, the largest room upstairs. It held a poster bed, built-in floor-to-ceiling cabinets with doors, a dresser with a basin and pitcher on top, a vanity with mirror and matching chair, and a rocking chair over in one corner. Faith pictured his wife sitting in that very rocker, perhaps holding and singing to one of her babies. Her heart squeezed at the thought. She wondered if the captain had immediately compared her to Sarah Beth upon first meeting her. She let her eyes wander to a peaceful painting of a mountainscape hanging on the far wall. Somehow, that combined with the Scripture she'd just read, helped to settle her nerves.

Now, with a sheet and lightweight blanket tucked up under her chin, she collected a few thoughts, weighing the pros and cons of marrying Joseph Fuller tomorrow. It did seem apparent the man had no other options, and she hated to be the cause of further stress in his life, not to mention lend even more instability to the children's. *Like Esther, had God placed her here for such a time as this—to help bring order from chaos? And if that were so, did she have what it took to fulfill that sort of task?* Isaac had put on quite a display before bed that night, cutting up and even sticking out his tongue at his father when Captain Fuller was turned away. His siblings had not told on him, and Franklin even got to giggling about it. As for Faith, she pretended not to have noticed. *Good gracious, what was she getting herself into if she assumed the job of stepmother? Would the children grow to despise her for marrying their father—or might her new role hasten a show of respect?* She flipped over on her side, bringing the covers with her. A frown played around her mouth as she watched a shadow dance across the ceiling—a tree branch bending in the breezes and the moon's reflection glancing off it.

"Lord, it's clear I'll need divine wisdom if I'm to take this job," she whispered. "What would You have me do?"

A portion of the Scripture she'd just read minutes ago from the first chapter of Joshua ran through her head. *"Only be thou strong and very courageous."* And the verse had concluded, *"…that thou mayest observe to do according to all the law…turn not from it to the right hand or to the left, that thou mayest prosper withersoever thou goest."*

As she pondered the passage, a calming effect began settling into her being. *Do not turn from God's law to the right or to the left. Could she take that to mean that if she did not marry Captain Fuller, she'd be turning away from God's plan? Or might marrying him be an act of disobedience?* Oh, how her head spun with a myriad of thoughts. "I need clarity, Lord."

In the stillness, with only the sound of her own breathing and a nearby hoot owl outside her upstairs window, a strong sense of God's gentle voice whispered into her, and the words, "Follow Me, child" repeated over and over. *Follow Me. Follow Me. What could it mean? Follow Him where? Back home to Columbus—or into a strange courthouse tomorrow morning?* Tears welled up until they had nowhere to go but down her cheeks and onto her pillow. A sob came out of her then. "Lord, I am willing," she heard herself say.

And just like that, her heart assumed a place of peace that passed even her own understanding. *What? Could it be that simple?* Without any prompting, her mouth turned up in the corners, and she had her answer. She wiped her eyes with the back of her hand and then quickly used her sheet to finish the job. Tomorrow, she would marry Joseph Fuller—and Lord help her if she'd misread His gentle nudge.

Morning dawned hours later. Faith opened her droopy eyes to a golden ray of sunshine beaming off the ceiling rather than that shadow of a tree branch from the night before. The sounds of children's voices below—someone screeching with annoyance, another laughing, and yet another sounding gruff and noncompliant—startled her fully awake. Captain Fuller's voice blended into the mix, raised and irritated in tone. *Joey*, Faith corrected herself. *If we're to wed, I must begin to think of him more familiarly.*

She tossed the covers off and rose in one quick move. The smell of bacon wafted up from the kitchen. *How long had she slept? Good glory! Was it noontime?* She certainly felt rested. She searched out the clock on the bureau and sighed with relief to find it only seven-thirty. Still, that was oversleeping by her standards. This was her wedding day! She ought to have risen earlier. Not that she had a single thing to do to prepare for it. By design, Joey had asked his brother Jack, and no one else, to attend the brief ceremony, to act as a witness and to sign the register, which would declare them husband and wife after they'd said their vows before the judge. According to Joey, it would be a quick affair, and nothing she need fret about. And so she hadn't—until now. Gracious, she had yet to even give him her final answer. His nerves must surely be more strained than hers.

She dressed in a hurry, donning her underthings first and then a gown of light green satin and white lace with a scooped round neck and belted waist. Overall, it was a plain dress, suitable for a day of travel or light housework, but certainly not for reciting wedding vows. Still it would have to do, as this was not the sort of wedding that demanded fancy attire. She pulled on her stockings, and last, stepped into her sensible, black low-heeled pumps. A bit of regret singed her insides at the realization that the wedding of her dreams had passed her by with Frederick Holland's sudden desertion. Not that she held to any long-lost feelings for him, but that he'd deprived her of her girlish fairytale. *And her best friend.* She brushed away the thought, then reached behind her and fastened one final hook at the back of her dress, then moved to the mirror to tend to her hair. She had tied it in a dozen or more rags last night to ensure she'd have a head of curls this morning. However, with the clock already registering twenty minutes before the hour, she would have little time to fuss over it, so she made a hasty decision to undo each rag, give her hair a thorough brushing, and then draw it up into a chignon and secure it with a fancy comb.

She seated herself on the cushioned bench much like the one she had back home and took up her horsehair brush. While working on her locks, she studied her face, thankful that at least it was free of blemishes, save for the still somewhat swollen upper lip that even this morning looked worlds better. In haste, she whipped her hair up into a tight bun, snatched up the shiny comb and carefully inserted it so as to secure the twist. She drew down a few strands of hair to frame her face, then sat back and gave herself another quick perusal. "Aargh! I am certainly no Sarah Beth Fuller," she scoffed. She breathed deeply, then blew out the air. She made a face of disdain at herself, then rose from her seat with a loud sigh and moved to the door, her heels clicking on the hard wood. Swallowing, she took one last breath for courage, opened the door, and then walked out into the hallway.

∽

Joey sighed in exasperation. "Isaac, help Franklin set the table."

"How come *she's* not down here to do the job?" he groused.

"She must be very tired. Yesterday was a long day for her."

"Yeah, it was a long day for all of us, but we all got up an hour ago."

"Shh, that's enough complaining. Finish your job."

"This is a girl's job. Why isn't Beth doing it?"

"Because she's stirring the eggs for me. Just do it, please. It's not like you have to do it every day."

The boy's shoulders slumped, but at least he resumed his task. Franklin moved around the table putting silverware in place, yawning and too tired to complain.

Miriam came in carrying her doll and dragging a blanket on the floor, still wearing her nightgown. "Miriam, I asked you to get dressed a while ago. Why didn't you do it?"

"I can't find the dress I wanted to wear."

Joey's eyes narrowed as he scanned the messy kitchen and the unkempt house that somewhat resembled a battlefield. His insides churned with worry. Perhaps Faith hadn't come down because she was too busy figuring out how to tell him she planned to use her return ticket to Columbus today. Perchance the right words just weren't coming, so she needed time to mull them over.

"Ouch!" Beth wailed.

He turned on his heel and rushed to the stove. "What happened?"

"I burned my finger on that dumb pan."

"Ha ha! Beth is a clumsy oaf, Beth is a clumsy oaf," Isaac chanted.

Rather than deal further with Isaac, he moved the pan off the flame and set it on a marble slab. Snatching up Beth's hand, he gave it a quick inspection. A small red welt appeared between her thumb and forefinger where she'd accidentally grabbed the pan handle. He grabbed a rag from the dish pan of cold, murky water, rung it out, and placed it on the burn mark. "Here, hold this in place. You'll be fine."

"Daddy, I need help finding my dress," bemoaned Miriam.

"I know, I know." Then to Beth he said, "Take your sister back upstairs please and help her locate something to wear."

"I'm done," declared Isaac. "I'm going outside."

"No, you're staying right here. We'll be having breakfast in a few minutes, and I—"

The sound of throat clearing made him pause mid-sentence. All eyes turned toward the woman dressed in light green; everything about her looking refined and rested. "I'm sorry to have kept you all waiting. May I do something to help?" she asked.

Joey did his best to collect himself, hoping she wouldn't notice the beads of sweat coating his forehead, and gave a hasty smile. "Good morning, Miss Haviland. I hope you had a restful sleep."

She had a smile for everyone, as she let her gaze move from one to the other. "I did indeed. I hope the same for each of you."

Since no one had a single word of response, just stared open-mouthed at her, Joey hurried to reply. "We did, thank you. Right, children?"

As if they'd all just laid eyes on a three-winged bird, they did nothing but gawk, so Joey brushed his hands together and spoke. "Well, you're just in time for breakfast."

"'Cept I can't find my dress," said Miriam in her usual whiny pitch.

Beth stepped forward and took her sister by the hand, leading her right past Faith without so much as a second of acknowledgment. *Was Beth going to pose as big a problem as Isaac when it came to manners?* He'd not expected her to dislike the woman, but then he hadn't taken the time to speak to his children individually about his impending marriage, so how could he know how they felt about the arrangement? Of course, it remained to be seen if Faith would even go through with it.

Breakfast proved to be a mostly quiet affair, save for a few tidbits of conversation and the clatters of fork to plate as everyone scooped up their scrambled eggs, bacon, and fried potatoes. Joey and Faith sat in the captain's chairs at either end of the table while Franklin and Isaac sat across from Beth and Miriam. Of all of them, Miriam seemed the least affected by the newest member at the table, her attention falling mostly to the china doll sitting in her lap.

Isaac cleaned his plate first and quickly tossed his napkin on the table, then peered at Joey. "Well, what about it? Are you two gettin' married, or what?" The direct question had Joey gasping for a quick breath. Of all the things he'd expected to come out of his son's mouth that was not one of them.

"I—uh, well, Miss Haviland and I have to discuss—"

"Actually, yes, we are," Faith said, her unexpected words catching him off guard. She took up her water glass and swallowed a few sips, her eyes staring over the rim at Isaac. After another swallow, she set down the glass with a tiny plunk. "Your father and I talked about it last night, but I needed to pray about the matter before giving him my final answer. This morning, I am quite at peace and have decided to say yes." She directed her next words at Joey. "I'll sign that prepared document now—that is, if you haven't had a change of heart."

"Me? No!" It took some effort to collect himself. *Had she really said yes?* "This is excellent news. Isn't this good news, children?"

He hadn't expected a celebration, but neither had he expected such a lot of sullen faces, with everyone but Miriam staring at him as if he'd lost half his brain. And maybe he had. "Miss Haviland and I will be married at the courthouse today. Uncle Jack will go along and act as witness," he told his family. Then, to Faith, he said, "I made an appointment for three o'clock with Judge Cranston on the chance you'd say yes."

"You're getting married today?" Isaac grumbled.

"Yes, there's no time to dawdle. I have to report back to duty in a few days, Tuesday to be exact."

"I ain't goin' to no wedding," grumbled Isaac.

"Me neither," said Franklin.

"No one invited you," said Joey, grinning in spite of his sons' brashness. "Aunt Cristina has agreed to watch over all of you while we are out."

"Good, 'cause it sounds boring, and besides, Uncle Jesse wants Frank and me to go down to the birthing shed and help with the new calves."

"Well, that'll be fine. Beth, we'll drop you and Miriam off later on our way into town."

"Why do you have to go back to the army so soon?" Beth asked, her eyes filling with moisture. "You're always going away, and now you're leaving us with someone we don't even know."

His heart went out to her. "Well, you didn't know the other nannies either, Beth. There's a war going on, sweetheart. I'm needed."

"Well, don't we count?"

"Of course you count. Don't be silly."

"It won't be so bad, honey. I'll see to it that we have lots of fun together," Faith put in, her tone soft and reassuring.

"No nannies are ever fun, and you'll be just like the rest of them," Beth argued. "They all start out nice, and before you know it, they hate us." She pushed back in her chair before giving Faith a chance to respond, her eyes now dripping with tears. "She might end up being our stepmother, but she won't be no mother of mine!" At that, the girl turned on her heel and ran out of the room, making for the stairs.

"Hey, I thought you were gonna help me find my dress," Miriam hollered. But Beth ignored her, and after she reached the top of the stairs, her feet pounded all the way down the hall till her door opened and closed with a loud thud.

Miriam shrugged and went back to fussing over her doll, most of her breakfast still untouched. "What's wrong with Beth anyway?" she asked.

Hardly hearing Miriam's question, Joey laid down his napkin. "Well, I guess I should excuse myself and go have a talk with her."

"You should leave her be, Daddy," said Franklin. "You can't make her like Miss Haviland if she's already got her mind made up."

Joey opened his mouth to argue, but Faith spoke first. "He is absolutely right, Captain Fuller. Just leave her be for now. She needs time to adjust, as do Isaac and Franklin. Goodness, I myself am in for an adjustment."

"You can say that again," mumbled Isaac. Franklin giggled.

"Boys, that's enough," Joey said. "It will be your responsibility to set the example in the household."

"We always set the example," Isaac said, grinning and then nudging Franklin in the side.

Joey wasn't fond of their inference, but neither did he care to stir the already muddy pot.

Together, the boys stood, their grins still in place. "We're goin' out to the barn," Isaac announced.

"That's fine, but carry your dishes to the sink first." Beth's outburst still had Joey flustered.

Isaac stared at him as if he'd lost his marbles. "Why? We've never done that before."

Joey stared back, annoyed. "Yes, you have. Now, do as I say."

The boy huffed a loud portion of air from his lungs and cast his eyes at Franklin, his grin fading. Both boys carried their plates to the kitchen, but on the way there, Isaac mumbled something indiscernible. Too concerned about creating another eruption, Joey chose to ignore the remark, instead shaking his head at them as they disappeared through the archway and then out the kitchen door. That left Miriam, Faith, and Joey at the table, Miriam casting curious eyes from one adult to the other. To Faith, Joey said, "I'm sorry about that. They're rather...I don't know the word to best describe them."

"Willful?" Faith offered with uplifted brows. "Obstinate?"

"You could say that."

"Rude!" said Miriam without a hint of prompting.

Joey's eyes went round. "You are smarter than all of us put together, Miriam Joy."

Without missing a beat, Miriam went back to fussing over her doll. "I know that."

This prompted a much-needed burst of laughter from Joey and Faith.

11

"Understand that if I go into Columbus today, this will be my last favor, Stu. I want no part of your deceitful behavior."

Drunker than a skunk, Stuart had spent the night on Leon's sofa, not even stirring after Leon had fixed some supper. Now, however, he was eating like the hog Leon kept in a pen out by the shed—eggs, a slab of bacon, fried potatoes. Leon wanted him gone.

"I'm not expecting you to do anything wrong. Like I said, just check things out around town. See if you can learn anything pertaining to my butcher shop being closed and whether or not folks is talkin' about me."

"All right, but then you have to leave. You can't stay here more than a couple of days."

"Fine. I'll be out of your hair before you know it."

"I got errands to run anyway. I'm running out of some farm supplies, feed for the animals, chicken wire to fix some fencing, and beans. I have a bad craving for beans."

Stuart scooped up another forkful of food. "I'll be waitin' for y'. How long you think it'll take you?"

"I should be back by early afternoon, I'd guess."

Leon's gut churned at remembering Stuart's confession last night. Looking back, he never should have assisted him in burying Opal those many years ago, but back then, he had little confidence in himself, still lived under his cousin's influence, and certainly had no relationship with God. When Stuart said she'd died of natural causes, fallen asleep the night before and never woke up, he'd believed him, failed even to ask questions. He knew she'd been a sickly thing, so her passing hadn't surprised him. Now, though, he saw himself for the living fool he'd been.

They'd buried her on a deserted piece of Leon's land, out behind a ramshackle building. At least Stuart had built a box for her. *How long had he been working on it before he'd done the deed?* The thought made Leon's stomach roil. After Stuart had left that day, Leon had made a marker for Opal's grave, and as of last year, when he'd ridden his horse out there to check his fencing, he noted the marker still being there. It made him sick now to think about it.

"If you go into that eatin' establishment called Daybreak Diner, you might find out something. That's where Faith used to work."

"The woman you're trying to woo by showing her your fist?"

Stuart didn't even blink. "That's the one. Anyway, her aunt Martha owns the place."

"Yeah, yeah, I know the restaurant. I think I've eaten there a time or two."

"I'll pay you for your time."

"I don't want your money, Stu. Your leaving will be payment enough."

Stuart stopped chewing, laid down his fork, and set both arms on the table on either side of his plate. "Ain't that sort of unkind comin' from a religious man?"

"I'm a Christian, Stuart. I pray and read my Bible every day. Because of the relationship I have with God, I don't think He'd look too kindly on my harboring somebody who's running from the law, kin or not. That said, you can stay through tomorrow. But after that, you'll have to find someplace else to go."

"Oh, I'll be long gone by then. I've got to get Faith after all."

Leon rolled his eyes and shook his head back and forth. "Tend my animals, would ya? It's the least you can do."

"Maybe I'll butcher one. At no cost, o' course."

Leon glared at him. "Never mind. I'll tend 'em before I leave. Just—just leave my stuff alone, you hear?"

"Yeah, yeah, don't be so touchy."

Because he planned to pick up some supplies, Leon drove his two-horse team to Columbus and arrived by mid-morning. He directed his horses straight to the livery, where he paid the stableman to feed, water, and rub down his animals. His plan was to round up what supplies he'd jotted on his list, then have a good lunch at the diner. He'd talk to a few people and gather what information he could and then head home. Stuart Porter may be his cousin, but he had no obligation to go out of his way for him. He'd as much as confessed to killing his wife, for crying out loud, and Leon was harboring him. The very thought almost made him retch. *Lord, how shall I handle this? What would You have me do? I want to show him love and kindness, but it's a fine line for me of what's right and what is pushing the limit.*

He set off up the street in the direction of the hardware and general store to find what he'd need, his head full of thoughts and worries, and on his way, passed Porter's Butcher Shop. His chest went heavy as he walked by, noting the "Closed" sign on the door and the shades pulled on the windows. Again, that question of what he should do with the knowledge he'd gained from Stuart last night pestered his mind.

He opened the door to Grover's General Store and noted one familiar face, that of the owner, George Grover. Leon so rarely came to town, maybe three or four times a year, that he'd never made any friends, with the exception of George and the preacher at the Baptist church who'd introduced him to Christ fifteen years ago and had since moved on to a different congregation in another town. Leon liked George because they talked about spiritual matters when they had the opportunity. The fellow knew God, and he wasn't afraid to live out the gospel. Leon admired him.

At the jangling of the bell over the door, George looked up from his place at the cash register and gave a wave. "Leon! Good to see you. I'll be right with you." Leon nodded in return and set to wandering around the store a bit.

After about ten minutes, the store quieted down, giving Leon an opportunity to hand over his list of needs. George took the list in hand, glanced down at it, then looked at Leon. "Everything all right with you, Leon? You seem a little distracted."

The man had a keen sense about him. Leon tipped his head to the side. "I'm all right. Thanks. I noticed that butcher shop is closed."

"Porter's? Yeah, it sure is. The owner, Stuart Porter, got himself into some trouble. He's on the run. Authorities have no idea where he went off to, but I'm sure they'll find him. Sheriff Mumford's a pretty determined fellow. I understand there's a reward out for Porter's capture. If anybody knows of his whereabouts, they should let the sheriff know."

"That so? What did he do?"

"Porter? He assaulted a woman. She's left town too, last I heard. I sure hope the man stays clear of her. He's an odd duck, and now I'd consider him dangerous."

"I'd have to agree with you." In his years of knowing George, they'd only talked of spiritual matters, nothing personal pertaining to his upbringing or lack of a family. The fellow never had made the connection that his last name matched Stuart's, probably because there were a number of other Porters living in Columbus, none of whom were related.

George leaned in. "But that don't mean he don't need our prayers."

"You're absolutely right about that."

"How you doing? You still reading your Bible and listening for God's voice?"

"More than ever."

George smiled. "That's good news. You keep at it."

The door opened, and three more customers entered. Their time cut short, George completed Leon's order. He arranged for one of his stock boys to box everything up and deliver it to Leon's wagon at the livery.

They said their farewells, and Leon left Grover's to make his way to the grain store to buy feed for his animals.

He arrived at the diner around half past twelve, found a table at the back, and seated himself. "Hey, there, mister," greeted a pleasant faced woman balancing three lunch platters on her way to a table. "I'll be with you in a minute."

Leon nodded, removed his hat, and set the filthy thing on the table. He combed his fingers through his long hair and wondered if he ought to make a trip to the barber while in town. It couldn't hurt, especially since no matter how much he wracked his brain, he couldn't remember his last decent haircut. A copy of the weekly newspaper lay on the empty table next to him, so he rose from his chair and snatched it up, then sat back down and refolded it so as to review the front page. The first thing he read was the week's war news. In bold, block letters was the headline: "Battle of Petersburg: Union Forces Begin Digging Tunnels Under Confederate Lines." He skimmed the article until he grew bored, then let his eyes rove the rest of the page. Just before flipping the newspaper over to glance at the back, he caught sight of a small article in the bottom corner under the headline, "Authorities Still Seek Stuart Porter for Questioning." This earned his full attention. He sat up a little straighter and strained his tired eyes to read each word of the short piece. He didn't like the thought of protecting someone he knew to be a murderer, cousin or not. A deep sigh rolled out of him. *What should I do about it, Lord?*

"What you need, mister?"

He lay the paper down. "What's your lunch special?"

She rattled off something about fried chicken and mashed potatoes. "I'll take it," he said.

"Coming right up." She started to turn but stopped and gave him a questioning glance. "I don't think I've ever seen you in here. You new in town?"

"Nope, just don't get into town all that often. I'll take a tall glass of water, too, if you can spare it."

"You got it, mister. Water's cheap."

They exchanged polite grins before she turned on her heel and headed to the kitchen. He picked up the paper again and read some more, albeit with a distracted mind. The woman returned with his order in less than five minutes. He set the paper back down. "Fast service."

"We do our best."

She stood there waiting. "Take a bite, mister. I want to see your reaction."

He nodded and did as told, scooping up a juicy drumstick and helping himself to a good-sized bite. A bit of juice rolled down his chin, so he took up his napkin and swiped it. While he chewed, he closed his eyes and muttered, "I swear I ain't tasted anything better."

She laughed. "Ha! I'll be sure t' tell Miss Martha you approve."

"You do that." Leon chewed some more before taking another bite, then thought to ask, "Say, you wouldn't know anythin' about that Porter feller they're trying to locate, would you?"

Her brow furrowed, and she leaned in. "Not much, sir. Would you?"

"Me? Like I said, I don't come around these parts much. I was just reading the newspaper and came across this here article about him being sought."

She straightened and tipped her head down. "He attacked one of ar' waitresses, hit her square in the mouth, the nasty fellow. He's got some romantic interest in her, but she didn't reciprocate the feelings, so he showed her his mean side. Some fellow came along and rescued her. Course, Mr. Porter disappeared short after that, and good riddance to him. His butcher shop is closed down, and I don't expect it to open again. From what I hear, Sheriff Mumford's got a posse out lookin' for him, but they've made no headway. Sheriff thinks maybe he's crossed state borders by now and they might never find him." She leaned in even closer now and lowered her voice. "If you ask me, they suspect him of doin' more than just attackin' Miss Haviland. Otherwise, why would they have posted a reward for his return?"

"Yeah? What sort of reward?"

"One-hundred-fifty dollars is what it is. Wish I knew where he was. I could use that kinda money to buy me a new cook stove, maybe even an icebox too."

When he gave no further response, she returned to the kitchen.

Leon ate his meal with a great deal of reflection. A Bible verse kept coming to his mind from the book of Romans. *"Let every soul be subject unto the higher powers. For there is no power but of God: the powers that be are ordained of God."* He'd just read Romans 13 the other night after supper, and it spoke about obeying the laws of the land and the consequences for not doing so. His cousin's total disregard for the law didn't sit well with him, but what really concerned him was his own disregard for it. A pang of conviction stabbed him hard. He could not ignore the fact that Stuart had confessed to ending Opal's life. It was a secret the Lord wouldn't allow him to hold onto. He had to make a trip to the sheriff's office and confess it all—even the part he'd played in helping to dig Opal's grave. He had to tell it all. It was the only way he'd find peace, the only way he'd be able to sleep. He'd get that shave and much-needed haircut, then head to the sheriff's office and unload. Yeah, it would mean jeopardizing his already fractured relationship with his cousin, but he didn't see any way around it. He couldn't ignore what perhaps he'd half suspected for two decades: Stuart was a murderer.

12

Joey pulled his rig into a parking space in front of the Lebanon Courthouse, jumped down to the hard earth, looped the reins over a hitching post, and then jogged around to Faith's side of the wagon. "Here, let me help," he said, reaching up to grasp hold of her waist with both hands while she set her hands on his firm shoulders. He lifted her down and set her on the ground. Their eyes locked for the briefest moment. He was especially handsome today, dressed in his freshly laundered and pressed uniform. Faith *tried* not to take much notice. After all, this marriage of convenience did not call for any sort of mutual admiration.

"Are you ready for this?" Joey asked.

"Not at all." Faith's heart pounded in her ears, and she worried her shaky voice might reveal her tangled mess of nerves. She gave a shaky smile. "Are you?"

"I'm as uneasy as a cat in a tub o' water."

That was enough to merit a tiny giggle from her. "I'm not sure if that makes me feel any better."

He joined her in a chuckle then looped his arm for her. "Don't worry. Things will be fine." He glanced up and down the road at several parked carriages and a few horses tied to hitching posts. "I recognize Jack's horse over there, which means he's probably waiting inside. Shall we go in?"

"I suppose I'm about as ready as I'll ever be."

"Me as well."

She placed her hand through his arm then lifted her long skirt above her ankles to avoid tripping on the stairs.

On the way to the courthouse, they'd stopped at the telegraph office so she could send a wire to her family announcing the news of her marriage and also asking them to send her trunk. She'd kept the message simple, especially since Joey stood close by, and she couldn't be sure he wasn't gazing over her shoulder. It read:

Marrying Captain Joseph Fuller today (stop) please send trunk on next stage (stop) wish you were here (stop) will write soon with all the details (stop) missing you terribly (stop)

Once done, Joey paid the fee, and they'd headed straight to the courthouse, most of their ride filled with senseless, if not nervous, chatter, both knowing the seriousness of what they were about to undertake.

Inside, the courthouse was abuzz with townsfolk, some there to pay bills, others requesting permits, some inquiring as to deeds and property records, and yet others waiting for appointments with officials. It was unclear which category Faith and Joey fell under, so she did the dutiful thing and stayed close to his side. They stood idly for a minute or two before Joey finally spotted his brother Jack. He immediately approached them from across the room, a broad smile on his face.

"Hello there, brother and future sister-in-law. Are you both ready for this moment?"

"Funny, we both just asked each other that same question. We decided we are about as ready as two people can be who don't know each other."

"It's a big step, but I'm convinced it's a good one. Things will work out, and I've a feeling the children are going to benefit."

"I thank you for that vote of confidence, Mr. Fuller," Faith said.

"Please, call me Jack."

"All right then." She hadn't even begun calling her future husband by his first name—at least not aloud—but she supposed she would in time.

"Thanks for showing up, brother," Joey said.

"You're welcome, of course. In fact, it was my honor. Now then, which line should we get in do you suppose?"

There were four from which to choose, but just before they fell into one, a gentleman behind the counter caught sight of them and quickly motioned them over to his line. There were at least three others ahead of them, but the gentleman pointed at a gate off to the side. "I take it by the uniform, you're Captain Fuller, are you not?"

"Yes, I am."

"I thought so. Go on through there, Captain Fuller. Judge Cranston is expecting you upstairs in his chambers. Mr. Gray, his court clerk, will usher you in once you reach his office."

"Thank you." As if it were the most natural thing, he took Faith's hand and led her through the swinging gate, Jack following.

"You're quite welcome, sir. Oh, and I understand congratulations are in order."

At that, the room fell mostly silent, save for a few quiet gasps. The clerk's announcement slowed Joey's step, but it didn't last. He gave a tiny turn of the head and a quick nod. "Appreciate it." On the way to the stairs, he whispered. "Well, I guess my whole notion of keeping this marriage a secret was a foolish one."

Jack laughed. "I noticed the town gossip, Mrs. Greenleaf, standing in one of the lines. She's probably the one who gasped the loudest. By tomorrow, all of Lebanon will know you're remarried, brother. Maybe you should've requested we be permitted to enter through a back door."

"No matter," Faith said with a smile. "Let folks say and think what they will. It is just blather, and there's no point in our fussing over their words."

"I like your thinking. I'll try to remember it," Joey said.

Jack chuckled. "I think you're marrying a smart woman."

They walked down a long corridor till they reached a door with a nameplate reading "Ronald L. Cranston, Warren County District Judge." Joey turned the knob and opened the door, then stepped aside to allow Faith to go ahead of him. Jack dutifully followed them. Upon their entering, a middle-aged, balding gentleman sitting behind a desk with a tall stack of papers in front of him looked up. He gave a smile and a nod. "Afternoon. May I help you?"

"Indeed. I—rather, *we*—have an appointment with Judge Cranston."

"Oh, Captain Fuller, is it?"

"Yes."

Without hesitation, the fellow stood and looked all three of them over, then brushed his hands together. "Well, the judge is expecting you. Just one moment please." He scurried across the room and gave a little knock on a door, then opened it. "Sir, pardon the interruption. Captain Fuller and—er, his—ah, fiancée are here to see you."

"Good, good, send them in," the booming voice returned.

The man turned to deliver the message, but Joey had already taken Faith's hand and started ushering her to the judge's chambers. Jack followed close behind, and once they all entered, the clerk closed the door behind them.

"Joey, my boy, and Jack. My, how good it is to see you both." The large, bearded man stood and moved around his desk to meet them, a smile creasing his rugged face. "And this must be your intended, eh, Joseph?"

"Yes, sir, judge, this is Miss Faith Haviland from Columbus. I told you about her right after I heard she was coming to Lebanon by stage. Miss Haviland, meet Judge Cranston. He was a friend of my father's."

"How nice it is to meet you, sir."

The judge's crinkly eyes warmed at the introduction, and when Faith stuck out her hand, he quickly took it in both of his and squeezed. "My, my, it is lovely meeting you. Joey did tell me about your coming to Lebanon and his wish to marry you. Of course, he had no idea you'd be such a beauty." At this, Faith's face warmed, and she dared not even glance at Joey. Judge Cranston slapped Joey on the back but kept his eyes on Faith. "And meeting this fellow firsthand didn't make you turn tail and head back to Columbus?"

She couldn't help it—she laughed. "Well, there was the matter of the return ticket, but I chose not to use it."

"Lucky for Joseph then. Lucky indeed."

Faith instantly liked the man. Despite his prominent position in Lebanon, he was down to earth and approachable.

The judge's eyes traveled from Jack to Joey. "And how is the rest of the family? How's your wife, Jack?"

"She's well. We're about to have a baby come November."

"Wonderful, wonderful. And your mother? Is she just as ornery as ever?"

"Probably more so now that she's got that broken leg to slow her down," answered Joey.

The judge snickered. "I had a feeling that would pose a problem for her. My wife keeps saying she ought to take a drive out to visit her, but you know how time gets away from you." He gave Joey a good looking over. "And how is this war treating you, Joseph? Do you think an end is in sight?"

"I can only hope it's drawing nearer. Many theorize that Gettysburg and Vicksburg were key battles, maybe even turning points, putting the North in a position for winning, but it's probably still too early to predict. It's obvious we're much stronger in number than the South. I'm convinced General Grant's appointment will be a key factor, and I'd even go so far as to predict he'll lead us to victory. At least, I'm quite optimistic."

"From everything I've read in the newspapers, I'd have to agree." The judge slapped Joey on the shoulder. "At any rate, you look none the worse for all the time you've served fighting for the cause. I appreciate your service, and of course, yours too, Jack."

"Thank you, sir," Jack said with a quick nod.

"Well, then, shall we get on to the matter of this marriage ceremony?" Eyes on Faith, the judge asked, "Are you quite certain you wish to go through with this, Miss Haviland?"

"Actually, sir, I've covered it in prayer, and after much consideration, have decided that marrying Captain Fuller makes a good deal of sense, both for me and the children. I hope to do justice to my job."

The older man tilted his chin up a fraction and lifted his bushy brows. "Marriage is more than a job, my dear. It's a lifelong commitment."

His statement caught Faith slightly off guard. *Had Joey not fully explained the circumstances of their marriage?*

Joey put a hand to the center of Faith's back. "She is well aware, sir," he answered on her behalf. "As am I. We've both agreed to marry so that she can take over the care of my children until I'm relieved of my duties in October—at which time I will pay Miss Haviland an agreed-upon stipend for her trouble. I explained all that to you, if you'll recall—and she and I discussed it last night."

The man's smile dimmed just slightly, though a twinkle stayed put in his grayish eyes. "Yes, yes, of course I recall our discussion, but when I marry two people, it is always with the hope that they will stay together until death comes between them. When you say your vows today, I want you to say them with sincerity—and with the intent to stay together. Now, if something prevents that from happening, then we will cross that road later. Doesn't that make sense?"

Joey's eyes went round as two full moons and darted from the judge to Faith and back to the judge. "That wasn't—"

"It sounds like a smart way to look at it, Joey," Jack interjected.

Faith laid a hand on Joey's forearm. "I, too, am in agreement with Judge Cranston, Captain Fuller. We must say our vows with all sincerity and ask the Lord to bless us. We shall deal with the legalities of our marriage when the time comes—in October, that is, at the end of your term of service."

Joey's mouth slacked for three seconds before he found his voice. "We sh-shall?"

Her feet shifted, and she gave a fast, tense nod. A bead of perspiration popped out on her brow, which she fought the urge to wipe. "Yes, we shall." Her mind suddenly turned to the four Fuller children who needed love and attention. She inwardly prayed he wouldn't suddenly back out.

He bit his lower lip, pinched the bridge of his nose, then glanced down at his shoes. "That wasn't what we agreed upon, but I guess…"

It amused her how he'd been the one seeking the wife and now seemed to have the cold feet, whereas she'd been the wary one but now had a profound sense of peace and assurance. She had to combat the need to bolster his confidence, knowing it was best not to force the issue. This would all come to fruition if God intended it.

"Come on, Joey, this is no time for second thoughts," urged Jack. "You are the one who wanted this marriage. Think about your children, and also think about the fact that you've exhausted all potential nannies to be found in Lebanon."

Jack's words were no comfort to Faith, but she knew he no doubt spoke the truth. She was Joey's last and only option.

"I don't—*we* don't—know the future, Captain, but God does. All we really know for sure is that your children are in need of watchful care, guidance, and protection, and I am here to offer that. I will say my vows with the intention of keeping them, and I hope you'll do the same. It is God's way."

After a few seconds of painful silence, Joey lifted his face with all-new resolve and turned to the judge, grinning. "I believe my wife-to-be has spoken, sir."

The judge let out a breath and gave a low chuckle. "Well then, I believe it's time we get this wedding underway. After the ceremony, I'll have you sign a couple of documents prepared by Mr. Gray, my court clerk. Jack, as witness, you'll be signing the same documents. That will make things official. Oh, and perhaps after I declare you husband and wife, you can begin addressing each other by your first names."

This produced a little giggle from both of them—and the next thing Faith knew, she was standing next to her intended as he vowed, "I, Joseph, take thee, Faith, to be my wife, to have and to hold, from this day forward; for better, for worse, for richer, for poorer, in sickness and in health, to love and to cherish, till death us do part, according to God's holy law. In the presence of God, I make this vow." After Faith made her vows, Judge Cranston said a few words before the declaration that made them husband and wife.

It all happened so fast that Faith hardly realized the gravity of the moment. Even the kiss, which the judge decreed they do to finalize matters, went off in record speed, and the only thing she felt when his lips brushed against hers was a tiny flutter in her stomach, which she attributed solely to nerves. After today, there'd be no more touching except by accident, and she'd do her best to avoid even that happening. Last night, he'd given her his bedroom and announced that he'd stay in a closet-sized room at the end of the hallway whenever he came home for a visit. It had a narrow cot, he'd said, and while it wasn't the most comfortable, he'd make it work. The girls each had their own rooms, while the boys shared one, making a total of four regular-size bedrooms, a washroom, and Joey's "closet" on the second floor.

A hot sun scalded their shoulders on the ride back to the farm. After the ceremony, there'd been handshakes, words of congratulations, and a warm embrace from Jack, her new brother-in-law, who'd then dismissed himself and ridden back to the farm ahead of them. Where they'd made pointless chatter on the ride into town, both Faith and Joey now sat perched high on the wagon seat in utter silence, staring ahead and pondering what they'd just done. Faith's hands remained folded in her lap, and both of Joey's gripped the reins like they were some kind of lifeline. His knuckles even went white from clutching the leather straps so tightly in his fists. Several times, she'd opened her mouth to start a conversation, then closed it right back up for fear the topic might be too trite. When they were but a mile from the farm, Joey at last quashed the hush between them. "I suppose Ma will want us to stop by the house to let her know we did the deed."

The deed? He made it sound like some sort of surreptitious feat. "Yes, we should probably do that. I'm sure the children also are quite eager to know if we went through with it."

He gave a half chuckle. "No doubt. I'm sorry, I should have planned some sort of dinner—or something—to commemorate the event."

"No need. It's not like this was something we'd been planning for months on end. Besides, we already gathered last night at Jack's house for that fine turkey dinner Cristina prepared. I will get to know your family better as time goes by."

"I'm sure Cristina will be happy to accompany you into town from time to time. She's very nice and will be a good friend to you."

"I have no doubt about that. I liked her immediately. In fact, your entire family is lovely."

"Do you have particular concerns about my children?"

"Well, I'm sure it will be an adjustment for all of us. Perhaps tonight I'll watch more closely to see how you go about putting each of them to bed. I'll do my best to duplicate your practice so they'll feel comfortable."

He gave her a sideways glance. "You pretty much saw the procedure last night. I don't know as I have any particular practice. That was their mother's job—before she died."

"But she passed three years back. Surely, you've established some sort of routine with them."

"If you'll recall, I've been off fighting a war." His tone carried a hint of sarcasm. "I've left the bedtime exercise up to their former nannies."

"I see. Well, perhaps we can change that beginning tonight. You have a few more nights at home with them. A story and bedtime prayers would be nice. And then since this is Saturday, we'll see that they bathe so they'll be clean and fresh for Sunday church."

Now he gave her more than a sideways glance. He craned his neck full around to get a good look at her. "I thought I made it fairly clear I'm not much for church, haven't been since…"

"I know. Since your wife's passing. Did you attend before then?"

Joey paused before answering. "Uh—yeah, but…"

"Did she enjoy church?"

"Yes, she grew up attending church. She was very devout in her faith."

"Then she would be exceedingly upset with you for your lackadaisical attitude. She was a wonderful mother, was she not?"

"Of course."

"Then it would trouble her to no end to know you didn't place a great deal of importance on the Sabbath."

"I'm at war, remember? And the nannies always saw to it that the children were ready to go when Jesse and my mother stopped by to pick them up. It's not as if they aren't accustomed to attending."

"And when you are discharged from the army, is that how it will be, you making sure they're ready to go when your brother and mother pull up in the wagon?"

His brow scrunched, and he narrowed two twinkling eyes at her. "Are you always this bossy?"

"I'm not a bit bossy. Stubborn, perhaps."

Now he grinned. "Are you going to make me regret my decision to marry?"

She merely smiled and shrugged. "I don't know. Are *you*?"

He gave a loud snorting guffaw and turned his attention back to the road just as the horses veered off it and made their way onto the long, well-traveled two-track that would take them straight to the front door of the main house. Neither spoke another word, just jostled along, every so often bumping against the other's shoulder.

Mrs. Fuller sat on the porch, her hand up to her forehead to shield her eyes from the lowering sun. At the first glimpse of them, she sat a little straighter. Faith pasted a smile on her face, but the woman's shaded face did not reveal whether she returned one.

13

His shave and haircut complete, Leon went to the livery to pick up his team, then made his way to the sheriff's office. Once there, he parked his rig and walked up the wooden steps to the entrance door marked "Franklin County Sheriff's Office." Something in his gut turned over. *It was now or never, that single moment of truth.*

"Can I help y', sir?" came the voice of a male clerk behind the oak counter.

"Uh, yeah, is the sheriff in?" He absently removed his dirty hat, then took to turning it in his hands.

"You want to report a crime or file a complaint? I can help you with either."

"I want to talk to the sheriff."

No doubt the fellow heard the urgency in his voice, for he asked. "What is your name, sir? Can I tell the sheriff the purpose of your visit?"

"My name's Leon Porter."

"Le-on Por-ter," the fellow mumbled as he wrote. He paused and looked up, hazel eyes squinting at him. "You wouldn't be—no, never mind." He gave his head a fast shake and finished scribbling. "Now then, what's the purpose of your visit?"

"I want to see the sheriff."

"Yes, I know, but, well, can you tell me the nature of your—?"

"No! Just tell him it's urgent." A little bit of righteous anger rolled out of him, that and outright terror. He had half a mind to leave. *Did God really want him to turn in Stuart? Had he misread his inner sense?* No, he hadn't misread anything. He couldn't allow Stuart to go after that woman in Lebanon. *If his cousin had it in him to end Opal's life and had already slugged a woman named Faith, what else was he capable of doing?*

"All right, all right," the clerk said. "Just have a seat over there and wait. I'll be back shortly."

Leon let out a long, shaky sigh and watched the clerk disappear down a corridor. The fellow had been about to ask him if he was related to Stuart. He still marveled how George Grover had never made the connection. In less than a minute, the deputy clerk returned. "The sheriff will see you now. I'll escort you to his office."

Nervous, Leon stood and followed him down the hall. At the sheriff's door, he swiped his brow and walked inside. The clerk left after receiving a nod from the rather portly sheriff, who stood and extended a hand across his desk to Leon. His heart pounded loud enough to echo in his ears.

Leon wiped his right hand on his pants before shaking the sheriff's hand. "Thank you for seeing me."

"No problem. Have a seat." He pointed at a chair in front of his desk, and Leon sat down. "Now, then, what can I do for you?"

"Well, I got somethin' to talk to you about."

"I see. Go ahead then."

Leon cleared his throat and swallowed. "Stuart Porter is my cousin. I know where he is."

The sheriff's head jerked back and his eyes went round. "You've got my full attention, Mr. Porter."

⌒

"Are you really married to my daddy?" Miriam asked that night after their supper of pork, beans, cornmeal mush, and muffins. Miriam gazed up at her with wide blue eyes while Faith stood over the cast-iron sink with the convenient pump handle, dipping the dishes into the water to give them a good rinse, then making a stack on the cabinet counter next to her. Beth gathered the remainder of the supper dishes from the dining room table and carried them to another nearby counter. Isaac had taken a slop pail out to the hog pen and would join Franklin and Joey at the barn afterward to help the hired hands, Wendel and Jobe, with barn chores. Faith hoped this alone time with the girls might give her an opportunity to begin building a bridge, even though Beth's dour mood had not improved since the morning.

"I certainly am, lil' lamb."

"Beth says you ain't my ma, though."

"That's true enough, but I hope we can become friends."

The child chanced a peek at her older sister. "I don't 'zactly know. Are we allowed to be friends with her, Beth?"

"That's up to you to decide," Beth answered. She picked up a spare rag. "I'll go wipe off the table then come back and dry the dishes."

"Thank you, Beth. I appreciate you doing that without my even asking."

"It's what I did with the other nannies, so I figured I'd keep it up."

"That's very thoughtful. I had no idea what your former responsibilities were, so perhaps you could share them with me when you return."

The girl tarried for a second at the door. "I might be able to do that." Then she turned and walked to the dining room.

"I don't know what my 'sponsibilities is," said Miriam. "Do I have any?"

"Well, I'm not sure, honey. We'll check with Beth about that. Do you want some jobs?"

Miriam scrunched her petite nose, put a finger to the side of her chin, and tilted her head. "I don't know. Pro'ly only if they're fun."

Faith had to laugh. "I intend to see to it that we have some fun along the way, honey. What are some things you enjoy doing?"

"I like to play with my toys."

"What are your favorites?"

"All of them."

"You must have *some* favorites."

"My dolly Elizabeth is my favorite."

"Is she the one you brought to the table tonight?"

"No, that's Isabella. Sometimes Isabella gets left out, so I have t' give her extra attention."

Faith smiled. "That's very kind of you." She set down the final rinsed plate. Now to reheat the kettle of water at the hearth so she could let the dirty water down the drainpipe and start fresh. Beth returned and picked up a towel, armed and ready to begin her drying task.

"I'm not quite ready to begin washing the dishes yet. Perhaps we can talk a bit. Miriam has just been telling me about her favorite doll Elizabeth. Do you happen to have a favorite doll as well?"

"I don't play much with dolls."

"No? If I recall, I played with them till I was about ten or eleven. Some of my friends were interested in boys, but not I."

"Boys stink," Beth said.

That caused another smile. "I think I felt the same at your age."

"I can barely tolerate my own brothers."

"I understand that. Mine teased me mercilessly growing up. Just like you, I have two brothers and a sister, but they are all married and older than me."

Beth harrumphed, as if Faith's words held no interest for her. In truth, her eyes sparked a bit, but she made no attempt at furthering the conversation. Faith put a stopper in the drain and moved to the hearth to check on her kettle of water. Finding it beginning to steam, she used her apron to lift it by its handle and move it across the room so she could pour it into the sink. Miriam had vanished into another room, leaving Beth and Faith alone. Beth stood watching while Faith returned to the stove with the kettle then watched as she poured a little soap powder into the water. While Faith worked, she tried to think of topics that might interest Beth.

"Do you have any favorite games or things you simply enjoy doing in your spare time?"

"Not really," was her glib answer.

"No? Do you like to spend time in the barn? Tend the animals? Climb trees or go fishing? What about riding horses?"

"I don't know," the girl said.

Clearly, she had no interest in conversing, but Faith wasn't about to give up. "These are pretty dishes," she said, washing one and then holding it up to admire the dainty flowers lining the edges before handing it over to Beth to rinse and dry.

"Those were my mother's dishes. She got them from her mother, my Grandma Wilkinson. Grandma and Grandfather Wilkinson came here from Europe."

"Ah, how wonderful. I would imagine, being the oldest daughter, you'll inherit them someday."

"Maybe."

"Where do your Grandma and Grandfather Wilkinson live?"

"My grandma died even before my mother did, and my grandfather moved away from Ohio when he got married again. He don't ever write to us, so I don't even know where he lives."

"I see. Well, at least you have your Grandmother Fuller. She seems like a lovely person."

"Grandma's nice, and she's even nicer when she don't have a broken leg. Right now, she's a little grumpy."

"Everyone has a right to be grumpy from time to time."

Beth made a little grunting noise and shifted her weight. "Are you just about done with that dish?"

"Oh! Yes!" Faith handed the scrubbed plate to the girl, and while she tried to initiate more conversation with Beth while they stood there washing and drying the supper dishes, the child clearly didn't want to talk, and there was no point in forcing it. Everyone had a big adjustment to make, not the least of whom was Faith herself—now a married woman!

Approaching hoofbeats pounded the earth outside the barn. Joey and the boys looked toward the big double doors to see dust flying. They'd come out to help with chores even though their services weren't required. Wendel and Jobe had everything under control, although Joey always appreciated it when they gave jobs to his sons, which they did most days. Isaac especially needed to learn what it took to manage a farm. Joey enjoyed the chores and welcomed the distraction, for just about the only thing he could think of otherwise was his newly married status.

"Joey, you in here?" He recognized the male voice as coming from his brother Jesse. It carried a frantic tinge.

Both Isaac and Franklin took off toward the front of the barn. "Uncle Jesse, what's going on?" they asked in unison.

Out of breath, Jesse stood in the doorway, his bulky frame a silhouette against the late day sun. "What's up?" Joey asked.

"I need some help over at the birthing shed. I got a cow bleeding out. Her sack broke and the calf's not coming out. I need an extra set of strong hands."

Joey went into take-charge mode. "Frankie, go on up to the house and tell Faith where we're going. You can ride one of the horses over to the barn if you want to join us. Otherwise, stay at the house and wait for our return. Isaac and I will hitch up the wagon and meet you over there, Jess."

Quick as a flash of light, Jesse mounted his pinto and rode off, his horse kicking up another cloud of dust. Franklin could be seen running across the yard toward the house.

They arrived at the shed to the sounds of a mooing, moaning cow. Upon entering, Joey found his brother standing behind the poor critter, his arm around her back quarters, blood dripping out.

"Fill me in," said Joey moving up next to his brother. Isaac moved to the other side of him.

"She's a first-calf heifer, and she's not presenting right. There's been no progress in well over an hour, and when I went up there, I could tell that one of the calf's front legs is bent under. I think that's what's causing the internal bleeding. Not sure, but the leg might be deformed. I need someone to hold this girl steady so I can go in there again and see about straightening out the leg. If I can't, this cow won't be able to deliver, and she'll die soon. She's dilated, and the sac's broke, so she's ready, but she's growin' weaker. Isaac, run over there to that shelf and bring down that big can o' lard. I'll need it to use as a lubricant."

Without question, Isaac did as told, making Joey marvel for a moment at the speed with which his baby brother could motivate his son to act on orders. The boy jogged back in less than a minute and handed his uncle the big can. Jesse dipped a hand in and came out with a glob of lard in his palm. He eyeballed Joey. "Hold her steady. She's not goin' to like this."

"Come on over here and help me, Isaac."

Isaac moved alongside his father and together, they both took hold of the halter on either side of the heifer's head. Jesse inserted his arm, and the cow groaned and fought, although too weak to put up much of a fuss. After assessing, Jesse said, "I'm pretty sure the leg is just bent under. I—have—to—straighten—it—out," he said with great effort. It took a couple of minutes, but at last he said, "There. Okay. The birth canal is narrow, but I'm going to pull as hard as I can. If we can't get 'er out, we'll use the chains."

"Do what you can," Joey said. "Do you want Isaac to go get 'em just in case?"

Jesse didn't readily answer, just kept working, and the longer he worked, the more unsteady the cow became, faltering on all fours. "Yep, we're goin' to have to walk these shoulders out, and there's not much time."

"Go get the chains, Isaac," Joey said without consulting Jesse.

Isaac left and returned in a few blinks, the chains rattling as he ran. He handed them over to Jesse, who started attaching them to the two feet that were barely cresting. "Here, Isaac, you can help. You take this chain, and I'll take the other. When I tell you to pull, you give a good, long, steady pull until I tell you to let up. Got it? Slow, steady, gradual."

Joey looked over the cow's head to get a good view of his son. The boy nodded, his eyes sparking with life and energy. It occurred then that he was in his element, and a wave of pride rushed through Joey's veins.

"Pull, Isaac, pull! Keep pulling." After a few seconds, Jesse said, "Okay, let up a bit."

Joey held the cow's head, which had started to droop. The critter weaved and faltered, obviously exhausted.

"What's all that blood?" Isaac asked.

"Never mind that. All right, pull again. There we go, legs and head are coming nicely. Keep pulling." Another few moments. "Stop. I need to reach in there and rotate that baby to allow for the hips to pass through. Hold on, Isaac. Y're doin' real good."

Isaac remained calm, glancing over the cow at his father, who gave him a nod of approval. Once Jesse rotated the calf, he said, "Okay, now we're going to press downward, so this heifer can drop her calf."

About that time, the heifer started to go down herself, and while Joey did his best to keep her upright, she toppled in spite of his every effort, her feet giving way as she fell with a loud thump onto her left side. At that same time, the calf delivered, his mouth frothy from fighting for his first breath of real air. The new mother gave a pathetic groan.

Cows were a premium on the farm, so losing one milking cow amounted to lost money. "She's good, she's good," Joey said, lifting up the young cow's eyelid and then checking her heart and breathing rhythms. "We need to stand her back up though before she gets bloat."

That took some doing from all three of them, but they accomplished the task within minutes. The cow stood wearily, unmoving, taking in several loud, laborious breaths.

"Isaac, grab a rag and give that calf a good working over to get his blood circulating," Jesse said. "Your pa and I will see to this new mama." Isaac did as told, grabbing a rag off a hook and massaging the calf's body from head to hooves as if he'd helped birth a dozen calves before this one. It occurred to Joey then that he needed to play a more active role in his children's lives, particularly when it came to farming.

"Come on, mama," Jesse said to the cow, pushing her toward her newborn. Without much prompting, she sauntered over to her baby to investigate, and as nature would have it, started licking and nudging it with her nose. Jesse moved to her hindquarters and checked under her tail. "Bleeding's already letting up, so I think she'll be okay. Looks like we made it, men." Jesse patted Isaac on the shoulder and winked at Joey over the boy's head. "I couldn't have done it without you, Isaac. Thanks, both of you."

"We were glad to help, brother," Joey said. He turned to his son with a grin. "You were a real natural, Isaac."

The boy smiled, a rarity for him unless he was up to no good. "It was fun. I wanna help deliver more babies."

The brothers laughed. "Well, you'll have plenty of opportunities," said Jesse. "It wasn't until just recently you started taking a real interest, but now that you have, I'll take all the help you want to give me."

Isaac nodded and stood taller.

"Shall we go back home now, son?"

"I'd rather stay here in the barn for a while."

"I'll bring him home in about a half hour, how's that?" Jesse asked.

"If you're sure."

"Sure as rain. You probably should get home to that new wife of yours." Jesse's eyes twinkled with a tad bit of mischief. "How'd the ceremony go today? It sure didn't take long for Jack to get back to the farm. You must have recited those weddin' vows in record time."

"Judge Cranston didn't dawdle."

"Ha! Well, better you than me."

He might have reminded his brother that this was a temporary arrangement, but he didn't want to speak of it in front of Isaac. "Your day will come," he said instead.

"Naw. I'm a proclaimed bachelor. 'Sides, I've got no time for courting. Too much to do on the farm."

"It *is* a busy place, but you shouldn't let it dominate you. Might be a woman out there you haven't met simply because you don't choose to take time to meet anyone."

"I'm content living life my way."

"With Ma? Really?"

"She's not that bad."

"I love her, but I wouldn't want to live with her."

"She can be set in her ways, but I've learned to put up with her—just as she's learned to put up with me."

"Pfff, everyone knows you're her favorite."

They shared a few chuckles over that remark. Isaac had taken the can of lard back to the shelf and gotten sidetracked by another calf that was just a week old. He stood over its pen and patted its little square head, seemingly oblivious to Joey's and Jesse's conversation.

"You think he'll adjust to Faith?" Jesse asked in a low voice.

"I'm sure it'll take a while."

"He's a good kid."

"He's a rascal is what he is."

"He simply needs direction, brother. Maybe your new wife will have what it takes to keep him under control."

"I know he enjoys spending time with you. I appreciate the influence you've had on him."

"He can spend as much time with me as he wants, but I can't take your place, Joey. He really misses his father."

"I don't always see that in him. When I'm home he doesn't necessarily clamor to be with me. Frankly, I don't know what he needs or wants."

"Kids act out when they want attention."

"Listen to you, sounding like you know what you're talking about."

They laughed again, and about that time, Isaac started moseying back in their direction.

"You want to fill up the trough with some fresh oats for this new mama?" Jesse asked the boy.

"Sure. She need fresh water too?"

"Couldn't hurt."

Isaac grabbed a bucket and ran over to the feed bin.

"Well, I'll be on my way," Joey said, somewhat anxious to get home to his bride, but dreading it at the same time.

Jesse seemed to sense his apprehension. "Everything will work out as God wills it, Joey. You got to learn to trust Him."

He took a deep breath, then let it out. "Lately, I'm gettin' preached at from all directions. Apparently, I'm going to church in the morning."

"Well, glory be!"

"Yeah, don't get too excited. I'm only attending to appease my new wife. Next Sunday I'll be back on the battlefield."

Jesse removed his hat and finger combed his mussed hair, then plopped it back on his head. "Sometimes, I'm sorry I haven't done my part in the war."

"Don't be. Two out of three of us is enough. Ma couldn't have handled all three of us going to war. Besides, you needed to stay home and tend this farm. We're thankful you did. Otherwise, I'm not sure it'd be prospering as well as it is."

Isaac came back with a bucket of oats.

"I'll be going now. Isaac, Uncle Jesse said he'll bring you home after bit."

"Aw, can't I sleep in the barn?"

"What? No, you can't sleep in the barn." He ruffled his boy's hair then looked at Jesse and winked. "Thanks, Jess."

On the way back to the house, he took several deep breaths for courage. *I'm a married man again. This is going to take some getting used to.*

14

Stuart fidgeted, walking from one window to the next in hopes of seeing his cousin come over the crest in his wagon. Leon had been gone all day, and now dusk had settled in. *What was taking him so long?* The more time that went by, the more concerned Stuart grew. Something told him trouble was brewing, and he really didn't want to hang around any longer to determine its source. He had a strong suspicion Leon had gone to the authorities, and for all he knew, they'd detained him for questioning. His cousin had no friends that Stuart knew of, and even if he did, he wasn't one to socialize. *The dirty lickspittle.* He should've known better than to trust him. He made a snap decision to jump on his horse and escape now while he still had the chance.

He moved quickly, snatching every scrap of food he could find from Leon's kitchen cabinet and stuffing it into his backpack. Then he grabbed a blanket from the bed and a few other items to hold him over until he got far enough away to hunker down for the night. *No way would he hang around and wait for an arrest. No siree!* He snagged up his holster and pistol from the table and secured it around his waist, then he stuffed his spare one in his belt at the back. He gave a last hasty look around the rustic house. *No more time to dillydally!* But before he left, he grabbed a fountain pen and a piece of paper off the counter. "You dubble-crossen scum!" he scrawled across the paper. And just like that, Stuart ran out to his horse, hurriedly saddled him up, mounted, and galloped into the setting sun—in the opposite direction of Columbus. If he played his cards right, he'd arrive in Lebanon in the next couple of days. "Faith Haviland, I'm coming for you," he called into the wind.

⌒

Just as Faith settled onto the sofa with Franklin and Miriam in preparation for starting the first chapter of *The Children of the New Forest*, the sound of squeaky wagon wheels and neighing horses arriving in the front yard rent the air. Franklin leaped up and peered out the window. "Daddy's back, but I don't see Isaac. Beans! I should've rode over to the birthing shed. I wonder if that there cow done birthed a calf...or if they both died." His voice trailed off, and he looked pensive.

"Well now, I suppose you'll have to ask your father when he comes in," Faith said, her stomach all jittery at the sound of the approaching wagon, knowing at any minute her new husband would come walking through the door. Her *husband*. Just thinking the word gave her butterflies.

"I'm goin' out t' see. I'll help him bed down the horses."

"But—don't you want to hear the beginning of the story?"

"Naw."

Before she could say another word, he threw open the door and dashed outside, slamming it shut behind him. She'd seen nothing of Beth since finishing the supper dishes, only knew that she'd gone upstairs to her room. At the moment, Miriam seemed to be her only ally. Miriam yawned next to her. Faith glanced down at the sleepy-eyed child. "What do you think, Miriam? Shall we go upstairs and get you washed up before bed? Afterward, you can introduce me to a few more of your dollies."

"What about our story?" she asked in a groggy voice.

"Perhaps we can read a bedtime story in your room instead. It appears no one else is terribly interested." All of a sudden, she felt the need to escape, her shuddery trembles overtaking her. It occurred to her that being a married woman might very well take some adjusting. In fact, she almost looked forward to Joey's return to service, although those kinds of thoughts filled her with guilt. She certainly didn't wish any harm upon him.

She stood, and taking Miriam by the hand, pulled her up. She led her to the stairs, and up they climbed. Someone, probably her mother, had decorated Miriam's bedroom in a lovely, feminine fashion, with frilly white curtains on the dormer window, pink floral wallpaper, and white ornate furnishings. It was her first time actually stepping inside, as she'd only stood in the doorway of all the children's rooms the night before while Joey bade them all goodnight and tucked them in. She wondered how the rest of the nights would go when bedtime rolled around. *Would the children be receptive to her entering their rooms? And what would happen once Joey left home?* Perhaps she didn't want him reporting for duty after all.

"My nightclothes is in that top drawer, but I need to stand on that stool to reach it." Miriam crossed the room and pulled a pink wooden stool up next to the tall chest, then climbed on top of it to open the drawer and pull out a wrinkled nightgown. "This is my favorite. I have lots of 'em, but this one's broke in."

In spite of herself, Faith burst into giggles. "The broke-in kinds are the best."

The child undressed and only needed a bit of help with the buttons at the front of her gown. "Now that you're all set for bed, let's walk down to the water closet so we can wash you up for the night."

Inside the bathroom were an oval, wooden bathtub, a round, wooden table holding a basin and pitcher of water, and on the wall over it, a rectangular mirror. On the floor in the corner stood a chamber pot with a lid. A scrawled note tacked to the wall read, "Use only in the middle of the night." She had to grin to herself as she tried to guess who'd written it. No doubt one of the nannies if she'd been the one who had to carry it to the outhouse the next day.

She helped the child wash up and listened to her happy chatter. Of all the children, Miriam had the most delightful personality—so far. Time would tell if she'd be successful in drawing the best out of the rest of them.

Downstairs, the door opened, and Joey's deep voice echoed through the house, but she couldn't determine his words. Soon, light laughter sounded, and she knew that he and Franklin were enjoying a cordial conversation. *Why hadn't Isaac arrived home with him though? Had he received permission to spend the night with his grandma and uncle?* She hoped not. She wished to become acquainted with all the children before Joey left.

After Faith helped Miriam wash her face, hands, arms, and feet, and then toweled her dry, the child used the chamber pot, chatting all the while. When done, they opened the door to step out into the hallway and came face-to-face with Beth. "Well, hello, Beth. I've been missing you this evening," Faith said. "I hope you've found some interesting things to do in your room."

"I've been writing in my diary." The girl remained expressionless, but at least she responded.

"Ah, what a lovely way to spend your time, writing down your feelings and telling about the day's events."

"Yes, and I've written plenty. I'm going to wash up now, and then I'll be going downstairs to see Daddy." Her face showed no trace of a smile.

"Can I go see Daddy too?" Miriam asked, looking up at Faith.

"You don't have to ask Faith if you can see your own daddy. *Of course,* you can go downstairs," Beth answered, making a point to look directly into Faith's eyes rather than her sister's—as if she were the one in charge.

"Yes, we'll go see your daddy," Faith affirmed.

"No need," Joey said from the stairs. "I'm coming up right now."

His voice and the plodding sound of his big shoes on the staircase created a stir in her chest. That, combined with Beth's obvious dislike of her, put Faith's nerves on edge.

At the top of the stairs, he made the turn and met all three of them with a grin. "Well, I see my littlest is all ready for bed."

"Yes, and I didn't put up no fuss either—did I, Faith?" Miriam looked up at Faith, her big eyes seeking agreement.

Faith put a hand around her shoulder and drew her close. "Not even for one second." She turned to Joey. "How did it go down at the birthing shed?"

"It was a hard labor, but the cow and its baby are fine now," he said, combing his hair with his parted fingers.

"Oh, that's good to hear."

"Isaac will be home in a few minutes. He wanted to linger in the barn a little longer, so Jesse promised to bring him home within a half hour."

"Where's Frank, Daddy?" Beth asked.

"He's downstairs."

"Good, I'm goin' t' go talk to 'im."

"I thought you were going to wash up," Faith said.

Rather than look her in the eye, Beth walked past Faith and Joey, giving them her back. "I'll do it later."

Both adults watched her round the corner and then heard the skip of stocking feet going down the stairs. Joey looked at Faith. "I take it she's been giving you the cold shoulder."

"This is the first I've seen her since supper. She's been hiding out in her bedroom."

"I'll talk to her."

"Please, don't be hard on her. It's going to take all of them some time to adjust, especially after you leave."

"I'm rather dreading it—leaving, that is."

Her heart took a little somersault at the mere thought of him extending his stay beyond another couple of days. "I'm sure everything will be fine. We'll all manage to find a common ground."

"I've no doubt about that. It's just that..." His brown eyes penetrated hers. "I suppose I'm regretting how absent I've been."

"It couldn't be helped."

"I didn't *have* to enlist."

"There will be plenty of time to rebuild your relationships with your children, Joey. No sense in beating yourself up over something you cannot change."

"I guess you're right about that." They stared at each other for a full ten seconds, neither saying another word, until Miriam yawned and broke the silence.

Faith patted the child's head. "I believe it's time for you to tuck this one into bed."

He extended a hand to the child, and she took it, and then she glanced up at Faith. "You can come too," she said. Together, they walked down the hall to Miriam's room.

It was obvious the whole bedtime routine was a bit foreign to Joey. Miriam wanted a story, so Joey began reading the first chapter of the book Faith had tried to start earlier, but she quickly grew bored by his monotone voice. She then asked him to tell her a story rather than read one, but he said he didn't know any children's stories. "Just make one up," she said as matter-of-factly as if she were asking him to eat a teaspoon of pudding.

"Um, it's not that easy for me. Let's see." He crumpled his eyebrows, twisted his face into a frown, and gave Faith a pained expression. She couldn't help herself. She giggled and shrugged her shoulders. "You probably could do this much better than I, Faith." This he said with pleading eyes.

"Ah, but I'm enjoying watching your wheels spin."

"I just bet you are." He raised his eyes to the ceiling and thought. Suddenly, he brightened. "Okay, I think I have a story."

Miriam unclasped her hands, which had been resting on her chest, and clapped them fast, her lightweight blanket tucked up to her chin. "Oh, wheee! Tell it to me, Daddy."

He sat down on the bed next to her, so Faith brought Miriam's small chair over so she could sit close by and listen. "Once there was a very nice little girl named…um…" he started.

"Miriam?" the child cut in.

"No, no, not Miriam. Her name was—Mary. She had a very lively personality."

"What's lively?"

"Perky."

"What's perky?"

"Happy."

"What did she look like?"

"Well, I was just getting to that. She had brown, wavy hair that looked best in two long braids. She had large blue eyes and a smile that revealed one missing tooth on the bottom."

"Daddy, that little girl sounds like me."

"Yes, I suppose she does, a little. Now let me tell the story. It was a hot summer day in a small town in Ohio. As was usual, Mary had lined up her dollies side-by-side and told them to stay put while she went to make their noon meal. She decided to walk out to the garden to see what vegetables might be fresh for picking."

Just then, the other children, including Isaac, who'd obviously just arrived home, tiptoed up like three little mice and peered around the corner. If Joey sensed their presence, he didn't let on, just charged ahead with his story. Faith smiled to herself at the sight of their fascinated faces. *Was listening to their daddy's storytelling voice a rarity in the Fuller home?*

"Mary picked a few carrots and some other vegetables from the garden and walked back to the house," Joey continued. "As soon as she entered the house, she lay the vegetables on the kitchen table and went to check on her children. Because, of course, she always referred to her dollies as her children. When she got there, she noticed one of them had gotten up and walked away."

"Haw!" Miriam gasped. "Where did it go?"

"Well, let me tell you," he said, leaning in and putting a finger to the tip of her nose. "Mary walked into the parlor room and looked around but did not see her dolly. Then she walked into the dining room, and what do you think?"

"What, Daddy?" Miriam asked, all round-eyed and awestruck.

"She found her dolly taking a nap on the floor right next to the table leg. 'What are you doing there, Little Lady Jane?' she asked her dolly, but Jane did not answer because she was sleeping. So Mary picked her up and took her back to the living room, and sat her back where she'd been before. 'Now you stay there, Lady Jane. I must go make our noon meal.' And back to the kitchen she went."

By now, not only did Joey have Miriam in the palm of his hand, he also had his other children—and Faith! *What did he mean by saying he couldn't tell a story?* Why, he'd even picked up the proper voice intonations. Faith glanced to her left and noted that both Franklin and Beth had sat themselves down on the round braided rug. Joey paused in his storytelling, probably trying to think what to add to his developing plot.

"Keep going, Daddy," Beth urged him.

Joey turned around and winked at his older daughter. "I'm getting there. Be patient." Then he cast a quick, helpless expression at Faith as if to say, "Help me." She couldn't help but grin back at him with raised eyebrows.

"Well, after making some vegetable soup and slicing some bread, Mary returned to the living room to tell her children it was time to come to the table, but to her great surprise, every one of them had gotten up and left the room!"

"What? How did that happen, Daddy? Dollies can't walk."

"Well, apparently, Mary's could. She left the living room and walked into the parlor room, but none of her children were there. Then she walked into the dining room, thinking she might find Lady Jane and the others lying on the floor by the table leg where she'd earlier found Jane, but, no, none of her children were there either. She walked into the next room, which was the library, but she did not see them there either. The only thing she did see was the family collie named Gus. He was lying on the floor looking ever so innocent."

"Haw, Daddy! Did Gus take the dollies?" Miriam asked, her hands now clasped in a tight ball up close to her chin.

"Well, I don't know, but it's looking rather suspicious, isn't it? Mary stepped closer to Gus and asked him if he'd seen her children. At the question, he turned his head, and what do you think? There in the corner, right next to the bookcase, all lined up in a nice straight row, were her four children. Gus used his long, pointy, collie nose to show her right where they were. They were not one bit tattered or chewed, so we will never know if he moved them or not. Perhaps he was just lying there keeping an eye on them to make sure they didn't get up and go to another room without Mary's permission."

"Gus was a good dog, Daddy."

"He was indeed."

"Did they go eat their noon meal then?"

"They certainly did. By then, they were famished."

"What's famished?'

"Hungry. After they ate, Mary took her children upstairs to their bedroom and tucked them all into their wooden cradles, rocking each one until she went to sleep, and you know what?"

"What?" Miriam asked.

"They did not move from their beds, not even once."

"Pro'ly 'cause Gus comed in the room too. Did he come in to watch over them?"

"Indeed he did. And *that*, my dear, is the end of the story."

"Awww," Miriam whined.

"No awww-ing. It's time you closed those pretty blue eyes of yours— just like Mary's children did."

"Okay." Her voice carried a sleepy tone.

"How about we have a goodnight prayer?" Faith proposed.

Joey turned to her. He looked stunned and the color had drained from his face. "Uhhh."

"Daddy don't say prayers," Beth announced.

He gave his older daughter a sheepish look.

"How about I offer the prayer?" Faith suggested.

"Please do," said Joey.

When no one objected, Faith folded her hands where she sat and delivered a brief prayer, asking for God's watchful care over them. She then asked for His protection over the children's daddy as he prepared to return to war, then asked He grant everyone a good night's sleep and a pleasant day tomorrow.

After the "amen," Beth immediately wanted to know when her father had to report back for duty.

"I'll have to start out on Tuesday at first light, honey."

Her face dropped. "I don't want you to go."

"I know, but this last leg of duty will go fast."

"No, it won't."

"Well, let's not think about it now. We have tomorrow and Monday together, and I'll try to be better at writing letters home. How does that sound?"

"Can you come home again before October?"

"Oh, I can't promise that. I am not sure where our regiment will go next. In fact, I'm not even sure where they are now. I'm awaiting a wire from my commanding officer on Monday to determine where I'm heading."

Beth stuck out a pouting chin. Franklin and Isaac both walked away without a word, after which Beth soon followed. Joey shrugged his shoulders at Faith. "I can't give them any better than that."

"Don't worry. They'll manage fine. I'll make sure we fall into a routine that will make time move right along."

Miriam had turned over on her side and closed her eyes, so Joey stood, then fixed the covers around her neck. Once done, he straightened and looked Faith straight on, issuing a tiny smile. "Something tells me that you will be very good for my children. I'm not sure they will realize just how good though."

She smiled back. "I can do my job whether appreciated or not."

"I'm coming to believe that about you. And by the way, thank you for offering that prayer."

"I'm sorry if I embarrassed you. I'm afraid I wasn't thinking."

"I suppose these nighttime prayers are a good thing, even if they are not my normal routine. Shall we go to tuck the others into bed?"

"I believe I'll leave those honors up to you the next few nights. Your children seem to be hungry for your attention, and they need that time with you."

"Well, I appreciate that. How about I meet you downstairs in a few minutes?"

"That will be fine."

15

etting the others settled in for bed had taken longer than Joey
had expected and wasn't nearly as pleasant as it had been with
Miriam. All three were full of questions about Faith, questions he
couldn't answer because he barely knew her himself.

"Well, I'm not going to call her Mama," Beth reiterated for at least
the fifth time during the course of their nighttime talk, all gathered in
the boys' room.

"Has anyone asked you to or even suggested it?" Joey asked.

"No."

"Well then, I don't know why you would even give it a second
thought."

"I'm just making sure everyone knows it."

"I see." He tucked

"Forget calling her Mama; I'm not even going to *like* her," said Isaac.

"I can't force you to like her, but you had better show respect. I will
not have any of you chasing her off like you did your former nannies.
Understood?"

"Yes, sir," they all said in quiet response and with slow, uneven nods.

"I try to be good, Daddy, but Isaac talks me into doing stuff," said Franklin.

"Hey! I do no such thing!"

"Yes, you do," Beth declared.

"Do not," he argued. "You guys talk me into stuff."

"Stop," Joey said before the other two could get in another word. "The truth is, all three of you egg each other on. It's time you start treating others with kindness."

Isaac giggled. "But sometimes, it's kinda funny, Daddy—like the time Miriam sprinkled a bunch of salt on Mrs. Finch's roast beef when Mrs. Finch went back into the kitchen. You should've seen Mrs. Finch's face when she took her first big bite. She chewed and then spit it into her napkin. Then she took a great big gulp of water."

"And who told Miriam to do that?"

All three of them pointed at someone different. Joey frowned and shook his head. "I see no humor in your doing that," he said sternly, "and especially putting your little sister up to some shenanigans."

They rightfully sobered. "We were just having some fun."

"Spoiling someone's food does not equate with fun. I'm ashamed and highly disappointed that you three would find it entertaining to make life miserable for others."

"But all the nannies we've had were mean," Isaac insisted. "None of them liked us one bit. Mrs. Finch poured vinegar instead of syrup on Frank's pancakes once 'cause he wouldn't pick up a napkin that Miriam dropped. That was *mean*."

Joey frowned and scrunched his forehead. *Had one of the nannies truly done that?* He shook his head, deciding that if it *had* happened, the poor woman was probably at her wit's end. "It was wrong of you to not do as she asked, Frank," he said.

"Miriam's the one who threw it down. Why didn't she have to pick it up?"

"There is no point in getting into something that happened a long time ago. But that said, it is no wonder your former nannies haven't stayed. Your trickery and ill behavior had much to do with their dislike of you. However…" He cleared his throat. "Now that I am married to Faith, you must realize that not minding your manners and doing what she asks of you will provoke me even more because she *is* my wife."

They said nothing to that, just hung their heads again. After that, Joey wished them all goodnight, sending Beth back to her room and telling the boys to climb into their big poster bed. He turned down the lantern and left, the solemnity of the room's atmosphere putting him in a rather sullen mood that couldn't be helped. His children had needed a good talking to; he hoped it would stick.

He found Faith downstairs in the living room perusing the place, as if trying to decide if it'd been hit by a cyclone. "I'm afraid it's in need of some repair. It's been a while since I put any money into this house."

She spun around. "Oh! I wasn't thinking that. I did notice the draperies needing repair—or replacement. There's a panel missing."

"Yes, that's quite another story."

"Oh?"

"One of the children let a goat into the house last year, and it wreaked havoc. I believe that was the last straw for my second to the last nanny."

She slapped a hand across her mouth and muffled a laugh.

"I'm glad you can find some humor in that. It's more than Mrs. Harner did. From what I understand, she packed her bags that night, drove the children to my mother's house, and left them there with no explanation. She told Isaac to do the explaining. As soon as she dropped them off at my mother's front door, she drove away as fast as her horses would take her."

"Oh, my sakes, I can't imagine. There must have been many other incidents that led up to her leaving."

"You probably don't want to hear any of them."

Her smile remained in place. "You're right, I do not. I believe I'll be better off going into this whole experience without any further stories."

"Are you serious about that? You don't want to know what these children are capable of doing?"

"I think I've formed a pretty good idea."

"And does it scare you?"

"I'd be lying if I said I'm not somewhat nervous—but I know God will give me wisdom, patience, and guidance, so I'll trust Him."

Joey couldn't help but admire her faith, even wished he might have a fraction of it. Of course, he'd not be admitting that to anyone. He cast his eyes about the living room. "If you'd like to hire some work done in and around the house, it'd be fine by me. I intended to replace the draperies, but I just haven't had time."

Her well-sculpted eyebrows slanted upward. "I enjoy decorating. What did you have in mind?"

"I'll leave that to you to decide. The draperies are a must. As for the rest of the place, it could probably use some fresh paint here and there and maybe some new wallpaper. And if you want to purchase a few new furniture pieces, I wouldn't object."

Her face brightened as if he'd just told her tomorrow morning was Christmas. He still barely knew her. *Could he trust her not to spend his last dime?*

"Perhaps you should give me a budget so I'll not overspend."

Had she read his mind? "How about we go into the library, where I keep my files, and I'll bring out some paperwork? On Monday, we'll go to the bank so I can open an account for your household expenses. My former nannies shopped for food supplies at Griswold Brothers Penny Bargain Store. You'll find I have a standing account there. For children's clothing, shoes, stockings, and so on, you can shop at any number of Lebanon's general stores. All that's necessary is to give them my name, and they will take good care of you."

"I shouldn't think I'd need much. I will do my best to be frugal in all matters. As for food, I do love gardening, so I'll be taking advantage of whatever we harvest. I haven't had time to walk out to the garden yet, but I look forward to it. I'm afraid it's a little late for planting, but I'll give it my best effort."

He couldn't help but smile at her apparent enthusiasm. "I wish the last nanny would've taken interest, but she much preferred to buy most of her food at market."

"That's a shame. In my opinion, there's nothing much tastier than a good, creamy soup made with fresh vegetables from the garden." Her blue eyes twinkled, and she actually winked at him! *Good gravy!* "Kind of like the soup the little girl in your story made. Aunt Martha makes wonderful soups, and I am blessed to have many of her best recipes."

"Well, so far I've found you to be an excellent cook. I regret I won't have much more time to enjoy your meals."

She scrunched her brow in thought. "Speaking of cooking, I was thinking tomorrow after church, rather than eating inside...well, it might be fun to have a picnic."

"A picnic?"

"Yes. Tomorrow is your final Sunday at home. Wouldn't a picnic be fun?"

"A picnic," he repeated. "Sarah Beth used to love picnics."

"Well, then, she'd be thrilled to know her family is going on a Sunday picnic. We won't even tell the children, so it will be a nice surprise. I'll pack a lunch in the morning, we'll put it in the back of the wagon, and then after church, I'll leave it to you to drive us to a delightful mystery spot, someplace the children have never been."

"A mystery spot? I'm not even sure I know where that would be."

She laughed, a lighthearted sound, and gave him a little slap on the arm. "Oh, come on, Joey, use your imagination. Since listening to that fascinating story you told the children, I know you have one."

He gave a light chuckle. "I don't use it much—my imagination, that is."

She stared good and hard at him, then put her hands on her petite waist. "What, pray tell, do you do for fun?"

"Fun?"

"Yes, fun!"

"There's a war going on, Faith."

"And so you must punish your children because of that misfortune? Sometimes adults have to lay aside the cares of the day and make time for pleasant activities, especially for the sake of innocent children. A picnic will be most enjoyable, and your kids will be ecstatic."

He cleared his throat. "I suppose that does make sense."

"Then you're agreeable to the idea?"

He sucked in a deep breath and stared down at her. "First you talk me into going to church, and then you insist we go on a picnic. What have I gotten myself into with you?"

She laughed. "No need to worry yourself. You'll be gone in two days, if you recall."

Yes, he recalled all right. And the thought did not make him overly happy. He didn't have much of a relationship with his children, but somehow, over the course of the last several hours, since Faith Haviland had come on the scene, he'd started developing a desire to make things better between them.

⌒

"Blast!" Leon threw down the note Stuart had written. "I was afraid this might happen, Sheriff. Stuart grew suspicious when I didn't get back here soon enough. He knows by now the law is onto him. You can be sure of it. He'd be here sipping on his brew if he didn't."

The sheriff bent down to retrieve the note that had fallen to the floor and read it for himself. "Humph, where do you think he went?"

"Oh, no question he'll be heading for Lebanon. He's determined to get to that woman named Faith."

"Good chance she'll have married someone else by the time he gets there. I talked to Faith's parents, and if all goes well, she's marrying an army captain."

"That won't matter one iota to Stuart. He'll try to win her back, as ridiculous as that sounds. After his assault on her, I don't trust him."

Leon's gut churned with concern. The whole process had taken longer than Leon had anticipated. The sheriff had asked a lot of questions, even forcing him to tell in detail about the events leading up to Opal's burial and the part he'd played in it. But now Stuart was gone. Leon had wanted to wrap things up a lot sooner, but the sheriff had to do everything by the books. At least, after listening to his story, the sheriff hadn't thrown *him* in the slammer for the part he'd played.

"As long as you continue cooperating with authorities, Mr. Porter, I see no reason to hold you accountable for your cousin's actions," the sheriff had said back in town. "I believe you when you say you didn't know Opal Porter died from anything other than natural causes. But we'll still have to get a statement from Stuart when we capture him."

The sheriff studied the scribbled note a little closer before handing it back to Leon. "Well, we're going to have to hunker down here and start out at break of dawn." He looked at the four deputies who'd ridden along. "I trust you all packed your bags with enough vittles for a full two days of travel," the sheriff said.

A few murmurs rose up amidst the group of deputies, mostly affirming that, yes, they'd come prepared.

"There's room out in the barn to sleep, or you can sprawl out on my floor," Leon told them. "I don't have enough blankets to go around though."

"That's fine," the sheriff said. "We've already put you out enough."

Leon took a bit of consolation in the partial apology. "I wouldn't mind joining your search party. In the morning, I'll ride over to my neighbor's place up the road and ask him to tend my animals for a few days." Asking for favors was something Leon rarely did, but he knew he could count on Abner Stubbs. Being as their property lines butted up to each other, there were occasions when the two came close enough to share conversations, and over the years, they'd come to be quite good friends.

"That sounds fine. Might be you'll even be able to barter with your cousin when we do finally catch him."

"I wouldn't count on that, but I will do my best, sheriff."

"Well, make no mistake, we will locate Stuart Porter, and we'll bring him back to Columbus in short order. The fool has evaded us long enough, but his game is almost over."

"I hope you're right, sir. One thing I know, my cousin will do his best to avoid capture."

16

The Fuller family took up two entire pews at the Community Methodist Church. Jack, his family, and Jesse sat in the third pew from the front on the right side of the church, while Faith, Joey, and his children sat directly behind them. Faith surmised that Laura Fuller would have been sitting next to Jesse had she been able to attend church, and she could only imagine how much it must eat at her Sunday after Sunday to be cooped up in her big house, confined to that wheelchair. From what little Faith knew of her, she was a strong, stubborn woman, proud of her independence and rather set in her ways. Faith made a mental note to visit her often once Jack went back to war.

The congregation sang with great enthusiasm, the reverend preached a fine sermon on repentance and forgiveness, and after the service, congregants were as friendly as a whole batch of pups, surrounding Joey, her, and the children with words of welcome and well wishes. Apparently, word traveled fast around Lebanon, as everyone seemed quite aware that Judge Cranston had married Joseph and Faith. Some even hinted that there ought to have been a reception to honor them, to which some fellow in the crowd piped up, "Pro'ly wasn't time f'r that, as the captain has to return to duty, right Joseph?"

"Yes. That's right," he'd replied. "No time." He didn't elaborate on the fact that they'd only just met.

The children had left the church and gone out to play in the yard with the others, so once Joey and Faith, Jack and Cristina, and those still remaining finally departed the church, everyone milled in the yard for a bit to visit before calling their youngsters to their respective wagons. By the time Faith, Joey, and his children climbed aboard their wagon, Faith's stomach was aflutter with anticipation of what the day held. Long before the children rose from bed that morning, she'd snuck down to the kitchen to pack a lunch of sliced bread and butter, jam, tomatoes, carrot sticks, salted meats, and oatmeal cookies. Afterward, she'd filled a wicker basket with a checkered tablecloth, a jar of water, cups and plates, and the food goods, and then clamped down the lid. When Joey came down to the kitchen, she'd instructed him to carry the covered basket and a large blanket out to the carriage and hide it in the back. He'd lifted one brow at her. "You're serious about this picnic."

"Of course I'm serious. The children will love it. Now take this out-side, and don't argue."

He'd grinned. "I wouldn't dream of arguing." He picked up the basket, chuckled, and exited the kitchen, the screen door squeaking open then shutting behind him with a loud thwack.

Now, as Joey directed the horses down Silver Street and heading west toward Broadway, the children still had no idea of their plans to stop at some mystery spot for a picnic. As they rolled along, jostling against each other on the driver's bench, Faith leaned close to Joey's ear and whispered, "Do you have a particular place in mind?"

"It wouldn't be a mystery if I told you, now would it?"

"Oh, so you're keeping it a secret from me as well?"

He kept his gaze straight ahead while a grin played around the corners of his mouth, his jaw muscle flicking. A strange excitement welled up in Faith, but she dared not let it show lest the children grow suspicious.

"How did you like the morning service?" she asked him while smoothing out her skirt after a gust of wind kicked it up. Two barking dogs darted across the road in front of them.

"It was fine."

"That's all you have to say?"

Behind them, the children had found one thing or another to bicker about, but for now anyway, the adults ignored it.

"I suppose it was nice. I enjoyed the organ music, which I think lent to the fine singing."

"I noticed you knew all the songs."

"I grew up attending that very church, so, yes, I did know the songs."

"What is your favorite hymn?"

"Hmm. I suppose I'd have to say *Holy, Holy, Holy*. It's been a favorite since boyhood."

"I love that hymn as well. It speaks of the majesty and power of God Almighty."

"Do you also have a favorite?"

"Yes, mine is *Amazing Grace*."

"Hmm, that's my mother's as well. She continually tells us she wants that sung at her funeral, which, if I know Ma, won't be for years to come. She'll probably outlast us all."

"She is something, isn't she."

"Indeed. She's also very generous and goodhearted."

"Those are fine qualities in anyone." They hit a bump in the road, which knocked Faith against Joey. She righted herself. "The congregation was quite jubilant," she said. "After the service, I found them most friendly, and they all seemed overly happy to see you."

"Yes, they are a friendly bunch." The reins lay loose in his hands as the horses moved up the road at a steady trot. "I'm fairly certain my showing up at church this morning surprised the congregation as much as their seeing you for the first time. I haven't set foot inside that church since—since before my wife passed."

"I see. I suppose that *was* difficult. Hopefully, it will grow easier for you after today."

He gave her a sidewise glance. "I'm not making any promises about going to church. Besides, it shouldn't matter to you once I'm discharged."

That remark hit her like a hard clunk to the chest. Of course it was true. *Why should she care—since she wasn't even going to be here?* "I was thinking primarily of the children," she said, keeping her voice down. The children had stopped their arguing and had picked up some sort of "I spy" game. "They need you to set the example. Taking them to church is essential. Otherwise, what sort of message are you sending them?"

"You wouldn't be preaching at me, would you? I already heard one sermon today."

She giggled. "No, Joey, I wouldn't dream of it. I'm merely suggesting."

"Um-hum. You've been my wife for two days, and you're already making suggestions."

"As your wife, I have that right, don't I?"

The corners of his mouth turned up just so. "I don't know. It's a temporary position, remember?"

"All the more reason since my time is short."

This brought on an all-out chuckle. "You're a determined one, I'll say that."

"What are you two laughing about?" Franklin asked.

"Just silly things," he answered.

"I'm hungry," whined Miriam.

"Me too," echoed Franklin. "What are we havin' for the noon meal?"

"Something horrid, I suppose," said Isaac.

"You sampled Faith's cooking just last night, and I thought it was delicious," said Joey.

"Maybe that was the only thing she knows how to cook," said Isaac.

"Isaac, mind your conduct," Joey said. The boy's remarks didn't bother Faith. He had much to learn about her, and for now she would practice patience. She figured that, in time, he'd discover on his own what a fine cook she was, and when he misbehaved, she'd make him miss a meal and teach him a thing or two about manners.

"Well, what are we havin' to eat today?" Franklin asked again.

"You'll see." When Joey might have made a right turn to head toward the farm, he veered to the left instead.

"Hey, Daddy, you turned the wrong way," said Beth.

"Did I?" he asked. "As far as I know, I'm heading in the right direction." He stared straight ahead, a tiny grin playing around his mouth.

"Where we going?" asked Isaac. "Looks like we're headin' toward the Benson farm."

Even the horses were confused, as they raised their heads to look over their surroundings, their ears twitching. Joey took extra care to keep them moving forward.

"I guess you'll have to practice patience," Joey said.

"Are we goin' on an adventure?" Miriam chirped.

"Something like that," said Joey.

"Oh, wheee!" Miriam said, clapping her hands in the summer breeze. "That's exciting. Ain't that exciting, my kinsmen?"

That made everyone laugh, including Isaac.

"Where did you hear a word like that, Miriam?" Joey asked.

"In a book, silly Daddy. It means family."

"I know that. I just didn't realize you'd ever heard the word."

Faith supplied Joey with a smile, and he returned one. Miriam certainly had a way of keeping the atmosphere light and cheery, and she was smart to boot. She prayed an enjoyable mood would follow them throughout the day, and that instead of tension and arguments, the Fuller family would discover peace and pleasure.

Five minutes later, Joey parked the rig next to a lazy stream, and before he even set the brake in place, all four children bounded off the wagon and made a run for the water, whooping and hollering with excitement at the announcement that they were going to have a Sunday picnic.

At first, neither adult moved, just sat and watched the children scatter about the peaceful property. "This is Benson land, but I know Robert, and he won't mind if we picnic here for the afternoon."

"It's a lovely spot."

"I suppose you were right a while ago."

Faith swiveled her body to look into Joey's face. "About?"

"My taking the children to church. I've failed to set a good example for them. Ever since Sarah Beth died, they've had very little consistency in their lives. In a sense, they lost both of us."

"But you're still very much here. Don't ever forget that. And it's never too late to begin anew."

He surprised her when he reached up and removed a flyaway strand of hair from her face. He tucked it behind her ear, and the mere act, tiny as it was, sent a slight chill through her. *Silly, since he'd meant nothing by it.* "You're right, of course. Don't think I haven't taken your suggestions to heart. You've given me some things to think about when I head out on Tuesday morning."

Tuesday morning. It would be here before she knew it, and the thought of running the Fuller household without him gave her a bad case of the jitters. Albeit, his very presence made her nervous, but she was almost certain his absence would make her even more so. Goodness, she didn't know what to think of herself, one minute feeling confident she'd made the right decision, and the next, questioning her abilities. If she could be certain of anything, it was that in the coming days, she'd be spending a lot of time on her knees in prayer.

"I know the children are going to miss you terribly." She wouldn't even hint at missing him herself. She still didn't know him well enough to make such a statement.

He turned his attention to the children, the boys having pulled up their pant legs to wade in the water, and the girls standing on the bank watching them. Miriam bent down to pull up something from the ground, probably a wildflower, if Faith had to guess.

"Daddy, there's fish!" Franklin hollered, pointing into the stream.

Joey cast a smile at Faith. "Good thing I brought fishing poles."

Faith stared at him. "You brought poles?"

"Of course. I went out to the barn to get them after I loaded the picnic basket on the wagon this morning. I also brought a ball to toss back and forth."

"You did? Well, I'm as tickled as a June bug. I thought you weren't particularly happy about this outing."

Again, he reached up to snatch a piece of hair from her eyes. This time, though, he touched her cheek with the back of his hand and let it linger there, his smile still in place, his eyes boring into her. "Perhaps your enthusiasm for it started rubbing off on me."

"Oh." She sat dead-still, almost spellbound, unclear what to say next. Good gracious, he had her heart thumping and twirling with silly, unfounded emotions. Yes, he was her husband, but a temporary one. She'd do best not to allow any attraction to seep in. She found her wits and quickly adjusted herself in her seat, forcing him to drop his hand. "Well, shall we get down?"

He, too, snapped out of whatever had come over him. "Yes, wait there. I'll help you down." He jumped to the ground and ran around to her side of the wagon, then reached up and lifted her down, her hands clenching his sturdy shoulders.

Once on the ground, she gave her attention to the children. "They're as happy as can be."

He walked to the back of the wagon and retrieved the poles, setting them on the ground. Next, he brought out the picnic basket and began carrying it toward a large shade tree. "This looks like a fine place to spread out, don't you think?" he asked.

"It looks perfect! I'll start getting things ready."

Joey set the basket down and returned to the wagon. While he carried the fishing poles, pail, and other paraphernalia down to the riverbank, Faith spread out the large blanket and placed the checkered tablecloth on top. Next, she opened the basket and began removing items one at a time. Once done, she made herself comfortable, folding her legs at the ankles and sitting back just a bit, bracing herself up on her hands behind her. The boys had already taken to catching minnows in their net for future bait, and the girls had removed their shoes and stockings so they could wade in the water. They squealed with glee as they held up their skirts and tiptoed about. Faith swiped at her sweaty brow and thought about how refreshing the water must feel and how nice it would be to join them. Still, she reasoned, removing her shoes and stockings as the girls had done would be entirely inappropriate. To do that, she'd have to show a good share of her ankles, and that would never do. No, she would simply sit here in the shade and watch, which was almost as pleasant. A soft breeze played with the hair around her temples, reminding her of her reaction to Joey's touch when he'd stuck some strands behind her ear.

"Come on down, Faith," Joey called to her while he worked on one of the fishing rods.

She put a hand to her forehead to shield her eyes. "I best sit here and keep the flies away from our food. You all have fun. I'm enjoying watching."

"Daddy, look at all the pretty stones at the bottom of the brook," said Miriam. "Can I take some home?"

"Of course, take as many as you want."

Miriam bent to dip her hand into the water, drenching the hem of her Sunday skirt. When she found one, she held it out for her father's viewing. "Look at it. It's shiny as a diamond."

"Indeed it is," Joey acknowledged.

Beth bent and dunked both hands in the water, then splashed her face and laughed, the bottom of her skirt also dripping. "Daddy, the water's not even that cold."

"No? Well, maybe we should have a water battle after we eat."

"A water battle?" asked Franklin, walking up to shore to stand next to Joey. "That sounds like fun."

Faith couldn't help but smile. Watching the children interact with their father warmed her heart. They had just one more full day with him, and then he would be gone until October. The notion of his absence struck a chord of dread in her, no matter how irrational. She was only just starting to get to know him, and what she knew she liked.

Lord, help me with this unexpected attraction.

17

Stuart allowed his horse a little more time to graze and drink at the flowing stream. He had no idea how far he'd traveled, but he guessed it to be about twenty miles. Knowing he wasn't even close to the halfway point yet gave him pause, but it didn't deter his mission. He was Lebanon bound. Yeah, he might be crazy for thinking Faith would want anything to do with him, but he'd been watching her for years and waiting for that perfect opportunity to claim her. Even if she'd already tied the knot with that other fellow, he'd find a way to talk her into leaving with him. *What was marriage but a piece of paper anyway?*

After leaving Leon's house last evening, he'd traversed some out-of-the-way roads, paths that showed little evidence of other travelers, and then around midnight, had stopped to set up camp, building a small fire to ward off a slight chill in the air. Then at break of dawn, he'd eaten a bit of breakfast and set out again, following his instincts and hoping they were leading him in the right direction. So far, he'd only come upon one other rider. He'd kept his head down to avoid any confrontation, but the fellow had called out to him anyway. "Where you headed, mister?" he'd asked. Stuart guessed him to be a farmer by the look of him—overalls, tattered straw hat, muddy boots, and ruddy skin that had seen a great deal of punishing sun.

"Lebanon."

"Lebanon. I'll be. I got me a relative or two down there."

"Yeah? Anyone by the name of Fuller?"

"Fuller? Nope. My relatives is the Edward Hudson family. Cousins they is. Humph, you got a long ride ahead o' you."

"I'm aware."

"You might best get on a better road. There's a highway five miles north o' here that'll get you there a lot faster."

"I'll think about it," Stuart had lied. He fully intended to stay off heavily traveled roads for the first part of his jaunt to dodge the law on the chance they were trailing him.

"Why you goin' on horseback instead o' the train? Lebanon's a long way from here."

"I know that, mister. I got my reasons."

"Yep, I s'pose y' do." The fellow eyed him in a peculiar way. "Well, safe travels to y'," he'd said.

Stuart had tipped his hat at the old fellow and kicked his horse into a faster gait, glad when the farmer didn't try to detain him with further questions.

He sat on the riverbank and let the sun penetrate his shirt. What he wouldn't do for a nap in the shade about now, but there was no time for that. Not for the first time, he wondered if he'd made a mistake in assuming Leon had turned him in to the authorities. Perchance he'd just gotten waylaid in town…but, no. Leon had no friends that Stuart knew of in Columbus. The only thing that would hold him up would be paying a visit to the sheriff's office. He rose without a lot of pep in him and walked to his horse. He swallowed down the last of another bottle of whiskey and tossed the bottle to the ground. Good thing he had several more in his saddlebags. A few swigs every few miles did a body good. He reached his horse and withdrew a fresh bottle, unscrewed the lid, and threw back his head for a good swallow of the stuff. It burned going down but aided in soothing his otherwise sour mood. Time to set out again. He took in a deep breath of hot June air and mounted his steed.

After eating their noonday fare, the boys went back to fishing while the girls explored the riverbank, walking up and down its length but staying within Joey's clear view. Faith had walked down to the river to clean the soiled dishes. He probably should have lent a hand, but he found he much preferred watching her from his place on the blanket. He lay on his side, his elbow bent and hand propping his head so that he had a good vantage point. There was no denying he'd married a very pretty woman. Nope, no denying it at all. The notion that he only had one full day remaining to get to know her a trifle better nagged at him. He reminded himself that this marriage was just a temporary arrangement, and by the time his field duty ended, she'd be more than eager to collect her money, get the marriage annulled, and move on with her life. He gave his head a little shake to try to put some sense into it and then focused his attention on his children. They were all getting along so well, he could hardly believe it. Since they'd arrived at their picnic site, he hadn't heard a single utterance of complaint from any of them. Maybe Faith was onto something when she'd said this outing would be good for them.

Faith rose from her task of dishwashing and started walking back, arms full. A pretty smile made her whole face glow as she strolled in his direction, her long cotton skirt blowing in the breezes and some of her hair coming undone from its topknot. He couldn't help but return a smile. He sat up then and scooted over on the blanket to make room for her. "I was thinking I should have helped you with that chore."

"Nonsense. I enjoyed doing it." She carefully set the dishes in the picnic basket, then settled herself next to him, albeit putting a bit of distance between them. Once situated, she blew upward at the hair that had fallen across her eyes. When that didn't work, he reached up and removed the pieces himself.

"There you go," he said, noting the soft texture of her locks and longing to test it a little longer.

If she noticed his interest, she didn't let on. "My, it's a warm day, but that breeze does feel quite refreshing."

"I'll admit we couldn't have ordered a finer day for a picnic. Thanks for pulling the whole thing together."

"And thank you for going along with my idea."

"I've enjoyed myself. Do you think you'll do this often in my absence?"

"I'm sure I'll suggest it, as I'll be looking for interesting things to do. Keeping them busy will be important. Idleness breeds unrest, which leads to trouble. I'm going to do my best to make their days exciting and productive."

"Sounds exhausting if you ask me."

"Rearing four young children as a widowed father is a huge responsibility. I'm guessing you joined the army because it sounded less difficult."

He laughed a little. "What you say is painfully true. It gave me an escape, and looking back, that was selfish on my part."

"Joining the army is always honorable, Joey. You're not the only one to leave behind a family."

Joey sniffed and swallowed. "It's especially honorable when you do it for the right reasons. I think I can admit now that at least a part of me wanted to escape. Sarah Beth was only sick for a couple of months before she passed, so I didn't have much time to prepare for that. When she died, it nearly killed me as well."

"I can't imagine. And then to think of your children's grief and confusion."

"I'm afraid that, in my selfishness, I overlooked their own deep sorrow. That grieves me."

"As I've already said, it's not too late to fix it. I think Isaac especially needs to know he's loved. I will have to find ways to show him I care without embarrassing him."

A lump of emotion clogged Joey's throat. "You know, I actually believe you'll be able to pull that off. Thank you."

She smiled. "I haven't done anything yet."

"Oh, but you have." He dared reach up and touch her cheek. Rather than turn away, she leaned into his hand. In that moment, he almost kissed her, and might have if Miriam hadn't come running to them to drop her collection of rocks and pebbles on the blanket.

"Look, Daddy. Look, Faith. Me and Beth been finding lots of pretty stones."

"Would you look at that?" said Faith, quickly scooting back to make room for Miriam on the blanket. "Aren't they lovely, Joey?"

"I should say." Looking into Faith's blue eyes, somewhat shaded by her wide-brimmed hat, he marveled how he'd grown attracted to his new wife in just a few short days. "Lovely indeed."

18

For a change, Faith was the first to awaken on Monday morning. The sun had not even fully shone its face when she pulled the covers off her and slipped out of her nightclothes and into her dress. If she moved about quietly, she would be able to walk to the outhouse undetected and even get a head start on breakfast before anyone else got out of bed. At least, that was her aim.

After dressing, she quickly pinned her hair up into a neat bun, put a bit of pink in her cheeks, and then grabbed her Bible from the nightstand and tiptoed out of her room and down the hallway to the staircase.

Upon returning from the outhouse, she lit the oil lamps in the kitchen, stirred up the wood-powered stove, and put the kettle on to brew some coffee. She then opened the windows to let the cool air inside, knowing that by noonday, the kitchen would be as hot as a basted turkey. Finally, she sat at the table and opened her Bible. She wanted to get in a few minutes of quiet time before the household started stirring. She had been reading the New Testament since late April and had just launched into the book of Galatians. Turning the featherlight pages to the fifth chapter, she began prayerfully soaking up God's Word, taking her time as she read and prayed, read and prayed, asking for wisdom and compassion as she went about her day and to be a blessing to her new family. Just as she finished the chapter, she heard a stirring behind her. When she turned, she found Joey standing in the doorway. "Oh! Good morning! I didn't hear you come down the stairs."

He was dressed in neat attire and looking quite dapper, making her question whether her own appearance measured up. He was indeed a fine looking man, and she couldn't help but consider herself quite inferior. *Not that it mattered even an iota. Tomorrow he would be gone, and he would no doubt be glad to put her out of his mind.* Whether she would do the same remained to be seen.

"I didn't mean to disturb you."

"No, I was just finishing reading my morning Bible passage."

"It's quite noble of you to keep up a daily reading schedule."

"Not noble at all. It is my pleasure and the perfect way to start my day. You should try it. I think you'd find it helpful."

He leaned against the doorframe and gazed down at her as if to study her, his mouth slightly curved up.

"What?" she asked out of curiosity.

"Nothing, really. You fascinate me, I suppose."

"I don't know why. There is nothing very interesting or mysterious about me."

"On the contrary, I find you very intriguing."

"I can't imagine why." Slightly flustered, she put her bookmark on the page and closed her Bible. Then she pushed back in her chair to stand, hoping to divert his eyes from her. "Would you like some coffee?"

"No, stay put. I'll get my own coffee. Would you like some as well?"

"Um." She slowly sat back down, surprised by his offer. In fact, she hardly knew how to respond. In all her growing up years, she'd never witnessed her father serving her mother in the kitchen.

He moved to the stove, then gave a half turn in her direction. "I'll take that as a yes," he said, grinning. He withdrew two tin mugs from an upper shelf and began filling them with the steaming dark brew. Once the mugs were full, he returned to the table, set one in front of her, and then pulled out a chair and sat next to her.

"Thank you," she said.

"You're very welcome."

They both sipped, allowing the birdsong just outside the open windows to fill the quietness of the morning. He spoke first. "What is it you just read from the Bible?"

She welcomed his question, for it was the first time he'd been the one to initiate a spiritual conversation. "I've recently been reading from the book of Galatians."

"Ah, Galatians. I'm familiar with it. It's the apostle Paul's epistle to the people of Galatia."

"Yes. I'm impressed you knew that."

He raised his brow. "I'm not completely ignorant of the Scriptures. I used to read the Bible quite dutifully, actually. So tell me, what have you gleaned from today's reading?"

"For one thing, salvation is a gift from God, a result of His love, mercy, and grace. It's not something a person can work toward to achieve. Rather, it's a free gift. We need only ask forgiveness for our sins and then turn from them."

"I used to believe that."

"I have a hunch you still do. You're just too stubborn to admit it."

He tossed back his head and gave a loud chortle. "You think that, do you?" He sobered. "It's hard for me to believe God would allow such suffering in the world if He were truly a God of love."

"What sort of world would this be if there were no pain and suffering?"

He blew out another chuckle. "Heaven on earth, I guess."

"Exactly. So what you want is a world where no evil exists."

"That would be nice."

"But impossible. Sin began with Adam and Eve, and it has been with us ever since. The only remedy for it is salvation through Jesus Christ, God's Son."

He shrugged. "I feel like I do a pretty good job of getting along with people, holding my anger in check, and obeying the laws of the land."

"That's good, but being a good citizen on earth will not be enough to earn your citizenship in heaven."

He took another sip of coffee and stared at her over the rim of his mug. She smiled at him, hoping she hadn't offended him. "I didn't mean to preach."

"It's okay. When you're passionate about something, it just has to come out. My family is probably tickled to pieces that I've married a preacher woman."

"I'm not a preacher! Goodness."

"You should be. You could probably save a drunkard's soul."

"Not if I can't save yours!" she said, laughing.

He laughed too, and the mood lightened. "Shall we start breakfast?"

"You mean you want to help me?"

"I've been making breakfast for a long time, my dear. I'm fairly skilled at rustling up a meal."

"I'm just not used to a man working in the kitchen. My father wouldn't even have the first idea how to make a cup of coffee."

"Well, he hasn't been on the battlefield nor had to live without a wife for a few years."

Faith sobered. "You're right about that. Do you dread returning to war?"

They both pushed their chairs back and stood. "I will admit, I've grown awfully accustomed to being at home this time. I don't like the idea of leaving you behind—with my children, that is."

"We'll be just fine."

They went about working side by side. Joey cracked several eggs into a bowl, poured in a little milk, salt, and pepper, and then whisked the mixture with a fork. Faith peeled a few potatoes and sliced them thin in preparation for frying.

"Kids should be coming down soon," he said.

"That's what I was thinking. They had a big day yesterday. Lots of running, fishing, playing, and tossing the ball back and forth."

"Not much arguing either."

"Perhaps that is the key. Keeping them extra busy and having fun at the same time."

"Watch out for Isaac. He always has a dozen or more tricks up his sleeve."

"I'll be on the lookout."

Faith melted some grease in a skillet, then poured in the sliced potatoes. Beside her, Joey cooked the eggs in another pan, then pushed the eggs to the side and threw in some sliced bacon.

Funny how we adapted to each other's company in so short a period. God, help me not to worry about tomorrow, but to focus instead on each minute.

"I'll set the table. Shall we eat in the kitchen nook or the dining room?" she asked.

"There's probably more room if we sit around the big table," Joey answered.

"True. After you leave, we'll use the nook more." Using a towel, she clutched hold of the skillet handle and carried it to the butcher block. "I'll get the plates." She started to move to the big wooden hutch, where all the dishes were stacked, when a knock came at the front door. Outside, the farm dog barked a hearty greeting.

They exchanged glances, Joey's brow furrowed with curiosity. "Who would come calling at this hour?"

"Maybe one of your brothers?"

Frowning, Joey quickly moved the pan of eggs and bacon off the flame. "Maybe, but I can't imagine why." He wiped his hands on the sides of his trousers, then disappeared from the kitchen to answer the persistent knock. Faith continued the breakfast preparations, lifting down six plates and then removing the silverware from the bureau drawer. The front door squeaked open, and a male voice she didn't recognize spoke in a quiet tone. She attuned her ears for a clue as to who had come to call. She picked up the breakfast dishes, walked into the dining room, and set them on the table, then glanced through the archway into the parlor. She didn't know the gentleman caller, but she could read by Joey's expression that something was amiss. He turned his body and motioned for Faith to join them.

"Faith, this is Sheriff Charles Berry. Sheriff, this is my wife, the former Miss Haviland. Faith, I'm afraid the sheriff has some unfortunate news."

"Oh, dear." Faith's stomach took a quick flip. "Is it serious?" She didn't like the expression on Joey's face—or on the sheriff's, for that matter.

The sheriff, a middle-aged man with a dark, bushy mustache, removed his hat. "I'm sorry to trouble you folks so early in the morning." He set his eyes on Faith in particular. "An urgent telegram arrived in my office at six o'clock this morning. It came from Sheriff Mumford of Columbus."

A feeling of dread pinched Faith smack in the middle of her chest. "Yes?"

"Mrs. Fuller, it appears there's a fellow by the name of Stuart Porter who may be on his way to Lebanon. It is presumed he is on horseback, and he's thought to be armed, so he could pose a dangerous threat to you. Sheriff Mumford has formed a search party, and they believe they are hot on his trail." Sheriff Berry's brows tensed as he waved a finger at her. "I will need you to take every precaution to stay out of sight. My deputies are keeping an eye out as well. You can be assured we will do everything we can to keep you and our town safe."

Faith's chest constricted. "Oh, dear, I might have known Stuart would evade the law and then come looking for me."

Joey drew her up close to him, his muscled arm around her shoulder warm and reassuring. If she hadn't been so alarmed by the news, she might have taken more comfort in his nearness. "This is not your fault." His voice was soft and composed.

"But it *is*. I wanted to get away from him, and now he's coming to Lebanon."

"Well, there's a good chance they'll capture him before he gets here," Sheriff Berry said. "And as I said, we'll do everything we can to prevent any harm from coming your way. I'll assign a couple of deputies to keep a look out around the farms in this area. We'll be mindful until we're assured this Porter fellow is in custody."

Joey nodded. "Thank you, Sheriff. I appreciate it. I'm concerned for my family, but I have every confidence in your abilities."

The sheriff put his hat back on his head. "I'll be in touch."

"Thank you." Joey opened the door, let the sheriff out, and closed it behind him. He leaned his back against it and studied her, his brown eyes full of concern.

Just like that, two tears slipped down her cheeks. "I feel terrible."

He immediately stepped up and pulled her into an embrace, her head nestled close under his chin, his arms fully wrapping her frame. She couldn't help the natural impulse to hug him back, although doing so only opened the floodgate for more tears. "I never dreamed he'd do this," she spluttered. "I—I—don't even know how he found out where I am. Only my family knew, and Sheriff Mumford."

"Shh. Don't worry about it. Everything is going to be fine. Nothing's going to happen. I'm confident they'll catch him before he even steps foot in Lebanon."

She sniffed, knowing her tears had wet the fabric of his shirt. "I hope you're right."

"Ew! Daddy, why are you hugging the nanny?"

Faith jumped back at the sound of Isaac's voice, putting at least two feet between Joey and herself.

"Good morning to you too, son," Joey said. "And for your information, the *nanny* happens to be my wife, so I have every right to put my arms around her."

Knowing she had a few lingering tears, Faith lowered her head and gave her face a quick swipe with her sleeve. Isaac didn't seem to notice. "Well, it's disgusting. You hardly know her," the boy said.

"That is none of your concern. Go back upstairs and get dressed. We have a busy day ahead."

Isaac frowned. "Who was at the door?"

Joey threw a quick glance in Faith's direction. She felt his eyes on her, but she kept her own gaze pointed at the floor.

"Just—someone. Someone wanting to tell us something."

"What'd he want to tell you? Who was it?"

"Someone."

"Aren't you going to tell me?" Isaac's voice came off as sharp and impatient.

"Maybe later. For now, go back upstairs and get dressed."

Isaac turned and headed for the stairs, mumbling under his breath.

19

Stuart trained his eyes on the road ahead. It looked heavily traveled, if the wagon wheel tracks and horse muck were an indication. He wasn't sure it was wise to take it, but he'd had his fill of sticks and brush batting him in the face as he traversed narrow back tracks, so he decided to chance it—at least for the time being. He believed he'd ridden far enough by now that he wouldn't run into anyone who'd heard of him, so he relaxed a bit and pressed into his horse's sides to get him moving faster. It was only mid-morning, yet by the feel of the sun on his shoulders, he was in for a scorching ride. Stuart only hoped his horse was up for it. If not, he'd have to leave him behind and snag a better one off some unsuspecting farmer. Horse theft was a major crime, and if not hung for it, a person could count on spending time behind bars. Thus, he'd play it safe and wait till nightfall if the need arose.

He had no way of knowing how far he'd gone, but he guessed he had to be at the halfway point, past Springfield. He'd inquire of the next traveler he came upon, which might be sooner than he thought now that he'd decided to take a better road. He'd only passed a handful of folks since that one fellow who'd stopped him to inquire about his destination. Stuart wished now he hadn't divulged that information. *And how stupid of him to ask the traveler if he had any relatives in Lebanon with the name Fuller.* He supposed he'd had too much booze, making his brain foggy.

His stomach growled in response to the lack of grub he'd had for breakfast, his saddlebag supplies running low. It would be nice to come upon a trading settlement where he could replenish—or at the very least a farmhouse where he might encounter a friendly fellow willing to share what he had. He could play nice with someone if it meant getting a full belly. In the meantime, he'd keep an eye out for a squirrel or rabbit he could roast over an open fire when noontime rolled around.

His heart pounded at the thought of seeing Faith again. He knew now he should never have hit her. *Where had his common sense gone that morning?* He took a swig from the bottle he'd been carrying and thought about his plight. Somehow, he had to convince her he wasn't a woman beater. Yeah, he'd helped Opal to the other side, but that was years ago. He wasn't a bad guy, and every so often, when he'd catch a glimpse of himself in the mirror, he thought he wasn't bad on the eye either. *Why hadn't Faith recognized it?*

It was a quiet morning, not much stirring save for a tiny breeze that ruffled the leaves overhead. He thought about Leon and cursed aloud. *Had that fool gone and spilled everything about Opal's demise? Him and his religious ideas! He probably figured it was his duty to do it.* Stuart had been so drunk that night, he couldn't remember everything he'd sputtered, but he was pretty sure he'd confessed to ending Opal's life with that stupid drug the doctor had prescribed. His horse stumbled on a dip in the road. "Keep goin', ol' buddy. We got a lot of miles to put in. Don't you go lame on me."

Sheriff Mumford and a couple of his deputies got off their horses to study the surrounding area and walk over to a clearing. By the look of the makeshift spit and empty whiskey bottle left there, Stuart had built a fire and roasted something over it. Leon stayed seated in the saddle, having already stretched a couple of miles back when the posse got down to examine a disturbed area on the ground where it looked like Stuart had stopped to stretch and then finish off a bottle of his brew. It was all the empty pint bottles along the way that had kept them on his trail. Leon shook his head, bemused by his cousin's carelessness yet grateful for it all the same. *Stuart, Stuart, you don't even have the common sense to dispose of your bottles in a more discreet way.*

The sheriff took out his pocket watch. "Two thirty-five," he stated. He bent down and put a flat palm close to the fire pit ashes. "Still warm. He's not that far ahead of us. I think we'll have him in custody before nightfall."

"Let's hope so," said one of the deputies. There were five of them in total, including Leon, and every last man was intent on finding Stuart so they could end the pursuit and head back to Columbus. Leon's chest thudded at the thought of drawing nearer to his cousin. *How would it go down once they found him? Would he try to run away? Would he resist if captured? Would there be gunfire?* He prayed not. *Lord, give my cousin the ability to reason. May he open his eyes to see how foolish this whole pursuit has been.* He wanted Stuart brought to justice—but he also wanted it done in the proper manner. Everybody deserved fair treatment, and so he'd see to it that his wayward cousin got it.

Sheriff Mumford stretched, walked back to his horse, and remounted. Everyone followed suit. "Let's ride," he said, leading the way. Leon took up his position at the back of the line—right where he wanted to be.

⌒

"What are you thinking?" Joey asked Faith over a late lunch at the Golden Lamb Restaurant in downtown Lebanon, a favorite destination for travelers and citizens alike. They'd visited a few merchants in town that morning so Joey could introduce Faith to each one. They'd all been friendly and welcoming to the new Mrs. Fuller, informing her of their eagerness to serve in any way they could. Most about town probably assumed Joey would never remarry, so he could only imagine the whispers when he escorted his wife up and down Broadway, Lebanon's main thoroughfare. More than one in passing had tipped their hats, and he hadn't missed the occasional raised eyebrows and smiles of approval.

They'd also gone to the bank that morning. Joey had opened an account for Faith so she would have cash at her disposal for necessary purchases and to pay any bills that might come in. He'd also given the banker authority to transfer additional funds if his wife requested it. Everyone had been more than accommodating. But now, as he studied her from across the round table, she looked too distracted to eat. She'd barely touched her food—baked chicken breast, steamed green beans, and stewed potatoes—and he knew she had to be hungry. She'd barely eaten any breakfast either.

Faith looked up from her plate, her empty fork in her hand. "I'm thinking about that scoundrel Stuart Porter. I'm worried about the children."

He reached across the table and gave her arm a tender squeeze. "Don't be. Things will be fine, you'll see."

"But what if they don't catch him before you leave tomorrow?"

He looked at her, not wanting to let his own angst show. "Pardon me, but where is your faith in God now, wife?"

Her head shot back. "You're right, of course. I guess my humanness is showing through."

Joey gave a quiet laugh. "Since you're always after me to sharpen my faith, I figured I'd give preaching a little try myself."

She laughed in return, and it gladdened him. Regret settled in his chest as he thought about his leave-taking on the morrow.

"You're quite good at preaching, Joey."

A smile turned up his mouth. "I don't blame you for worrying, but try to have some confidence in our law enforcement. I believe they'll stay ahead of Porter. And if they don't, I'll talk to Jesse and Jack about keeping an extra eye on all of you."

"I hate to be a burden."

"You're no burden. Now then, young lady, pick up that fork and start eating—and remember, the God you're always reminding me about will watch over you."

She straightened in her chair, blue eyes twinkling. "You are absolutely right! Thank you for that little sermon." She dipped her fork into her potatoes, took a bite, chewed, and swallowed. "Hmm, delicious," she said.

He turned his attention to his own meal. After a few bites, he mulled aloud, "Starting this week, it'll be back to army grub for me."

She went sober. "It will be strange after you leave."

"Will it?" He tried to make light of it. "Does that mean you've come to like me?"

A bit of a pink hue touched her cheeks. "You're all right, I suppose." She took another bite of chicken.

"Just all right?"

She sniffed and kept eating.

He leaned across the table and whispered. "You're going to miss me, aren't you?"

Not a single muscle flicked. She merely picked up her water glass and muttered, "Did I say that?" Afterward, she put the glass to her mouth and took a few swallows.

He liked when she toyed with him. "Admit it. Things are going to be plain dull around the house with me gone."

"Not dull at all. I'm looking after your four rambunctious children, remember?"

"Meaning you'll miss me all the more."

"I wouldn't go that far." Now she avoided all eye contact and took another bite of food.

"You can't admit it?" He was chuckling now.

"I'm not admitting anything."

He shook his head and filled his fork with some vegetables. He didn't blame her. He wasn't ready to admit either that, besides missing his children, he would also miss his new wife.

20

The rickety farmhouse came into Stuart's line of vision once he completed the bend in the road. That single squirrel he'd shot for lunch hadn't been nearly enough to satisfy his hunger. And that last bottle of brew he'd polished off a few miles back hadn't helped either. He'd go knock on the door, act real friendly-like, and see what food and drink he could wheedle off whomever answered it.

He directed his horse up the long drive, hoping for good results. If he played things right, he'd walk out with a full stomach and a saddle-bag full of supplies, including whiskey, to last him the remainder of his trip. *Yes, indeed. He could be downright charming when the need called for it.*

After tying his horse to the hitching rail by the front porch, he climbed the two steps to the front door and gave a light knock. Right away, a scurrying sound came from inside, then, "Mabel, did I hear someone at the door? Mabel!"

"I'm comin.'" More scurrying, and then the door creaking open just a crack, and a pair of old eyes peering through the opening at him. "Yes?" came the squeaky voice. "What y' want, mister?"

He hadn't expected an old woman to answer. He quickly removed his hat and ran a hand through his greasy hair. "Afternoon, ma'am. I'm just passin' through and saw your house. I was wonderin' if y' might spare a hungry traveler a bit o' grub."

She widened the crack about an inch and looked him up and down.

"Who's at the door, Mabel?"

"Some feller askin' for food," she said, turning her head slightly without taking her eyes off Stuart.

"Some feller, you say? What's he want?"

"I jes' told y'. He wants food," she hollered back.

"I mean you no harm, ma'am."

"Are you a soldier?"

"No, ma'am. I'm just a regular citizen."

"If you was a soldier, I might've let y' in."

Darn! He should've told her he was a soldier...even if he wasn't dressed in army attire. "All I'm askin' from y' is a little grub." He tried to make himself sound as down-home as possible, even picking up a bit of a country drawl.

"Does he look harmless?" the man asked.

Rather than respond to his question, the woman kept on with her up and down perusal of Stuart. "You got a gun on y'?" She gripped the door so tightly that her gnarly knuckles went white.

"Uh, yeah, you want t' see it?"

"I want y' t' lay it on one o' them chairs right there, that's what I want."

"Oh!" He removed his pistol. "Sure thing, ma'am." He walked over to set it on a rickety looking chair. Of course, he failed to mention that he had another pistol stuck in his belt under his shirt at the back. *The less she knew, the better.* Once he did that, she opened the door and stepped back to allow him passage. She and her old man had to be in their mid to late seventies by the look of their wrinkled, sun-parched skin, craggy faces, and thin white hair. The way she moved, slow and with a slight limp, made him question whether she even knew how to cook a decent meal anymore.

"Sit y'rself down right there, mister. What's y'r name?" she asked, pointing him to a chair a few feet away from her husband who had yet to say anything to him. Instead, the old guy just gaped at him through empty eyes, leaned forward, and gripped both hands around an ancient walking stick. *Besides being partially deaf, was he also dim in the eyes?*

Stuart had to think fast. "Moore, Harold Moore."

"Harold Moore, eh? We's Hank and Mabel Middleton. Where you an' your horse headed?"

"Lebanon."

She crossed her arms over her thick, round waist and crinkled her brow at him. "That's a far piece. Why ain't y' on a train?"

He swallowed down his impatience. It wasn't like he had all the time in the world to converse with the old bag. He merely wanted to eat and be on his way. Still, he had to put on a friendly demeanor to get what he wanted. "I like to enjoy the scenery as I go. I been takin' my time, enjoyin' nature, and doin' some huntin. Sleepin' out under the stars too. Goin' to visit some relatives for a short spell. That's the purpose of my trip," he lied.

"You say somethin' about Lebanon?" asked the old man.

"He said he's on his way to Lebanon. Lebanon," his wife repeated.

"Lebanon. Hm. That right?" the man muttered.

To Stuart, Mabel whispered, "He's deaf as a post and can't see much better than he can hear."

"I see." Stuart swiveled his gaze to the old guy.

The man rubbed his white whiskered jaw. "We don't know nobody in Lebanon. That's a far piece."

"That's what I just said," she told him, folding her arms.

"What's that?"

"Never mind," she hollered.

"You wouldn't know how many more miles I got to travel, would you?" Stuart asked Mabel.

"Nope, don't know, but I'd guess you got a good full day's ride ahead of y'."

"I was hoping I was a bit closer. Not sure my horse is up for that."

"Humph, maybe you shoulda planned better. Where'd you start out from?"

"Columbus area."

"Humph." She had a rough-around-the-edges manner about her.

"Well, so's you can be on y'r way, I'll fix y' some beans an' bacon. I got some cornbread left over from breakfast too."

"That sounds right good. I'm much obliged. Um, might y' have some homemade brew on hand?"

She turned down her mouth. "Nope. We ain't much for the strong stuff. I sure do smell it on you though. You'll have to beg some off the neighbors 'bout two miles up the road."

That made Stuart nervous. Having finished off all the bottles he'd brought, he desperately needed to restock. Otherwise, he'd get the jitters.

Mabel moved to their little kitchen and set about gathering what items she'd need. She didn't move any too fast either, which served to agitate Stuart all the more. To cover it, he cleared his throat and struck up a conversation with the old guy, who still held tight to his overlarge walking stick.

⌐

"Look up ahead! That's Stuart's horse tied to that post," Leon whispered to the sheriff as he pulled back on his reins. "I'm sure of it."

"You're kidding." The sheriff stopped abruptly and held his hand up to halt his party.

Leon had ridden up next to the sheriff a couple of miles back after they'd found yet another whiskey bottle alongside the road. There was an overall sense now that they were closing in on Stuart. Leon's heart stepped up its beat at the sight of the old gray gelding. He'd know it anywhere with the markings on his rump and side.

"Let's get off this road," Mumford said in a low, excited voice. "Everyone take cover in that brush over there." Quietly, they all led their horses to an area behind a thick cluster of trees, well out of sight. "We need to plan our next move and be mighty vigilant about it. First, Leon, are you sure that's his horse?"

"Yes, I'm sure. See that big black heart-shaped spot on its rump? I used to joke about it to Stuart, saying that black heart was the color of Stuart's—and aptly placed too! I also saw a red blanket that he stole from my house hanging off the saddlebag."

The sheriff's light brown eyes glittered. "All right, then, I say we come up with a plan."

"What sort of plan, Sheriff?" one of the deputies asked.

"I'm thinking about it. Give me a minute."

Everyone sat atop his horse, eager for word as to how to proceed. Sheriff Mumford nodded to himself, then patted his horse on the neck. "First, we have to bear in mind there are innocent folks inside that house. We can't do anything that would jeopardize their safety. Second, whatever we do, we must do it right the first time. There is no room for error."

"Agreed," someone said while the others nodded.

"We've finally caught up with him, but how we carry out seizing him will be another story. We can't just go up to the house, bang on the door, and demand he come out. He could easily take someone hostage if we do that. Instead, we need to lure him out."

"I have an idea," Leon said.

"I'm listening," said the sheriff.

"Is there someone here who could make a specific bird call or a dog's bark—or a baby's cry? If it sounded realistic enough, Stu might come outside to investigate."

For a moment, they all sat atop their horses, gaping at one another. "A baby's cry?" said one of the fellows. "I could do that. I live with a baby, and I got her cry down pat."

"No kidding, Zeke," the sheriff said. He scrunched his face up. "Can't imagine why that would make Porter come outside though."

"If it's convincing enough, I would think it would draw just about anybody outside," Leon interjected. "Folks have a soft spot for babies, and I don't think Stu will be an exception. He'll be curious. And think about this: Stuart has been short on common sense this whole time,

Her Steadfast Heart 169

throwing bottles alongside the road, setting campfires in open spaces. He's probably half-drunk right now and not a bit suspicious that we're on his trail."

"You might be onto something," the sheriff said. "So, here's the way I see it. We dismount, spread out, and carefully advance on the house from different directions, taking care to stay secluded. I'll situate myself at the side of the house closest to the front door. When you see me pull my gun on him, the rest of you move in quick as lightning, y' hear?"

"Yes, sir!" they all said as they speedily climbed down, tying their steeds to low-lying branches. Overhead, the birds' singing ceased, as if they sensed some impending excitement.

"Choose your positions carefully. Zeke, we're counting on you to sound like a real baby."

He gave a sheepish grin. "You got it, Sheriff. We got seven kids, and all of 'em have the same wail."

"Well, all right then. No room for errors, men." At that, the sheriff tipped his hat at everyone, and they all set off, bodies low as they crept away in various directions like clever foxes.

Leon's heart almost boomed out of his chest as he, too, squatted low and departed into the thick woods heading up the side of the property toward the house.

⌒

"That's smellin' mighty good, ma'am," Stuart said.

"My Mabel's a fine cook. She weren't always, but she learnt some cookin' tricks from 'er maw early on. Ain't that right, Mabel? Course, it never has taken much to satisfy my belly." The old man chuckled and rubbed his round gut. Stuart pretended interest, granting him a forced smile.

"She makes a fine pot o' beans, you'll see," he went on.

"Oh, stop talkin' the poor man's ears off, Hank. You'll have him rushin' out o' here 'for he has his first bite."

"What's that, Mabel?"

"I said stop talkin' so much!" she screamed.

"No problem, ma'am," Stuart said. "I'm just enjoyin' conversin' with your man. He's been tellin' me all about y'r farm and the livestock you used to have as well as what you used to farm. Now he says you do well to keep up your garden."

"He's right." She moved the pot of pork and beans away from the flame and started setting the table. "We was real prosperous at one time. Now we live off ar' garden and rely on them chickens outside to give us plenty of eggs. About three times a year, we buy a good supply of dried meats and salted pork from the neighbors, and I do a lot of pre-servin' in the fall, so we do jus' fine. A peddler stops by with his wagon of goods 'bout once a month so's we can trade with him. We give him produce and whatnot to sell and he provides us with what we need. Y' can't always trust them fellers, but he's one o' the good ones."

Stuart had to grit his teeth to keep from rolling his eyes.

Mabel filled three tin cups with water from a pitcher and carried them to the table. "I best go out to the pump and fill this pitcher up with water so's we can have plenty for ar' meal."

"I can do that," Stuart said, anxious to stretch his legs.

"Oh, that's mighty nice. Thank y' kindly. You'll see the pump on the other side o' the porch."

He walked across the room and took the pitcher. "No problem a'tall." He'd be glad to escape their banter. Just as he approached the door, pitcher in hand, a screeching sound coming from outside stopped him dead.

"What in tarnation was that?" asked Mabel.

"What? I din't hear nothin'," said Hank.

"That's 'cause you're deafer than a board, ol' man. It sounded like—like a—baby or something."

"What's that about a hay bale?"

Stuart stepped up to the window and pulled back the curtain. He *saw* nothing, but he'd definitely *heard* something, and Mabel was right. It sounded like a baby's cry.

"I sure don't see no baby," said Mabel.

"Me neither."

She went to the door, opened it wide, and peered out. Another wobbly, wailing cry rent the air. "Lordy, there it is again! Where's it comin' from? Good gracious, sounds like Moses in the bulrushes, but t'ain't no river near here."

"What is it, Mabel?" asked Hank.

"It's a baby!" she answered back.

"I'll go have a look," said Stuart, stepping past Mabel and finding himself in the middle of the porch. He walked to the chair and set the empty water pitcher down next to his pistol. *He might've picked it up, but what would he need that for if he was seeking the whereabouts of a baby in the woods?* Besides, he still carried the one tucked behind him in his belt. He raked the whole area with his keen eyes, looking from one side of the house to the other, but determined the sound was coming from one direction only—the woods on the east side of the house. *Had some mother deserted her infant with the intent of leaving it for some unsuspecting stranger to discover?*

He took another cautious step, trying to determine the location of the wailing. He looked around and saw not a soul—but then there came that pathetic little cry again. That did it. He moved forward, then stepped down from the porch and advanced toward the woods, slowly and with caution lest the mother be lurking nearby and perhaps be mentally deranged.

And just like that, before he had a second to react, a hard poke came to the center of his back, and he froze where he stood. He'd been duped. "Don't move, Porter. Stop right where you are and point them hands to the sky."

He cursed so loud that even the old man in the house would've heard him.

"I said, put 'em up, Porter. Your little game stops right here."

"Wull, I'll be dingswiggled, what's goin' on out here?" Mabel asked from the porch.

"They got the wrong man, Mabel," Stuart shouted. "Take my gun off that chair there and shoot this guy."

"Not so fast," came a male voice. Stuart squinted at the sight of a man emerging from the woods, who grinned and let out a whimpering sound. *The baby.* Stuart cursed again. They'd played him for a giant fool.

"No need for a gun, ma'am. This here's a wanted man. I'm Sheriff Mumford from Columbus, and we been trailin' this rotten scum for a couple o' days now."

"Well, I'll be a green-bellied weasel. I had no *idear,*" she muttered.

By now, old Hank had heard the commotion and hobbled out to the porch to stand next to his wife, his walking stick acting as his third leg. "What's happenin' out here?"

"We been housin' a criminal, Hank. Can you imagine? Don't know when we've had this much excitement 'less y' count the time that deer smashed clear through ar' winder five years ago."

"What's that, Mabel?"

"Never mind."

"Huh?"

"I'll tell y' later," she yelled into his ear.

Stuart had yet to put his hands in the air as the sheriff had instructed, which led to his thinking about that pistol in his belt. "Ain't y' goin' to at least let me enjoy the fine meal Mrs. Middleton took the time to prepare for me, Sheriff?"

"Just shut up and put your hands up." The sheriff's gun poked him so hard he winced. He had to think fast because the mere thought of spending time behind bars gave him nervous trembles. "Come on, Sheriff. All I did was give Faith Haviland a little punch to the face. I don't see how that warrants this circus-like behavior."

"Uh-uh, Porter. There's the little matter of your wife's death—and your burying her body on your cousin's property—then telling folks she left you if they happened to ask." The sheriff put his mouth close to Stuart's ear, making his hair stand on end. "Remember that? Or did that little incident slip your mind?"

Leon! He would kill that dirty, double-crossing dog the next time he saw him. A real man didn't do that to his own flesh and blood. Anger reared up in him so that a growling sound came out from deep within.

He whipped his arm around, snagged hold of the gun at his back, shoved away from the sheriff, and pointed his pistol dead center at the lawman's head.

"Hey, easy, easy, Porter!" one of the deputies called out. "You don't want the law's blood on your hands. You'll be hanged."

"Shut up! Now, every one of you drop your weapons to the ground." When no one did, he screamed the order again, adding that he would take the sheriff out at the count of five if he didn't see every single weapon hit the ground. One by one, their guns hit the dirt. "Now, Mrs. Middleton, you be a real good gal and bring me that pistol sitting on that chair."

"You ain't draggin' me into nuthin'," she said, her chin pointed out in a stubborn display.

"You best do it if you value that old man's life." Stuart darted his pistol from the sheriff to Hank and back to the sheriff. "I could pick him off in one shot."

"You best do as he says, ma'am," the sheriff urged. "He's not kidding."

"Get in the house, Hank," she screamed in the old man's ear.

The man turned and started to hobble back, but then he hesitated and turned back around. "I ain't goin' nowhere, Mabel. Hand me that gun on that chair there."

"Don't you do it, Mabel," said Stuart. "I swear I'll shoot."

"No, you won't," came a familiar voice from behind. "Drop it, Stuart."

Something he could only assume was a gun poked him hard in the back. "Leon, you're no better than a rat's behind. I'll get you for this."

"Drop it, Stuart, or things are going to get a whole lot worse for you. Do the right thing for a change."

What choice did he have? Not only did his cousin have a gun pointed in his back, but now the old man had Stuart's pistol in hand—and he had no idea how good a shot he might be. With a begrudging growl, he dropped his gun, and just like that, everything happened faster than a moving train. The sheriff whipped him around and snagged his hands, cuffing them behind him, and then every other man picked up his weapon while giving out loud whoops of celebration—at his expense.

Well, at least he'd scared them all plenty, even if he'd failed miserably in the end. He narrowed his eyes at Leon and shook his head in disgust. "I'll get you for this, Leon. You ratted on your own kin."

"I would feel bad about that if I thought I did the wrong thing, but it's time you fessed up, Stuart, beginning with what really happened to Opal."

"I did not bury her. *You* did."

"So you admit someone buried her, do you?" the sheriff asked, tugging at his arms.

"Ow!" Stuart's insides started to shake. "I c-can't go to jail, Leon." Actual tears started forming. Just the thought of being confined behind bars set his head to spinning. "Tell 'im, Leon. Tell 'em I can't do it, will you?"

"No can do, Stu. You have to pay for your crime. Think of it—you'll finally have a clear conscience after all these years."

The sheriff tightened Stuart's wrist cuffs. "Stuart Porter, you're under arrest for the murder of Opal Porter."

Stuart's lower lip quivered, but to cover his fear, he blurted, "Pfff, she was dying anyway. May as well have helped her along. She wasn't nothin' but a nuisance anyway."

The sheriff took him by the arm. "And for your assault on Faith Haviland. You have the right to remain silent…" He finished reading his rights, then apologized to the Middletons for any inconvenience. Stuart didn't so much as glance in the old couple's direction. *If old Mabel would've hurried things along in the kitchen, he wouldn't be in this predicament.*

The sheriff gave him a little push toward the end of the driveway. "Come on, Porter. We got a long ride ahead of us. And once we arrive back in Columbus, you'll have a nice, long stay in a cozy prison cell. You may as well kiss that meat market goodbye."

"Pfff. Don't bother me none," he said, feigning bravery even while trembling from the top of his head to the soles of his worn-out boots.

21

Tuesday morning brought drenching rain, the kind that soaks to the bone if a body steps out into it for even a second. It came down in torrents, pounding the windows with its wind-slanted gush, forming instant lake-like puddles in the driveway and beyond. Faith worried that the garden would flood, but she supposed it would survive. It wasn't much to brag about anyway since she'd had no time to work in it yet. Perhaps tomorrow she'd carve out some time. *Tomorrow.* An aching feeling nagged at her insides at what that word implied. Joey wouldn't be here. It would just be his children and her.

While Faith cleaned up after breakfast, Joey and his brood moved to the living room to spend a bit more time together before Jack stopped by in his buggy to drive Joey to the train station. She wished to spend a bit of time with him herself, but she didn't want to impose on the remaining moments he had with his children either. Her mind was a jumble of thoughts—first, that, yes, she would miss Joey, regardless that she'd refused to admit it yesterday; and, second, Stuart Porter was out there. She'd barely slept more than a few winks last night just thinking about that horrid man. *Would he truly try to find her, or was it just a ploy on his part to scare her?*

A streak of lightning flashed across the sky, illuminating the kitchen for all of three seconds. Close on its heels came a thunderous crack that shook the house. In the other room, Miriam let out a screech and Faith heard Joey's comforting words to his little one. "Don't worry, honey. Here, come and sit on my lap." Faith finished drying the last breakfast dish and placed the clean dishes in the hutch. Once done, she glanced into the living room and caught Joey's eye.

"Come and join us," he invited.

"Oh no, that's fine. You should spend this last hour or so together without my interference."

"Yeah, she's right," said Isaac, ever the doomsayer.

"Isaac!" scolded Joey. "This is goodbye for all of us, including Faith. You shouldn't be selfish."

The boy hung his head, but only for a moment, for the sound of wagon wheels and a loud "Whoa!" competed with the storm.

"Is that Uncle Jack already?" Isaac jumped up and ran to the window.

"It shouldn't be," Joey said. "I'm not expecting him till closer to nine o'clock, and possibly later if this rain doesn't let up."

"It ain't Uncle Jack. Don't know who it is," said Isaac.

Franklin and Beth joined him at the window. "It's the sheriff's wagon, I think," offered Beth.

Joey and Faith exchanged looks. He rose from the sofa and made for the front door, opening it wide for the sheriff's entry. Faith's stomach gave a sickening turn, her nerves creating an awful case of jitters.

Sheriff Berry stepped inside and stomped his wet boots on the front rug. When he removed his hat, water dripped off its rim. "Phew! It's wet out there."

"Indeed it is. Morning, Sheriff," said Joey. "I presume you brought some news."

The sheriff grinned, and Faith dared to let down a bit of her guard. She found herself stepping into the living room so that she might hear whatever announcement he'd come to deliver.

"I certainly did bring news. This morning, I received word by way of a telegram from Sheriff Mumford that Mr. Porter's been arrested. You can rest easy."

A loud, breathy sigh escaped Faith's lips, and she found she had to take hold of the back of the chair she was standing behind.

"Who's Mr. Porter?" Beth asked.

"No one you need to worry about," Joey told her. "Isaac, would you please take your brother and sisters upstairs so I can talk to the sheriff?"

"Why do I have to go upstairs? I'm the oldest," he groused.

"Precisely why I'm asking you to do this little thing."

Isaac gave a growl, turned, and ushered the others up the stairs. "Let's go to Frankie's and my room."

"Thank you for taking charge, son," Joey called after him.

"Yeah, yeah."

"I don't have a great deal of information," Sheriff Berry said once the children were out of sight. "I can only tell you that a telegram came this morning telling of Stuart Porter's arrest. They located him in the residence of an elderly couple some thirty or forty miles northeast of here. They had been on his trail for a couple of days."

"Oh dear, I hope he didn't do any harm to the couple," Faith said.

"I don't believe so. It sounded like he was just holing out there for a bit. If I learn any further details about his capture, I will be sure to pass them on."

"Please do, Sheriff. I'll be heading back to my field duty today, but I know my wife would appreciate it if you would keep her informed."

Faith found she rather liked Joey referring to her as his wife, no matter that their marriage might only be temporary.

The sheriff turned his wet hat in his hands. "Well, you be safe, er, *Captain* Fuller. Here's hoping you return to Lebanon safe and in one piece."

"I appreciate that."

Sheriff Berry plopped his hat back on his head, then tipped it at both of them. "Good day then."

Joey opened the door for him, and the sheriff stepped out into the rain just as another bolt of lightning ripped across the sky and a thunderous clap filled the air.

"That's a close storm. I doubt Jack will want to drive in this, so it might be he'll wait it out before driving over."

"But don't you have to catch the train?"

"I do, but I don't mind waiting at the station for the next train if I have to."

He glanced upstairs. "The kids are quiet. Want to sit down on the sofa and have a private chat?"

Her heart skipped a beat or two. *Foolish me*, she chided herself. "Of course. Perhaps you can give me some last-minute instructions."

"I think we went over all the instructions last night before we all went to bed. I want you to write letters to me informing me of the children's behavior. Tell me if they pull any tricks on you so I can keep a running record of their wrongs."

Naturally, she would write to him, but she had no intention of listing *all* their wrongs. *Good grief, he'd have his hands full with punishments if she did that.*

"That was something lacking with the other nannies. Our communication was sparse at best."

"I'll be sure to write to you. That I can promise," she said. "And I don't want you worrying. You'll have enough on your mind. Like the sheriff said, just come back in one piece."

"I plan to do that. I'm afraid I'm not much of a letter writer. If I'm hiking from one spot to another, it's usually a day-long hike with very little time for writing, and of course, it's next to impossible if I'm on the battlefield."

She smiled. "I wouldn't expect you to lay down your weapon so you could jot a few lines to me, Joey."

He grinned at her. "But I might be thinking about you, just the same."

"Not while in battle, I would hope."

"You never can tell. The mind does have a way of wandering even at the most inopportune times."

"Is that so?" Faith could feel her cheeks flushing.

When they sat down on the sofa and sank into the cushions, their knees brushed, creating a tingling sensation that shot through her veins. *Saints above and mother of mercy!*

He made a low sound in his chest. *Had he felt it too?*

"Sit back," he coaxed. "We may as well take advantage of these few minutes of peace and quiet."

She tried to relax, but in vain. Another thunderous boom filled the house. "Peace and quiet, you say?"

Joey slipped an arm around her shoulder and began to rub it as if this were the most natural thing in the world to do. "It's a great relief they've found Porter," he said.

"Indeed it is. A huge burden off my shoulders."

"But you're still so jittery. Is it because I'm leaving?"

"Yes, that's—that's part of it. On the one hand, I'm excited about accepting the position of caring for your children, and on the other, I'm worried I might not be all that you hoped for. What if I fail miserably?"

"I have every confidence that you'll do just fine. In the short time I've known you, I've witnessed a strength that probably even you don't know you have."

"Really?"

"Yes. I genuinely admire you for many things, including your faith in God."

"That's kind of you to say that. Of course, I'll be sure to include daily Bible reading in the children's routines." She lifted her gaze at him. "Did you pack your Bible?"

Joey gave a little chuckle. "Yes, I sure did. I might even be given to reading it every now and again."

"Every now and again? It should be the first thing you read in the morning and the last thing at night. Your faith will increase the more you read it."

"I'm beginning to believe that little by little."

"You are?" Excitement welled up. "I'm happy to hear that."

"It's your fault, you know." His voice had a teasing tone.

"I don't mind taking the blame."

His fingers kept tracing little circles on her shoulder, increasing the number of chill bumps mounting on her skin. It was a most delightful sensation, but it also frightened her. She dared not grow attached to her husband lest he return in October and expect her to leave on the first train going out of Lebanon.

She took to twiddling her thumbs in her lap and staring down at them.

"Is there anything else you'd like to say?"

She scowled a little. "Yesterday, I didn't want to admit it, but I might—I might miss you a little bit."

"Really?" She almost heard the smile crack his face.

"On the other hand, I might not. Perhaps I'll be so busy keeping house and dealing with your children that thoughts of you will be few and seldom."

"Oh. I hope you think of me often."

Now she felt guilty for having blurted that. "I will pray for your safety every single day, morning and night. When I think of you, that is."

His light laughter tickled her ear. "I didn't used to believe prayer really worked, but I'm beginning to have a tiny change of attitude."

"I'm glad to hear you say that."

He shifted his weight a bit in the sofa, turning himself so his body almost faced her. "I've been thinking about something lately."

That sparked her interest. "Oh?"

"Remember that pathetic kiss I gave you at the courthouse after Judge Cranston pronounced us husband and wife?"

She bit her lower lip. "It wasn't so bad."

Without warning, he cupped the right side of her face with his callused hand. "I think I can do better. You deserve the sort of kiss that you'll remember while I'm gone."

"What? Oh, I—I don't know if that's—"

But he didn't give her time to finish her sentence. Instead, he closed in and planted his mouth squarely over hers, rather firmly and with purpose to begin with, but then softening and melding after the first few seconds until she nearly melted into the cushion beneath her. *Lord above, this is quite divine.* She should have pulled away, should have explained the impropriety of such a kiss when neither of them had even proclaimed their love. But rather than discourage the kiss, she leaned into it, stunned and even mesmerized, amazed by what he was capable of doing to her. Not even Frederick Holland, her former fiancé, had had the ability to make her insides dissolve into a pool of mush as Joey was doing now. *Would she ever recover?*

The kiss continued, and she even participated in it when she adjusted herself so as to put her arms around his broad back and cling. But when another crack of thunder split the air, and then the padding of rushing feet rumbled on the stairs, she quickly pushed herself back from him and set to smoothing out her skirt. She pushed several strands of hair out of her eyes and made a fast swipe of her perspiring brow.

The children bounded around the corner. "Frankie saw the sheriff leave, but you never called us back down, so we comed anyway," said Miriam. "Are you in trouble with the sheriff, Daddy?"

Joey laughed, looking fully recovered. "Hardly, darlin'. Everything is just fine."

"What'd he want anyway?" asked Isaac.

"Perhaps Faith will tell you sometime."

"Perhaps I will," she said. "If you're good."

Isaac scoffed. "Pfff. Never mind. I don't need to know."

rain should be arriving any time now, Captain," said the fellow behind the ticket window. "What company you stationed with anyway?"

Jack had left Joey at the station some forty-five minutes ago. He'd wanted to stay and wait with him, but his responsibilities at the farm prevented it. The rain had finally let up, leaving the air heavy and humid and the sun fighting to get through an array of grayish clouds. Joey had been leaning up against the building, hardly noticing the ticket master, but he turned to him now to answer his question. "Ohio Twenty-Seventh Infantry. I've been on a two-week furlough."

"I see. Must've been nice to get y'rself a break from the war. You think it'll end soon?"

"I can't say. Everyone wants to know the answer to that question. I would say the North has a definite edge...but the South isn't about to surrender yet."

The fellow shook his head. "It's a shame all the lives lost. You killed anybody yet?"

Joey cringed. It was one of those questions people wanted to ask but usually didn't—if they had any common sense about them.

"I may have. It's war, mister."

He wasn't in much of a mood for conversing considering he'd just left his new wife and his children. He couldn't stop thinking about them, so the man's question especially annoyed him.

"Yeah, it's war. Let's hope everyone can come home soon and that them Rebels will surrender their guns. It's high time, don't you think?"

"Yeah. Excuse me, sir."

"O' course."

To rest his weary legs, but also to escape further talk, he walked to a wooden bench and planted himself on it. In the distance, he heard a train whistle—his train, no doubt. He'd be glad to get on it, he supposed, if for no other reason than to sit next to a window and wallow in his lonesome thoughts. These last few months of duty would drag unless he got so caught up in battle that he had no time to think about it. *Not that he wished for that.*

He recalled the sheriff's visit that morning and the feeling of relief that had come over him to learn of Stuart Porter's capture. Hopefully, the fellow would never see the light of day again. A trial would no doubt ensue, but Joey doubted the loathsome fellow would be able to trouble Faith any further.

He thought about the prayer Jack had offered when they'd all gone outside to form a circle before he and Joey climbed aboard Jack's rig. It had been a prayer asking for protection over Joey, but also a prayer that Faith and the children would build a friendship as well as a mutual respect for each other. He also prayed that even in their absence from each other, Joey and Faith would form a lasting bond. Joey didn't quite know what to think about that last part of his brother's prayer. *Did he want that, and more importantly, did Faith?* Yes, he'd thrown caution to the wind when he'd kissed her this morning, and they'd never had a chance to discuss it before he left because of his children's interruption, so he had no idea how she felt about it. *Why had he done it?* Probably mostly out of curiosity. He'd gotten a tiny taste of her lips on their wedding day, and so it just felt like the right thing to do—to kiss her again, and do it right this time. Whether it was more than that, he couldn't say. *He did know that he'd enjoyed getting to know her in the short time he'd spent with her, but did she feel the same? Would she be counting the days till his return so he could make good on the monetary allowance, or would they both recall the judge's words about doing their very best to keep their vows?* These were things for which he had no answers and only time would tell. At any rate, he'd look forward to her letters.

The train rumbled into town, its shrill whistle informing the whole of South Lebanon of its arrival at Deerfield Station. Add to that the screeching sound of brakes against steel tracks, and not even a deaf person could nap through it. He hefted up his knapsack and fell into a line of other travelers, none of whom he recognized. *Thankfully.* He didn't cotton to sitting next to an acquaintance and feeling the need to converse. In fact, he'd do his best to find a seat by himself so he could reflect in silence. Bellows of smoke from the incoming locomotive filled the air as the monster screeched to a stop. A door opened, and out stepped the conductor. "Step aside, please, so other passengers can debark. You'll all get your chance to climb aboard. Hold y'r horses," he called.

Joey shifted his weight, swiped at his wet brow, and tried to hold his dour mood in check. It occurred to him then that the very last thing on earth he wanted to do was go back to war—and he had a strong suspicion that besides his children, one slender-framed blond woman was responsible for his regret at having to do that.

～

Faith had invited the children to come out to the garden with her, as she wanted to assess its needs and perhaps pull some weeds. At least it wouldn't require watering for a few days after the good dousing the ground had gotten that day. No one but Miriam jumped at the chance to follow her, but that was fine. The rest of the children had sullen moods, and so she decided coaxing them into doing something they had no interest in would do little to increase their liking for her. She would have to think of something else.

On the way to the garden at the back of the yard, Miriam slipped her hand into Faith's. Faith gave it a little squeeze and then swung it back and forth with each stride. "I miss my daddy," she offered.

"I'm certain you do, but we'll do fun things every day to make the time go faster."

"Like what?"

"Oh, I don't know, perhaps you can help me think of some things. Tell me some of your favorite games to play and things to do."

"Play house with my dollies. That's number one."

"Is it now? Then we'll make sure to do that together. Does Beth ever play dollies with you?"

"Sometimes, but sometimes she just wants to read by herself."

"I understand that. Everyone needs his and her own space."

"I like to help feed the chickens and collect the eggs, but that's mostly Frankie's job. I like to play with the kitties in the barn too."

"It sounds like you enjoy a lot of things."

"I like to swing, too, but nobody never pushes me."

"I'm sorry to hear that. I'll be happy to push you sometime."

They reached the garden. Faith surveyed it with a keen eye. She and her mother had always maintained a pristine garden, but this one was certainly lacking. To her surprise, the nanny before her had indeed planted several vegetables, but most of them were strangled by weeds. She bent at the waist and pulled out a few weeds, then tossed them to the side. Miriam went down next to her to play in the dirt.

"Do you know why my brothers and Beth doesn't likes you?"

Her ears perked as she gazed at the girl. "No, I don't, but I'd like to know."

"They thinks you're goin' t' be mean, but I tol' them you was nicer than Mrs. Whatsername."

She laughed a little. "Have I been mean yet?"

Miriam shook her head. "Nope. You been real nice."

"Why, thank you."

"They also doesn't like that you married ar' daddy."

"I sort of gathered that." She pulled a few more troublesome shoots. "How do you feel about that?"

"I like it real good. Y're pretty too. My real mommy was pretty."

"I know she was. I have seen her portrait on the wall over the fireplace." Faith picked through the plants and found more weeds. She yanked them one by one. "Do you want to help me?"

"I don't know which is weeds an' which is good."

"Well, let me show you." For the next while, she schooled the child in telling the difference. "Weeds can sometimes be pretty, but they aren't usually as sturdy as the plants we want to keep. You'll find weeds are easier to pull out."

"This one's pretty," said Miriam, starting to give it a yank.

"Oh, don't pull that one. That's a lovely tomato plant. Those little flowers will someday sprout tomatoes."

"I don't know if I like tomatoes."

"I bet you do. They're red and juicy."

"Like an apple?"

She giggled. "Well, no. A tomato is juicier and has a completely different flavor."

They continued chatting. "Weeds make the other plants die if you don't pull 'em," said Miriam.

"You are absolutely right. That's why we have to pull them out of here. Goodbye, weeds!" she said with a giggle, tossing more of the pesky things to the side and moving down the row, their knees soaking up the dirt.

"My teacher taught me about weeds."

"Your schoolteacher?"

"Well, no, my Sunday school teacher." Miriam studied the plants before her, miraculously identified a weed, and gave it a good pull, then added it to Faith's pile. "She said weeds is like ar' sins. The more we gots inside us, the more trouble we'll have growin' a good garden in ar' soul. Or somethin' like that."

"Your teacher was right. If we let sins grow like weeds inside us, then it will be harder and harder to live a healthy life for Jesus."

"Um-hm. That was the day I asked Jesus to kill all the weeds in my heart."

Faith went stark still. She turned to the child. "You mean you asked Jesus to forgive your sins and live in your heart?"

"Yep. And He did, too! That very day!" She grew a big smile, which made her eyes glisten.

"When was that, honey?"

"Hmm." She put a finger to her chin and looked off. "When the other nanny was still here."

Faith's heart swelled. "Oh, my goodness, did you tell your Sunday school teacher about asking Jesus to forgive your sins that day?"

Miriam shook her head.

"What about your grandma—or your Aunt Cristina?"

"Nope, I jus' kep' the secret right here." She put a hand over her heart. "Until I tol' you just now."

Faith's own heart nearly melted. "Oh, sweetheart." Faith couldn't help it. Dirty hands and all, she drew the child into an embrace, clutching her close to her chest. Tears formed at the corners of her eyes. *Oh, the precious faith of a child!* After a moment, she held Miriam at arm's length. "I am so proud of you for making that decision—and then for sharing it with me. Would you mind if I tell your brothers and sister tonight at bedtime?"

She shrugged. "I guess. I mean, it ain't a secret anymore."

Faith laughed, her heart as light as a duck's feather, and she gave the child another tight squeeze. "You know what we should do this very minute?" she said.

"No. What?"

"We should go swing. I'll push you higher than you've ever gone before.

"You will?"

"Try me."

They jumped up and, hand in hand, ran to the giant rope swing.

Joey arrived in Cincinnati later that afternoon. Major James Dieters, his commanding officer, had wired a ticket and sent word that, upon his arrival there, he was to board a train to Marietta, Georgia. However, since the train to Marietta wasn't departing for another two hours, he found himself with time on his hands, so he decided to go in search of a restaurant for a bite to eat. He was in for a long train ride, so he told himself he might as well head out on a full stomach.

He found a diner and seated himself at the nearest table. Almost immediately, a fellow at the next table struck up a conversation with him. He'd been feeling somewhat low, if not lonesome, so he welcomed the chance to talk and hopefully get his mind off himself. "Where you headed, soldier?" the man asked.

"I got my orders to go to Marietta."

"Hm. Atlanta area, eh? You think the Union's plannin' to capture the city?"

"I'm sure that's the plan."

"How much longer you got?"

"I enlisted in September of sixty-one, but I believe my mustering out date is in mid-October."

The fellow wagged his head and took a swig of coffee. The waitress placed a tall glass of water in front of him, then took his order for a cup of chicken broth, loin of lamb, a baked potato, and some French peas.

"Who you stationed with?" the fellow asked after she left. Joey didn't mind the chatter, as it made time pass faster. "I'm with the Ohio Twenty-Seventh Infantry. When I left, Sherman was in the process of concentrating his armies along the Western and Atlantic Railroad. I left in the middle of a skirmish at Gilgal Church along Mud Creek."

"Ah, then you left at a good time," the man said with a hearty laugh. "I served with New York's One-Hundred-Twenty-Ninth Division. Mustered out three months ago. Never so glad to have made it home."

"Good for you." He hadn't realized he'd been chatting with a veteran. He relaxed and welcomed further conversation. The fellow talked about some of the battles in which he'd fought then asked Joey where he'd been, so he gave a few details.

"From what I'm told, Union forces pushed the Rebs back to a new line on Kennesaw Mountain just outside Marietta," the fellow said. "I wouldn't doubt there'll be another engagement. I also heard several hundred new recruits just joined forces with your company."

"How'd you hear that if you're discharged?"

"I got some friends servin' under Sherman."

Hearing about new recruits was welcome news. "Have there been any recent major conflicts that you may have heard about?"

"Not since the two sieges in Petersburg. Pfff. Those were complete failures," the man said.

"You're not kidding. Still, I'm not too concerned. Confederates have far less victories than us, and I doubt it'll take much more for them to surrender."

"I sure hope you're right, but about the time I think this rotten war is coming to an end, something like Petersburg happens, and I lose my confidence."

Joey sniffed and gave a little laugh. "Yeah, the trick is not to grow too overconfident."

Fast as a bullet, the woman returned with his food order, so the fellow gave Joey a nod. "I'll let you enjoy your meal now, soldier."

"Thanks. Nice talking to you."

"Likewise."

23

"W"e don't usually eat cake unless it's Christmas or some-body's birthday—or some other reason to celebrate," said Franklin, gobbling his generous slice. "This is good."

"I'm glad you're enjoying it," Faith said. "I just thought it would be nice to bake a cake for a change. I don't eat it often either."

"There ain't no occasion—except Daddy's gone, and that's no reason to celebrate," said Isaac, suddenly glum-faced. He'd said very little over supper, but he certainly didn't waste any time wolfing down his beef ribs, stewed tomatoes and peas, and mashed potatoes. On top of that, he'd just finished devouring his cake.

"I certainly agree with that, but cake does a body good, especially when it's lonesome."

"I s'pose," said Beth.

"I—I gots a good reason to celebrate," said Miriam in a tiny voice.

Faith held her breath. All eyes turned to their little sister as their bodies quieted. "What is it?" asked Franklin.

"Yeah, what is it, Miriam?" Beth asked.

"I wasn't goin' t' tell y' till bedtime, but I'll tell y' now. I asked Jesus in my heart when I was in Sunday school, and I tol' Faith about it today—and now I'm tellin' you."

A hush fell over the room as they all stared wide-eyed at their baby sister.

"That *is* good news, isn't it?" asked Faith.

"I did that once, asked Jesus into my heart," said Beth. "But I don't think it stuck."

"Of course it stuck, Beth—if you were sincere in your decision."

Beth squinted and wrinkled her brow. "I never felt any different though."

"Becoming a Christian is not about a *feeling* as much as it's about *faith*. Romans chapter ten, verse thirteen, tells us, '*For whosoever shall call upon the name of the Lord shall be saved.*' It's really no more difficult than that, except that when you pray, you must pray in faith, believing that Jesus hears you and is in that very moment cleansing you from the inside out. You also must be sorry for your sin and want to turn away from it." She looked down at Miriam. "And that's exactly what your little sister wanted to do that day in Sunday school. She wanted to turn from her sin."

For a change, there wasn't a single snide remark made around the table. Faith kept holding her breath and waiting for it, but when it didn't come, she softly exhaled and gave her hands a single clap. "So, what say we all celebrate with Miriam by going outside on this lovely night and playing a few games?"

"Games?" asked Isaac, turning his chin a tad and throwing her a suspicious glance. "Frankie and me don't play baby games."

"I bet I know a number of games that aren't too babyish."

"Like what?" Isaac challenged.

"Oh, let's see. There's Statue Tag; Dodge That Ball; Run, Run, as Fast as You Can; Muffin Man; Hide and Seek; Come Over, Red Rover; Don't Wake the Tiger... Want me to keep going?"

"What's Don't Wake the Tiger?" asked Franklin, his blue eyes sparking with interest.

"Well, we'd have to go outside so I can show you."

"Okay, let's go," said Miriam, leaping up from her chair. The others followed suit.

"Wait. Just. A. Minute. First, I want you to grab your plates and silverware, along with one other dish from the table. Carry them out to the kitchen and set them on the butcher block. We can rinse, wash, and dry later. Usually, I like to get all the dishes washed and put away directly after a meal, but we can make an exception today."

Everyone dutifully acquiesced, then, one by one, filed into the kitchen, set down their dishes—and then made a mad dash for the great outdoors.

Outside, they all gathered in the shade of the big oak tree with the rope swing, and Faith explained the game Don't Wake the Tiger. "One person is the tiger, who is sleeping, and everyone else runs around teasing him and trying to get him to rouse. You never know when the tiger might awaken, so you best beware! If the tiger jumps up and touches you, then *you* must be the tiger."

They jumped into the game with much enthusiasm, and Faith found herself entering in with a full amount of joy herself. It was wonderful to hear their laughter. For the moment, they all forgot about Joey not being there.

After that game, they played Statue Tag and Red Rover, followed by Hide and Seek. They ended up playing Hop-Along Tag, whereby everyone had to hop on one leg in an attempt to run away from whomever was "it." There'd been merriment and plenty of cackles, lots of falling down and getting back up, and even a couple of tears when Miriam skinned her knee. Overall, the after-supper games had been exactly what everyone needed, and when added to Miriam's announcement about asking Jesus into her heart, it made things all the more perfect.

Out of breath and dripping with sweat, Faith said, "Come on, let's go sit down for a bit."

"Okay," said Miriam. "But only for a minute 'cause sitting is boring."

They all made their way back to the big oak tree and plunked down in the shade. The boys stuck their legs straight out, their dusty dungarees stained and showing signs of wear. The girls spread out their skirts; Miriam's cotton plaid dress that went just past her knees showed a multitude of dirt and stains, while Beth's longer cotton floral dress with puffy sleeves fared only a little better.

"Where do you suppose Daddy is now?" Beth asked, eyes on the hole Miriam had started to dig.

"I've been wondering the same thing," Faith answered. "All I know is he received word by way of a telegram at daybreak this morning that he's to go to a place called Marietta, Georgia. His first stop will be Cincinnati, but whether he'll stay there for the night or move on, I'm not sure. His last assignment was in the Atlanta area, and I don't think Marietta's far from there. Sometimes it can take several weeks for the army to capture a specific area."

"Is he ridin' on a train?" Miriam asked, glancing up from her digging. She swiped at her hair and put a large smear of dirt across her forehead.

"Yes, honey. I believe he'll be taking the train all the way to his destination. However, it might not be the same train the whole distance."

"I never rode on a train before," she said. "Have you?"

"I've ridden a train a few times, but not overly much. I had to ride a train to arrive in Lebanon."

"Do you think Daddy misses us?" Beth asked.

"I am certain he does, especially now that his army service is nearing its end. I imagine he's thinking about the fact that next time he comes back, he'll be home to stay."

"Of course, you won't be here," Beth said with about as blunt a tone as one could ever make.

"Well—I—"

"What does *that* mean?" Miriam asked in a loud whine. "Why wouldn't Faith be here?"

"Don't you remember, dodo bird?" said Isaac. "Daddy tol' us he pro'ly wouldn't stay married. Faith's ar' nanny."

Miriam started tearing up. "I f-forgot." Faith wished Joey hadn't divulged that detail to the children. *Did they really need to know it? And what of the vows the judge had told them they should try to keep?*

"Don't call your little sister a dodo bird, Isaac. That's not nice."

"Are you leavin' as soon as Daddy gets home?" Beth asked.

"I don't know—how things will play out. It might be I'll stay awhile. It will depend on what your daddy says."

"Why? Don't you get a say in it?" asked Franklin.

"I—I suppose, but it's not for any of you to worry about now."

"I ain't worried," said Beth. "If you stay, you stay. If you don't, you don't. Doesn't bother me one way or the other."

Faith studied the eight-year-old. She wore a tough exterior that made it hard to determine what lay underneath. *Had she been hurt by nannies always coming and going, not to mention her own father and the loss of her mother? Was she too afraid to open up to another soul lest she suffer one more disappointment?*

Miriam leaned into Faith, so Faith stretched an arm around her and brought her closer.

"Let's spend the rest of the day thinking nothing but happy thoughts," Faith muttered to anyone who would listen, her chin resting atop Miriam's head.

"That's hard to do when Daddy's not here," said Franklin.

"Indeed it is," said Faith.

"I'm thirsty," said Beth.

"Shall we go get a cold drink from the well?" Faith asked.

Everyone agreed at once and scrambled to their feet. "Race y'!" Faith yelled, setting off at a run. The boys overtook her, and then so did Beth. Faith slowed so that Miriam could outrun her, and they all arrived breathless and giggly. Beth went into the house and returned shortly with several tin mugs, handles hooked over her fingers, and passed them around. "Thank you, Beth," Faith told her with a smile, but the girl only shrugged in reply. They filled their cups with fresh water and drank till they were satisfied.

Franklin tugged on Faith's sleeve. "What do me and Isaac win for comin' in first in the race?"

She'd almost forgotten about the little footrace. She thought a minute. "Hmm. What *do* you win?" In an instant, she tossed a cupful of water at both of them. "How's that?"

"Hey!" Although she'd barely sprinkled them, that was cause for "war" in the boys' minds, and so the water battle began—with lots more squeals and even more laughter. When it was all said and done, they were soaked to the skin, but at least they were all refreshed.

"Hey," said Franklin, "let's go down to the creek for a swim!"

"Yes, let's!" shouted Isaac.

"Me too!" said Miriam.

"All right, let's do it, and this time, I'll beat you there!" said Faith, setting off ahead of the rest, down the hillside, around a small bend, and to the creek that ran through Fuller property.

They played for nearly an hour, the boys running upstream to see if they could catch a turtle—or anything moving, for that matter—and the girls collecting pretty stones, as was their want. Exhausted, Faith lay herself down on the grassy bank and thought about Joey, missing his smile and his friendly chatter. Of course, with that came the memory of his kiss earlier that morning and the questions surrounding it. *Had he kissed her for one reason only—because the one he'd given her on their wedding day was lacking? Or had he kissed her because he felt something for her that went beyond friendship? Did he want her to remember it over the course of his absence?* Her heart longed for more of him, and yet, the notion that the next time she saw him might coincide with her having to say goodbye gave her pause. *Dare she lose her heart to him? Or was it already too late?*

She closed her eyes for just the briefest moment and allowed her mind to wander. Soon, the faintest rustling sound had her opening her eyes. There, not more than two inches from her nose, was the frolicking tongue of some hideous reptile. She saw its eyes too, which set her body in motion. In less time than it would take a squirrel to scamper up a tree, she was on her feet, screaming, leaping around, and flapping her arms. There stood Isaac holding a snake and squawking with laughter, Franklin at his side.

She pointed her finger at both boys. "You get that—awful—slimy thing out of here this instant, Isaac Fuller. What is your middle name anyway?"

"It's Allen," offered Franklin.

"Thank you." She shook her finger at Isaac. "Put that thing back where you got it, Isaac Allen Fuller, or I'll—I'll withhold all your meals for the next week and give you bread and water instead! You hear me!?" Even she couldn't quite believe the pitch of her own voice. The girls came running, their eyes huge at the sight of the snake, and they positioned themselves behind Faith, Miriam clinging to her skirts.

Isaac stood there as calm as could be. "It's not slimy for your information. It's warm and smooth. Wanna feel?" He took a step toward her.

She stepped back. "No! Just—put—it—back—in—the—creek!" she shrieked.

"We didn't find him in the creek. He was on the bank."

Faith took in a deep breath. *The Lord is my shepherd; I shall not want....* Thinking of Psalm 23 stilled her fear, and she swallowed hard. "That's. Simply. Lovely." Two calming breaths. "Now, say goodbye to it and put it back."

Both boys shook their heads and laughed, then turned and headed back upstream, the snake dangling between them.

"Phew! Well"—she turned to look at the girls huddled behind her—"that was interesting. I guess you just witnessed me at my finest."

The hint of a smile played around Beth's pretty mouth. "I guess we did." Gazing out at the boys, she scratched her head and added, "And I guess Isaac and Frankie found y'r weak spot."

Faith dropped her shoulders. "Aaargh!"

24

Before dawn's first light, Faith awoke to the tiniest stirring of a brand new day. She lay there, covers up to her chin, enjoying the chill in the air, knowing it wouldn't last. She thought about the day before, Joey's morning departure, the children's grumpy spirits, her successful attempt to bring them out of their doldrums...and the incident with the snake. In all, the day ended well, with a bedtime story, everyone gathering in Beth's room for a change, then Bible reading, and finally a nighttime prayer in which they thanked God for His blessings, for Miriam's confession of faith, and for protection over their daddy. Afterward, they each walked off to their rooms with a simple goodnight, except for Miriam, who'd insisted on being tucked in. Contentment settled in around Faith. *Had she managed to put a tiny crack in the children's tough façade? Was it too much to hope that they might all be friends in time?* "Thank You for this day, Lord," she whispered into the dark. "May it be a day of honoring You, but also one of building friendships with the children."

Slowly, she pushed the covers off, lit the lantern closest to her bed, and then walked across to her bureau to open her drawers in search of fresh underclothes and a lightweight cotton dress.

Once dressed, she glanced around her husband's bedroom, almost sensing his presence as she studied each of his possessions—his chest of drawers, his dresser with a vanity and mirror where surely Sarah Beth once sat to brush out her long locks, the serene painting on the wall depicting a lovely pasture, and the floral pitcher and bowl resting on a wooden table. The fireplace mantel held a few trinkets, one of which was a tintype of Sarah Beth. Faith had come across it while dusting the day before and thought then how much her memory filled the house. *If Faith were to end up staying here after Joey's return, would all these mementos of her also stay?* She gave her head a little shake. Such a foolish thought to entertain so early in their marriage. She took up her Bible and sat in the rocking chair to start her morning devotions. She'd soon have to go downstairs, get breakfast ready for the children, and then sit down to write a list of daily chores, including some chores for them. She prayed that hearing that they'd been assigned regular tasks would not undo the fragile friendships she was building with them.

Joey debarked the train at Marietta at exactly four o'clock the next afternoon. It had been a long trip with many stops, starts, and layovers, but at last he'd arrived and could finally stretch his tall, tired body.

"Captain Fuller, is it really you?"

He turned at the voice of Private Lester Harrison. The man shoved his shoes together with a click and gave a formal salute.

"At ease, Private. How are you?"

"Good, sir. How was your trip?"

Joey rolled his aching shoulders. "Long, I'm afraid, but I made it in one piece."

"That's good. Glad to hear it. Are you hungry, sir? There is some grub at the canteen."

"No, Private, but thank you. I ate a bun and a turkey leg at our last train stop."

"I see. Well, the Major is waiting for you in his tent whenever you're ready to see him. Would you like me to take your gear and set it somewhere? I could set up your tent for you if you like."

"That's mighty nice of you, Private. I just might take you up on that. You'll find my tent in this brown duffle here."

"Yes, sir. I'll get right to it. Is that spot over there by that pine tree a good one? It's a bit removed, providing you a measure of privacy."

He took a gander at the area and laughed at the irony. "Home, sweet home."

"Yes, sir, that it is."

He left the friendly fella and went on his way.

He found Major Dieters sitting on a folding chair outside his tent with five other officers. The major rose to his feet. "Joseph, you're back. Good to see you, Captain."

Joey saluted his superior officer, who returned the gesture and then drew up a chair for him. "Here, sit," he instructed as he himself took his seat again. "I'll catch you up on the latest goings on. You want some coffee?"

Joey put out a hand to the major's attendant standing nearby who stood ready with a tin mug. "No, thanks."

"All right then, I'll get right to business." He paused a minute and looked Joey square in the face. "I s'pose I ought to ask you how your leave went, but that can wait."

The major never had been overgenerous with niceties. Joey didn't expect him to start now.

"No worries, Major. Plenty of time for that later."

"All right then. Let's talk strategy. Johnston's got his men on a line centered on Kennesaw Mountain, but it's a thin line from what Major General Sherman says. Sherman's convinced they're positioning themselves for attack, so we must be ready. Our numbers are better, so I'm sure they'll be strategic if and when they move on us. The plan is to make a frontal attack on the mountain within a couple of days—before they move on us. I'm still waiting on further orders as to when, but as of now, tell your men to prepare for an artillery bombardment. In the meantime, reinforce your stockades and prepare for battle. Everybody clear?"

"Yes, sir," the men said in unison, some of them nodding, Joey included, even though he couldn't say he'd worked up their same level of enthusiasm. In fact, he sat there in somewhat of a fog. *What? Had he just been given his assignment?* He tried to recall each word.

"You all right, Captain?" Dieters asked after the other men dispersed. "Y're lookin' a bit lost."

Joey snapped out of it. "No, sir, not lost. I'm fine. Just fine." He quickly stood and brushed off his lapel, then saluted.

"At ease, Captain," Dieters said. "How'd that furlough go? You get everything squared away on the home front?"

"Yes, sir. I got married, sir."

The major's eyes bulged. "Married, you say?"

"Yes, sir."

"Joseph, I had no idea you had a wife waiting for you back home. Why didn't you tell me that before you left?"

"I didn't know I had a wife back home either." Joey gave a slight chortle.

Dieters frowned. "What in tarnation? You're talkin' in circles."

"I suppose I am. All right then. I had need for another nanny for my herd of youngsters, so rather than hire a sixth nanny, I married one."

The major, a rather short, stout man, had to look up to make his expression known. It showed a tremendous amount of confusion. He shook his head slowly. "You married someone you didn't know?"

Joey nodded. "Yes, that about sums it up." He went on to explain his plight and the reasoning behind marrying as opposed to hiring.

"I s'pose that makes a bit more sense now that you explain it to me. I wish you the best, Joey. And your wife, of course. With a little luck, maybe you'll find yourselves compatible with each other and you'll manage to stay together. It takes a mighty strong woman to keep the home fires burning whilst her husband's off fighting."

"Yes, it does."

"I'm grateful for my own faithful wife, Lorene."

"I don't believe you've ever mentioned her before, sir."

Dieters removed his hat, scratched his head for a moment, and then put it back on. "She's a fine woman."

"You have children?" Joey asked.

"Yes, two, but they're grown and married. They'll be starting their own families one of these days."

It was the first personal talk Joey had had with Dieters, and it surprised him when the major opened up. He was always so direct and no-nonsense. As if also bewildered by their little conversation, Dieters straightened his shoulders and sniffed. "Well, then, you have any questions about your orders?"

"No, I think I'm prepared, thank you."

"That's good then. Remember, you're not home anymore. You got a company depending on you for instruction and survival."

He stood pin-straight. "Yes, sir!"

"For the moment, you gotta forget you're married, forget that new wife's off watchin' after your rascal children, and keep your mind on this war."

"I understand."

"All right then. Dismissed."

Joey set off, wondering about that brief glimpse into Dieters' private life…and wondering if Private Harrison had managed to set up his tent yet. If so, Joey was going to crawl inside and write his first letter to Faith. He could talk to the men later.

⌒

The next several days went off as smoothly as a new wife and stepmother could hope for, considering most days Faith hadn't a clue what she was doing. Over the last week, she'd written two letters to Joey, come up with a daily schedule, and tried out some new recipes on the children, a few of which ended up in the farm dog's dish and in the pig's sty. Fortunately, they had heartily gobbled up most of her meals.

Monday was wash day. Tuesday was the day for baking loaves of bread and pies as well as shaking rugs, dusting, sweeping floors, and polishing silver. Wednesday called for odd jobs like sewing, mending, darning socks, and a trip into town with all four children, unless Isaac and Franklin chose to work with their Uncle Jesse instead. Thursday meant tending the garden, pulling weeds, and filling pails from the well pump to water the vegetables if it hadn't rained for a few days. They were already beginning to see the fruits of their labor. Friday was visiting day—meaning driving the rig over to the main house to see the children's grandmother and carry out odd jobs for her, and then driving over to see Cristina and her children, allowing the children time to play with their cousins. Saturday was set aside for Sunday preparation, choosing what to make for the Sunday meal, and getting everyone's clothes ready. Saturdays were also bath nights, much to the children's chagrin, unless it meant bathing at the creek on a hot night. It was also a day of recreation, playing ball, games, fishing, or doing whatever else the children had in mind. Finally, Sunday was a day of rest, albeit after completing the typical farm chores.

Every day included collecting eggs and feeding the chickens, pigs, goats, and horses in the barn. Wendel and Jobe oversaw all of the farm tasks, but Faith enjoyed involving the children as much as possible, regardless of their fussing and complaining every time she assigned them some random duty. She could just count on it.

She'd been delighted when her trunk from Columbus had finally arrived. Beth and Miriam hung out in her bedroom and watched her unpack it, Miriam especially eager to help her decide where to place everything, Beth mildly interested, but still hanging back. For some reason, she simply did not wish to like Faith, and that was fine by her as long as she continued to see subtle signs of growth in the girl. As for the boys, neither appeared to take much interest in their stepmother, though she wondered if it wasn't just pretense. They didn't *want* to like her, so they made every effort not to, even when she did all she could think to do to make life pleasant for them.

One Saturday, Faith and the girls were out in the garden, checking on the tomatoes and other vegetables. The boys were out in the barn with the hired hands to help them stack hay, something Faith hadn't even asked them to do. Every day, she waited for some sort of prank, knowing it was sure to come.

Wheels of an approaching wagon stirred up dust, as did its horses' hooves. "It's Uncle Jesse," Beth declared, running off to meet him. Miriam followed on her heels, squealing with delight at the sight of him. They surely loved both of their uncles, but Jesse seemed to be the most playful of the three brothers, probably because he had no children of his own on which to dote.

"Whoa!" he called out, jumping down from his rig and looping the reins over the hitching post in front of the house. He held out his arms to both girls and folded them close when they reached him.

"Did you go to town?" Miriam asked stepping back to gaze up in his face.

He laughed. "How did you know?"

"'Cause you gots supplies on the wagon."

"Yes, I do."

"Did you bring us something?"

Another good laugh came out. "Well, I just might have."

"What? What did you bring us?"

He reached deep into his pants pocket and withdrew a handful of candy sticks. "Here, but share with your brothers."

By now, Faith had reached the house. "Hello, Jesse. Girls, what do you say to your uncle?"

"Thank you," they said in unison.

"We'll go give the boys their candy," Beth announced. "Come on, Miriam."

"Don't spoil your supper," Faith called to their backs as they ran as fast as jackrabbits, their skirts flaring and braids flying.

Both adults watched until they disappeared through the big open barn doors. Faith then turned her attention to Jesse with a smile. "You made their day! Do you always do that? Bring them something from town?"

He grinned. "Absolutely. It's an uncle's duty. Do the same for Jack's kids. I'll have to drive over there after this."

"Oh, my goodness. You do like to keep them spoiled."

"Naw, no such thing. I just love them, that's all."

She wondered if he'd ever marry and have children of his own, but she dared not ask such a personal question.

"How are you managing the household?"

"I think I'm doing all right. At least I haven't threatened to leave yet."

"So the children have been behaving?"

"For the most part."

He issued her a slanted expression. "Let me know if you need a male's influence. I can deliver a lecture if need be."

"And ruin your reputation as the fun uncle?"

Jesse laughed. "Well, I suppose that would tarnish my good name to a degree. But seriously, let me know if you need my input."

"Thank you. I appreciate that. I'll try to keep things under control."

"I think the marriage certificate was an extra measure of reassurance for my brother. He hoped it'd serve as a deterrent for you to consider leaving. Plus, I understand he's giving you a financial settlement at the end."

She didn't like to think about the end. "That is the plan."

"Oh! Speaking of Joey, I almost forgot." He fished into a different pocket than the one that had held the candy sticks. "I stopped in the post office today and the postal clerk handed me this letter for you."

Her heart jumped at the notion that Joey had written to her, and she could hardly wait for Jesse to leave so she could tear into the letter. Still, she managed nonchalance and slipped the missive into her apron pocket after quickly perusing her husband's neat handwriting. "Thank you so much for delivering it. The children and I went into town on Wednesday. I received a couple of letters from my mother and sister, but I knew it would be too soon to hear anything from Joey."

Jesse gave her a wink. "Ma always insists I visit the post office when I go into town, usually on Tuesdays and Saturdays. I'll be happy to check for you every time I go. I can also stop by on my way to town to deliver any letters you might want to go out."

"That would be wonderful, although I don't wish to be a bother."

"You're no bother at all. Besides, Ma wants me to keep an eye on you. Even though we know that scoundrel who meant to do you harm is in jail, it's still a good idea to stay alert. You never can tell what he might have in mind to do. Fellows like him cannot be trusted. You do know where Joey's rifle is, don't you?"

"Yes, he made me aware. I hope never to have to use it though."

"I hope the same, but one cannot be too careful. Well, I best be getting back to work. I've got some supplies to unload and then a field to tend before nightfall. You take care now." He tipped his hat at her, unwound the reins from the hitching post, and fairly leaped into his rig like a deer. All three brothers had similar builds and features, but Jesse seemed to be the most wiry. To be sure, in her mind, Joey was the most handsome, although Cristina would probably disagree with that assessment.

She gave her brother-in-law a smile and wave and watched him head down the long drive. As soon as it seemed appropriate, she darted up the steps and into the house, closing the door behind her and hoping the children wouldn't come barreling inside. She made herself comfortable in a soft chair, then, using a great deal of restraint, she slowly removed the seal and unfolded the paper. She'd fully intended to rip into it, but soon thought better of it when realizing that she would want to keep his letters neatly stored in a box for future rereading.

Sitting back, she breathed deep and set to reading.

Dear Faith,

As you will have guessed by now, I have safely arrived at my camp just outside Marietta, Georgia. I will try never to bore you with any details of war—unless you wish to know, in which case you'll have to tell me. I don't want you or the children to fear for my safety, but I should say that war is a reality we all must face.

I fared just fine on my train ride here, but I will admit to feeling a bit lonely for my family after having spent two weeks at home with them.

I trust that you are doing alright with my busy children. Do not hesitate to dole out the punishments as needed. I am not opposed to the switch if it calls for that. I know they can be a troublesome lot when they all start to plotting. By the way, if by chance you allow them to read this, they will see firsthand that I mean business about their behavior.

Would you believe me if I told you that I have been thinking about you? You are after all my wife. I trust you haven't forgotten our vows to each other. Of course, our time together will be limited. I'm sure you must be glad about that.

Well, someone has come calling at my tent, so I must close for now. Please write to me as often as you can—a couple times a week if possible. A man gets a trifle lonely out in the wilds. And now that I've admitted that to you, you must think me some kind of weakling.

My best to you.

Your temporary husband

Joey

P.S. Please tell my children that I love them very much and miss them even more. Also, you will be happy to know that I have not been able to get the reverend's sermon out of my mind. Yes, I have given quite a lot of thought to prayer and Bible reading and shall be reading my Bible before I go to sleep tonight.

Faith smiled to herself, then gently folded the letter and held it to her chest, knowing that she would read it several more times before finally tucking it away in a box. She would read it to the children before tucking them in for the night, too. Perhaps she would skip over the parts about the spanking and then hope that Isaac didn't ask to read the letter for himself.

So much to ponder about Joey's words. She could try to read between the lines and imagine that he meant to say he missed her as well, but she had no idea if he did, especially since he made no mention of their kiss. *Had he even thought about it?* And she could pretend that he meant to say he didn't wish for her to be his temporary wife, even though he'd clearly written it. Oh dear, she could work herself into a frenzy if she thought too long and hard about it. Best to stick it in her pocket and try to put it out of her mind for now.

She stood and walked through the kitchen to the back door. She would spend a bit more time in the garden, then go back in the house and start supper. *What could she make tonight that would please everyone?* She didn't want another meal going to the animals.

25

From one end to the other, Stuart paced the rotten cell Sheriff Mumford had thrown him into after sarcastically telling him to make himself at home. He shared it with one other fellow, someone who'd robbed a bank in another town but lived in Warren County. He didn't know the fellow's name, nor did he wish to, only that he went by Stubbs, probably because he was missing a couple of fingers at the middle knuckle. He hadn't asked him about it because he didn't care to know a single detail about him. Why they'd thrown him in the same cell with such a nasty person, he'd never know. *What had he done to deserve such maltreatment?* As crooks went, he didn't even come close to Stubbs' criminal category. *He'd robbed a bank, for Pete's sake!* All Stuart had done was help his wife to the other side, which took very little effort, and then he'd slapped Faith Haviland. *One tiny little slap. That's all it was!* He'd always operated a decent butcher shop and did a fair business. That ought to count for something. Sure, he'd cheated a few ancient, nearly blind, patrons by putting a heavy finger on the scale or not giving them their exact change, but those were minor issues. *Didn't every businessman do that from time to time?* He'd even taken some cash out of Mr. Somers' satchel once when he'd left it on the counter to run across the street to the shoe repair shop to drop off some boots. The old guy never mentioned a word about missing any money, and he'd continued to buy Stuart's meats.

As far as Stuart could see, nothing he'd done warranted his being cooped up with this smelly Stubbs character. He complained plenty to Mumford, but a lot of good it did. Mumford told him he was sitting there because he'd murdered Opal Porter then buried her on his cousin's property. "With my cousin's help!" Stuart pointed out. *Looked like Leon wouldn't be spending one second in jail, though, probably due to his aiding them in finding him.* "It happened some twenty years ago anyway, Sheriff. That ought to count for something."

"Sorry, Porter. Ain't no statute of limitations on murder," the sheriff said.

"At least put me in a different cell!" he yelled to Mumford's back just before the big steel door slammed shut.

"You ain't givin' up, are y', loser?" said Stubbs, looking up from his reclined position on his cot. "I'll be gettin' out o' here long before you. Bank robbery ain't nothin' compared to murder."

"Shut up!" Stuart groused. "What do you know about anything?"

"Apparently more than you. This was my first offense. I'd lost my job and needed to feed my family. And I only took from the clerk what money I thought I'd need to get me through the month. I learned my lesson too. Won't never be doing that again. Now, why don't you quit pacing and find y'rself somethin' to do?"

Stuart spat on the floor. Judging by the look of the stained concrete, a hundred other jailbirds had done the same thing before him.

His stomach burned with a mixture of hunger and panic. He couldn't eat because of his nerves, and he couldn't sleep due to his outright fear. *Was he going to live out the rest of his days in jail? How would he manage? How would he live?* "You need God, Stuart." His cousin's words came back to haunt him. He lifted his upper lip and sneered. *I don't need God. I need to get out of here.* But he had a sinking feeling he might never see the light of day again.

After days of plotting and conferring, General Sherman drew up an attack order with Union Generals McPherson and Thomas to break through Confederate lines at select points on Kennesaw Mountain. Joey had known it was coming, as he'd been meeting daily with his superiors at Major Dieters' quarters. Every day, a new wire concerning maneuvers came in, and army captains were instructed to keep their companies well informed.

He'd propped his Bible on his chest, his head reclining on his plumped up backpack. He'd been reading from the book of John and found that even though he'd read it many times in the past, the last time had been so long ago that it all felt new to him. He attempted a simple, silent prayer that went something like this: *I'm a failure when it comes to spiritual matters, Lord, but I trust You'll lend me an ear anyway. I've wandered away from You over the years, blamed You for lots of things, and made excuse after excuse to not serve You. I'm still not convinced about a lot of things, but I'm willing to start looking at things differently if You'll guide me along the way. I have no idea even where to start, so I'll just start with these three words: Help me, Lord.* And that was the extent of it, having no idea if God had heard or even cared.

Joey had received two letters from Faith, both of which he'd pored over whenever he had the chance, but his return letters were sparse, and he worried that she'd think he'd forgotten about her and the children. First chance he got, he vowed to sit down and scrawl a note to her, no matter how brief—just to reassure her that he hadn't stopped thinking about home. He might even confess that he'd thought a great deal about that day in the courthouse and the vows they'd recited, along with the judge's suggestion that they do all they could to adhere to them. But reading her letters gave him no indication she wanted to remain in the house when he returned, and she never mentioned the last kisses they'd shared. *Had she forgotten all about them?*

One thing in Faith's second letter that had struck an emotional chord with him was when she'd mentioned Miriam's decision to invite Jesus into her heart. His eyes had teared up while reading it, and he'd had to swipe at them to avoid blurring the words on the paper. Perhaps that news was what had spurred him on in his Bible reading. *If a five-year-old could have enough faith to believe in a saving, loving, and forgiving God, why couldn't he?*

The six o'clock drum roll sounded, alerting everyone to an early start to another day. He'd been lying awake, awaiting the call, dreading the sound, and knowing he must prepare himself for battle. That meant laying aside all thoughts that did not pertain to his duty, putting on his army gear with single-mindedness, carrying himself with confidence, and delivering orders with authority and a level of brashness so that none would cower under pressure. War had little room for cowards, even though they walked among each other every day disguised as brave, triumphant warriors. It wouldn't even be human not to experience fear. Fear usually kept people alive.

He dressed in a hurry, rolled up his bedding, packed his gear, and stepped out of his tent. A few fires were already burning, and the smells of coffee and some sort of venison penetrated the air.

"Coffee, sir?" came a distant voice. He turned at the sound, then gave a wave to Private Reginald Dunkin, one of the fellows in his company. "It's going to be a busy day from what I hear. May as well start it out right with a stiff cup of brew."

"I don't mind if I do, Private. Thanks."

He approached the young fellow and sat himself down on a log by the fire. He took the mug in hand and downed a hot, bitter swallow. "Ahh. That'll wake a soul up."

They sat in silence, each sipping his coffee. Soldiers all around them were moving about, some folding up tents, others just milling and carrying on quiet conversation. Tents almost always came down in the morning—with the exception of the last several days, when they'd stayed in one place. Only time would tell what today would hold. Moods were difficult to read this morning, but generally, men were quiet when they were introspective, or even a bit morose. They knew what was coming, and they were busy mentally preparing themselves. It was just what you did when you knew a battle was nigh.

Joey finished his coffee, thanked Reggie, and made for Dieters' tent, knowing he'd be pacing and wanting to get matters underway. Joey wanted to make sure he had every detail in place so he'd not be responsible for leading anyone astray.

As expected, the stout major had already worked up a sweat from walking in a large circle outside his tent. Several other officers had arrived and continued to arrive, descending upon Dieters' quarters until there was a good-sized gathering, all seeming eager to get on with their duties. They just needed clear direction and then the go-ahead. This morning, there were no casual offers of coffee or genial conversation, only formal salutes. The atmosphere around the major's campfire was somber and tense.

"All right then," Dieters at last began in a loud, clear voice. "A rider came to my tent at four-thirty this morning with a message that Major McPherson, who holds the Union's left, is going to open fire on Kennesaw Mountain at precisely eight o'clock. Major General Thomas, who holds the center, will also open fire. Word is at least fifty cannon shots will sound. Our duty will be to prevent Rebel forces from shifting positions to Little Kennesaw or Pigeon Hill, where the terrain is denser. It will be quite an ascent, and the brush is thick, so warn your men to gather all their strength. It could be a very tough fight. Still, we shall remain confident and strong and not grow weary in giving it our best effort. I'll sound a single rifle shot when it's time to proceed, so keep alert. When you hear it, instruct your troops to advance."

"Yes, sir!" came the rousing agreement. Not even one question followed. Of course, they'd been discussing maneuvers and then putting them to practice on the open fields for days so everyone already had a good idea of how things would go. It was just a matter of receiving the final word.

The morning seemed to drag—until seven-thirty arrived. Soldiers suited up, checked their rifles and ammunition, and got into formation. Joey walked up and down the line to inspect each one from head to toe. With all sixty plus members of his company, he made eye contact and saluted, then moved onto the next. It was the same with every company and their battalion leaders. All told, there had to be at least one-hundred-thousand Union soldiers ready for combat today. But questions remained. How many Confederates stood ready and waiting on Kennesaw Mountain? What sort of artillery did they have? And how prepared were they for battle?

Just as expected, the first cannon fire sounded at eight o'clock, shaking the ground beneath everyone's feet in earthquake-like waves. Regiments held their positions, and then another round of cannon fire blasted the air, nearly splitting eardrums with its booming timbre. On the mountain, great explosions of smoke ripped through the atmosphere, blotting out the blue sky and creating enormous gray billows. Union soldiers stood at attention awaiting orders to advance, some on foot, some on anxious mounts. The air smelled of horse dung, smoke, and sweat. When all cannon fire finally ceased, there came a deafening silence—and then a single rifle shot. "Forward, men!" Joey shouted. All up and down the line, orders from other commanding officers rang out, and soon the sound of pounding soldiers' boots and the horses' mighty hooves hitting the ground in marching rhythm filled the air, along with shouts and whoops like thunder. The fight was on!

They tromped through brush so thick that some men could barely see those ahead. Some became so tangled in the mesh of weeds and thicket that they fell and then struggled to get up. For what seemed like hours, gunfire from both sides rang out. To Joey's great dismay, he had to step over several fallen men, some of whom had already lost their battle, and others barely hanging on. He bent over several and encouraged them to keep fighting, assuring them that help would soon come. True to his words, medics trained only for tending the wounded crawled low to reach casualties. It was one of the worst encounters Joey could remember having with the Rebs. He did not falter, but shouted encouragement; he did not stumble, but pressed forward, lending a hand when someone staggered or covering for someone who moved ahead of him in combat. There seemed to be no relief from the Confederates' punishing musketry, as gunfire whistled past his head, and he prayed, *God, help me—God help us all!* The firing went on for hours with little advancement on the part of the Union. Some managed to cut through the brush with machetes, leading the way for others to follow, but most became stuck in the mire, so that avoiding gunfire became their biggest challenge.

By eleven-thirty, commanders called a halt to the firing. Even though Union troops had shelled the enemy entrenchments for hours, took down several hundred Rebels and captured even more, it was not enough to call it a Union victory. The Confederates prevailed, surprising the men in blue with their strength and preventing them from advancing any further.

They had lost the battle, and while moods were gloomy, Joey didn't hear a single soldier complain that they'd given up too soon. Still, it was a loss, and no one liked losing. Tired and spent, Joey trudged down the bumpy slope with his squadron, his own spirits dry as tinder dust.

Would this war ever end?

26

Each day presented its own kind of challenge, none easier than the day before. No matter how hard she tried, Faith could not win over the three oldest children's affections, and they often tried to pit sweet little Miriam against her. The poor dear wanted her siblings' approval, but she also had no argument with Faith, so it put her in a tough position, one for which Faith would never fault her. Gone was the feeling of certainty that she could win their friendship. No, something in them had determined to make life miserable for her, and so they went out of their way to accomplish it. One day, she'd found a dead beetle in her soup; fortunately she had discovered it on her spoon whilst bringing it to her mouth. She couldn't pinpoint the culprit, but the boys had thought the whole thing terribly humorous. Rather than overreact, she'd dismissed it.

"Well, would you look at that," she'd said. "A beetle found its way into my soup bowl. I must have carried it in on my clothes while hanging the laundry." Of course, the boys' faces went long at that pronouncement because they hadn't gotten quite the attention they wanted. She'd merely carried her soup bowl to the back door, shuddering to herself as she did so, and pitched the remainder on the ground for the chickens to peck at.

While she was putting some folded clothes away in her room, having given each of the children their own pile to take to their rooms, a frog jumped out of her stack and landed on her bed. Startled, she screamed—but only briefly. Then she went into the hallway and hollered for Isaac.

"What?" he said, peeking out from his bedroom, Franklin at his side.

"Get down here immediately."

Isaac came willingly, then stood in the doorway, eyes big and as innocent-looking as a newborn foal.

She pointed at the green critter soiling her bed linens. "Take this—this thing—off my bed and put it outside."

"What is it?" he inquired, stepping inside.

"You know very well what it is. Now, pick it up and get it out of here." She carefully lifted the remainder of her clothes, skirts, tops, underthings, and stockings. "Is there another one in here?" she muttered.

He stepped up next to her, picked up the frog, and stuffed it into his trouser pocket. "Doesn't look like it. Hmm. I wonder how it got in here."

She stared wide-eyed at him, buttoned her lip, and pointed one finger at the door. It was all the instruction he needed to disappear into the hallway and glide down the stairs, his happy little footsteps echoing in her head.

Last week, she thought she would surprise them with vanilla custard for dessert, but just one spoonful was all it took for her to realize that someone had added no less than half a cup of salt to the custard she'd spent several minutes laboring over at the stove. Apparently, no one liked custard, or they wouldn't have ruined it. And she did note that none of them ate any, not even Miriam, who'd no doubt been warned not to taste it. At any rate, she'd said little, and in fact, blamed herself for her carelessness in mistaking the salt for sugar. "Silly me," she'd scoffed. "Well, next time I'll be more careful." And they'd commenced to cleaning up the supper dishes, making no bones about gawking at one another for the way their trick had backfired.

Yesterday had been the final straw when she'd lifted the lid off the can of lard in preparation for making pie crusts and discovered a pile of stinking worms at the top. This time, no one was in the house, so she had no faces to study. She growled to herself and mumbled over and over, "I will not give in, and I will not quit. I will not give in, and I will not quit."

She had chosen not to mention a solitary word about the worms in the lard, which she figured would irk the guilty party or parties even worse than if she'd lined them up for questioning, threatening their lives if they didn't confess. She figured silence was a better weapon than pointless shouts of anger. Then again, she could be wrong. This entire experience was new to her, and she hadn't a clue if she was doing any of it right.

June had come and gone, making way for a stifling July, the first several days dry and hot as a pone cake. To date, she'd written at least ten letters to Joey's three, and none of his missives contained much news even though she'd expressed interest in learning about his typical day. His only response to her request was that no two days were ever alike. He had told her that they were preparing a siege on Atlanta, but beyond that, he gave little information. Perhaps he didn't know, or maybe he wasn't allowed to reveal much in the way of combat detail. At any rate, the children missed him and looked forward to his letters. She figured that his absence only contributed to their ill behavior. The less he saw or knew about their antics, the more pranks they could pull. At least that was their theory. So far, she had not divulged anything to Joey about their tricks, and she wasn't sure how much good it would do anyway. *What could he possibly accomplish in the way of discipline stationed way out on some battlefield in Georgia? And what good would come from telling him? Didn't he have enough on his mind without having to worry about his children's behavior?* No, this was her battle to fight, and she was just determined enough to win.

The house was quiet since the children had gone to their Aunt Cristina's house to play with their cousins. Cristina had promised to return them in time for supper, which gave Faith the opportunity to visit her mother-in-law, something she'd only done once by herself since Joey left. Besides, she looked forward to the chance to leave the house without four complaining youngsters trailing behind, for even Miriam could be a little handful at times, especially with her siblings egging her on.

Much to her surprise, when she gave a little knock at Laura Fuller's front door, stepped inside, and called out a greeting, she found the woman sitting on the living room sofa, a cane leaned against it.

"Well, hello, dear," Laura exclaimed with a bright smile. "How wonderful to see you."

Faith had a difficult time closing her mouth. "Your wheelchair. You're—not sitting in it."

She clapped her hands together. "I know. Isn't it wonderful? Jesse drove me into town to see Doc Withers, and he removed my cast. He wanted to see how well my leg had healed, and since it's done so well, he decided not to put on a new cast. I can now walk with the use of this cane, but he's made me promise not to overdo it. Pfff." She flicked her wrist and laughed. "He doesn't know me very well. I've already taken a little walk out to the garden."

"I thought you were to have started with crutches."

"As did I, but he said the cane should serve me just as fine. He said the bone seems to have knitted back together remarkably well. Of course, I told him I'm sure the Lord had much to do with my healing."

"And to that I would say 'Amen!'"

"Enough about me." She patted the place next to her on the couch. "Come and sit by me so we can talk. Tell me how everything is going with the children. And by the way, where are they?"

"Cristina came to pick them up an hour or so ago. She plans to return them before supper. I thought their being gone would give me the perfect chance to pay you a visit."

"Well, isn't that sweet of you? I'm honored you chose to do that over stretching out on your bed for a nice afternoon nap. Heaven knows you deserve one after watching over my ruffian grandchildren."

"They haven't been so bad."

Laura tilted her face at Faith and gave a doubtful look. "Is that so? Why am I having a difficult time believing you?"

Was it that evident? "Well, they've been somewhat of a challenge, but I'm winning."

The doubtful scowl remained. "You can be honest with me, dear. I know my grandchildren well. They are a handful, but I've no doubt you will get a handle on them before Joseph's return. You are different from the others."

Faith's heart snagged. "I am? In what way?"

"Well, let me see. For one thing, you're younger than all the others were, so you naturally have a level of energy and patience that they lacked. You're loving, caring, and kindhearted, whereas the others treated their positions like mere jobs, lacking compassion and a natural love for children. My grandchildren sensed it and often told me stories, some that I wasn't sure whether to believe due to their ability to exaggerate, but since they all quit I'm prone to believe some of what they said was true. At any rate, I must tell you I haven't heard a single negative word from any of them about you, and I know Isaac would be the first to come running to me if you'd done or said anything contrary."

Faith released a sigh. "Well, I'm relieved to hear he hasn't done that yet."

"Have they been behaving?"

She hesitated to tell the whole truth. "I'll just say most of the time."

"Spare the rod, spoil the child. It's in the Bible," Laura said, lifting her chin.

"I'm well aware, but in their case, they need an entirely different approach."

"You're probably right. Lots of love, attention, and kindness is what they need, sprinkled with rules and boundaries, of course. I hope you're not too discouraged yet."

"What? No, I'm not even a little bit discouraged. Well, perhaps I'm a trifle, but not to the point of quitting like the nannies before me did. No, I would never do that."

Laura gave a full-out smile, and Faith couldn't help but notice her innate beauty. Her sons came by their handsome looks quite naturally. "I'm thrilled to hear that. Not that I ever thought you would."

They changed topics a few more times, and then somehow landed on one that Faith had been wanting to cover with Laura, the subject of Sarah Beth.

"Joey's told me a few things about her, but not much. I wonder if you could share a little."

Laura eased back in the sofa and smiled, lifting her face to the front window to gaze off for a bit. "She was a lovely woman," she said in a reverent whisper. "A caring wife and a doting mother. When she passed away, it took a terrible toll on Joseph and the children."

"It must have been dreadful. What else can you tell me?"

"Hmm, well, she was quite pretty, a fine cook I suppose, and, oh, she loved to read books. Oh my goodness, she could bury herself in a book and almost forget she had a family to tend."

"So that's why the big library collection."

"Yes, the library. She obtained many books from her grandparents in Europe. They shipped them over, then had them delivered by the wagonload. My, she had so much fun arranging them all according to author and in alphabetical order, though I'm not sure they've remained that way. Let's see, what else can I tell you? Oh! She enjoyed sewing, to a degree, and gardening, though neither of those things captured her fancy nearly as much as books did."

"Oh, I love to garden. Pulling weeds and watching lovely things grow is a favorite pastime for me. Of course, I enjoy reading as well, but gardening has my heart."

"Yes, I enjoy it as well."

"Tell me more."

"Well, Sarah Beth was friendly, yes, friendly, but in a rather reserved way. She was a fine Christian woman, although not overly outspoken about her faith."

"Oh, then the opposite of me," Faith said, her voice dropping.

"Yes, quite opposite—in most ways."

She felt her spirits fall.

"Not in a bad way, dear." She quickly covered Faith's hand with hers. "We wouldn't want you to be just like her."

"I know, but I had hoped there might be something about the two of us that would be similar so that Joey…" She let her words trail off.

"You think that Joey prefers a duplicate of his first wife?" Laura hurried ahead. "Faith, I'm glad my son married you. I think you will be a wonderful match for him. It is true you are nothing like Sarah Beth, but that's good. Life would be boring if everyone was alike. I've been praying for someone just like you. Someone to love his children, to take care of the household, and to point him back to God. Joey's been in an argument with God ever since Sarah Beth's passing."

"I believe I have already sensed a softening. He told me in a letter that he had begun reading his Bible again."

Laura put one hand to her chest and gazed upward. "Ah, thank You, Lord. Did you tell him in a letter about Miriam's decision?"

"I did, and I'm sure that must have affected him."

"As am I."

"Well, I've certainly stayed longer than I expected. I must be going, as I have some chores to do before the children return home. Thank you for today. I've enjoyed it."

"No more than I have. I shall be praying for you and the children. Never lose sight of God's purpose, dear. He brought you into our family for a reason."

Faith carried that thought with her the remainder of the day, and that evening over supper, she told the children about her visit with their grandmother. "You are blessed children to have such a lovely Grandma."

"We know," said Beth. "She would've took care of us after ar' nanny quit if she hadn't broke her leg."

"I know. I'm sorry she didn't have that chance."

"Me too," said Beth, not in the least concerned about her lack of tact.

"Well, tell me what you did with your cousins today," she said.

"We went down to the barn to see the goats, and there was a baby there. I named it Wobble," said Miriam after scooping up some mashed potatoes on her fork.

"Wobble? That's a different sort of name. How did you come up with that?"

She chewed and swallowed. "'Cause he was trying to stand, but he was so wobbly, and kept falling over."

"Ah, I see. Hence, Wobble."

"Rosie had kittens," Beth offered. "She had seven. Aunt Cristina said we can't pick them up quite yet though because they was just born a few days ago. Could I have one of the kittens when they get bigger? Aunt Cristina said I could."

"Well, perhaps we can. We'll give it some thought."

"Elias got his own horse," said Isaac. He wasn't one to chatter much at the table, so she turned her full attention on him. "He named it Champ. He's all broke in. Uncle Jack bought him off some guy in town."

"That's wonderful. He must be so proud."

"Yeah. Made me wish I had a horse. Elias and me could ride together if I did."

"I'm surprised you don't have one. Have you and your father discussed it?"

"Yeah, I've asked him, and he says I can, but he's gone, so we never have gone looking."

"I see. Well, it won't be too many months and he'll be home for good. You can talk to him again about it."

"We can ride any ol' horse we want out in the barn," Franklin said. "You don't need a new horse, Isaac."

"I want one that's just mine," he said.

Faith nodded sympathetically. "I can understand that, Isaac. However, responsibility comes with owning another living creature."

"I know. I already help out in the barn."

"Well, like I said, talk to your daddy about it when he gets home."

"That's a long ways off."

"If Beth gets a kitten, I want one too," Miriam said.

"I'll take my own goat," said Franklin.

"There's plenty of goats in the barn, Frankie," said Isaac.

"Just like you got your pick o' horses," Franklin returned.

"Oh my goodness, we'll be overrun with animals if everyone gets a new one," said Faith. "Let's just finish our supper for now and talk about these things later."

They all went back to picking at their plates while Faith picked at her own brain. *Could it be? Did Isaac's problems stem from lack of responsibility? Would things change for him if he had a horse all his own, something to care for, to clean up after, to bathe and brush?* Yes, he could ride any of the horses out in the barn, but taking responsibility for just one could make a difference in his life. She would have to think on this.

"Well," she said after everyone finished, "what say we all go down to the creek after we wash these dishes?"

"Do we have to help?" asked Franklin.

"Yes, you do. Everyone does his and her part, remember? We all carry our own dishes and at least one other dish from the table. And we make a second trip if there are still dishes on the table afterward. Then we take turns with washing and drying. Tonight, it's Frankie's turn to wash and Beth's turn to dry."

"Aargh," they both groaned.

"Come on, it's not the end of the world."

"Just about," said Beth.

Faith laughed in spite of herself.

"Hurry, the quicker we get done, the sooner we can all go swimming."

"Oh, all right," Franklin said.

"I'll help," Faith said.

"Me too," said Miriam.

"Not I," said Isaac. He turned and left the room.

27

After the battle at Kennesaw Mountain, there'd been another brief scuffle there a week later, followed by one at Nickajack Creek from July 2 through July 5. After that, Joey's regiment moved on to Ruff's Mills, and then the Chattahoochee River, where they remained through July 17. Everything seemed to be leading up to a siege on Atlanta. The South was determined to capture the city, but the Union would prevail. Joey was certain of it. He was also certain that his body had grown quite battle-weary, and he wanted to go home. His change in attitude surprised him to a degree because he'd always been a dedicated soldier, but things were different now, and he had a feeling his marital status played a part—even though Faith gave no indication she wished to remain married upon his return. In fact, her letters, informative as they were, failed to mention anything about their marriage agreement or that final kiss they'd shared. No, they contained tidbits from the Sunday sermons and reports about how his brothers were doing, her visits with his mother, what the children were up to, and how her garden was coming. Nothing, however, about his return and how things would go between them once he came home. If she had any expectations for staying married, she never let on.

He probably had himself to blame because his own letter-writing fell under the "pathetic" category. When he did write, which wasn't often, his missives were sparse in detail. He had little to say since the army was no place for a woman, surrounded as he was by the stink of mud, horse dung, human sewage, tobacco smoke, and the occasional wild meat cooked over a campfire. On those occasions when he did write, he failed to bring up the matter of their marriage, so it was no surprise that she also avoided the subject. He also never quite knew how to sign off. He had signed one letter with "Your Temporary Husband" and could have kicked himself later for that blunder. Another time, he'd signed off with "Captain Joseph Fuller," another mistake. Looking back, Joey assumed he'd done it out of habit, having just finished signing several government documents for Major Dieters, but surely its formality must have put her off.

It was a rainy day, a good day for writing a letter, he told himself. He'd try to come up with something to make it halfway interesting. For a change, they weren't doing drills in the rain or digging trenches. Instead, except for those on guard duty, everyone was told to take the afternoon off. A rare opportunity indeed. Joey had read and reread all of Faith's letters so many times he had them practically memorized, but now, he reread just the last one to give him a starting point by which to write one in return. As he read, he pictured her sitting at the dining room table writing it, or perhaps at the vanity table in his bedroom, where Sarah Beth used to sit when doing her hair.

Just as he set his duffle bag on his lap and his Bible on top of that to serve as a sort of hard surface for penning a letter, he heard someone call out "knock, knock" at the opening of his tent. Joey set his letter-writing supplies aside and bent over to lift the flap. Of all people, Major Dieters stood there, holding an umbrella.

Joey jumped up, preparing to salute…but then realized it would be a poor sort of salute, since he could not stand fully upright in his awkward little canvas space. "Sir!" he said. "I didn't expect you on this rainy day. Is something wrong? Did we receive some unexpected orders?"

"No, Captain, I merely wished to bring you some news."

Joey gave his tiny tent a quick gander. "I wish I could invite you in, sir, but it's a bit cramped."

"No bother. I have my umbrella. You might wonder why I didn't wait till the rain let up to talk to you, but I thought you might appreciate a bit of good news."

"Good news, sir?"

"Yes, it's regarding your discharge date. I've been going through some files of late and came across yours."

"My files? Any problems?"

"No, not at all. Captain, what was your exact enlistment date into the army?"

"My exact—I guess I'd have to pull out my own paperwork, sir. It was sometime in September of sixty-one."

"Hmm, just as I suspected. The papers I have back at my quarters indicate you joined up on October fifteenth of sixty-one."

"No, sir, that would be incorrect. It was a full month before that, closer to September the fifteenth."

Major Dieters nodded his head. "Weren't you wondering why your discharge date fell in the middle of October?"

"I guess I hadn't thought much about it. I figured it had to do with furloughs and weekends off."

"No, no, there's been a simple administrative error. It appears your mustering out will come a month earlier than expected."

Joey felt a little surge of joy bubble up inside, but he tried not to show it. "Really? That's interesting."

"Indeed. Now for my question. You wouldn't be interested in reenlisting, would you? You're a fine soldier with keen leadership skills, and, well, there are benefits, of course, increased pay, a nicer pension, a—"

Joey waved a hand. "No, thank you, sir. But I appreciate the offer."

"Hmm. That's right. You got yourself a new wife back in Ohio. Well, I can't say I blame you. I guess that's all then, Captain. I simply figured you could use a little good news."

"You were right about that. Thanks again."

Without so much as a salute, the major turned and moseyed back to his own tent, the light rain not worthy of a hurried gait.

⌒

Leon really had no desire to visit his cousin in jail, but he hadn't quite been able to shake off his sense of duty to at least pay him a call. Besides, God had nudged him to do it—and it was one of those nudges he couldn't ignore. Jesus Himself, in the Gospel of Matthew, said visiting someone in prison was the right thing to do. He and Stuart had grown up together and been through a lot of similar circumstances as kids, especially in their manner of upbringing. It seemed the least he could do was see how his cousin was managing and judge whether authorities were giving him fair enough treatment. Yeah, Stu was a murderer, but everyone deserved fair treatment. There'd be no trial in Stuart's case, since he had pleaded guilty. All that remained was waiting for the judge's final sentencing. No doubt Stu would receive twenty-five years to life in the state prison. Leon had sent a note to Sheriff Mumford, requesting permission to see his cousin, which was granted. Now, here he was, standing on the top step of the county jail, taking a deep breath and swallowing down a lump of nerves before swinging wide the door and stepping inside.

Sheriff Mumford was there to greet him. "Ah, you're right on time. I told Porter you were coming, so he's expecting you. I don't know how happy he'll be to see you. He's ornerier than a trapped coon."

"Yeah, I was kind of wondering about that. I know he hates trapped quarters."

"He'll have to get used to it. He's heading for state prison one of these days."

"When will that be?"

"Soon, I'm sure. Don't have a date yet. The place is full at the moment."

"I see." Sadness he hadn't known for a long time swept over him. In some ways, Leon was responsible for his cousin's imprisonment. But he had to remind himself it was Stuart who'd done the awful crime.

The sheriff scratched his bearded cheek. "I guess I never knew the real Stuart Porter when he ran his butcher shop," he mused. "I can't say he was ever overly friendly, but I never had a run-in with him either. I heard a few grumbles around town about his business practices, but no one ever filed any formal complaint against him. Which reminds me, that butcher shop of his sits empty. The judge authorized someone to go in and dispose of any perishable items. He does have quite a lot in the way of equipment, however. As for his horse, he's over at the livery, where they're taking good care of him. Any idea what your cousin plans to do with his possessions?"

"None whatsoever. I've had no contact with him since the day we brought him back to Columbus, and we rarely saw each other over the years. He's my cousin, yes, but I've managed to keep my distance from him because, as kids, we got into our share of trouble. My life's different now, and the two of us have nothing in common."

"Hmm. I see. I s'pose there's not much chance then of him appointing you his power of attorney."

"Doubtful, but I could always inquire."

"I'd appreciate it. Might be someone out there who could put the building to good use."

"Could he potentially sell it?"

"He could, but he wouldn't have access to the money. At any rate, due to taxes, the building and its contents will eventually go to the county if he doesn't do something with it."

"Humph. I'll see if I can talk to him about it."

"Good. Now then, before you go see him, I'm afraid I'll have to check your pockets. If you have any weapons..."

"Oh, of course." Leon turned his pockets inside out and then unbuckled and handed over his gun belt.

"And your hat?"

Leon removed his hat so the sheriff could look it over. Satisfied, he motioned for Leon to put it back on. "I'll take you to the prisoner now."

Leon found Stuart lying on a cot reading a newspaper, a cellmate doing the same on another cot. "I see they at least give you the weekly paper, eh?"

Stuart jumped at the sound, then sat up at the sight of Leon and tossed down the newspaper. "What are you doin' here?"

"Hello to you too, cousin."

"Pfff." Stuart stood and moseyed across the room, then wrapped his fingers around the steel bars and pressed his face into them, staring hard at Leon. It gave Leon an instant chill, so he made sure to keep his distance. The sheriff had left, informing him that he had fifteen minutes in which to visit. "Why'd you do it, Leon? Why'd you snitch on me? Y're family, and family's s'posed to be loyal. You dirty-crossed me."

"I couldn't let you go after that innocent woman, Stuart."

"Yeah, but then you had to go an' tell them about Opal. That was dirty."

"What you did to Opal was dirty, Stuart. There comes a time when people have to pay for the wrongs they did. This is your chance to make things right, Stu, not only with the law, but with God. Haven't you been running long enough?"

Stuart spat on the floor and cursed a red streak. There was a day when Leon would've done the same, but God had changed his heart. Still, he wouldn't let Stu's foul language deter him from what he'd come to say. "God loves you, cousin."

"How many times I gotta tell you not to preach at me?"

"I know, I know, but just hear me out this once, would you?"

Leon noted Stuart's cellmate laid his paper down on his stomach to stare at the ceiling. *Perchance he would listen as well. It couldn't hurt.*

Stuart rolled his eyes and switched his weight from one foot to the other, his fingers still firmly gripping the jail bars. "I s'pose I don't got much choice. Say your piece."

"You and I had rough upbringings. Our parents were drunks, for the most part, and you even found your mother dead in her bed. That was rough on you."

"I survived it just fine."

"Did you? Look around. Do you call this surviving?"

More eye-rolling. "The worst part, besides being locked up, is I got no booze to calm my nerves."

"God can help you with that, Stu."

A half grin appeared. "You sayin' He can get me some booze?"

"I'm saying He can take away your need for it. Why don't you give God a chance to prove His love for you?"

For the first time, Stuart had no retort. He stared at his shoes.

"Would you take a Bible if I brought one to you?"

Still, no sound out of him, not even a grunt.

"I would," said his cellmate.

Leon looked over Stuart's shoulder and smiled at the man. "I'll bring you one when I come back."

"I don't need your pity visits, cousin," Stuart said, ignoring his cellmate.

"That's good, 'cause I don't pity you. I'm just comin' 'cause I don't know how much longer you'll be here before they transfer you."

"I heard I'm goin' across town to the state pen. What if I don't live through it, Leon? That's a big place." Now his eyes were pleading. Leon couldn't help it. He stepped closer despite the danger and reached a hand through the bar to touch Stuart's wrist. The bars were close, so it was a tight squeeze. "You'll live through it, Stu, but you'd handle it better if you'd invite God into your heart."

"Don't preach at me."

"All right, I won't, but promise me you'll think about it."

Stuart went into silent mode again. Leon withdrew his arm and stepped back again, deciding to change the subject. "You might like to know I drove my wagon out to Hank and Mabel Middleton's place."

At that, Stuart lifted his gaze. "Y'r kiddin'. Why'd you do that for?"

"I wanted to make sure they were okay after what went down there. You scared them plenty, but they survived it."

Stuart gave a low chuckle. "They turned out to be tough ol' birds, especially that Hank fellow."

Leon grinned himself. "Yeah, he stood up to you even when you threatened to shoot him."

"Hmm. Guess he didn't figure I'd go through with it."

"And you probably wouldn't have," Leon said.

"How do you know?"

The truth was, he didn't. "It's just a hunch. Hey, I need to talk to you about something else."

"What?"

"Your butcher shop. What do you want done with it?"

"What do you mean?"

"Stuart, have you even thought about the fact you won't be going back there?" Stuart simply stared through the bars at him. "Do you want to appoint me your power of attorney so I can look after the business end of things?"

Stuart gave a gruff laugh. "Oh, I get it. You want to sell it and take all my money."

Leon kept his composure. "No, Stuart, I don't want your money. I'm perfectly content with what I have. Shoot, there was a reward out for your capture, one-hundred-fifty big ones, did you know that? But I didn't take it when they offered it. I'm just suggesting you should probably appoint someone to take care of your finances. The sheriff informed me that if you don't sell it, the county will take it over at some point because you'll start owing taxes and whatnot. If you want me to sell it for you, I will. And then I'll make arrangements with your banker to deposit it in your account. You won't be able to draw on it, but with a power of attorney, you could let it collect interest and at some point at least designate where you want it to go. Or look at it this way. Maybe you won't be in prison for the rest of your life. Might be they'll release you for good behavior. If that were the case, you'd have money waiting for you in an account."

"Ha! Fat chance of that happening." Stuart rubbed his hand down his face then looked up again, his eyes suddenly bright. "They had a reward out for me, huh? That's a good amount."

The door at the end of the hall opened. "Mr. Porter, your time is up." It was one of the deputies.

Leon gave Stuart a good, hard look. "You be thinking about what you want to do about your shop, all right? I'll come back next week."

"You don't gotta come back."

"I want to."

"Besides, he's bringin' us Bibles," said his cellmate.

Now, Stuart rubbed the back of his neck. "Yeah, yeah." He turned around and headed toward his cot. Then, with a backward wave of his hand, he muttered, "Get out o' here."

28

It was a hot day in late July. Faith and the children had just returned from a visit with their grandmother. While there, Laura had enlisted the children's help in washing all of her upstairs windows. They'd groaned and moaned at her request, until she offered them warm cookies and icebox milk afterward. "Can we have as many as we want?" Isaac had asked.

"You certainly can."

"You can have three, but that's the limit," said Faith.

"All right, three," Laura said, winking at Faith across the room.

Each child was assigned a bucket of water and a rag with which to wash the windows, after which Laura would walk from room to room to inspect and then wipe down each window. While they worked, Faith slipped out to the barn to talk to Jesse. He grinned at the first sight of her. "Well, I'll be, first prettiest thing I've seen in this barn since little Miss Miriam brought me a bouquet of dandelions."

She couldn't help her gust of laughter. "She brought you dandelions?"

"She sure did, pretty little things too. We rubbed them on the end of our noses to see if we like butter."

"To see if you like butter?"

"Of course. If your nose turns yellow after rubbing a dandelion on it, it's a sure sign you're a fan of butter, and what do you know? We both are!"

She laughed again. "It's no wonder those children clamor for you."

Jesse stood his shovel up against the wall, took off his hat, and hit it against his leg to rid it of dust, then hung it on a hook and brushed his hands on his pants. "What can I do for you?"

"Well, I have a question for you—or maybe a favor."

"You name it." He took hold of her elbow and led her to an open window where a bit of breeze blew through.

She gazed up at him. A ray of sun shone through the big open door and bounced off his cambric shirt. "I'd like to surprise Isaac with a horse he can call his own."

"Really?" He raised his eyebrows. "I know Jack just got one for Elias. Is that what prompted this?"

"Yes, I'd say so, but it's more than that. Isaac continues to tell me that he wants a horse, but in my mind, he *needs* one."

"A horse is a big responsibility. It requires daily attention and care. You think he's ready for that?"

"I'd like to know what *you* think."

"Me? Oh, yeah. I think he's more than ready. And I know what you mean by saying it's as much a need as it is a want. Isaac needs to know his own value. Sometimes I think he lacks that and to gain attention, he acts out. If he had something to keep him busy, a hobby or a critter to care for, it would give him an added purpose in life."

"Exactly!"

"What does Joey say? Have you talked about it in your correspondence?"

"No, I wanted this to be a surprise—perhaps for both of them."

His eyebrows shot higher this time. He rocked back on his heels, saying nothing.

"Do you think it's a bad idea?" she asked.

"No, no, I think it's a great idea. I just—I'm not sure it's something you should do without Joey's blessing."

"I wondered the same, but Isaac told me his father has had every intention of getting him a horse, but he's never home long enough to see to it. I thought maybe you could...you know keep your eyes open for the perfect buddy for him. I'd want a gentle horse, already trained."

He gave her another grin. "I see your mind's pretty much made up. I'll tell you what. I'm going into town tomorrow. I'll talk to a few fellows and see what I can come up with. I'll also talk to Jack and inquire where he picked up Elias's horse."

"I intend to pay for it with my own money. I want this to be a gift from me."

There went those eyebrows again—and that warm smile. "That's very generous, Faith. I'll keep that in mind when inquiring as to price. I'm sure I can find a good horse at a very good bargain, perfect for a boy going on fourteen."

Her heart felt full to brimming. They talked on about a few more details and then she returned to the house, glad to have walked in unnoticed. The children were all sitting around the table, enjoying cookies, milk, and a lively conversation with Laura.

When they returned home, they all kicked off their shoes and walked into the living room.

"What are we gonna eat for supper? I'm starving," Isaac said.

Faith shook her head. "How could you be starving? You just ate several cookies and drank two full glasses of milk at your grandmother's house. I watched you with my own eyes."

"I know, but my stomach ain't full yet."

"Isn't full," she corrected. She'd been casually working on their grammar in hopes that it would begin to stick over time.

"What are we going to eat?" Isaac asked again.

"That is a good question," she said. "Hmm. Shall we pack some food in a basket and go down to the creek bank to eat?"

"Yes!" they all shouted in unison.

"All right then, give me some time to put our supper together, and we'll head down."

"I'll help," Beth volunteered.

"Me too," said Miriam.

"Wonderful!"

Lately, she'd noted a sort of warming coming from Beth. *Thank You, Lord.* The boys scooted upstairs to change into their swim clothes, so Faith and the girls walked into the kitchen to get things ready.

Later, their picnic basket full with bounty, they sought shade under one of the trees down at the creek, Beth spreading out a blanket on which they could all sit. They all plopped down on the blanket, and Faith removed the lid on the basket and began taking out what food she'd packed: apples, bread and butter, strawberry jam, dried beef, and some tin cups. "Isaac, since you carried down the jug of water, would you mind filling our cups?"

"Okay," he said without a hint of rebellion.

"I wish Daddy was here," said Miriam after they all settled down and began to eat.

"Me too," said Beth.

The boys agreed with silent nods.

"Oh!" Faith finished chewing on the bite she'd taken from her apple and swallowed. "I have some news!"

"What is it?" Beth asked.

"Your daddy told me in letter he's coming home a whole month earlier than he originally expected."

"He is?" they asked in unison.

"What date?" Franklin asked.

"I believe he said September the fifteenth."

"When is that?" asked Miriam.

"It's about six weeks," Faith said.

"How long is six weeks?" she asked.

"It's a long time, moppet," Faith said.

"Don't keep asking; you'll never figure it out," Isaac added. "That means he'll be home for harvest. We don't go back to school till after harvest."

Faith nodded. "You're right about that, Isaac. I'm sure your uncles will be happy for the extra help."

"I'm anxious for my daddy to stay home," said Beth.

"Me too," said Franklin.

"You won't be here," said Isaac, eyes squarely on Faith. He didn't say it with a malicious tone, however, merely factual. Still, she wasn't sure how to respond, so she just took another bite of her apple and looked out at the creek, where a few ducks had landed and were busy fishing for their own suppers. Overhead, more ducks flew by, squawking loudly to one another. It reminded her of the way the children sometimes bickered back and forth.

"Do you like living here?" Beth asked.

The question so surprised Faith that she choked a little and had to take a quick drink. Once she recovered, she answered, "Yes, yes, I do."

"You're our fifth, or maybe sixth, nanny," Franklin stated. "I can't keep track."

She gave a light chuckle. "I know there've been many."

"And you prob'ly won't be our last," said Isaac. He chewed and swallowed his last bite of bread, then took a drink of water. "Nobody ever stays."

"It's possible I'll stay. You never can tell," said Faith.

"We won't need a nanny once Daddy comes home," said Beth.

"I'm not sure what your father has in mind," Faith said. "He'll be working out in the fields. I would think he'll have to hire someone to watch you children while he works during the day. Or perhaps you boys will start working alongside him every day and you girls will go to your aunt's house or your grandma's during the day. Something will work out, I'm sure—if I'm not here, that is." She wanted to sneak in that tiny bit of hope that perhaps she wouldn't be going anywhere.

They ate several more bites in silence. No one seemed eager to jump up and play, not even the boys, who'd had plans to play catch with their ball. Nor did anyone mention swimming, even though they'd brought towels. Something had happened to change the tone, and she suspected it had to do with the possibility of her leaving in September. *Was it possible? Were they going to miss her if she left?* If so, no one, not even Miriam, would admit it.

Back at the house, the boys in their room working a wooden puzzle on the floor, and the girls in their rooms dressing for bed, Faith went into her own room to lay out her bedclothes. She had established a routine whereby she lay out her things while the children were readying for bed, then, once they were all tucked in, she put on her own nightclothes then went downstairs for a cup of hot tea and time to herself, usually with a book from the library or her Bible. Although she had come to enjoy the busyness of daily household chores, she also valued her quiet times.

She walked to her chest of drawers and pulled open the top drawer where she kept her undergarments. The box that held her button string lay undisturbed in the front corner of the drawer. She picked it up and thought how heavy it had gotten, perhaps weighing as much as seven or eight pounds by now. She would never wear it, but it was fun to admire it every now and then. Somehow though, it had lost its luster from days of old when she'd first started collecting, and she sometimes asked herself why she continued holding onto it.

She lifted the lid then slowly removed the long, heavy string of buttons. Some still shone as bright as new while others had dulled over time depending on the material from which they were made.

"What's that?" came a girlish voice. She turned to find Beth standing in the doorway.

"Oh, it's my button string. Would you like to see it?"

Without hesitation, Beth stepped inside. The girls had grown accustomed to Faith plaiting their hair every morning, either before breakfast or directly afterward, so they'd grown more comfortable with entering her room. "What's a button string?"

"Have you never heard of one? Oh, my goodness, you must come close so I can show you." She carried the chain of buttons to her bed and lay it out lengthwise. The thing must have stretched a good four or five feet when laid straight.

Beth gave a little gasp. "Jumpin' jack rabbits, that's a lot of buttons!"

Faith laughed at her euphemism. "Yes, it is."

"Why you got so many?"

"Well, why don't we sit down on my bed so I can tell you?"

"Okay."

None too shyly, the normally quiet child leaped up on the high bed. Faith warmed at the sight of her sitting there in her nightgown, her pretty legs and bare feet dangling off the side. *Could it be? Was she truly making progress with her older stepdaughter?* Faith herself sat on the edge of the bed next to her and picked up one end of the strand, then slowly began to disclose the history of her button string and the meaning behind it. Before long, Miriam joined them and then the boys. And before she knew it, she was pointing out various buttons and sharing memories of who'd given it to her and when.

"How many is on the string?" Isaac wanted to know.

"You know, I lost track at around nine hundred and fifty, I believe. I don't recall the exact figure."

"That's a lot!" he exclaimed.

"I hope I get a button chain someday," Miriam said.

"You're too little," said Isaac.

"Huh-uh. Am I too little, Faith?"

"There is no set age at which a girl may start her button collection. In fact, the sooner one starts, the more likely she is to have enough by the time she is betrothed."

"What's betrothed?"

"Engaged to be married."

Miriam wrinkled her nose. "Well, I'm not gettin' married, so I guess I don't need a button string."

"Someday you'll marry, honey, but five years old is far too young to be thinking about such things."

Beth adjusted her seating. "How old were you when you started?"

"I think I was right around twelve."

"Then that's when I'll start collecting."

"This is getting boring," said Franklin.

Faith giggled. "I imagine it is. What say we all go to the boys' room now so I can read our Bible story and have our bedtime prayer?" She picked up the string and carefully set it back in the box, then walked over and put it back in the top drawer.

For a change, there were no arguments. Everyone filed out and headed down the hall. Faith could hardly believe it. *Was this the quiet before the storm? Or were these children finally learning how to be compliant? Oh, Lord, may it be so.*

29

The next day told a different story. All morning, a storm had been brewing, both outside and within the house. Faith couldn't put her finger on it, but something wasn't right. She sensed it. The thunderstorm itself had ended a couple of hours ago, but a gray cloud of unnamed sullenness hovered in the home. To keep everyone busy, she'd put Beth to work polishing silver, Miriam picking up and straightening her toys in her bedroom, Franklin sweeping floors, and Isaac outside pounding the dirt out of the rugs. While they did carry out their assigned chores, they made sure to grumble about them.

"Our other nannies never made us do housework," said Isaac. "How come you do?"

"Why do I have to sweep the floor? That's woman's work," moaned Franklin.

"I hate polishing silver," whined Beth. "You always make me do it."

Even Miriam had something to say about having to go to her room. "My room's clean enough. Why do I gots to make it cleaner?"

Faith tried to ward off her concern by keeping her own self busy in the kitchen rolling out dough for baking a couple of pies for the week ahead, thankful that at least when she'd opened this can of lard, no worms greeted her. Every so often, Franklin and Beth would exchange quiet words, although she couldn't make them out. She didn't wish to interfere with their chatter, but at the same time, if they were plotting something, she wanted to put a halt to it. There was always a fine line determining the right way to handle things under this crazy roof, where one moment it seemed like things between them were improving and the next, she was sure a bomb would go off. She went on with her rolling until she'd formed a nice thin layer perfect for setting on top of her pie plate. Next, she fitted it onto the plate and trimmed off the edges, then went about rolling out the remaining dough for the next pie.

Outside, the sound of an approaching wagon drew her to the side window. Of all people, her lovely sister-in-law Cristina was just pulling up to the front of the house in her two-horse buggy. Faith wiped her flour-covered hands on her apron and hurried to the front door, the children nearly beating her there, but not quite. "Cristina!" she called from the porch while shielding her eyes from the sun that had just peeked through the clouds. "What brings you here?"

Cristina smiled from her high perch, turned herself around, and carefully stepped down, her growing belly slowing her movements. She looped the reins over the hitching post and climbed the porch steps. "I wanted to pay you a visit, if you don't mind."

"Mind? I'm elated."

"Where's Uncle Jack?" Franklin asked.

Cristina ruffled Franklin's sandy-colored hair. "He took Catherina and Elias into town with him. He wanted to wait till the skies cleared. After they left, I thought it was a nice time for me to visit your stepmother. I hope I'm not interrupting anything."

"No, not at all." Faith glanced down at Beth and Franklin. "Why don't you take a break from your jobs for now and go play?"

"Yes!"

"I'll go get Miriam," said Beth.

"And I'll go out back and tell Isaac," Franklin announced.

And just like that, they vanished, Beth running upstairs and Franklin disappearing behind the house.

"I've never seen anybody so happy to get out of a job in my life! You would think I've wrapped a ball and chain around their ankles, the way they've been complaining today. I've been thinking maybe none of us should've gotten out of bed this morning."

Cristina laughed. "Some days are like that."

Faith wanted to say that most of her days were like that, but she kept that thought to herself. "Come into the house, Cristina. It will be so nice to have an adult conversation."

They walked through the parlor, past the library, and into the living room to sit on the worn sofa. Cristina glanced around the room. "Looks like this room could use some sprucing up."

"Yes, Joey and I discussed that when he was home. I expressed interest in decorating it, and he was fully in favor, but since he left, the children have kept me so busy, I've not taken any time to even think about picking colors and furnishings."

Cristina frowned. "I'd be happy to help. I happen to know a fine seamstress in town who could stitch some new draperies. I know you're a seamstress yourself, as am I, but neither of us has time. She works fast and could probably have them ready for you within a week." She glanced around again. "The room could use some new wallpaper, too, and perhaps a couple new pieces of furniture. We could take the children into town sometime soon and make a day of it. I know this all sounds a bit overwhelming, but with all of them together, they'll entertain each other."

It did sound overwhelming—even exhausting—but with Cristina's help, it could be fun and adventurous. Somehow, her enthusiasm for the house project she'd mentioned to Joey started to return. "He's coming home a month earlier than planned, on September the fifteenth."

"Well, then, we should get busy so that it will all be done by the time he returns. Why don't you refrain from telling him about it so that when he walks through the door, he'll be met with a nice surprise."

That thought lifted Faith's spirits.

They sat on the couch for the next hour, sipping coffee and talking about a lot of things, including the story of how Cristina met Jack and he captured "her rebel heart," as he liked to put it. They also talked about Cristina's pregnancy, her due date of mid-November, and how excited Elias and Catherina were about having a baby brother or sister. Faith could only dream about one day having a child of her own.

"Now tell me about your life, your family, and how you happened to decide to marry a complete stranger," Cristina said after taking another sip of coffee. Just minutes earlier, Faith had refilled their cups with piping hot brew.

"Oh, goodness, my story is boring compared to yours."

"I doubt that. I heard tell that your former fiancé ran away with your best friend. He sounds like a scoundrel. And then, of course, you had that hideous incident with that man who murdered his wife. I'd hardly call that boring, my dear. But, please, give me the specifics, as what I heard came from Jack, and he's not very good when it comes to details."

With that encouragement, Faith shared her story, and before long, another half hour flew by, and she was sure she'd taken up far too much of Cristina's time. "I'm sorry. You came to visit, and I feel like I'm doing all the talking."

"Not at all. I'm lovin' this chance to get to know you better. We get so busy in our own homes, we forget to call on those closest to us. I did hear that you've been visiting Mom Fuller. She told me how much she enjoys you. I do hope you and Joey can hold your marriage together because, if you don't, a lot of us—including Laura—will be disappointed."

"I hope so as well, but nothing's been mentioned about it in any of his letters home to me. He even signed one of them *your temporary husband*, as if I needed reminding."

Cristina frowned. "Well, we'll see what the Lord has to say about it. I do believe He brought you into this family. Even the children seem so much better off since you came."

"Do you really think so?"

"I sure enough do. The nannies before you were already starting to complain to Laura by the second week. I'm surprised any of them lasted to six months, but a couple did. None of them seemed to genuinely care for the children, nor did they take them to church as you've been doing. It was always Jesse's and Mom's job to pick them up on Sunday mornings."

"Oh dear, that explains a lot about their behavior then. I'm sad that they've had so many bad experiences along the way, not to mention losing their beloved mother at such young ages."

"Yes, that surely has affected them in deep ways, especially Isaac. But even he seems pleasanter to me since you arrived."

"I hope you're right. We had a good day yesterday—for the most part. They all came into my room last night, and I told them the story of my button string."

"You have a button string? Oh, my goodness, I've heard of them, but I've never actually seen one. Isn't it an English tradition?"

"It is. My mother's parents came over from England, and it was my grandmother who started my mother on her collection and my mother, of course, who started me on mine. The children seemed fascinated by it last night."

"Would you, could I—?"

Faith smiled. "Would you like to see it?"

"Oh, could I?"

"Of course. Come upstairs, and I'll show you."

They stood and both smoothed out their dresses, then headed toward the stairs. "I don't believe I've ever seen Joey's upstairs before. In fact, I've only been as far as the living room, seeing as there was always one nanny or another here, none of whom seemed very friendly or eager to get to know me. I'm so happy to have gained a friend in you."

"As am I," said Faith, meaning it with all her heart. Since leaving her family in Columbus, she'd longed for companionship, but visiting with Cristina caused a big chunk of that loneliness to fall away.

They reached the top of the stairs. "I've been staying in Joey's room; the children's rooms are down that way." Faith pointed in the opposite direction. "Follow me."

They entered her room. "Have a seat on the bed." Faith giggled. "You can even bounce on it, if you like. That's what the girls did last night." Cristina laughed and sat down while Faith walked to the bureau and pulled open the top drawer. Immediately, she noted the drawer's messiness, and when she started to dig around, a feeling of deep dread came over her. She turned quickly and scanned the room. *Had she forgotten to put the box of buttons away last night?* No, she clearly remembered doing it, and then she recalled seeing it early this morning when she'd pulled open the drawer to take out some clothing.

"Is something wrong?" Cristina asked.

"It's gone."

"Gone? What? Your button string?"

"Yes. I showed it to the children last night, then afterward, put it away. I have always kept it in a silver box given to me by my grandmother. The box is gone."

"Oh dear, what do you think—oh no, you don't think one of the children—"

"Why would they do that? Don't they know I'd realize immediately it's missing?"

"Well, maybe *they* didn't do it. Perhaps only one of them is responsible. Which one do you think would be most likely to take it?"

"I would say Isaac, as he's been the most conniving. But what on earth would he want with my string of buttons?"

Cristina wrinkled her brow and scratched her temple. "I'm so sorry, Faith. This is awful. Whoever did this knows better. Shall we go look in their rooms?"

Faith thought a moment. "I hate to drag you into this as it's truly my problem."

"But they are my nieces and nephews by marriage, and they come to my house often. I want to get to the bottom of this as much as you do. However, if you'd rather handle it on your own, I will respect your wishes."

Faith bit her lower lip and fought back a combination of anger and disappointment. "Let's go check their rooms."

Cristina slowly rose from the bed, and they both headed down the hallway to check all three rooms. Unfortunately, their search rendered nothing—no trace of the silver box or the string of buttons. They searched drawers, looked into toy boxes, and lifted blankets to look under beds. Nothing. Faith's heart sank to the floor. "It could be anywhere," she said sadly. "In fact, if they were going to take it, the last place they'd hide it would be in the house."

"You're probably right. I'm sorry this has happened, Faith. You must be very hurt and confused."

Tears formed in the corner of her eyes. "I don't quite know what to do to earn their favor."

"Just continue being yourself and doing your best. It will pay off, but it'll take time."

"We may as well go back downstairs."

"And I'm afraid I must be going, as I have to start getting supper ready."

They took the stairs in silence, and just as they reached the bottom step, the kitchen door squeaked opened, and the sound of children's voices filled the house. Cristina turned around. "Do you want me to stay and talk to the children? Maybe I'll be able to get the truth from them."

"No, I think I better take it from here. But I'd welcome your prayers."

Cristina squeezed Faith's hand. "I'll definitely be praying, and I'll tell Jack to pray as well. We won't say anything to Catherina and Elias though."

"Thank you. I appreciate that."

Cristina headed toward the door just as the children entered the living room.

"Are you leaving, Aunt Cristina?" Beth asked.

"Yes, I've already stayed longer than I intended. I have to go home and start supper."

"What are we having for supper?" asked Isaac.

"I want to talk to you before we talk about supper."

"About what?" asked Beth.

"You'll see. Go sit on the couch."

"Why?"

"Just do as I say."

Cristina and Faith exchanged glances. "I'll be going now," Cristina said. Faith walked her to the door, and from the porch, Faith watched her climb aboard her rig, then turn her horses toward home. Cristina gave a final wave and a tiny smile then mouthed, "I'll be praying."

30

The battle for Atlanta had been raging for days with no end in sight. Every day, orders remained the same: seize the rail and supply center of Atlanta, move forward, don't back down, do not give up. Press on, press on! Soldiers fought from morning till night with cease-fires at various points throughout the day and also ceasing at dusk. If they weren't fighting, they were drilling, inspecting arms, hunting for food, or sitting against a tree, rifle in hand, sleeping. Sickness had over-taken the camp, and even Joey acquired a mild case of dysentery that he was able to ward off after a few days. It had left him weak and depleted, but he didn't let it slow him down. Some in the camp had recently passed away, one from typhoid and a couple others from whooping cough. Medics had quarantined patients in covered wagons, and there'd been no new cases in the past week. Over the last three years, the army had learned a thing or two about sanitation and the passing of disease from one soldier to another. Still, disease remained prevalent and a constant worry to the government.

It was nearing suppertime, and the smells stirred Joey's empty stom-ach. Food had gotten scarce, and he wondered if he hadn't lost a bit of weight. Confederates and Federals alike often crossed over boundary lines to forage off the land for food, but much of the land, once fertile and verdant with crops aplenty, had been trampled and turned to muddied fields. Farmers who'd counted on bountiful harvests bemoaned their losses, and soldiers, hungry for something other than stale hardtack and salted pork, often ate what little they had on hand and prayed a shipment of rations would arrive the next day. Joey stationed himself against a tree and prepared to reread his most recent letter from Faith. In the distance, constant gun and cannon fire rent the air, but having grown accustomed to the sound, Joey blocked it from his mind. Just because a battle was raging didn't mean every soldier was engaged. There were periods of rest when certain companies stayed back and others went out. He sipped on a warm cup of coffee that tasted more like dirt and read the soiled letter.

Dear Joey,

Everything here is fine as silk. The children have been well-behaved for the most part, and I am enjoying my station here at the Fuller farm. Last week Cristina came to visit me, and we had a lovely time together. She is a good conversationalist, and so I'm sure we'll get together again soon. We seem to have a lot in common.

Time is flying. I can barely believe it's already August. You'll be a regular citizen before you know it. I pray for your health and well-being every day. I pray that you sense God's presence on the battlefield and you'll be able to avoid every bullet that comes your way. Lord, may it be so!

I visit your mother at least once a week, sometimes twice, depending on my schedule. On one of our visits, your mother put the children to work washing her upstairs windows. Their reward was fresh-baked cookies and milk. It's miraculous the way her leg healed. You would be pleased to see how well she is walking with her cane. We do serve a loving, faithful, and healing God.

Last week's sermon at church was about repentance, and how just receiving Christ as Savior is not enough. We must also turn from our sin and live a new and clean life. He definitely challenged me to change a few areas of my life. Sometimes, I am not the most joyful individual, so I am working on becoming better. Life has its share of hardships, as I know you are experiencing in this moment, but always, even in the midst of war, we can find little slices of joy throughout the day. I hope you are getting a glimpse of those slices, even if tiny.

Well, today I am taking the children into town to buy them each a new pair of shoes and perhaps some trousers for your growing boys. I shall write again soon, if not tomorrow then the next day.

Sincerely,

Faith Haviland Fuller

Joey liked that she'd signed her full name. Other times, she'd simply signed "Faith." He wondered what caused her to sign it this way for a change. He studied her perfect, feminine handwriting, then thought about his hen-scratch in comparison. Surely, she must frown every time she read his letters. Hers were newsy and cheerful while his ranked up there with boring, if not bleak. He generally had not one cheerful thing to share, with the exception of his newfound interest in reading the Bible. Her comment about repentance rang a bell with him. *Yes, he had asked Jesus to come into his life as a boy, but what had he reaped from that decision since becoming an adult? What had he done to help cheer or bring hope to another soldier?* He'd made a recommitment to God, but he had yet to tell anyone about it or share the good news of God's love with anyone. While staring down at the letter, he quietly prayed that God would somehow choose to use him in some way, if not today, then at least some day before he mustered out.

"You got a letter there, Captain?" One of the fellows in his squadron, Sergeant Louis Pinkley, plopped down beside him. Pinkley was a godly man who used to get on Joey's nerves, but only because he was so vocal about his faith. Lately, though, Joey had come to respect him more, and they'd even had a few conversations about God. "Seems like you been gettin' lots of mail lately. Those all from your new wife?"

"Most of 'em, yes."

"You anxious to see her again?"

He thought about the question before replying. "Yeah, I am."

"You don't sound too sure of yourself."

"Well, I told you about our arrangement. I don't know what to expect when I return."

"Do you want to stay married?"

"I—I think so....I don't know. I have no idea."

Pinkley laughed. "It's usually the woman who's the indecisive one, but not in your case. I'll pray things work out for you. I know it would be God's plan for you to stay together. I'm sure you'll do the right thing."

"It goes two ways. She'd have to want to make it work."

Pinkley nodded. "Right you are, and I'm sure she's back in your hometown of Lebanon thinking the same thing about you. *He'll have to want to make it work.*"

Joey nodded back. "I can't say I'm in love with her. I don't even know her really."

"There's time for that, my friend. God can put a deep love in your heart for her."

"If it's meant to be, I suppose."

Pinkley gave a chuckle. "Uh, it's meant to be, Captain. You're married."

Joey returned a light laugh. "I see what you're saying. I'm married now, and, therefore, it's His will that we stay together."

"Exactly. I wonder how your kids are gettin' on with her."

"You know, she never has anything negative to say. Either they're doing well, or she's not telling me the full truth."

"Ha! Kids will be kids! She might think you need protecting."

Joey thought about that. "That's occurred to me.

⌒

The last several days had been difficult ones, with friction aplenty. Ever since the incident of the missing button string, in which no one professed his or her guilt, the children were on edge and at each other's throats. When she'd told them that one of them had to have taken the string, they all turned on each other, Beth saying it was Isaac who had done it because he was always the instigator.

"Am not, and no I didn't. It was you. You even told me you took it!" he'd yelled back.

"I did not!" she'd wailed. "Tell him he's lying, Frankie," she'd pleaded.

But Franklin had only shrugged. "How do I know? I think you took it, Beth, 'cause you were really admiring it."

"No, I wasn't. I thought it was stupid."

Their bickering had grown to such an extreme that Faith had to cover her ears. "Stop!" she'd ordered. "We'll drop it for now, but whomever took it, I'd appreciate if you'd put it back in my drawer. When it's returned, I will not ask any questions. I'll just be thankful to have it back."

But no one returned it, and every day, tensions mounted. She didn't know what to think, and since that day, she'd not brought it up again, hoping that one day soon, it would simply turn up due to someone's guilty conscience.

Exactly a week after she'd spoken to Jesse about acquiring a horse for Isaac, Jesse arrived at the house eager to speak with Faith. The children had run out to greet him, but after he gave them each a candy stick, he announced his need to talk to Faith about something and asked that they give them privacy.

"What's it about?" Beth asked, squinting up at him.

"Well now, if I told you that, it wouldn't be private, would it?"

"I guess. Is it about her leaving?"

"What? No, why would you ask that?"

"I don't know. Things has been kinda bad around here lately. I thought she had her fill of us."

Faith's heart turned into a puddle of mush. She so longed to hug Beth, but she wasn't sure how the child would react. Instead she tried to reassure her with words. "Honey, I am not leaving you, and I'm not angry with anyone, so you can relax about that. Your Uncle Jesse just wants to talk to me about something, so if you all will go out to the barn or go back in the house, we would both appreciate it."

All four of them moseyed out to the barn, candy sticks in their mouths.

"What's up with them?" Jesse asked.

"Oh, goodness, we had a little incident a week or so ago in which something very dear to me went missing. One of them took it, but no one will confess to it, so it's been rather tense around here as I wait for the guilty party to return the item."

"Do you want me to talk to them?"

"Cristina asked the same thing, but I think I'll manage. It's bound to come to a head at some point. Now then, did you happen to find a horse for Isaac?"

"I did, but are you sure you still want to give it to him? What if he's the one who stole your item?"

"I'm putting that whole matter to rest. I'm confident it will resolve itself, and I still feel very strongly that Isaac needs a horse. Tell me all about it."

Jesse said he'd procured a fine horse at public auction just that morning, a twelve-year-old mare, trained and mild mannered, but plenty spirited when the need called for it. He assured her that the mare would make a suitable starter horse. Jack had been with him at the sale, and they both agreed she would be a perfect match for Isaac. Excitement bubbled up in her. "When can we give her to him?"

"She's at my barn right now. If you want to bring the kids over in, say, an hour, I can have her saddled up and ready to go."

"Did you also purchase a saddle?"

"No, we already have sufficient bridles, tack, gear, rugs, and saddles in the barn that Isaac uses whenever he takes out one of the farm mounts, so he's equipped. Everything's in good shape, but we'll leave it up to Joey to suit him up with new gear if he wants."

They discussed price, and she promised him she'd bring the correct amount of cash in exchange for the horse. She thanked him, and shortly afterward, he mounted his own horse, gave her a wave, and off he went.

She found the children in the barn with the hired hands, Wendel and Jobe. "Howdy, Mrs. Fuller," said Jobe. "We's jes' talkin' to y'r youngins 'bout some chores we got for 'em."

"That's wonderful. They love chores," she said, smiling.

"I don't," said Miriam. "I jes' like to take care of the kitties."

"We know," said Isaac. "That's all you ever want to do out here."

"That and chase the chickens," added Franklin.

"I like to feed the goats," said Beth. "But I hate mucking stalls." She wrinkled her nose.

"Me too," said Miriam. She shook her head and squeezed her nose shut with her thumb and index finger. "It's too stinky."

Faith laughed. "I'd agree with that." She looked at the hired men. "What sort of chores did you have in mind for them?"

"Wendel and me was thinkin' they could help stack them hay bales up on the loft."

"That'd be fun!" said Franklin.

"That's fine, but I need them to come in the house soon and get cleaned up. We're going to Grandmother Fuller's house soon."

"Why we goin' there?" Beth asked.

"It has to do with Uncle Jesse's visit. Sort of a surprise."

"Ohhh, I love surprises!" squealed Miriam.

Faith smiled at the men. Jesse had spoken to them a few days prior and asked them to ready a stall in preparation for a new horse's arrival. The other morning, when Faith had gone out to the barn to help Beth collect eggs, Wendel had taken her aside and told her the stall was ready. He tossed her a knowing wink now. "I'll send them to the house in a few minutes, ma'am," he said.

To Faith's surprise, when they arrived at the main house, everyone from the family was there, including Jack, Cristina, and their children. They all sat with Laura on the front porch. They'd no doubt wanted to watch Isaac's reaction.

"Why is everyone here?" Beth asked.

"Perhaps they just came for a visit," Faith said.

When she brought the horses to a stop in front of the house, the children jumped down and ran up the steps to hug their grandma one by one. "Where's Uncle Jesse?" Isaac asked no one in particular.

Jack grinned at the lad. "If you turn yourself around, you'll see him walking this way now."

Everyone turned to watch his approach, a saddled, cream-colored horse at his side. "Did Uncle Jesse get a new horse?" Isaac asked.

"He sure did," said Faith. "Isn't she a beauty?"

"Yeah." His eyes wide, Isaac stepped off the porch ahead of everyone. "She's a fine horse, Uncle Jesse. Never seen a prettier one. Where'd you get her?"

"Got her at auction just this morning. Your Uncle Jack was with me."

Everyone stepped down from the porch to gaze at the mare.

"She's a pretty one all right," Laura said, stepping up behind Faith.

"What's her name?" Isaac asked, stepping up to rub the horse's forehead. The horse nuzzled in close to Isaac, and everyone laughed.

"She likes you," Beth said, as if she'd started picking up on the surprise. She and Faith exchanged knowing glances.

"I guess she does," said Isaac.

"I'm told her name's Rose."

"Rose. That's a pretty name. Hello, Rose," Isaac said, nuzzling the horse's head with his face.

"You like her, Isaac?" Jesse asked.

"Sure, who wouldn't?"

"Do you like her well enough to take care of her?" Faith asked, walking up behind Isaac and reaching around him to pet the mare's strong neck. The boy swiveled around and jerked his head up. He locked eyes with her.

"What do you mean?"

She smiled. "I mean—do you want her? I asked Uncle Jesse to pick out a fine horse for you, and this morning he and Uncle Jack bought her at auction. It's my gift to you."

For a second, he simply stared, mouth sagging and instant moisture collecting in his eyes. "Wh-what? F-for me?" he stammered, emotion clearly clogging his throat.

The family stood quiet. Not even Miriam made a sound. In fact, the only sounds were those of clucking chickens moving about the yard and a gentle wind whirring across the fields.

"Well?" asked Laura. "What do you have to say about that?"

"I—I don't even know what to say." More tears gathered. "Th-thank you?"

Faith rested a hand on his shoulder, and wonder of wonders, he wrapped his arms around her for a hug. "You're very welcome, Isaac."

He pulled back and smiled up at her, as sincere a smile as she'd ever seen. In fact, it might have been the first *real* smile he'd ever given just her. She would take it.

"She's really mine?" he asked.

She nodded. "She is definitely yours. Why don't you take her for a ride?"

Jesse handed over the reins. "Here you go, Isaac. You do know that owning a horse will mean a whole new level of responsibility, don't you?"

Isaac took the reins with an eager sort of reverence. "Yes, I know. I'll—I'll take good care of her, I promise."

"I have every confidence you will. Jobe and Wendel are always around to help, so don't hesitate to ask them if you have any questions. I'll be happy to give you some training tips too."

"I'm sure I'll be askin' y' for help." Then to Faith, Isaac swallowed hard, then broke into another smile. "Thank you, Faith," he repeated, this time with even more sincerity, making her heart leap.

Perhaps this would mark a turning point in their relationship. She could certainly hope so anyway.

31

It was August 27, less than a month before Joey's return. A new deep blue, velveteen French Royal sofa and two matching armchairs had arrived yesterday from J. N. Oswald Furniture Store, carried in by two men who also hauled away the old furniture. Over a three-day period last week, hired workers from Lebanon had removed the old wallpaper and hung the new pattern she and Cristina had chosen, and today, Wendel and Jobe were coming into the house to hang the new drapes the seamstress had dropped off this morning. That would put the finishing touches on the living room. She liked the way it had turned out…all except for the bronze-framed, massive picture of Sarah Beth that still hung over the fireplace. The woman's light blue eyes seemed to follow Faith wherever she went in the living room, as if judging her for the colors she'd chosen, not to mention the wallpaper's pattern. *Would she have selected something altogether different? And what of the furniture? Would she have gone for a more lavish style, as had been there before, or would she approve of Faith's choices? And how would she feel about the brocade draperies she'd purchased?* She bit her lower lip as she worried about it, then quickly scolded herself. *What would it matter anyway?* Chances were, Joey would come home and want to fulfill his end of the marriage agreement, pay her what he owed her, and send her on her way. Afterward, he could do what he wanted with her furniture choices— keep them or return them and pick something more to his liking.

At the side window, she craned her neck to look toward the barn and watch the children. Beth was carrying around a baby goat, Miriam was chasing a couple of chickens in the yard in hopes of catching one, and Franklin was helping Wendel haul buckets of water to the livestock. Meanwhile, Isaac was riding Rose—"'cause she's beautiful like a rose"— in the corral, working on figure-eight patterns and other training techniques. He'd been so enthused over his horse that often he wanted to skip meals just to be with her. In fact, most mornings, he made it out to the barn before the other children got out of bed and certainly before Faith had a chance to finish making breakfast. He and Rose had formed some sort of bond that only a boy and his horse would understand.

By all appearances, one would consider the children happy and carefree, but underneath, there remained a current of cheerlessness, and Faith thought it stemmed from the missing button string. She refused to bring up the matter again, praying that one day soon, one of the children would confess to taking it. In hopes of winning their favor, she'd been preparing their favorite meals, baked an apple butter custard pie, made raisin cookies, bought them all new shoes, and purchased fabric for making the girls new dresses, even allowing them to choose the patterns. They'd been appreciative, even thanked her, but it hadn't changed much of anything. Most times, she still wondered what they thought about her. No one ever expressed a great desire for her to stay on after their father returned, but then neither did they want to talk about it. *Was she expecting too much of these children?* Perhaps a close friendship would never come. Maybe their past experiences with nannies had ruined them for trusting her. Thank goodness, Miriam remained full of cheer and happy smiles. *What would she do without her?*

She had a kettle of peeled potatoes sitting on the butcher block ready to put on the stove for a low boil; in the Dutch oven, a round of beef had been slow cooking for two hours and the smells made her stomach rattle with hunger. There would also be fresh corn and for dessert, rice pudding. She hoped and prayed for a peaceable dinner and perhaps afterward some outdoor games. It was Saturday, after all, and with tomorrow being the Sabbath, she longed for good moods and a bit of family unity. She decided to walk out to the barn to check on things and ask the hired hands when they could hang the drapes.

"Howdy, Mrs. Fuller," Jobe called out when he stood up and noted her approach. He was a dark-skinned man who'd apparently been with the Fullers for the past twenty years. He tipped his hat at her. Franklin took his bucket back to the pump and dropped it on the ground, then started walking back in their direction.

She put a flat palm to her forehead to shade her eyes. "I thought I would come out to check how things are going."

"Wendel and me was thinkin' we'd come hang them drapes soon. We jus' gotta wash up beforehand."

"That would be lovely, but there's no hurry. If tomorrow is better…"

"No, we're lookin' forward to it, ma'am. Frankie here lent us a hand so's we could finish on time. He's a good worker."

"Yes, he is," Faith said. "Don't know what I'd do without his help around the house."

Wendel came up beside Franklin and ruffled his thick, sandy hair. "He ain't too bad," Wendel teased. The boy dipped his head as if embarrassed.

"Now that one out there," Jobe said, pointed his head in Isaac's direction. "He ain't got eyes for nothin' but that horse these days."

They all turned to cast their eyes at Isaac. "He does love that horse."

"Yes indeed, he do. That was a mighty fine purchase," said Jobe.

"Yeah, 'cept he don't wanna do farm chores now," said Frankie.

"I'll have a talk with him," said Faith. "He still has to carry his weight around here."

"Yeah, you hear that Isaac?" Franklin yelled out to his brother.

Isaac looked up. "What?"

"Faith said you gotta start doin' some chores around here."

"I did not say that, Frankie."

"I *do* chores!" he called back, directing Rose to stop so he could converse.

"We'll talk later, Isaac. Carry on," Faith said.

"Hey, Frankie, you wanna ride over to Uncle Jesse's? You can saddle up Annabelle."

"Not now, boys. It won't be long till we eat supper, and you have to go down to the creek to wash up beforehand. Tomorrow is the Sabbath, and we have things to do to get ready." Isaac climbed down from Rose, opened the gate, and led her out. "Awww, me and Frankie will be home in time for supper. I wanna show Uncle Jesse some of the things I been teachin' Rose."

"No, not tonight. You can show him on Monday." She put firmness in her tone. "Like I said, you need to go down to the creek." She glanced at the girls. "In fact, you're all in need of a good washing. Maybe I'll walk down there with you."

"I don't feel like goin' down to the creek," Isaac argued.

"Me neither," said Franklin, lifting his chin. Of course, Franklin would agree. She swore he'd swallow a cup of vinegar if Isaac told him to.

Like the smart men they were, Wendel and Jobe left her to settle their own dispute.

"All right then, you can wash up in the house, but you will have to put some water in the bathtub and get those feet clean."

"What's wrong with my feet?" Isaac asked, sticking one black-bottomed foot in the air. Faith might have laughed if she hadn't sensed his challenging tone. She was not up for an argument. "Just take care of Rose and then come in the house, both of you." She started to walk toward the house.

"Yeah, but Uncle Jesse's expecting me."

She stopped and slowly turned. "Did Uncle Jesse specifically tell you to come and see him tonight?"

"S-sure," was his weak reply.

"He did not, Isaac," said Beth.

"Shut up, what do you know? Uncle Jesse always tells us to come over."

"All right, that's enough back talk. If it was any other night, I wouldn't have a problem. But it's Saturday, and we have things to do to get ready for church tomorrow. Besides, I've cooked us a nice meal. All I have to do is put on the vegetables, and dinner will be ready. Come on, let's go up to the house. Besides, Jobe and Wendel might need your help hanging the drapes."

In anger, Isaac dug his boot into the dirt and gave a good, hard kick, sending a stone flying through the air that hit Beth on the cheek. She started crying and immediately held her face.

"Isaac!" Faith scolded in a loud voice. He simply stood there, saying nothing

Faith gently removed Beth's hand from her face to see a good-sized red mark. She turned and give Isaac a hard stare.

"What? It was an accident," he said, lifting his shoulders.

Not considering his thoughtlessness worth arguing over, she turned her attention to Beth and gently spoke, putting an arm around her shoulder. "Come on, honey, let's get you to the pump where we can splash some cold water on this and have a closer look."

Before leaving, Beth turned to Isaac, "I hate you!" she screamed.

"So what!? That don't hurt my feelings none."

"Go put Rose away and get in the house, boys," she said. Then to Beth she muttered, "You don't hate your brother. He didn't mean to do it."

"Yes he did."

At the well, Faith started pumping the handle. After she got a good flow, she cupped a little water in her hand and splashed it on Beth's upper cheek.

"Isaac's mean."

"Well, he's grumpy, that's all. I'm sure he'll apologize later."

"Not unless you make him."

"Then I'll make him." She inspected the small wound. "It might produce a small bump, but it's nothing serious," said Faith. "Let's go inside."

In the house, Miriam took Beth's hand, and like a little mother, walked her to the new sofa, where they sat. Wendel and Jobe followed shortly after, so Faith showed them which drapes she wanted where, and once done with that, walked into the kitchen to start cooking the potatoes and corn. Neither boy had returned to the house, but she was too tired to go after them now. If they didn't come in soon, they'd pay the consequences by going to bed hungry. And it would give her pleasure to issue the punishment.

After fifteen minutes, the men had successfully completed hanging one set of drapes. It helped that she'd had the necessary tools and hardware handy, except that Jobe did have to run out to the barn once to get another tool. Upon his return, he announced he had seen the boys in the hayloft. He'd told them to get down, but whether they'd minded or not remained to be seen. Faith shook her head in frustration. *What was she going to do with them?* She said a silent prayer asking for wisdom, then thanked the Lord that at least they'd partially obeyed by not riding off to visit their Uncle Jesse.

The second set of drapes went up faster, and Faith really enjoyed the warm tones of color and pattern. Even Beth remarked how pretty they were. Her cheek had turned red and a bit swollen, but at least she'd stopped complaining about it.

"Let's not let any goats into the house to destroy these new drapes, please," Faith joked.

"Never again!" Beth said with a tiny giggle. "That made Mrs. Hutchins so mad. She went running through the house after that goat with a big, long spoon. The poor goat ran toward the window, thinking he could get out that way, but then he got tangled in the curtain. His foot got stuck in the hem, which tore the fabric, and then Mrs. Hutchins got all the madder. She shrieked loud as the wind. When Frankie finally got hold of the goat and put 'im back outside, Mrs. Hutchins said, 'That's it! I'm packin' up and leavin' first thing in the mornin' and I don't care what happens to you naughty little monsters.'"

"Oh my!" Faith said.

Jobe nodded. "I believe she's right, Mrs. Fuller. That Hutchins lady weren't too friendly, and her patience was about the size of a peapod." He started putting the tools back into the box Faith had provided the men. Suddenly, the front door flew open and bounced off the wall.

"Help! Come quick!" Franklin's face was blood red from running. "It's Isaac! He fell through the hayloft, and he's lying on the ground, and he's not moving!"

"What?" Wendel cried out.

"Oh, dear God, no!" On instinct, Faith took off on a run for the barn, everyone following behind and Jobe yelling from behind, "Don't move him, ma'am!"

She reached the barn ahead of everyone, and just as Franklin had said, Isaac's lifeless body lay on the hard floor. She knelt over him and spoke close to his face. "Isaac, Isaac, wake up! Isaac." Frantic, she picked up his hand and gave it a squeeze but got nothing in return. "Isaac!" she said again, this time with more desperation. Jobe and Wendel both knelt on either side of the boy, Jobe easing Faith over with a gentle nudge. He put his ear to Isaac's chest. Faith held her own breath, waiting, her heart racing with fear and hideous angst.

"He's breathin'," Jobe said. "His heart's poundin' too. He's knocked out cold though." Someone go get me some cold water." Without another word, Franklin took off at a run for the house. Faith glanced up at Beth and Miriam, who had wrapped themselves in each other's arms.

"Dear Jesus," Faith prayed aloud. "Please, dear Jesus, wake him up. Please, Lord."

"I best take the rig into town and get Doc Eldred to come out here," said Wendel.

"Would you?" Faith asked, so full of fear she could barely think what to say or do.

Wendel jumped up and took off running to the back of the barn to fetch the farm horses. Faith heard him take down the harnesses from their hooks, then lead the wagon team outside.

"Oh, Isaac, please wake up," she said again, bending close to the boy. "Why isn't he moving, Jobe?"

"I don't know, ma'am. I think it's God's way of protectin' 'im from the pain right now. He's sure to be in a might of it when he comes to."

"What if he don't wake up?" Miriam asked. Of course, leave it to the youngest to utter the unthinkable.

"He will, Miss Miriam. You just be thinkin' all the best thoughts you can."

Both girls started weeping, but there was little Faith could do to comfort them. Their brother was lying partially on his side, his left arm tucked awkwardly under him, and one foot twisted in a strange way. "Do you think he's broken some bones?"

Jobe looked up with a glum face. "I cain't say, Mrs. Fuller. We best not move him though till the doc gets here." He gazed up at the hayloft. "He done fell about eight or so feet." He studied the boy from top to bottom, looking at every exposed part he could find without removing any clothes. "He don't appear to be bleeding bad 'cept for a few marks here and there."

Franklin returned with a pail of water. "Here," he said in a breathless, shaky voice, handing over the pail. Jobe took it and cupped his hand in the water, then dripped some over the boy's face. Dirt rolled off his face in little streams, but he didn't move, didn't even make a sound. Beth cried louder, causing Miriam's whimpers to increase as well. Jobe repeated the action, this time rubbing his dark, wet hand over Isaac's face, and then up and down the one arm that wasn't tucked under him, but getting no response.

Faith reached a hand out to the whimpering girls, but they were so wrapped up in each other's arms that neither noticed. "Girls, it will be all right," she said, not at all sure of her own words but knowing with surety that she had to be strong for them. If she herself grew hysterical in the situation, it was certain they would follow her example.

A full twenty minutes went by before they finally heard the fast clip of horses' hooves and the rumble of a wagon coming up the drive along with Wendel's loud "Whoa!"

The doctor, a slightly graying man with a short beard and medium build, ran into the barn, a large black bag in hand. "Move aside please," he instructed, all business. Everyone did his bidding. He opened his bag and withdrew a few instruments, then went down on his knees and immediately lifted Isaac's eyelids. "Pupils are somewhat dilated," he said. "But not overly so."

"What does that mean, Doctor?" Faith asked.

Seemingly lost in thought, Doctor Eldred did not reply. He brought out his stethoscope and listened to various areas on Isaac's chest. "He has a good, steady heart rate, and he's breathing well."

"That's good," Faith responded, kneeling next to the doctor and silently praying with every ounce of mental and spiritual energy she could muster.

The doctor very carefully removed Isaac's left arm, ran his fingers along it, and inspected it. "Remarkably, he appears to be quite unscathed."

Isaac gave a quiet groan. "Isaac?" the doctor said. He repeated his name a few times, and Faith had all she could do not to shout at the boy to wake up. The doctor continued to examine Isaac and stopped at his left ankle. "This might need to be wrapped. It's swollen. I'm most concerned about his inability to wake up. There's no real evidence of bleeding from a wound, but there's no guarantee he's not bleeding internally." He bent down close. "Isaac, can you hear me? Isaac! Can you open your eyes?" Still no response. "If he landed on his head, there could be some swelling around his brain that is causing his coma-like state. I say coma-like because he did let out that groan, which indicates part of his brain is still functioning, and by that, I mean he's responding to pain. I really need to get him into the house so we can remove his clothing and I can do a more thorough exam."

"Of course," said Faith.

To Jobe and Wendel, the doctor said, "Do you have a flat board that we can carefully move him onto so we can carry him into the house?"

"We sho' does, Doc. Me an' Wendel will find something and be right back." Both men took off toward the back of the barn.

"And Mrs. Fuller, do you have a cot on the main floor of the house that we can lay him on?"

Faith thought of Joey's cot. "No, but there is a small cot in an upstairs room that Jobe and Wendel could bring down. We could set it up in the library."

"That would work fine."

"Is he goin' t' die, Doc?" Franklin asked, his voice quivering.

The doctor gave the boy his full attention, his face solemn at best. "I can tell you this. I'm going to do everything in my power to see that he doesn't. I'll also say this. If you believe in God, it wouldn't hurt to start talking to Him."

"We do!" Franklin answered. "All of us does."

"I'm a Christian," declared Miriam, her voice a tad stronger than it had been before. "And I know God listens to us when we pray."

"Me too!" said Beth, her eyes round with hope and eagerness.

The doctor gave a kind smile to all three children. "Then I'm certain the good Lord will listen extra closely. You just keep those prayers going up to heaven."

Jobe and Wendel had found an old door and placed a couple of clean horse blankets on top of it. Very carefully, they helped the doctor move Isaac from the barn floor to the makeshift gurney. It garnered another moan from Isaac…but it was not enough to awaken him.

Once they got in the house, they set Isaac down on the floor, then, while the doctor tended him and the children hovered, Faith took Wendel and Jobe upstairs to the tiny room with the cot. Looking at it now, she could barely believe Joey fit on the thing. Perchance he'd chosen to sleep on the floor instead. "That should be real easy to move," said Jobe.

"Yep, you take the mattress, and I'll carry down the frame," said Wendel.

"And I'll carry the bedding," said Faith.

Faith stepped up and tore off the bedding so Jobe could remove the mattress. When he walked out the door with it, she noted something familiar on the floor underneath the bed frame: her button string box. Wendel made no mention of it, just lifted the small metal frame, turned it on its side, and managed to maneuver it through the door without

bumping against the door frame. She knew she ought to hurry downstairs behind him, but she couldn't resist bending down first and lifting
the lid on the box. Sure enough, there lay the button string. Apparently,
it had been there since the day it went missing. *But why under Joey's cot?
And why hadn't anyone confessed?* She closed the lid, quickly scooped
up the heavy box, hurried down the hall to her bedroom, and slipped
it back into her top drawer. Without wasting another second, she has-
tened downstairs with the balled-up bedding in her arms.

32

Everything leading to the seizure of Atlanta had been going on for weeks, months really, but it looked to be coming to a close with the North the clear victors. Since late May, soldiers from both sides had traversed up mountains, through forests, down into ravines, and across rivers, but it was the Union troops who guarded bridges, stations, railways, and intermediate depots, diminishing enemy forces and charging forward, ever on the defensive and having the decided advantage in numbers, reinforcements, supplies, and fighting force. Joey couldn't help but feel good about it, as did Major Dieters and other commanding officers. Yes, there had been casualties, some 1,700 at the crossing of Peachtree Creek on July 20, but nearly twice that many inflicted on the Confederates. Not to be dissuaded, Confederates, led by General John B. Hood, attempted a second attack just two days after the Battle at Peachtree Creek, this one a surprise, but the Federals had positioned themselves in such a way as to defeat them yet again, this time inflicting 6,000 casualties on Rebel forces compared to the Union's 3,700. Undeterred, General Hood initiated a third battle on July 28 at Ezra Church, this one costing Hood 3,000 men to the Union's 632. But Hood had tenacity, and it wasn't until the last line fell in the midst of yet a fourth Union victory that he admitted defeat and began evacuating the city. After that, it became clear to most that the end of this bitter war might well be drawing closer, the fall of Atlanta proving to be the blow from which the Confederacy might never recover. Still, now was no time to let down defenses, become overconfident, or grow slack, so when a battle wasn't raging, troops continued drills, weapon inspection, and practicing maneuvers.

It was August 29. In wartime, soldiers usually lost track of exact dates—unless they were soon to muster out. Then every day and minute counted. A soldier's routine was to awaken at dawn, dress in a hurry, then roll up his bedding. Afterward, he usually drank a cup of coffee or got a drink from the nearest stream and ate a few bites of salt pork and dry bread. If he was lucky, he might get an occasional egg or a rare piece of in-season fruit. Early morning formation followed, then physical and individual training, some having administrative duties and others assigned to something as menial as digging trenches. Days and even weeks in a soldier's life melded together in a mundane fashion. Joey knew the date though; he had been keeping good track since he'd returned to duty back in late June and could recall the dates of every battle, from Kennesaw Mountain on June 27 to Atlanta on July 22, and then to the Battle of Utoy Creek in Atlanta during the first week of August. To say he was exhausted didn't quite describe his body's condition, but there was no time for reflection or even much rest because they'd gotten their orders that they'd be starting out for Jonesboro tomorrow morning. They had one day to drill, inspect firearms, write letters, and catch up on what rest they could get. Yesterday, Major Dieters had told Joey he suspected that, after Jonesboro, they'd be lingering around the Atlanta area for the next several weeks, guarding stations and rail lines and evacuating the last of Atlanta's citizens. Atlanta belonged to the Union now, and General Sherman wasn't about winning any popularity votes with the South. In fact, to prove his point, he'd ordered regiments to commence with burning down most of the city, including private residences, entire cotton plantations, storefronts, and warehouses.

Joey grew more anxious to muster out with every passing day. At the same time, he had a strong sense of duty to his country and company, so while he wanted—even needed—to get home to his family, his emotions were mixed. It made no sense to him, but he couldn't deny it either. And then there was the matter of Faith. He'd tied a string around the pile of letters she'd written and wondered if she'd saved his as well. The big surprise was that she seldom, if ever, mentioned behavioral problems with his children. *Was it too good to be true to think there weren't any, or was she merely keeping the entire truth from him?* He suspected the latter.

Joey was stationed with his back against a tree, reading his Bible. Over the past few months, he'd read the entire New Testament, and while his reading stirred up questions, his newfound faith made up for them. He'd never understand the way God worked or why He allowed certain things to happen, but he'd finally concluded that doubting God's love or casting blame only led to bitterness, and that was no way to live.

"You want some fish, Captain? Edwards caught a couple of big trout down at the stream." Joey looked up. Under his nose was a plate of fresh-fried fish. His taste buds went a little wild.

"Are you kidding? I knew I smelled something cooking, but I couldn't distinguish it. Thanks, Sarge." He reached up and took the offering.

Sergeant Ralph Meyers crouched down, resting his arms across his bent knees. "I notice you been reading that Bible every chance you get lately."

"That I have. I discovered it holds the answers I've been running from for years now."

"Glad to hear it, Captain. I believe it myself, you know. I'm quiet about my faith, but I know God has a purpose in all things. It says so in Romans chapter eight, verse twenty-eight." He started to quote the verse, and soon Joey joined in so they finished it in unison. "*And we know that all things work together for good to them that love God, to them who are the called according to his purpose.*"

They smiled at each other, and the sergeant stood. "Well, you enjoy that fish. I'll stop by later to pick up the fork and plate."

"Thanks. I appreciate it."

"Gentlemen." They both startled at the sound of Major Dieters' solemn tone. Ralph straightened and saluted, and Joey set down the plate and stood in an instant.

"Sir," Joey said, saluting as well.

The major nodded, his face still a picture of solemnity. "At ease. I—uh—need to talk to you, Joseph." *What in the world?*

Without further ado, Sergeant Meyers made a fast exit.

"What is it, sir?"

The major looked around. It was quiet, save for a few soldiers milling in the distance. Joey had specifically picked a remote area in which to read his Bible. In fact, he'd been surprised that Ralph had even found him to deliver the fish. Perhaps it'd been providential that they'd recited the Bible verse together. He swallowed down a hard knot because he knew beyond a doubt that something wasn't right.

Major Dieters gave a hard sniff and extended his hand. "This telegram just arrived at my tent. For you."

A sudden pang of worry made Joey's stomach take a giant flip. With reluctance, he took the paper and began to read.

Isaac suffered tragic fall (stop) in coma state (stop) doctor says in God's hands alone (stop) your brother Jesse (stop)

Joey's heart skipped several beats as terror swept through his body and even overtook his ability to think. *What was he to do?* He wasn't due to leave for another couple of weeks. *Would his son still be there?* His brow furrowed in a desperate attempt to hold his emotions intact. He raised his eyes to the major and, for the first time ever, read true compassion in his face.

"If it weren't for the fact you're mustering out soon, I'd tell you to buck it up, but I can't in good conscience do that. I want you to gather your things and go home to your family."

"Wh-what?"

"You heard me. Things sound grave. You'll have to go through the necessary channels to officially muster out, but as of now, I am granting you an honorable discharge."

Joey had no words. He wanted to show his gratitude, but a hug was definitely out of the question. Instead, the major reached out his hand, and they shook rather than saluted. "I wish you and your family the best, and especially your son Isaac." It was a gesture Joey would never forget.

⌒

"Any change today?" Doctor Eldred asked as soon as he walked through the front door.

Faith quietly closed the door behind him. "Not much. I will say he's opening his eyes more, and he's taking small bits of water and spoonfuls of broth. I can't get him to speak to me though, although his eyes seem to follow me." She wrung her hands. "Unless that's just my hopeful imagination. Laura is with him now."

"That's good. He needs a certain amount of stimulation, but lots of rest is also most vital. I've been reading all the medical journals I can get my hands on to learn more about comas and their causes. It can result from many things, even infection, but most are due to injuries such as the one Isaac suffered when he took that fall. There is swelling around the brain, which is preventing him from functioning normally, and only time and God can get that swelling to go down. I wish I had some ideas for specialized treatment, but alas, I am just a regular doctor with no experience treating coma patients."

"I understand you've been doing the best you can, Doctor. The family appreciates your efforts. Everyone has been taking their turns sitting at Isaac's bedside during the day, holding his hand, looking for subtle changes, and giving him sips of water or broth. Reverend Stanton from Community Methodist Church stopped in this morning to offer a prayer and read some Scripture. Isaac stirred a bit when he was here, even opened his eyes and tried to focus, but then he went right back to sleep."

The doctor nodded and quietly studied her face. "You're looking tired, my dear. You need your rest, or you'll be no good yourself."

"I've managed to nap a bit during the day when someone is here, and during the night, I sometimes lie on the floor next to him."

He shook his head. "That's not sufficient, at least not long term."

"I appreciate your concern, but I'll be fine. I'm strong."

He lifted his bushy, graying brows and turned up his mouth a tad. "I've certainly witnessed that. Has Joseph been notified?"

Her throat clogged with emotion. "Jesse sent him a telegram, but he has a full two weeks before he musters out. I just hope…" She glanced toward the library where Isaac lay sleeping.

The doctor touched her arm. "I know, my dear. We all hope, but we must remain positive throughout the process. The boy is making progress, I can assure you of that."

She gave a sluggish nod. "I hope and pray you're right."

"How are the other children holding up?"

"They are doing as well as can be expected, but they miss their brother. The last words Beth said to him were 'I hate you,' so she's been continually repenting of that and telling him she didn't mean it. I feel so badly for her, but there's little I can do. Miriam kneels at his bedside and daily prays aloud for him. It is both touching and inspiring. Her faith is truly strong and righteous for one so young. Franklin mostly mopes and blames himself for the accident, even though I tell him he had nothing to do with it. He's also tending Isaac's horse, spending as much time with her as Isaac would, and I think it's been rather healing for him. He goes out and talks to her and tells her Isaac will return to her as soon as he's able. Jobe, our hired man, had no idea there were a couple rotted boards in the hayloft, so he, too, is carrying some guilt. It's been repaired now, thankfully. The whole thing is tragic."

"Indeed it is, but you all must bear in mind it was an accident."

"The children are with their Uncle Jesse now. He does well at keeping them occupied. He had errands to run in town, so he took them with him an hour or so ago."

"Glad to hear it. I'll go look in on our patient now."

She followed him to the library, and as soon as he entered, Laura stood up from the chair she'd been sitting in next to the cot. "Doctor

Eldred," she whispered, stepping aside. She too looked weary, certainly older than her late fifties. "Thank you for coming."

"Of course." He stepped up to the sleeping boy. "How are we doing today, Isaac?" Faith liked the way he always spoke to Isaac as if he were listening. She'd been doing the same during bedside vigils. So far, she'd been handling nighttime on her own, even though Laura and Cristina and even her brothers-in-law had offered to take their turns. With Cristina's pregnancy progressing, her sister-in-law needed her rest, and the men had a farm to tend. They couldn't afford to miss a good night's sleep.

"Let me have a peek at those hazel peepers of yours, my boy." Doctor Eldred lifted Isaac's eyelids for a look. "Uh-huh, a little brighter today, I'd say. It's good that the pupils respond to light, and they're not fixed. Good sign indeed." He removed his stethoscope from his bag. "I'm going to listen to your breathing now, Isaac." He placed the stethoscope at various places, then turned him on his side so he could place the instrument on his back. Isaac made a whining sound. "A bit sore, are we? Well, you fell a good distance. It's no wonder." He glanced up at Faith and Laura. "By the way, it's another good sign that he's annoyed with my disturbing him." He rolled the boy to his back again. "Let's see if you feel this, Isaac." He lifted the boy's arm and pinched the skin on his forearm. Instinctively, Isaac withdrew. "Excellent, that's very good, Isaac." He pulled the covers off of Isaac and tested his reflexes. "Excellent," he told the women. "See how he responds?" He removed the wraps on Isaac's ankle, checked on the swelling, and then rewrapped it. "The bruises have changed color, which is to be expected. Overall, he's in good shape. Has he been relieving himself?"

Faith nodded. "Yes, but not often because I can't get him to drink much. I've put that large pan under the cot, as you can see, and I keep fresh bedding and underdrawers handy at all times."

"She's taking excellent care of my grandson, Doctor," Laura said.

He smiled and nodded. "I can certainly see that. I assume you've also been rolling him to his sides periodically? We want to make sure he doesn't acquire any bedsores from lying in one position too long." They both nodded. "His lungs sound clear, and he has a good, strong heartbeat. I noticed, too, he took some good, deep breaths. That's important. Sometimes, patients who lie flat for extended periods develop pneumonia, but so far, he's not showing any signs." He turned his attention back to Isaac, brought the light blanket back over him, and then gave him a pat on the shoulder. "We just need you to wake up, young man." The sleeping boy gave no indication he'd heard him.

Doctor Eldred put away what items he'd withdrawn from his bag, closed it up, and then smiled again. "He's moving in the right direction, ladies, so you can be glad about that. I just can't predict when he'll awaken. It could be tomorrow, it could be next week. And when he does, I don't know what we'll face. Will there be some brain damage? Possibly. The sooner he wakes, the closer we'll be to determining the answers. I'll be back tomorrow. If there's any change at all that warrants my attention, send someone to fetch me."

"Thank you, we will," Faith said, walking him to the door, while Laura remained in the library.

She stood on the porch and watched him drive away, but just as she started to turn to go back inside, she caught sight of Jesse's wagon rounding the corner. The two wagons stopped next to each other, and it appeared from what little she could see that the doctor and Jesse were conversing, but soon, the doctor went on his way, and then Jesse's wagon proceeded up the drive, drawing closer with every second. At closer inspection, Faith noted an extra body. *A man.* Her eyes widened. She shielded them from the sun. Could it be—no, it wasn't possible. Hesitant to believe it, she merely stood there, still as a tree stump, eyes carefully trained on the extra passenger. That's when Beth called out from the back of the wagon. "Faith, look! It's Daddy! Uncle Jesse wanted to surprise you."

She put a hand to her mouth, and for a couple of seconds, did nothing but stare. But then her better judgment left her. She lifted her skirts, took one giant leap off the porch, and broke into a desperate run toward the approaching wagon, tears already streaming down her cheeks, sobs coming intermittently. Joey bounded off the moving wagon to meet her halfway, and just like that, she was in his arms, releasing a flood of tears that she'd held in for three long days. "Joey, oh, Joey, I'm so sorry. I'm so sorry," she said between sobs.

"Shh. It's all right." He held her tight to him, rocking her back and forth, one hand cupping the back of her head and the other splayed across the middle of her back. Her own arms wrapped tightly around him, as if clinging for life, her face still deeply buried in his chest, his chin resting on her head.

"I didn't know—I shouldn't have—"

"No, no, don't talk like that. Jesse said it was an accident. Shh. We'll talk later, all right? For now, let's just go inside. I'm home now."

She pulled away, knowing she looked a dreadful sight, her face probably red and swollen. She hadn't even had a decent bath in three days. She searched his face. "For good?"

"Yes, for good."

Jesse had driven past them on his way up to the barn, so it was just the two of them standing in the middle of the long, dusty two-track. He set her back from him to study her face. Then he gently removed several strands of hair from her eyes and, with his fingertips, he wiped away the tears that lingered on her cheeks. "I'm happy to see you, but I must go inside to see my son. Tell me what to expect."

She pondered how to answer. "He looks like he's sleeping, and that's all I can say."

He breathed in deep through his nostrils, then slowly let the air back out. Then, straightening, he stared at the house. After seeming to gather his wits, he said, "All right then. Let's go inside."

33

Stuart glanced around his dingy cell. It had been his "home" for too many weeks, and soon, he'd be looking at four new walls at the state penitentiary. He had no idea when to expect the guards to come for him, only that it would be sometime today. *Whatever.* He'd reached the point of not caring. Loneliness such as he'd never known had settled in on him. His former cellmate, the infamous bank robber, had been transferred to a different facility, but news was his sentence only amounted to three to five years, nothing compared to Stuart's twenty years to life. Stuart's defense lawyer said it was the best he could hope for, considering his crime. "If you mind your manners, you might get out in twenty, so keep your nose clean," he'd said.

Leon had visited him several times, an accomplishment for Leon considering he rarely came to town. Stuart had come to appreciate his visits, had even learned to listen more and talk less, a real feat for him. He'd even taken to reading the Bible Leon brought, and before his cellmate left, they'd had a discussion or two about some of the passages. Stuart wasn't the best reader so he struggled with several of the words and lengthy chapters. *Would he ever make sense of it? And if he did, would it even matter?* Religion was good for some, but he wasn't sure he himself was cut out for it. *He'd murdered his wife, after all—he'd admit that now—and how could someone who did that ever expect forgiveness, even if Leon told him repeatedly God loved him despite his insufficiencies?* That was what the cross was all about, Leon had said, Jesus giving His life as a once and for all sacrifice for the sins of all mankind. He didn't *choose* who was worthy. No, Leon said, salvation was for all. Even the thief hanging next to Jesus on a cross asked for forgiveness in his final breaths, and Jesus promised he'd be with him in paradise that very day.

And then there was the matter of Faith Haviland. Somehow, in his convoluted manner of thinking, he figured she'd see something in him, no matter that he was several years her senior. *What had he been thinking? And why had he treated her so wrongly? Had his years of drinking so twisted his mind that he'd lost all common sense?* Now that he'd not had a drop of booze in months, his head had cleared, and he saw himself in a totally different light. He was not a good person. Far from it.

Lord, I don't know. If You're real, maybe You can reveal Yourself to me somehow—someday. I'll leave that up to You.

The door at the end of the corridor rattled open, then shut with a loud clang. Footfall echoed in the hall as it drew closer. Of course, he couldn't see who it was because of the steel bars. He breathed a sigh of great relief at the sight of Leon's face. "You came one last time."

"You doubted that I would?"

"I wondered. I don't know what time they're taking me to the state pen."

"Later this afternoon is my understanding. It's not like you're going on a long ride. I don't know when I'll see you again though. I'll have to first learn their visiting policies. I suspect they're probably much different than at this here county jail." Leon nodded thoughtfully. "But I will visit you if I can, Stu."

"Don't be worryin' about it, cousin. I ain't worth visiting, and I'm not sayin' that to earn your sympathy or favor. I'm just seeing myself for the man I am, and I don't much like myself."

Leon smiled. "I once viewed myself in the same way. I did a lot of things I wasn't proud of, Stu, but I had to reach a point of saying, 'God, here I am. I don't have much to offer, but if You want me, I'm Yours.' And you know what? He wanted me. And that's exactly how He views you. Think on it, Stu, but don't wait too long because every day that goes by that you don't trust God with your life is a day wasted."

"I'll think on it."

They changed topics several times, discussing everything from the war to politics to news around town. That led to the subject of Stuart's butcher shop. "I been thinking, Leon. I want you to sell my shop and put the money in my account. I also want you to take twenty percent of the profits."

"I'll be glad to handle the sale of your business, but I won't be taking any of your profits. We're family, Stu, and we do for each other, expecting nothing in return."

They argued about it for a few minutes until it became clear Leon wasn't going to budge. "Well, I need you to tell my lawyer to visit me at prison so we can settle some things and I can appoint you my power of attorney."

"I'll be glad to do that for you."

"Nothin' like waitin' till the last minute, eh?"

Leon chuckled, then stepped back to study him from head to toe. "You've changed, Stuart Porter."

"Have I?"

"If I didn't know better, I'd think you'd started growin' some common sense."

"Hah! Maybe I have. I think it's the lack of booze."

"You been readin' that Bible I gave you?"

"I have, bits of it anyway."

Leon nodded. "You keep it up, and before you know it, you'll be a new man, might even be preaching to your cellmates."

Now it was Stuart's turn to laugh. "Wouldn't that be a miracle?"

"Don't laugh. God's in the miracle-working business."

Joey found he had to divide his time between his four children. Even though he'd wanted to devote every minute of the last few days to attempting to awaken Isaac, the other three also sought his devotion, hardly taking their eyes off him except to sleep. Even now, as he sat in the library holding Isaac's hand, he had Miriam on his lap, Beth holding his other hand, and Frankie sitting on the bed next to Isaac, his and Joey's knees touching. His mother Laura and brother Jesse had left an hour ago, and Faith was in the kitchen preparing some supper.

They felt like a family, although not a complete one. For one thing, Isaac was present…and yet he wasn't. And Faith was still under his roof, no doubt thinking about her future, although neither of them had brought up the subject. Surely, with Isaac in this sickly state, she wouldn't want to leave just yet. She'd certainly been overly attentive to Isaac, even insisting on sleeping on the floor next to him at night so Joey could have the couch in the other room. "You've been sleeping on the hard ground for three years. It's time you slept on something softer," she'd said. He'd tried to argue with her, but she'd have none of it.

Try as he might, Joey couldn't imagine his house without her, managing his children, seeing to the housekeeping, handling farm chores. It was all too much to think about just now—at least while his son lay in this semi-comatose state, as the doctor called it. He wanted Faith under his roof, but how to go about telling her so without coming off sounding selfish and needy would be the trick.

Over and over, he'd relived that moment when Jesse had steered the wagon onto his property, and he'd caught sight of Faith standing on the porch. Once she'd determined it was him sitting next to Jesse, she'd left that porch in one leap and come running to meet him, her skirts flying, her hair all undone, her eyes brimming with tears. He'd instinctively jumped off the moving wagon to meet her and swept her up into his arms without a second's hesitation. It had all felt so natural. After all the letters she'd written him over the past months, he felt he'd come to know her so much better. *Did she feel the same?* He wanted—needed—to talk to her…and yet the very thought of it gave him the jitters.

There was a bit more conversing over dinner that evening than on the previous nights, with the children doing the greater share of talking while Joey and Faith slipped in a few words here and there. Even after three days at home, he didn't quite know how to feel or act around her. When he'd first met her back in June, he'd been bold and forthright. Shyness hadn't played into his emotions. Now, though, he viewed her in a different manner, caring what she thought about him and wondering if she had grown any feelings for him in their absence.

At the same time, he had Isaac in the library, sleeping his life away, seemingly unaware his daddy had come home, and hundreds of miles away, a war raging in which he no longer played a role. His world felt strange, surreal, and dreadfully unsettled.

"I'm happy you're home, Daddy," Miriam said for at least the hundredth time since she'd jumped into his arms at the train station on Tuesday afternoon.

He snuck another peek at Faith, but she was staring down at her plate while trying to balance some peas on her fork. "I'm happy as well, my lambkin."

"Are you sure you're not going back to that bad war?"

"I'm sure."

Beth picked up her water glass for a quick drink, then smiled. "I'm glad too, Daddy." And suddenly, her lips turned down into a frown. "I feel sort of strange though."

"What's making you feel strange?"

"I don't know. I have to try to get used to you being here and Faith being gone." She pouted.

Faith slowly raised her head at the comment, but he couldn't read her expression. She slipped the forkful of peas into her mouth and silently chewed.

"That does sound like quite an adjustment," Joey said. His throat went as dry as sand, so he, too, took a swig of water.

Beth's face sobered as she looked at Faith. "We haven't always been our nicest. You probably can't wait to leave."

Faith's blue eyes grew bigger than usual. "Well—that *is* true."

"What's true? That we ain't been nice, or that you don't want to stay?" asked Franklin.

She took up her napkin and dabbed at her mouth. "Um, perhaps—a little—of both. I don't know. That is something for your father and me to discuss."

"Your letters didn't inform me of their ill behavior," Joey said, looking across the table at her. They sat at the ends with the children on the sides, Isaac's chair conspicuously empty.

"I didn't wish to worry you unnecessarily."

"You never told Daddy about ar' bad behavior?" Beth asked.

"I wasn't bad," Miriam clarified.

"You weren't perfect," Franklin said.

Faith smiled. "None of you were terrible, and none of you were perfect."

Beth hung her head. "I just can't believe you didn't tell Daddy."

Joey cleared his throat. "Nor can I."

Faith gave a little shrug. "I didn't think it necessary."

There was a soberness around the table—until Miriam made a little squealing sound. Her mouth formed a circle, and a gasp escaped. "I just remembered something I got for you, Daddy. Can I be excused for a minute?"

Joey gawked at his youngest. "It can't wait?" Miriam shook her head violently, braids flying. "Then—yes, I guess—although you haven't finished your meal."

"I know, but I will." She jumped up and disappeared around the corner. No one could miss the sound of her fast little feet tramping up the stairs.

He trained his eyes on Beth and Franklin. "I'm sorry to hear you gave Faith a difficult time, particularly since I lectured all of you about using your best manners before I left."

"Please, they were just fine," said Faith, setting down her fork, her hands lowered to her lap. "They helped me a great deal around the house and in the garden. Really, I have very few complaints. There were a few pranks now and again, but we also had fun, didn't we?"

"She's makin' us sound better than we was," said Franklin.

"No, I'm not, Frankie," Faith said. "Life has been difficult for you, and I understand that. I knew that your acting out came from a deeper source, so I forgave it." She reached for her napkin and dabbed her mouth, then smiled and added, "Of course, I had to pray a lot."

Joey's heart tightened in his chest. He wanted to know just what sort of pranks they'd played…but then again, maybe it was best left between Faith and the kids.

Miriam's return to the table was a lot quieter than her retreat. In fact, her glum face when she sat back down said she wasn't happy.

"What's wrong?" Faith asked.

"It's gone," she said.

"What's gone?" asked Joey.

"Yeah, what are you talkin' about?" Beth wanted to know.

Miriam looked from one to the other. "The string. I forgot you moved the lil' bed to the library for Isaac. I wanted Daddy to find the string. I put it under there."

"What string?" Beth asked.

"The button string."

Beth gave an extra loud huff. "What?! It was *you* who took the button string? Why didn't you tell us? Why didn't you confess it to Faith?"

Miriam's face screwed up into the angriest frown Joey had ever seen on his little one.

Faith put a flat palm to her mouth and simply stared.

"Miriam, you stole it and never told Faith! That was naughty," Franklin scolded.

Miriam burst into tears. "No, I didn't mean it to be stealing. I—I'm—sorry. I—put it under Daddy's lil' bed so he could—find it when—he comed home—and…" Her words became indecipherable, lost between her heaving, ragged sobs. She gave a loud moan and began anew. "I—w-wanted Daddy t-to give the last button to Faith—so she'd have her millionth button!" she wailed. "Then—then they'd be 'fficially married." Then her sobs turned into a scream directed at Joey. "Now—now I don't even know how to find it!"

He felt completely helpless. *What on earth was happening under his roof?*

"It's not a *million* buttons, silly," Beth said. "It's a thousand." That only made the poor little girl howl the louder.

Joey reached his arm across the table to comfort her, but Faith jumped out of her chair to run around the table and enfold the child in her arms, kneeling next to her and patting her little back. "It's all right, honey, I have the button string. It's back in my drawer where it belongs. I found it when Wendel and Jobe carried the cot downstairs to the library."

The girl sniffed and pulled back. "You did?"

"Yes, don't worry about it."

"Are you mad?"

"No, I'm not mad."

"You should be," said Beth, her indignation showing. "You're very forgiving, Faith."

"Well, I don't think Miriam quite looked at it as stealing." She turned her full attention on Frankie and Beth. "I am sincerely sorry I blamed you. Will you forgive me?"

They both nodded. Beth said, "I guess she didn't know better. It's okay, Miriam."

Joey's youngest daughter continued to release a few wracking sighs before eventually finding her voice again. "But—are—you goin' to give the string to Daddy?" she asked Faith.

It was all starting to make sense to Joey now. Faith's bridegroom was supposed to complete the chain with its one thousandth button. He grew a trifle uncomfortable, and Faith's cheeks turned a pretty shade of pink. "Well, I—"

Thinking it necessary to change the subject, Joey quickly interjected, "Maybe we should think about dessert. I recall seeing a pie…"

A moaning sound and then a yell coming from the library had everyone instantly forgetting about the button chain and shoving back in their chairs to make a beeline for Isaac. Faith beat them all there, and to Joey's great elation, he found his son lying on the cot, eyes open, though certainly looking confused. "Isaac, you're awake!" Faith said, running to his side and kneeling next to his bed. She turned to seek out Joey. "He's awake!" Faith took Isaac's hand and brought it to her cheek. "Oh, Isaac." If the boy objected to her handling, he didn't show it. Instead, he turned his head slightly to take in the sights around him, then let his eyes slowly roam from one person to the other, as they all gathered around his bed.

"Isaac," said Beth, stepping up to touch his shoulder, "I didn't mean it when I said I hated you."

Miriam swiped at her still wet and swollen eyes. "Did you wake up 'cause I was screaming? I'm sorry—no, wait, I'm not 'cause we wanted you awake. I been praying for you every day, Isaac."

Franklin patted his brother on the arm. "I missed you."

Joey came up behind Beth and leaned over her slender frame to touch his son's head. "Hey there, buddy. I'm home now. To stay. What do you think about that?" Isaac turned his face upward to see Joey full on, but rather than speak, he merely furrowed his brow.

Everyone became quiet and held their breath, awaiting Isaac's first words. *Did he have any? Was he even capable? What had happened to him in those days he lay sleeping? What thoughts danced around in his head? Did he even have any? Was his brain ever going to function normally again?*

After a full minute of utter silence, he opened his mouth and started to move his lips. However, nothing came out.

"What is it, son?" Joey asked, his heart racing with a mix of fear and excitement.

Isaac closed his mouth, swallowed, and opened it again, his eyes trying to focus on Joey and his hand still clasped in Faith's. "I—th-thirsty."

"He's thirsty!" everyone said at once.

"I'll get it," several said, but Frankie made it out of the room first, returning in a matter of seconds. He handed the cup to Faith.

Joey stepped around Faith and put a supportive hand around his son's back to lift him. "Here, son, let me help you up a bit so you can take a sip."

Faith put the cup to his mouth, and he drank, though just a few swallows, then waved his hand to indicate he was done.

"Would you like a little soup, Isaac?" Faith asked.

"She makes good chicken soup, 'member, Isaac?" Beth asked.

Isaac turned his head to look at Beth. "Who?"

"Faith," she said.

He slowly moved his gaze from one person to the next. "F-Faith. That's you," he said, eyes finally stopping to rest on her.

She smiled. "Yes. Do you remember me?"

He blinked. "I'm—I'm confused."

"Of course you are, son. You've been mostly sleeping for a number of days," Joey told him.

"I—have? Wh—why?"

"Don't you remember?" Frankie asked. "You fell from the hayloft." The boy slowly shook his head. "Hey, don't worry about Rose. She's doing great, but she misses you. I been takin' good care of her for you."

"Rose?"

"Your horse. Remember? Faith gave her to you."

Isaac merely stared at Frankie. Joey worried his memory might not return in full.

"Do you want some soup?" Beth asked again.

"I'm—tired."

"Of course you are," Joey said. "But before you go back to sleep, let's pray and thank God for Isaac's progress."

Everyone laid a hand on Isaac, and Joey, shy as he was about praying in front of anyone, even his own family, thanked the Lord for the miracle they'd all just witnessed. He asked the Lord to continue the healing in his son and to restore his memory so he could return to life as usual. When he gave the final amen, they all opened their eyes—except for Isaac, who had drifted back to sleep.

34

With every passing day, Isaac improved, and Doctor Eldred said he had no reason to believe he wouldn't make a full recovery. His bruises had faded, and even the swelling in his ankle had gone down so that now he moved around fine, but with a very slight limp. He was able to care for and ride Rose once more, but he couldn't recall all the training techniques Jesse had taught him to use with her. Still, he was riding, and that was a big positive in Faith's mind, although she worried about him falling and constantly reminded him not to try anything foolish. He still had no memory of climbing up into the hayloft or any of the events leading up to it, and the doctor said that portion of his memory might never return.

"You must've made me climb up there, Frankie," he'd said one night while they were all sitting in the living room talking about the incident. September had rolled in with a storm and a cold front, then a week later transitioned back to hot and humid. So far, Joey had not mentioned a single word to Faith about her leaving, nor had she brought up the subject. She'd been so busy tending to Isaac that it seemed best to wait till he fully recovered before mentioning it. The whole thing felt awkward to her and no doubt strange to Joey as well.

"No, I didn't. It was your idea. You were mad at Faith about something, and so you said, 'Let's go in the barn.'"

"Why was I mad at Faith?"

"I don't remember."

"I do," Faith chimed. She had *The Pilgrim's Progress* in her lap and had been sporadically reading while also listening to the children's lively chatter. Joey sat on the new sofa, newspaper in hand. He laid it down when she spoke. "You were mad at me because I told you to come in the house instead of going to your Uncle Jesse's. It was Saturday afternoon, and we had things to do to get ready for Sunday church."

"So, we didn't come in the house, but we didn't go to Uncle Jesse's either," Isaac said. "We half obeyed then."

She laughed. "I suppose that's one way to look at it."

"Did we go to church on Sunday?" he asked.

"No, silly. You fell out of the hayloft!" Beth answered. She was sitting on the floor with Miriam playing with dolls.

"Oh. Well, how would I know that? I don't even remember falling."

Faith put her hands on her hips. "Do you remember being naughty?"

"Me? Never! I have been an angel from the moment I was born."

That produced a laugh from everyone. Even Miriam thought it funny.

One thing Faith would say about the family since Isaac's accident; they'd all drawn closer together with much less arguing. Somehow, life had taken on a new meaning, and even the children recognized it as a precious a gift. *Whether or not this new attitude would last remained to be seen—and would she even be here to witness it?*

Another thing she'd noticed was that they all seemed to have softened toward her. Whether it was due to Joey's being home or the way she'd taken care of Isaac, she couldn't say. She only knew that things were different and she'd come to love them all with a deep tenderness she never would have dreamed possible. She'd not earned any goodnight hugs from the boys yet, but Beth and Miriam were generous with them, something that made her heart swell with gratitude. As for their father, she'd come to care deeply for him as well, perhaps even love him if she dared think it, but she had no idea what thoughts or emotions ran through his head. He didn't express them, and if anything had grown somewhat distant. *Was he worried about how she would take it when the day finally came to tell her he no longer required her services?* They certainly had not been living together in the way a normal husband and wife would, he taking over the cot in the library after Isaac was well enough to return to the bedroom he shared with Franklin. Oh, he never uttered an unkind word to her, and there was never a hint of impatience. But there weren't advances either, so she had no way of knowing what to think.

Joey had taken to working the farm again every day, and as harvesttime drew nearer, the workload increased. If she were going to leave, and he were going to find a replacement to watch the children during the day, it would seem to her now would be a good time for him to start looking. Her heart and mind were a scrambled mess as she tried to imagine her future.

"I s'pose it's about time to get you whippersnappers off to bed," Joey said.

"Awww," came the usual groans. "Do we have to?"

"The hour is getting later."

"Yes, your father is right," Faith said, laying her book on the table next to the chair.

Everyone moved like tortoises, but eventually the bedtime routine was set in motion; stories were told, prayers were said, and covers were tucked up close to four youthful chins as Joey and Faith closed the doors on the three bedrooms. Once done, they stood in the hallway and briefly looked at each other before one of them spoke.

"Well." Joey brushed his palms together. "I can take care of turning down all the lights downstairs if you want to stay up here."

Her heart sank. "All right."

He stared down at her for just a second. "Good night then."

Why did everything have to be so awkward between them? She felt shy and downright tongue-tied. "Good night."

They both turned and started walking, he heading for the stairs, she for her room—*his* room, actually. She stopped in her tracks, suddenly tired of the whole charade. "Joey," she said.

He stopped in an instant and turned. "Yes?"

"Do you want your bedroom back?"

"My bedroom—you mean—tonight?"

"I mean—" *Goodness, what did she mean?* "It is your room, after all."

"Are you saying you want to—share the bed?"

Good gracious! She hadn't meant that! *Or had she?* There came that awful gawkiness again. But now that he mentioned it, they were husband and wife after all. "Perhaps—we could—*talk?*" *How utterly embarrassing! He probably had no intention of talking—not if they were going to share the bed.*

"Of course. We *need* to talk, actually."

Finally! He admitted the need. "It's probably time," she said.

"To talk," he said.

"Yes. To talk."

He pointed a thumb over his right shoulder. "I'll just go down to the library and get a few things."

"All right then."

"And—I'll extinguish all the lights."

"Yes, the lights."

He turned again and headed for the stairs a second time. *Was it her imagination, or was his step a little lighter?*

⌒

He could hardly believe it. She'd brought up the matter of their sleeping arrangements. Perhaps that meant she was entertaining the idea of staying. *Was it too much to hope?* Joey moved through the house, snuffing out one lamp after another, eager to return to his room and, for the first time in a long while, sleep in his own bed. He would be careful not to touch her, although he'd had a taste of her lips back in June. He wouldn't mind another. But he also wouldn't push it. He had no idea what thoughts circled her head, how she was feeling about things, or whether she'd only stayed because of Isaac.

To say that he himself knew exactly what he wanted wasn't altogether true either. He'd spent the past three, almost four, years single. *Was he ready for marriage in its entirety?* At the same time, he'd said vows to her, and even though he hadn't meant them that day in the courthouse, he had made a recommitment to God. *Shouldn't honoring his wedding vows be topmost on his priorities?* And then there was the question of love. *Hmm. Love. Could he ever love her to the full extent—as he'd loved Sarah Beth?* It worried him that he might never get there. *What kind of marriage would that be?*

To add to his stress, he'd been suffering nightmares, and a couple of nights since arriving back home, he'd awakened in a pool of sweat, dreaming about running from a group of Rebels, blood running down his arms and legs. He'd heard that soldiers coming off the field often had terrible dreams, but he'd not been fully prepared. He extinguished the last lamp in the library, picked up his Bible from the little stand next to the cot, and headed for the stairs, his stomach suddenly tied in a million knots. *Lord, I'm a mixed-up mess.*

He found Faith lying in the big poster bed, the blankets pulled past her neck so that only her face showed. Even her arms were covered, and it was a warm night. Both windows were open to let in some air, but it was still stuffy to be sure. She'd let her hair down, so he did get a glimpse of her flowing blond locks spread out against her pillow. He sat on the edge of the bed and removed his boots, lining them up perfectly—as he'd been accustomed to doing for the past three years. Then he took off his shirt, his back to her.

"You have a scar," she said.

He reached around to the center of his back and rubbed the protruding slash. He'd never actually studied it with a mirror though, so he had no idea how bad it looked. "Shrapnel, I'm afraid. Happened during the Mississippi Campaign in November of sixty-two. It's what advanced my rank to captain."

"That's awful—the wound, I mean. Did it hurt terribly?"

"It laid me up for a while. Is it ugly? I've never looked at it."

He heard movement from behind, and then felt the touch of her fingers against his back as she traced the scar. It gave him a jolt.

She withdrew right away. "I'm sorry."

"No, it's fine. It's just—it's been awhile since anyone's touched me there."

He heard her go back under the covers. "No, it's not ugly. It's beautiful, really."

"Beautiful?" He folded his shirt just so and set it neatly atop his boots.

"It represents who you are—and what you did for our country. You should be proud of every single scar you acquired."

"I guess I've never looked at it that way."

"You should."

He stood and walked across the room to extinguish the single glowing lamp atop the chest of drawers, then made his way back to the bed in the dark, the moon and stars his only light. He pulled back the covers on his side of the bed and lay down, taking a deep sigh of pure pleasure at the familiar feel of the old mattress as he settled in.

"Comfortable?" she asked.

His eyes had adjusted to the dark, and in the shadows, he could make out her silhouette as she lay on her back staring at the ceiling. "Very much so. You?"

"It's a very lovely bed. Almost as comfortable as the one back home in Columbus."

"Almost?"

She gave a light giggle. "Well, it was my bed for twenty-plus years."

"So you miss it, do you?"

"I didn't say that."

They lay in silence for a bit, the only sounds being the ordinary squeaks and squawks of the aging farmhouse. Outside, nothing stirred as far as he could tell unless it was a few swaying branches from the gentle breeze. In another month or so, those branches would drop their leaves, and he wondered if Faith would be lying next to him when they did.

"I'm sorry I haven't had a lot to say since I got home."

"You've had a lot on your mind."

"It's a relief that Isaac is recovering so well. Must be all those prayers."

"I'm convinced it is. Things could have been so much worse."

"I hate to think of it."

"As do I."

A brief pause and then he spoke again. "I don't know if I ever adequately thanked you for getting a horse for Isaac. I think it was exactly what he needed. I should have done it a year ago, but I wasn't sure he was quite ready. So...thank you."

"You're welcome. I was slightly worried you might not approve—or might want to be the one to have given it to him. Even Jesse questioned the wisdom of my going ahead with the purchase, but in the end, I just took the leap—and hoped you wouldn't be upset with me."

"Upset? No, not at all. I'm glad you took the initiative."

"Good. I'm glad too."

More stillness passed between them. In fact, neither so much as moved a muscle. He wondered if her heart were racing as fast as his. To have her so close and yet not touch her was a sort of torture he'd never experienced, even worse than burrowing down in a fresh-dug trench and wondering if you'd dug deep enough to avoid soaring bullets.

They both spoke at once.

"I don't know—" she said.

"I've been wondering—" he said.

"You go first," he said.

"No, you," she insisted.

He smiled in the dark. "I was going to say, I've been wondering what the future holds."

"And I was about to say something similar."

"Any thoughts?" he asked, holding his breath.

"Well, I know we had an agreement."

"Yes, we did—*do*. I'm willing to honor it if that's what you want."

"It isn't what *I* want, Joey. It's what *you* want."

"Isn't it what we *both* want? I know you had plans for going out on your own. I had promised you a large sum. I don't think I should go back on that promise."

"So you're saying you want me gone."

"No, I didn't say that. I mean to say, I don't want you thinking I don't keep my promises, and now that I'm home, it's convenient that you're here because you cook fine meals, and you do a great job of keeping the house clean and tidy, and my children…"

"So, you consider me to be your housekeeper then?"

"No, not that. I'm not making myself very clear."

"It seems like you are."

Frustrated, he quick as lightning flipped onto his side to face her. She didn't, though. She kept on her back and stared at the ceiling. "What I mean to say is, if you want to stay, I'd—well, I'd like you to stay."

"But why?"

"Why?"

"Yes, why do you want me to stay?"

"Didn't I just explain that?"

"Not very well."

He inhaled a deep breath. "I want you to stay. There. But only if you want to."

He could almost hear her eyes rolling. Almost.

Without giving his next move much thought, he went up on one elbow and got closer. She turned her face toward him just a fraction. "I want you to stay," he repeated.

She said nothing, just stared at him with those deep blue eyes. He leaned down closer now, close enough to feel her uneven breaths against his mouth and to see the outline of her petite nose and full lips. He couldn't help it; he kissed her, at first with a slow, tentative, and even thoughtful intent. But soon, the warm moistness of her mouth sent him into a dizzying swirl, and he set to searching her mouth with much more intensity. She kissed him back, and then her arms came out from under the covers, and she hugged him, trembling, drawing him closer yet. They kissed—and kissed—until it seemed inevitable that he would take the next move, if she were willing—but then he thought better of it and drew back, flopping on his back to catch his breath.

Both of them lay there, staring at the ceiling, and then he asked, "Does this mean you'll stay?"

"Because we kissed, you mean?"

"I mean…" He wasn't sure what she wanted him to say. "I already told you I wanted you to stay."

"So I could be your housekeeper."

"I never said that."

"Do you want to be husband and wife?" Her voice carried a hint of annoyance. "Or do you want a housekeeper?"

"I—both?" *Was she fishing?* He wasn't good at reading women. He'd never succeeded with Sarah Beth, and he had a feeling he wasn't going to be much better with Faith. *Did she want him to tell her he loved her?* Because if that was what she wanted, he couldn't say it. Not yet anyway.

A deep sigh rolled out of her. "If I stay…" She paused as if trying to choose the right words. "If I stay," she repeated, "I would like you to—"

He decided to take a stab at it. "You want me to pay you?"

"No!" She hauled off and slapped his arm. "You don't pay a wife!"

"Good grief, then what is it you want?" He was plain stumped.

"There is no way to say it but to come right out with it."

"Then do it."

"That portrait of Sarah Beth—over the fireplace."

"Yes?"

"It's—it's big."

"A good friend of my father's painted it as a gift to me. He did a superb job. It is her exact likeness."

"And she was very beautiful."

"Yes, she was."

"Could—could you take it down?"

Now it was his turn to be indignant. "What? No. It's been there since before she died. She was my wife."

"And now *I* am."

"And she is the children's mother. They like looking at her every day."

"Do they? They've never once told me that."

"If they don't have her portrait there, they may well forget what she looked like."

"Perhaps you could—I don't know—put it away and then give it to one of them at a later date—or have duplicates made so they can each have a copy."

"What? I've never heard of such a thing."

"I don't know. It was a passing thought."

"Well, it can just keep passing right on by then."

"All right then."

"All right then."

He turned over, facing away from her, and she did the same. "I have no idea why you would ask that of me," he said.

"Because it's important to me."

"Well, that painting is important to me," he countered.

She said not another word, so that marked the end of their conversation. It took a long time for them to drift off to sleep, but at last, she slept, and then he did as well. But it wasn't a restful sleep. In the middle of the night, he awoke from a bad dream. He found himself in the trenches, bullets soaring overhead, men shouting, gunpowder clogging the air and making it hard for him to breathe. And when he looked around, he discovered Sarah Beth on one side of him and Faith on the other. "It's time to choose," Sarah Beth said. And that's when he awoke, his face buried in his pillow as he gasped for breath and his body drenched in sweat. Next to him, his wife lay sleeping, her breaths deep and even, her hair cascaded around her face. Soon, dawn would be upon them, and he'd be eating a quick breakfast and heading out to the fields.

Lord, I've really done it. I let the sun go down on my anger.

He went back on his side, facing away from her, and pinched his eyes shut, trying to get back to sleep. *I cannot take down that portrait. I won't take it down. There is no reason I should have to, none at all.*

As hard as he tried, he couldn't fall back to sleep, and so he very quietly pulled back the covers, dressed in the dark, and left the room to go down to the kitchen and make some coffee.

35

The days passed in steady succession with harvest in full swing, food preservation underway, and thoughts of school starting once the busiest part of the season passed. Miriam would attend for the first time, walking the mile and a half with her siblings to the one-room schoolhouse up the road. Lately, she'd been asking Beth a lot of questions about what to expect, and her eagerness for attending grew to great lengths. On the one hand, Faith was happy for her, but on the other, the house would be empty and painfully quiet. Oh, there were never dull days on a farm. There were still animals that needed tending and eggs to collect, but really, those weren't her tasks. Jobe and Wendel reminded her often that they'd been hired for barn chores and she needn't concern herself with such things. There were also hired hands to tend to cows and bulls in other big barns several acres over, mend fences, and process the milk for market. Fuller Family Farms was no small operation. Even in wartime, it thrived, and thrived well.

She and Joey had talked, and he'd apologized for his lack of sensitivity and also for having gone to sleep the night of their argument without asking for her forgiveness, but the painting of Sarah Beth remained in place, and she found herself dusting it every now and again—and even growing somewhat used to it. *Perhaps she'd been wrong to ask him to take it down. Perhaps.* She'd wanted to discuss it with Laura and Cristina, but it seemed a trivial matter the more she thought about it, and so she kept it to herself. The three of them had enjoyed their time working in Laura's kitchen—making winter jams; drying, salting, and smoking their meats; preserving vegetables and fruits; and filling shelves in their individual root cellars. *But the question remained: would she even be here come winter?* Yes, she had said her wedding vows in the courthouse, even halfway meant them, but to date, they hadn't even consummated their marriage, forget that they'd continued sleeping together, and he'd kissed her several more times. *Was she a wife or a housekeeper?* She couldn't tell, and the question had started gnawing a hole in her heart. *Was she that difficult to love?*

She'd written several letters to her mother about the situation, as personal as it was. She had the urgent need to talk about it with someone. *If not Cristina or Laura, then who but her own mother?* Her mother's return missives were always full of love, concern, and promises to pray, but never advice, the one thing Faith most wanted and needed—someone to tell her what to do. Instead, Audrey Haviland always ended her letters with Bible verses, telling her to stay in God's Word and lean on Him to tell her how to handle the matter of her marriage.

It was early Sunday morning. The sun had not yet begun to rise, but that was because fall had set in, meaning shorter days. She always rose ahead of everyone, even Joey, on Sundays. She wanted to cook a good breakfast before heading to church, and then of course, there was much to do to prepare for Sunday's dinner. Today, she'd invited everyone to their house for the meal. Cristina's due date was fast approaching, and it was getting harder for her to navigate all the chores that went with being a farmer's wife, not to mention a pregnant one. It seemed the least she could do was to offer to make dinner for the entire Fuller clan. In fact, she looked forward to it. Naturally, the children were excited as well, for that meant a visit from their cousins.

She slipped out of bed, thankful that Joey didn't budge but continued his deep, long, steady breaths. Last night, he'd tossed and turned a great deal, but when she'd whispered, "Are you all right?" she got no response, so she suspected he was having a bad dream. It wasn't the first time he'd spent a restless night, but always when she asked him the next morning how he'd slept, he gave the same curt answer: "Fine." Clearly, he didn't wish to discuss it.

She lingered for just a moment to study the contours of his handsome face, the shadow of his whiskered face giving him that rustic too-busy-to-shave look. He lay on his side, one muscled arm lying outside of the blanket. Quietly, she gathered her things, then walked down the dark hallway to the bathroom. Another busy day, although the blessed Sabbath, lay before her, and she didn't know whether to be happy about it or to dread it. She loved going to church. She loved the hymns and the wonderful sounds coming from the organ pipes, and she always looked forward to the Sunday sermon, but lately, her heart weighed heavy, and thoughts of taking the train back to Columbus, if only for a visit, kept knocking at the corners of her mind. She still had that return ticket. It lay in her top drawer next to the box holding that ridiculous button string.

She slipped into the bathroom, lit the lamp, and began preparing for her day.

⌒

Joey watched his wife scurry around the kitchen after church. He asked if there was something he could do to help, but she said no, that Beth was setting the table, Frankie was filling the water glasses, Isaac was laying out the folded napkins, and she herself had already made the gravy, mashed the potatoes, and put the beef roast with carrots on the silver platter. All that was left to do was carry the food into the dining room. "Well, at least let me help with that," he said. But, oh no, she said she had it all under control. He was to go into the living room and entertain their guests. "They're my family. They don't need entertaining," he told her, trying to eke a smile out of her, but getting none. *Something wasn't right with her today.* He'd known it since breakfast. Even during church, she didn't seem her normal, cheerful self. He worried he'd done something to offend her, but if he had, he couldn't think what. They'd had no arguments since that last one concerning Sarah Beth's portrait, and lately he'd caught her dusting it and seemingly admiring it, judging by her gaze and the time she spent on it.

A bit frustrated, he left the kitchen. When he got the signal a few minutes later to invite everyone to the table, he did so, and his family eagerly moved in the direction of the dining room.

"My goodness, Faith, you've outdone yourself," Laura said.

"Looks wonderful," said Jesse.

"I so appreciate this, Faith. Everything smells and looks delicious," said Cristina while waddling to the table. Jack pulled back a chair for her, then pushed it in as soon as she lowered herself. Thankfully, the table had two extensions, making more than enough room for all twelve members of the Fuller family to sit. Joey remained standing and offered the prayer.

After the "amen," Laura beamed. "Joseph, you can't possibly imagine how it warms my heart to hear you pray. I always knew you'd find your way back to the Lord. It seems to me your beautiful wife had a lot to do with it."

Joey smiled while seating himself. "I won't argue with that, Ma. She insisted I take my Bible with me when I returned to duty, and I'm glad for it. It was in those final few months that I really started reevaluating my life. I knew God had been chasing after me for some time, but I had become pretty good at running away. No more, though. I'm back on track, and I have everyone's faithful prayers to thank for it."

From there, the topics ran the gamut, the adults carrying on about a variety of things while the cousins spent their time giggling and nudging each other in the arms. After dessert, they quickly asked if they could be excused to go outside to play. "Of course," Joey told them. "Just don't go up in that hayloft!" They ran out the door, the last one closing it with a loud thump that made everyone wince.

Joey had kept his eyes on Faith throughout most of the meal, watching for signs of discontent, but if she felt it, she covered it well, remaining cordial to everyone, jumping up to see to everyone's needs, and seeming to enjoy the opportunity to serve them. When it came time to clear the table, she refused the help, insisting that everyone remain seated and that she would happily clean up later. While Laura and Cristina adamantly insisted on helping, she was equally adamant about tending to it later.

"Well, I taught my boys from childhood to help around the house with chores, so Joseph is well-trained in washing dishes. You be sure to put him to work."

Faith laughed. "He has been very good about offering to lend a hand when needed, so my grateful thanks to you for training him." Joey took special note that she seemed to want to avoid making too much eye contact with him. *Something was definitely up, but what?* He felt about as dumb as a stick when it came to figuring her out.

"Hey, why didn't all that training rub off on you, Jack Fuller?" Cristina asked.

"He knows better," Laura said. "Although, he was the one who seemed to grumble the loudest when it came to washing dishes."

Jack put out his callused farm hands for everyone to see. "Do these look like the sort of hands that belong in dishwater?"

In unison, the women all said, "Yes!"

"Ha! You're outvoted," Cristina said, giving Jack a playful nudge on the arm.

The banter continued until early afternoon when the men all talked about what needed to be done on the farm. As a rule, Sundays were a day of rest, but there were still certain chores that couldn't be ignored, and so even though Faith argued about it, when everyone stood, they each grabbed their plates, utensils, and whatever other dish they could carry, and took them into the kitchen.

"Are you sure I can't stay and help?" Laura asked.

"I'm positive," Faith answered. Then looking at Cristina, Faith said, "And as for you, I want you to go straight home and lie down for a bit. You're looking a little weary."

Cristina put a hand to her bulging stomach. "I believe I might take you up on that little directive."

It didn't take long for the house to clear, and with the cousins leaving, Isaac and the others came back inside, their faces red from romping.

"Why don't you all go down to the creek to cool off?" Faith suggested. "Joey, you go with them. I don't want Miriam down there without an adult."

"But I was going to help you in the kitchen," he said.

She waved a hand. "I can manage. After they cool off, they'll be going to their rooms for a Sunday rest, and I expect you'll be meeting up with your brothers out in the field."

"Yay, come on, Daddy, let's go down to the water," Miriam said, tugging at his arm.

"Don't you need to put on some swim clothes?" he asked the child.

"These aren't our Sunday best, Daddy," Beth chided. "We changed after church. Faith says we can wear our play clothes in the creek."

"Oh, well, if Faith says it, then I guess it's all right," he said, glancing at Faith and giving her a little wink. She favored him with a tiny smile in return, but not the usual sort. Something nagged at him. "Are you all right?" he asked her.

"Me? I'm fine. Why do you ask?"

He studied her a minute even as Miriam tugged at his arm. "No reason, I guess. Just wondering."

"Oh. Well, wonder no more."

And at that, they all ran down to the creek, the boys challenging him to a race. No question, Isaac was back to his old self. Faith, on the other hand…

36

She was going to do it. She was going back to Columbus. This would be the deciding factor for the direction their marriage would take. It was the only way she'd ever know how Joey really felt.

Last night, after tucking the kids into bed, she'd been willing to talk, to tell him what was on her heart, but as soon as he put his head to the pillow, he'd gone straight to sleep. She'd stood right over him, hands on her waist, staring down at him and willing him to wake up, but instead, he'd started snoring! "For heaven's sake!" she'd muttered. Then, as if that wasn't enough, in the middle of the night, she'd awakened to his tossing and turning, and whose name did he mutter in his sleep but Sarah Beth's. He'd been dreaming about his former wife! *That was it. She would never measure up to the beautiful woman in the bronze picture frame. Never.*

This morning, after Joey had gone out to the fields and the children had run out to the barn to do some chores, Faith sat down at the table and wrote Joey a note, then left it on the butcher block in the kitchen where he'd be sure to find it when he came in for lunch. She'd packed a small bag, tidied up the house, and saw to a few last minute details, one of which was to scrawl another note to Joey to tell him the children were

with his mother. Afterward, she went out to the barn to collect the children and tell them they were going to go to their grandmother's house
for the day. No questions asked, they gladly obliged, but on the way to
Laura's house, she told them she planned to take a trip to Columbus to
visit her parents for a few days.

Miriam whined about it. "What day are you comin' back?"

"I don't know exactly."

"But you are coming back, right?" asked Beth.

"Of course. All my things are here anyway." Whether she stayed
long after that was yet to be determined, although that was a discussion
for another time.

Isaac then said, "I guess you probably miss your parents, right?"

"Very much," she'd said, wanting to keep the conversation short and
simple.

"So, then are we staying home with Daddy—or what's going to
happen to us?" Isaac asked, a bit of concern in his tone.

"That will be up to your daddy to decide, but you are not to worry
about it. He'll come get you at your grandma's today once he's done
working."

That seemed to quiet them for the remainder of the ride.

Upon arriving at the big house, the first person they spotted was
their Uncle Jesse standing by the barn talking to one of the hired hands.
Isaac and Franklin said hasty goodbyes to Faith then jumped down and
made a beeline for the barn. Miriam gave her a tight hug and clung for
an extra second, then jumped down and followed her brothers. Beth
hung back, climbing up on the buckboard next to Faith. "I hope you
don't stay away too long."

"I'm sure I won't, honey."

Beth clasped her hands in her lap and looked down at them. "I'll—
miss you while you're gone."

"You will? That's so sweet. I'll miss you too."

"I know we didn't start out very good when you first came, so I hope
you're not goin' back to Columbus 'cause we are too much trouble."

"Oh, Beth, no. No, that's not it at all. I—need to see my parents. It's been several months."

Beth raised her head and looked Faith square in the eye. "Are you really going to miss me?"

"Terribly."

"And the rest of us?"

"You can be sure of it."

"What about my daddy? Will you miss him?"

She paused before giving an answer. "Yes."

"Good. I want you to miss all of us. I want you to miss us so much you won't be able to stay away."

"Oh, honey. I will." She pulled Beth into an embrace, and the way Beth clung to her made her heart ache with premature loneliness. She prayed for more time with them—and she prayed that these days away from Joey would make him long for more than just a housekeeper. *Lord, may it be so.*

Once inside Laura Fuller's house, while the children played outside with Jesse, Faith spilled the whole story to her, then asked if she'd be willing to watch the children for the next few days—or however long it took for her to sort things out. Laura reluctantly agreed. She didn't like the idea of Faith going back to Columbus any more than Beth did. They, too, embraced, but this time, Faith couldn't hold back her tears. In fact, they both freely shed a few. "I just hope that boy of mine wakes up because if he doesn't, I will personally go out to the barn and find a board big enough to thwack him a good one across the side of the head!"

Despite her glum mood, Faith laughed. "I love you, Laura Fuller," she said.

"And I love you, child," Laura replied.

Faith had made arrangements with Jobe to drive her to the train station at ten o'clock, so at a quarter to the hour, she left Laura's house and drove straight to the barn. She was going back home—using the return ticket Joey himself had given her.

It was an early autumn scorcher. Joey mopped his brow with a rag he grabbed from his pocket. His stomach growled, reminding him that Faith would have a tasty lunch waiting for him. Things had not been great between them. He'd known yesterday something wasn't right, but after a long day of playing with the kids and a bad night's sleep the night before, he'd been too exhausted to talk about it. Shoot, he never even heard her come to bed. *Fine husband he was.*

His thoughts and emotions were all over the place. One minute, he envisioned telling her he loved her and would until his dying day, and the next, he caught himself thinking about what life had been like with Sarah Beth. He'd loved her thoroughly, but his feelings for Faith were growing every day, and he didn't want to ruin things with her. No doubt about it; he had to figure this thing out. *Lord, erase every last doubt and let me be completely free to love again.* His mind and heart were a jumbled mess. He'd even had another dream about Sarah Beth last night, and while he couldn't remember the exact details, he clearly recalled saying her name in his sleep and waking at the sound of his own voice. *Good grief, what was all that about?* She'd been gone now for almost four years. *Wasn't it time she quit entering his dreams? Was he losing his mind?*

He gave his head a fast couple of shakes and mounted his horse to make the short trek home. On the way, he passed Jack, who also looked to be making his way back to the barn. He waved at his brother and kept riding.

The house was strangely quiet when he entered through the front door. "Hello?" he called. No response. "Hmph." *Perchance everyone was in the back yard working in the garden?* But no, this was Monday, Faith's designated wash day. Well, maybe she was outside hanging up clothes. *That was probably it.* He tromped through the parlor, then passed the library, wishing now he'd kicked off his dirty boots at the door like Faith had asked him to, then walked through the living room. He liked the new furniture she had picked. And the wallpaper. And the drapes. *Had he mentioned enough how appreciative he was to her for making his house feel so much more like home?* He frankly didn't know how she did it, taking care of four scraggly kids, keeping a clean house, washing everyone's clothes, plus making wonderful meals three times a day. He could go on. But right now, he was too busy looking for her.

"Hello?" he called again. "Faith?" He looked outside, then opened the back door in the kitchen that overlooked the garden, the barn, and the outbuildings—but nothing. All he saw were horses grazing and some cows in the distance. And those pesky, free-roaming, squawking chickens pecking at the ground. He closed the door. *Upstairs. That's probably where she was.*

But then as he glanced around the sparkling clean kitchen, he suddenly realized there was no lunch waiting for him. That's when he spotted a couple of folded up pieces of paper, a rock sitting on top of them to keep them from blowing off the table due to the open windows. Curious, he walked to the table and picked up one of the notes.

The children are at your mother's house, so you can pick them up at the end of your work day. Faith.

"Hmph," he muttered to himself. *What were they doing at his mother's place?*

He picked up the second piece of paper and unfolded it as well. This note was longer, and he had a sinking feeling he might want to sit down to read it. He lowered himself to the nearest chair at the table.

Dear Joey,

I am going back to Columbus. I don't know for how long. I need to sort things out. I know we are married, but it doesn't feel like we are. I don't know what you want from me, whether you want me to be a wife or a housekeeper. You did ask me if I wanted you to pay me. That sent me a rather clear message.

One thing I have learned is that I cannot compete with Sarah Beth. She is gone, but you have not been able to let go of her long enough to see me for who I am. I do not blame you. I understand she was your wife and the mother of your children, and I would never want you to forget her. Never. I just want you to look at me—if you can—and realize that I am here and very much alive. And I care very, very deeply for you.

We had an arrangement at the onset of our marriage. Do you want to honor the original arrangement, or do you want to remain married? It is your choice. But I will tell you this. If you want me to be Sarah Beth, I cannot do it.

It appears you have a choice to make: either remain faithful to your first wife or choose to start anew with me. I will await your decision, but please do not take too long, as I, too, have some decisions to make.

Your wife,

Faith

Joey refolded the letter, then sat there at the table and stared out the window. So much had changed since she'd come into his life. She'd made his house a home, brought order to the chaos, showed his children unconditional love, set a Christlike example, and even brought his pathetic garden back to life. He looked out at it now and saw the rewards of her efforts. "Lord, what have I done?"

Panic settled in, real and raw, but he didn't want to act on racing emotions. He needed to think things through so he could start over and do this thing right. The kids were fine for now. What he needed to do first was head over to his oldest brother's house and have a good heart to heart with him. Jack had a good, level head on his shoulders. He'd have some wise words for Joey. He tossed down the letter, forgot altogether about his empty stomach, and headed for Jack's.

His brother wasn't very helpful. "What do you mean, she went back to Columbus? What did you *do*? And what'd you say to cause her to leave—or maybe, I should ask, what *didn't* you say?" The questions shot out of Jack's mouth like cannon fire. It was not the response he'd expected from his usually calm, sensible brother, but at least they were outside, out of earshot of Cristina and the kids.

Joey kicked at the dusty drive and sent a little pebble flying. "I don't know, I guess it's more what I didn't say. I'm pretty sure she wants to stay married, but I haven't let her know what my thoughts are on the subject. Our agreement was temporary."

"I know, and it was a stupid arrangement if you ask me."

"Do you think you could try to be a little more understanding? I didn't come here to be yelled at."

"Well, it's possible you need a little sense knocked into you. You are aware she is the best thing that's happened to you, aren't you?"

There was no denying it. "Yes. I do know that."

"Have you told her?"

"Not—not in those words."

Jack took off his hat and finger combed his coffee-colored hair then stuck the dusty thing back on his head. "Come on, let's go find a place to talk this thing through."

They found a grassy spot down by the creek and sat in some shade. "All right, start from the beginning," Jack said.

Joey told him about the note she'd written him and then about the events leading up to it, how he'd had some moody days since getting home from the war and about the nightmares that came out of nowhere. He told Jack how nervous he was about fully committing to Faith and how she'd asked him to take down the portrait of Sarah Beth and the argument that ensued when he told her he couldn't do that. Through all of it, Jack listened and said little. He didn't even react when Joey admitted they hadn't yet consummated their marriage, just slept in the same bed and shared a few kisses.

A full minute went by before Jack responded. "First, I understand about the nightmares. I had them too. They've let up, and yours will too. War does a number on a soldier, but with God's help and an understanding woman, you'll get through it. You need to talk to Faith about it though. Don't keep those dreams bottled up, or they'll get worse. Second, marriage is for good, brother. The Bible is clear on that. But it also says if a man is unfaithful to his wife, she has a right to divorce."

Joey grew defensive. "I haven't been unfaithful, not for a second."

Jack frowned at him. "I want you to think about something. By keeping Sarah Beth's big-as-life portrait hanging there for everyone to see, you're sending a message to your current wife that Sarah Beth takes precedence over her. You're saying to her, 'I may be married to you, but I will always love my first wife more than I love you'—if indeed you even do love Faith. And by the way, do you love her?"

The question rocked him right down to the center of his gut, and he had to ask it of himself before he could answer his brother. A gentle breeze whistled through the trees overhead as he pondered it, and the ever-flowing stream reminded him of the inevitable assurance of God's love first and then the very real love he had in his heart for Faith. He sucked in a deep, cavernous breath that went clear to the bottom of his lungs. When he let the air back out, it was as if he'd been washed anew.

"Yes, yes I do love her. No question."

Jack grinned and swiveled enough to give Joey a soft punch to the arm.

"You don't need anything from me, brother. You have only to listen to your heart—and to God's voice. What's He telling you to do—and what's your heart saying? Do they mesh?"

Joey nodded and grinned back. "I believe they do, yes. But I need to talk to my children."

"You don't need their approval."

"Oh, I know that. They are not the decision-makers in my family. But I want to talk to them before I take down their mother's portrait."

Jack turned his mouth down a tad and raised his thick eyebrows. "So, you're taking it down then? Don't be persuaded by my words. It must be your decision alone. And another thing. If you are truly honest and forthright with Faith, assuring her of your love, she may well tell you to keep it there as a remembrance of days past."

"You know, she might. But I am taking it down more for myself than for her, and I'll make that good and clear to her. I am moving on with my life, and I know it's way past time that I do."

"All right then."

The brothers stood, and as natural as the stars are to night, they hugged. "Don't waste any time bringing Faith back home where she belongs."

"I don't intend to, but perhaps it will be nice for me to meet and visit with her parents. Plan on my being gone for a couple of days."

"We managed without you for a few years. I think we can manage a couple of days."

Joey picked his children up at three o'clock. He might have known his mother would be waiting for him, all ready with a few choice words for him concerning what he'd done to chase Faith back to Columbus. He quelled her by telling her not to worry, that he was boarding the first train in the morning to Columbus, and he planned to do everything possible to convince her of his love and his deep desire to stay married. She breathed a loud sigh of relief and told him to bring the children back in the morning with enough clothes to last a few days.

"Why did Faith go back to Columbus?" Franklin asked just as soon as they walked into the house. "Is she really just going back to visit her parents, or do you think she plans to see if she can have her old job back?"

Joey hadn't thought that far—that she might possibly talk to her aunt about returning to the restaurant. His own stomach clenched a bit.

"She's coming back, right, Daddy?" Beth asked.

"Uh, yes, of course she is." He tried to put a positive tone in his voice. It was nearing the supper hour, and he had to figure out something to feed his family. That's when it hit him yet again. He loved Faith and would never again take a second of her presence in his house for granted. She made it a *home*.

"When's she coming back?" Miriam asked.

"In a few days, lambkin. I'm going there tomorrow to meet her parents."

"Can we go too?" asked Franklin, following him into the living room.

"No, not this time. Let's all sit in the living room, shall we? I want to talk to you about something."

Isaac had been quiet on the ride back to the house. In fact, all of them had been, but once they seated themselves, Isaac spoke. "Are you sure she didn't go back to Columbus because of us?"

"No, Isaac. You had nothing to do with her going."

That didn't satisfy Isaac. He went on. "After Faith left Grandma's house this morning, I went into the house to get a drink of water, and it looked like Grandma had been crying. I asked her what was wrong, and she told me not to worry, that everything would be fine. Is everything going to be fine, Daddy? Because if Faith went back to Columbus because of me, then I want her to know how sorry I am."

"I know she didn't go because of you, but I'll be sure to tell her you said that, Isaac. She'll appreciate it."

Now Miriam started to whimper. "I love Faith."

"Me too," said Beth. "Faith was the nicest, funnest nanny we ever had."

"Don't talk about her like she's in the past. It's not like she's not coming back. I'm going to see to it that she knows we love her."

"Do you love her, Daddy?" asked Beth.

"Yes, I do, very much."

"Good, 'cause we want her to live with us. Always."

"Yeah, we do," said Franklin.

Joey's heart warmed at their words. He took a breath for courage. "And now I have a question for all of you." He glanced up at the portrait over the fireplace. "What would you all think if I took down the painting of your mother?"

They all raised their heads to glance at it. Then one by one, they shrugged.

"I don't know," said Beth. "I guess it's okay. I don't really look at it very often."

"I don't really care either, Daddy," said Franklin. "It's probably been up there long enough."

"It's fine with me," Isaac said. "We all got ar' own memories—well, all of us but Miriam. I don't need Mama's picture there to remind me of her every day. Now that you're finally done fighting in that war, I would like us to start making some new memories around here, memories with Faith."

Joey nodded. "That sounds good to me. I'll be taking it down after you go to bed tonight."

"What are you gonna put up there in its place?" asked Isaac.

"I haven't thought that far. Should we let Faith decide?"

"Yeah!" they chimed in unison.

"All right then." Joey set his hands on his knees and prepared to stand.

"But, Daddy," Beth blurted, "I just thought of something important!"

"What is it, pumpkin?"

"The button string! You have to find at least fifty buttons before you go to Columbus. You have to give them to her so she can make her chain complete."

"Yeah, 'cause that makes her be y'r 'fficial wife!" said Miriam.

Joey's mouth gaped as he stared at all four of his youngsters. He pointed a finger at Beth and said, "You, my dear, are a genius! Right after we eat something, we are going for a buggy ride. We need to find us some buttons!"

"Where?" asked Beth.

"I don't know—your aunt's house, your grandma's house, the neighbors." He threw up his hands. "Downtown Lebanon!"

37

*F*aith and her parents sat in the living room conversing about life in general. She had arrived yesterday afternoon, to her mother's utter shock and great dismay, while her father was at the blacksmith shop. "It didn't work out?" were her mother's first words. No "Hello, I've missed you so much," or "It's wonderful to see you." Just, "It didn't work out?" And she'd looked so disappointed as she drew Faith into a massive hug, the kind that only a mother can give. Naturally, Faith had cried. She'd shed her tears with Laura too, but when she'd seen her own mother, she'd truly wept, an all-out, slobbery, no-holding-back kind of cry, the sort that made a body tremble.

"Stuart Porter's been transferred to the state pen across town," Albert said. "There was a brief article about it in the newspaper yesterday."

"I'm relieved to hear it," Faith said.

"I've heard talk around town he has a cousin who lives in the area. Leon Porter's his name. Charley Hardy—you remember him, Faith. He's a regular customer at your aunt's restaurant. Anyway, he came into our shop the other day and told me Stuart's cousin Leon is a man of great faith who's been visiting Porter on a fairly regular basis. Perhaps his positive influence will rub off on him."

"That would be wonderful," said Faith. "If anybody needs the Lord, it's him."

"Is Joseph a Christian man?" Albert asked.

"He is, but he only recently rededicated his life to God."

"Since marrying you, then," he said.

"Yes, but I think his involvement with the war had much to do with it. He simply came to the realization that he needed the Lord in his life to find true peace."

Albert nodded. "That's certainly good to know. I wouldn't be surprised if you had something to do with his decision."

"If I did, it's only by God's grace."

"Do you love this man, Faith?" her father asked.

"I do, Papa, but I needed to come home to sort things out."

"I understand that. Your mother told me last night about the talk you had with her yesterday. She mentioned Joseph might be having a difficult time letting go of his first wife."

"He still has a portrait of his wife over the fireplace, Papa, and every time I walk through the living room, it's all I see. I asked him if he would take it down, and he became irate with me, as if I'd asked him to perform some impossibly difficult feat—like—like walk a tightrope."

"Well, perhaps it never occurred to him that her likeness would bother you. Men are not the quickest at reading women's minds—nor the most sensitive. When you made the request, it no doubt took him by surprise, and so he reacted in a defensive manner. After all, she is the mother of his four children. Perchance he keeps it there more for the children than for himself."

"He told me that was his reason, but I've never once heard the children mention it."

"Perhaps it is too painful a topic for ones so young."

"Yes, perhaps. I have, however, heard him mention Sarah Beth a number of times, and in fact, he called out her name in his sleep the other night."

"One has no control over his dreams."

"Papa, it sounds like you're defending him."

Albert gave a half grin. "I always try to understand why people say and do things. And I wonder if you've given him enough of a chance. You must remember, he's been fighting a war for three years. It is my understanding he left only months after his wife's passing, so perhaps he didn't give himself enough time to adequately grieve his loss. He went from one tragic circumstance into the heat of battle for these United States. After that, he went through one nanny after another in search of someone who he could trust with his children. Now it appears he's finally found one in you—but you have come back to Columbus to sort things out? How do you think the children will handle knowing that after they've come to know you and hopefully grow fond of you, they might again have to start all over with someone new?"

Tears formed, for she could appreciate his words, as difficult as they were to hear. "I don't want to cause them a minute of worry."

"Before you left for Lebanon, you said that you believed God was leading you," he continued.

"And I did."

"Do you also believe He would endorse divorcing the man to whom you spoke vows?"

"But it was the agreement we both settled on."

"I understand that. But you didn't answer my question. Do you believe God would approve if you divorced your husband?"

"Is it right for me to stay in a loveless marriage?"

He tipped his head at her. "Have you considered how much time you've given him to fall in love with you? How much time have you truly spent together? The equivalent of a month, a few weeks? Perhaps you are expecting too much too soon. And another thing..."

She sighed and let go a little laugh, even through tears. "You mean there's more?" She looked to her mother. "Mama, is there no way of stopping him?"

Of course, she meant it in jest, but Audrey shook her head. "When your papa gets serious, I have learned to listen because he speaks with the wisdom God gives him."

Faith sobered. "I know you're right. I'm listening, Papa."

"Have you considered the real reason you came back to Columbus?"

She sniffed, and through a jagged sigh asked, "Wh-what do you mean?"

"Could there be a hint of jealousy—of his first wife? Is that the real issue? The memory of another woman lingers in the house, and you can't shake it. Even though you never met her, her portrait hangs above the fireplace, and you are just a trifle jealous. Am I right?"

She considered the question and the realization struck. "I *am* jealous of her! I didn't want to admit that in so many words, but it's true."

"How about you begin to ask the Lord to give you a love for her?"

"But—she's dead. How can I love someone who's not even here?"

"Perhaps respect is a better word. Think about this. She birthed four lovely children, albeit difficult ones from what you've indicated in your letters home. Your mother gave birth to four as well, and I can vouch for the fact that all of you caused us a number of headaches in your growing up years. Still, we wouldn't have traded any of you for the world, and I have a feeling you're beginning to feel the same way about Joey's children."

"I am, Papa. I've come to love each one in a unique way."

"And who do you have to thank for that—besides Joey? His first wife, of course. Perhaps you have to consider that a part of Joey will always love her, but that doesn't mean his heart is not large enough to love you as well—if not in full yet, then someday. Can you not give him time to develop these feelings—without undue pressure?"

Tears now spilled freely down her cheeks.

"I didn't intend to make you cry, dear daughter. I only wanted to—"

She leaped up from her chair before giving him a chance to finish and threw her arms around his neck. "Oh, Papa, what you say is so true. Your words were exactly what I needed to hear, so don't apologize. Mama is right, you are full of wisdom."

She stood back up, wiped her tears away, and looked from one parent to the other. "I've been selfish. I know that now." Then she looked her father straight on. "Do you think there's a train going to Lebanon this afternoon?"

"This afternoon?" they both said in unison, mouths sagging. "You only got here yesterday," Audrey said.

Albert grinned. "Trains come and go all the time. I s'pose there's only one way to find out if one would take you to Lebanon yet today. I'll drive you to the station, and we'll look at the schedule."

Now a vague smile found its way to Audrey's mouth as she lifted her shoulders then let them drop. "Well, your visit was nice while it lasted."

"Come with us to the station, Mama. If there's a train leaving yet today, we'll be able to say our goodbyes from there rather than here." Then she looked from one to the other, as they sat side by side on the sofa, and bent to put an arm around both their necks in a three-person hug. "Oh, I love you so much, both of you. Thank you for everything."

The train station buzzed with people, folks just arriving and others preparing to depart. Faith's father had walked up to the ticket booth and learned that indeed one of the trains sitting at the depot was departing for Lebanon in twenty minutes. He hurriedly purchased the ticket even though Faith offered to buy it. "No, honey, this is my little gift to you. I want you to go back to Lebanon and give this marriage everything you've got." He put the ticket in her palm, then with both hands, folded her fist around the paper stub and held on for a minute, his look tender.

"I will, Papa. I promise."

One more hug from both of them was all the time they had for their goodbyes. The conductor had already called, "All aboard!" She headed toward the door to the train and, just before boarding, turned and blew them both one quick kiss, then climbed the stairs with her single piece of luggage.

⌒

Joey watched the bustle of folks gathered at the Columbus depot to either say goodbye to outgoing passengers or hello to those just arriving. He navigated past the jumble of people as he made his way around the building to find a lineup of one- and two-horse hansom taxis awaiting folks who needed assistance in reaching their ultimate destinations. Also parked were privately parked rigs, so he had to study each wagon to determine which ones were taxis and which were not. He found one and headed in that direction. Once he was there, the driver met him. "Help you, sir?"

"Are you familiar with the location of the Albert Haviland family home?"

He gave his head a slow, thoughtful shake. "Can't say I am, but I do know there's a Haviland and Sons Blacksmith Shop. Would that be the same family?"

"Absolutely. Could you drive me there? I'm sure someone there will be able to tell me where the home is located."

"Yes, sir. Climb aboard. Here, let me take your satchel."

He prepared to hand over his bag when a male voice from behind asked, "Joseph Fuller by any chance?"

He swiveled to find a bearded gentleman and a woman, possibly his wife, both wearing curious, if not eager, faces.

"Yes?" That's when a crazy notion dawned on him. "You wouldn't be—"

The man stuck out his hand. "Albert Haviland and my wife Audrey."

"Well, I'll be." They shook hands. The man's face drew into a sudden frown. "In case you're wondering, Faith just boarded the train back to Lebanon. It's leaving in a few minutes." In fact, in that moment, the whistle blew a warning signal of certain departure.

"Oh no, you must hurry!" cried Audrey.

In less time than it would take an arrow to leave its bow, Joey set off at a run toward the waiting train, then he noted two different tracks. He stopped and turned. "Which one?" he called.

"The first one—the one closest to you!" Albert returned.

Joey raced on. At the steps, he started pounding on the door. The conductor waved him off, shouting, "No more passengers! We're leaving."

"No!" He pounded some more. "I have to get someone off the train!"

"Sorry," the conductor said through the small window.

"Faith!" Joey yelled as loudly as he could. "Faith Haviland Fuller!"

The conductor stepped back a bit, making way for a passenger, someone wearing a hat over her golden locks and dressed in yellow, from what he could tell through the cloudy glass. She took a step closer to the door, then turned and said something to the conductor. At last, he opened the door.

"What are you doing here?" she asked, looking down on him from the train car.

To his eyes, she was even prettier than she'd been two days ago—if that were possible.

How did she see him right now? He'd gone to a barber yesterday for a real shave and a haircut. He'd even gone into the general store to buy a new pair of trousers and a button-up shirt. And then there was the matter of the button string, which he carried now in his haversack—with an additional fifty buttons that he'd begged off his mother, Cristina, a few ladies in town, and some shop owners.

"I missed you," Joey told her.

A tiny smile turned up at the corners of her mouth. "I wasn't even gone a full two days."

"It felt like a week."

"That's sweet."

"It looks like you were about to go back to Lebanon? Did you get some things sorted out in your mind?"

The train's whistle sounded. "Hey, this is all sweet and nice, you two, but make up your mind, miss," the conductor said with irritation. "Are you staying in Columbus or heading to Lebanon?"

Joey extended his hand to her. "She's staying here—at least for a couple more days."

Now her smile grew a fraction more, and she put her hand in his so he could help her down. He instantly took her piece of luggage, she put her hand through his arm, and they set off in the direction of Albert and Audrey Haviland's wagon. The pair stood arm in arm, watching their approach with full-out smiles.

"Mama, Papa," Faith called out to them. "This is Joey!"

They both laughed. "We know, honey. We've met. Sort of," said Albert, his eyes twinkling.

Albert pulled the wagon up close to the house. "Welcome to our home, Joseph," he said. "My wife and I are delighted to have you here."

"Thank you, sir," Joey said. "I'm glad to finally make your acquaintance." He squeezed Faith's hand, sending delicious tingles up her spine.

"Well," Albert said, his lips turned up in a smile. "Audrey and I are going for a drive and will probably wind up visiting with some friends. But Faith can show you around."

At that, Joey took hold of his haversack as well as Faith's satchel, then told her to stay put until he rounded the wagon. Once there, he set down the two bags and then reached up to help her to the ground.

When Albert set the wagon in motion and it was just Joey and Faith standing in the front yard, reality began to sink in. They turned to face each other, and her heart nearly burst with pleasure at the sight of him. Goodness, he was handsome in his fresh haircut and clean-shaven face, not to mention his new attire. "You clean up well, Captain."

He grinned down at her, then touched the tip of her nose. "And you, my dear wife, have never looked prettier."

Despite the unseasonably warm air, a few chill bumps raced up her arms. *What had happened to change things between them?* One thing was certain: she intended to find out. "Shall we go inside?" she asked.

"After you, darling." He picked up the bags and followed her up the porch steps.

Darling? He'd never once called her that. *Was this a dream?*

She opened the door and entered first; he quietly followed and then shut it behind him.

"Let's go into the kitchen, shall we?" she suggested.

Once there, she opened the oak cabinet icebox and removed some lemons to make a pitcher of lemonade. Joey hovered nearby as she worked at the counter, once leaning down to kiss her neck. She couldn't help the nervous giggle that escaped.

She filled a pitcher about three-quarters full with water from the sink pump, added a bit of sugar and the sliced lemons, and gave the drink a few stirs. She took two glasses from an upper shelf inside the two-door cabinet and filled them both. "Shall we go sit in the living room or here in the kitchen?"

"I would like to sit wherever you want to sit."

She gave another giggle. "My, we are so agreeable."

"Seriously, I have a number of necessary things I want to say to you, so perhaps we will be more comfortable if we sit in the living room."

She tried to settle her jittery stomach. They each took a glass and moved into the living room, both lowering themselves to her parents' elegant sofa. They took several sips from their drinks then set them on the round platter Audrey always kept on the maple tea table in front of the sofa.

"All right then," Joey said, sitting back and drawing her closer to him with his arm. "I will start."

He started by telling her how her note in the kitchen had shaken him up, and how he'd gone straight to Jack's house for a long talk. He said his brother had set him straight on a number of things, primarily that he was married to Faith and, if he were smart, he'd start treating her like his wife.

"Did he really say that?" she asked.

"I don't remember his exact words, but he did tell me I might need some sense knocked into me. He also said you are the best thing that's happened to me, and I told him I very much agreed. You are, you know."

He also told her that since returning from war, he'd had some pretty gruesome nightmares, and that Jack had admitted to having some as well when he'd first been discharged. A physical ache built up in Faith's chest. "Please promise me you will talk to me when these nightmares happen. I want to help you through them."

Joey nodded. "I will try. Jack also told me it was God and the love of his understanding wife that got him through those night terrors. I appreciate that you want me to talk about them."

He took her hand then, and they stared into each other's eyes for a brief time. Nothing more, just took each other in, as if seeing the other for the first time.

"How are the children?" she asked finally.

"They're fine, but they wanted to make sure I was coming to Columbus to bring you back home. Isaac especially worried that perhaps you'd come back here because he'd crossed over the line one too many times with you. He asked me to tell you he is very sorry for the pranks he pulled. And Miriam and Beth both said they love you."

"Oh…" Faith put a hand to her mouth and fought back a round of tears, her heart feeling tender. "I love them as well."

"Would any of those feelings of love happen to carry over to me?" He positioned himself on the sofa so that he looked her straight in the face, while still holding her hand. She felt a blush heat up her cheeks. *How could she answer such a question if he hadn't proclaimed his love for her? Must she be first to express it?*

"I—perhaps," she managed. "There is something I want to settle with you right now though."

A worry line flashed across his brow. "All right."

"It's about Sarah Beth's portrait. I want you to keep it right where it is."

"I took it down last night."

"What? But I was being purely selfish. I know that now. I think it's important that the children never forget her."

"Isaac reminded me that he didn't need a portrait of his mother to spur on his personal memories. In fact, they were all in favor of taking it down and letting you choose something of your own liking, something that will go with the rest of the living room décor—which, by the way, has wound up being the coziest, most comfortable room in the house. I don't know if I adequately thanked you for taking the time to bring it back to a true feeling of home. Every time I walk inside now, I find I want to sit down on that sofa—or in one of the chairs next to the fireplace."

"I'm glad you like it, but as for the portrait…"

"It's already been settled. I put the picture in storage. Someday perhaps one of the children will want it for his or her own home. That's far in the future though."

"But—don't you want to look at it yourself?"

"I don't need to. Like Isaac said, her portrait isn't something I need to call up important memories. And do you want to hear something nice that Isaac said?"

She sat up a little straighter now, eager to hear his next words. "Yes, tell me."

"He said now that I am back from the war, it's time we make new memories—with you."

"Oh my, he did?" Fresh tears surfaced when she compared the new Isaac to the one she'd first met back in June.

"I'm so thankful to our loving Lord for protecting him in that awful fall. It could have turned out so differently."

"Indeed. I thank Him every day."

"I'm glad you found your way back to God."

"You had much to do with it. I needed that extra little push you gave me as well as your prayers. I felt those prayers out on the field."

"I'm glad you came home in one piece. So thankful, in fact."

"Which brings us to the subject of our marriage, doesn't it?"

Before she responded, she found herself nervously licking her lips and then biting down on the bottom one. "I suppose it does."

"I believe I told you once that I want to remain married."

"Yes, you did. And I believe I asked you if you wanted to remain married so that we could be husband and wife or so that you could have a housekeeper."

"And I obviously gave you the wrong answer."

She smiled. "I agree we sort of fell off the tracks at some point. Do you suppose we can get back on?"

"I'm sure of it, as long as you know I love you and sincerely want to honor the vows we said that day in the courthouse. They didn't mean that much to either of us back then, but now that I recall them, they mean the world to me. And I *do* love you, Faith Haviland Fuller."

"And I love you, Captain Joseph Fuller."

In that very special moment, he touched his lips to hers, then gathered her fully into his arms for several warm, delicious kisses. Suddenly, he dropped his arms and sat back. "Don't move."

"What?" Confusion raced around her head.

He jumped up and quickly made for the haversack he'd set down by the door. He opened it and searched around before finally withdrawing something. When he stood, she recognized the silver box. Her pulse quickened. "Blessed saints—what have you..."

He sat back down and put the box in his lap, slowly lifting the lid and pulling out the long string of buttons. With a silly grin, he said, "Last night, the children and I counted every last button on this string. There were exactly nine hundred and fifty-three."

"No. You didn't."

"Indeed we did. Then, after we grabbed a bite to eat, we rode from one place to another gathering buttons. And we added more buttons to your string. At the moment, my dear, sweet wife, there are exactly nine hundred and ninety-nine buttons on this string."

She gasped. "There are not!"

"You don't believe me?"

She put a palm to her mouth and laughed. "Oh, my stars, Joey, I never dreamed this day would come."

"But it has, hasn't it?" He kissed her again, a short peck that made her want more. He pulled back and reached into his pocket to withdraw the shiniest button she'd ever seen. It glistened off a ray of light that shone through the front window and fairly danced with color.

"This opal button," he said solemnly, "was from my mother's collection. She said it came from my grandmother's wedding dress. I thought it would be suitable to finish off your string."

A little sob came out of her. "It's—perfect," she whispered.

"Shall we put it on the string then and tie it off?"

"Yes, oh yes!" She watched his big fingers fumble with the fine string and marveled at how they could swing a heavy sledgehammer yet do such intricate work as well. He tied it off, and she found herself clapping with glee. "I love it—and I love you. Thank you, Joey."

"No, thank you, darling." There was that sweet endearment again. This time, she initiated the kiss—which developed into several more thorough, searching ones.

"How about that bed of yours?" he asked just an inch from her mouth. "The one you said is even more comfortable than mine? Do you think it will fit us both tonight?"

Her heart fluttered and thrilled at the thought of sharing her childhood bed with her husband. And her stomach did a massive flip. "It might be rather crowded, but I have no problem with snuggling."

"Nor do I. Snuggling—and *so* much more."

And as they buried themselves in more delightful kisses, Faith's steadfast heart beat with perfect love.

Epilogue

Christmas 1864

Laura Fuller's house rang with excited Christmas chatter, good-hearted laughter, and the occasional sound of a wailing baby—Jack and Cristina's baby boy, six-week-old Martin Jack. Joey loved the fact that Jack had named their new son after their deceased father, who'd been gone for six years. A fine Christian man, Martin Fuller had left an indelible mark on his three sons, and Joey had only God to thank for His divine providence. He glanced across the living room at his mother, the matriarch of the family, and marveled at her strength and sheer grit. Oh, she could be a bossy one, but the Fullers wouldn't be much without her, and looking at her now, doting over her newest grandson as she rocked and cuddled him, put a longing in his heart. Just last month, Faith had expressed her desire for a baby, and he had inwardly groaned. *Wasn't four kids enough?* But just watching her when she got the chance to hold baby Martin affirmed in his mind that she deserved the experience of birthing her own child—and so they delighted in trying to make one. *And who knew?* One child could very well lead to another—and another. He might end up having to build a bigger house someday.

Standing against the fireplace where a warm fire glowed, he sought out Faith and found her sitting next to the family's guest. It had been the biggest surprise of all when Faith had announced her wish to send an invitation to Leon Porter for Christmas dinner. Naturally, she had checked with Laura first, and she'd been more than agreeable. The man deserved to share Christmas with someone, his mother had said. In fact, he would stay in the spare room next to Jesse's for the duration of his stay, she declared. A hermit of sorts, it was clear he felt somewhat out of place sitting in the midst of this friendly, if not rowdy, bunch of folks, but Joey bet his last dollar he'd eventually lose any uncomfortable shyness before dusk settled in. The Fullers didn't put on airs, and he hoped Leon would sense it.

It still amazed him how Leon had come to be with them today. He'd sent a letter to Faith in late October, having gotten her address from her parents, introducing himself as Stuart Porter's cousin. They'd grown up together, he'd explained, and so he had a certain affinity to Stuart that no one else had. He described himself as a lifelong loner who lived on a quiet piece of property some fifteen miles outside of Columbus, and so it was just God and him. Leon explained he was writing to honor Stuart's request to let Faith know how sorry he was and ask for her forgiveness. Leon explained that he'd given Stuart a Bible and, by God's grace alone, the man's heart was beginning to soften toward the Lord and His ways. The letter had brought Faith to tears, giving her a sense of closure concerning the assault. She had let Leon know that she not only forgave Stuart, but would pray for him during her morning Bible reading sessions.

Joey knew that his wife was a wonder. Every day, she did or said something that made him love her even more.

"Come on, Daddy, we're going to go out to build a snowman," said Miriam, tugging on his sleeve. Her cousin Catherina tugged on his other arm.

"We are? Do you think there's enough snow?" They'd only gotten a couple of inches, just enough for a sparkling white Christmas day.

"Uncle Jesse says it's the perfect kind 'cause it's wet."

Joey moved away from the warm fire and caught Leon's attention. "Come on, Leon. Let's show these kids how to build a snowman."

To his surprise, the bearded fellow stood. "Why not?" he said. "I haven't built one since I was a boy, but I think I remember."

"Just don't lose track of time," Laura said from her place on the couch. "My turkey will come out of the oven in about an hour."

"Ma, the smell of that bird alone will be enough to call us all back inside," Jesse said while donning his coat, his nieces and nephews all doing their best to beat him out the door.

Three rather pathetic looking snowmen later, with stomachs full from a scrumptious dinner of turkey and all the trimmings followed by pumpkin pie, everyone sat around the living room, sated and peaceful. There had been two gifts for each of the children: an extra-long candy stick Laura had bought at the general store, and then a toy of some sort that she'd carefully selected. After opening them and expressing their thanks, they had all gone into the parlor room to settle down and play, leaving the adults to sit in the living room around the Christmas tree that Jesse had cut down and decorated with Laura.

Joey drew Faith up close to him on the sofa, one arm slung over her shoulder. His fingers made little circles in her arm, every so often producing a shiver in her that made him laugh softly. She'd gaze up at him with that look of love he'd grown so accustomed to seeing, and once he even bent down and kissed her cheek because he couldn't help himself, not caring one iota who noticed.

"God's been good this year," Laura said. "He's brought another of my sons safely home from the war, brought us a new family member in Faith, a brand new baby in precious Martin Jack, and a new friend in Leon." She looked across the room at their visitor. "Don't you dare be a stranger now, you hear? We'll expect more visits from you."

"I appreciate that, ma'am. It's been a pleasure joinin' you all in your Christmas festivities. I must say, I've never had a better Christmas, never in my life. It's just plain amazin' to me the way the Lord works His wonders. Just three months ago, I never would have thought I'd be sittin' in this here room with this good family enjoyin' a warm fire and fine company. Never. Just goes to show what a faithful God I serve."

"Amen to that," said Jack.

"I echo that," said Jesse.

"We're all grateful for His bountiful blessings," said Joey.

Laura spontaneously began to sing *Silent Night*, and one by one, the others joined in. It wasn't the most beautiful rendition Joey had ever heard, considering the few slightly raspy voices, some on key, others a little off, but his heart swelled none the less.

Outside the Fuller house, light snow fell past the window, a reminder of the ever-changing seasons of time, the ever-constant love of God... and faith.

About the Author

*B*orn and raised in west Michigan, Sharlene MacLaren attended Spring Arbor University. Upon graduating with an education degree in 1971, she taught second grade for two years, then accepted an invitation to travel internationally for a year with a singing ensemble. After traveling for a year, she returned to her teaching job, then in 1975, she reunited with her childhood sweetheart, and they married that very December. They have raised two lovely daughters, both of whom are now happily married and enjoying their own families. Retired in 2003 after thirty-one years of teaching, Shar loves to read, sing, travel, and spend time with her family—in particular, her adorable grandchildren!

Shar has always enjoyed writing, and her high school classmates eagerly read and passed around her short stories. In the early 2000s, Shar felt God's call upon her heart to take her writing pleasures a step further, so in 2006, she signed a contract with Whitaker House for her first faith-based novel, *Through Every Storm*, thereby launching her professional writing career. With almost two dozen published novels now gracing store shelves and being sold online, Shar gives God all the glory.

Shar's novels have won numerous awards. Most recently, *Their Daring Hearts* was named a 2018 Top Pick by Romantic Times, and

A Love to Behold was voted "Book of the Year" in 2019 by *Interviews & Reviews*. *Her Steadfast Heart* is the second book in Shar's Hearts of Honor series. The first one, *Her Rebel Heart*, centers on Joey's brother Jack and his wife Cristina, and the third, *Her Guarded Heart*, releasing in January 2022, features Anna Hanson, a widowed mother, and the youngest Fuller brother, Jesse.

Shar has done numerous countrywide book signings and has participated in several interviews on television and radio. She loves to speak for community organizations, libraries, church groups, and women's conferences. In her church, she is active in women's ministries, regularly facilitating Bible studies and other events. Shar and her husband, Cecil, live in Spring Lake, Michigan, with their beautiful white collie, Peyton.

Shar loves hearing from her readers. If you wish to contact her as a potential speaker or would simply like to chat with her, please send her an e-mail at SharleneMacLaren@Yahoo.com. She will do her best to answer in a timely manner.

Additional resources:
www.SharleneMacLaren.com
www.instagram.com/sharlenemaclaren
twitter.com/sharzy_lu?lang=en
www.facebook.com/groups/43124814557
(Sharlene MacLaren & Friends)
www.whitakerhouse.com/book-authors/sharlene-maclaren

QUESTIONS FOR GROUP DISCUSSION

1. What did you like best/least about this book?

2. Did you happen upon a favorite quote from the book that you'd like to share?

3. How did you feel about Faith marrying a man she'd never met, especially seeing as the marriage was first intended to be a temporary arrangement?

4. What emotions, if any, did this book evoke in you?

5. How did you feel about the way Faith handled the children when problems arose?

6. What are your thoughts about Joey's parenting? Do you think he escaped parental responsibility by joining the Union Army?

7. What do you think was the author's primary purpose for writing this book? What concepts was she trying to bring to the forefront?

8. Did the story line feel realistic to you? Were the characters believable?

9. Did you learn anything new from reading this book? What questions do you still have?

10. Did this book leave you wanting more? Do you see yourself ever rereading it?